THE ASSASSIN LOTUS

David Angsten

NowHereBeBooks
LOS ANGELES
2014

ALSO BY DAVID ANGSTEN

DARK GOLD

NIGHT OF THE FURIES

This is a work of fiction. All of the characters, organizations, and events portrayed in this novel are either products of the author's imagination or are used fictitiously.

THE ASSASSIN LOTUS. Copyright © 2014 by David Angsten. All rights reserved.

ISBN - 10 : 1502442485

ISBN - 13 : 9781502442482

Buddha illustration by Arthur Aguirre

No part of this book may be reproduced or transmitted in any form or by any means, electronic or mechanical, including photocopying, recording, or by any information storage and retrieval system, without the express written permission of the author.

DavidAngsten.com
davidangsten.blogspot.com
Twitter: @DavidAngsten
davangsten@gmail.com

To my brave and loving 90-year-old mom,
against whom the enemies of Western civilization
do not stand a chance.

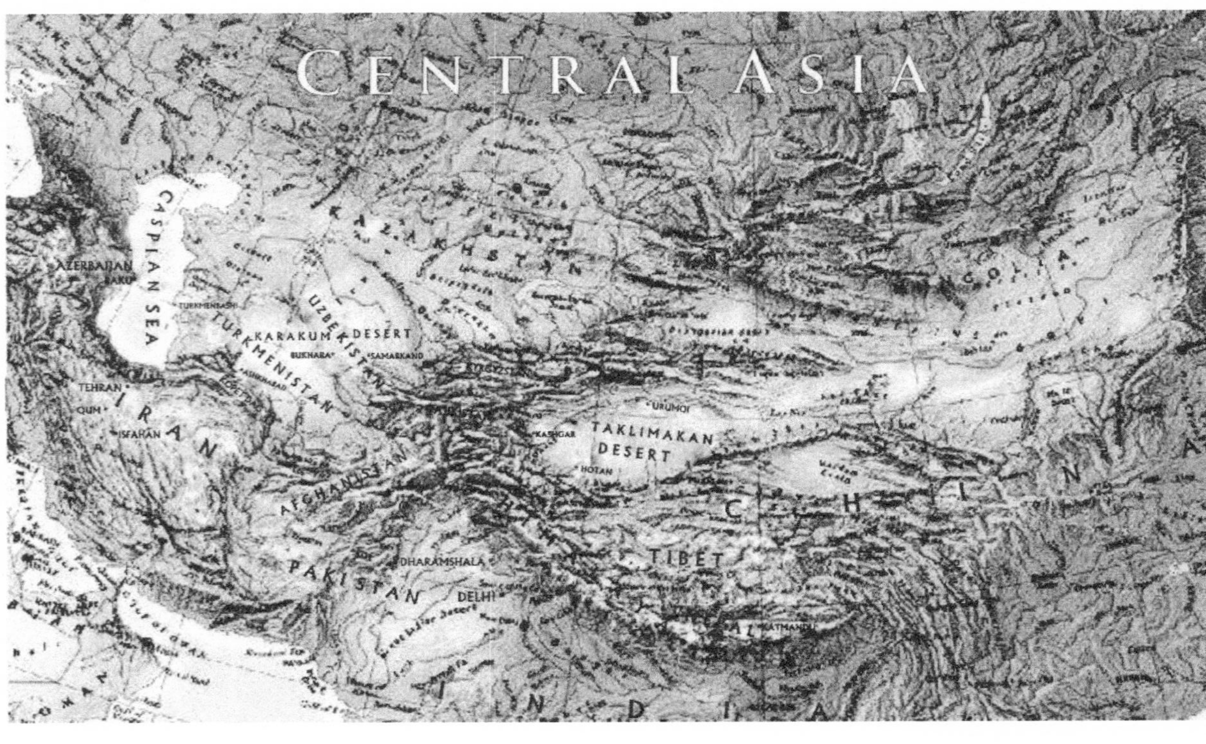
CENTRAL ASIA
CASPIAN SEA
AZERBAIJAN
BAKU
TURKMENBASHI
KAZAKHSTAN
UZBEKISTAN
TURKMENISTAN
KARAKUM DESERT
BUKHARA
SAMARKAND
TEHRAN
QUM
ISFAHAN
IRAN
AFGHANISTAN
PAKISTAN
DHARAMSHALA
DELHI
KASHGAR
URUMQI
TAKLIMAKAN DESERT
HOTAN
TIBET
KATHMANDU
MONGOLIA
CHINA
INDIA

OM MANI PÄDME HUM

The jewel is in the lotus

Nirvana is in samsara

The Buddha is in the world

Rome

1.
I Awoke from a Dream

I awoke from a dream in the dead of night, that hour when your fear lays bare the truth that you've been hiding. My dream was like that song they write a thousand different ways, the one about the love you lost, the girl that stole your heart, the face you can't forget. In mine she's sitting still as stone beneath an ancient oak, staring off inscrutably, unaware I'm there. Her beauty takes my breath away. Her glance would stop my heart. However hard I try it seems I cannot turn away from her. The woman has enthralled me. Longing is my fate.

It's a cynic's dream, I realize, now that I'm awake. A jilted lover's pity party. An alibi for apathy; no surrogates will do.

Which only begged the question: Who was this unfortunate woman lying beside me now?

Her snoring had woke me up. Open mouth gasping through the tangle of her hair, face half-buried in her pillow. What *was* it we'd been drinking? All I could remember was that single red carafe. A deep fatigue still dragged me down; I could not seem to shake it. Studying her face, I forced myself awake.

She hadn't been on the tour, that much I remembered; she'd joined up with my group of students later at the club. Half-Asian, half-Caucasian, an alluring blend of East and West, yet so gregariously American she fit right in among them. Something about the woman had reminded me of Phoebe. Her spirit, her "spark." The immediate attraction. But I could not remember now the color of her eyes—always a bad sign. And then it occurred to me, lying there beside her in that crappy *pensione*, I couldn't even remember her name. Glenda? Gwyneth? I know it started with a G. Gina? Ginny? Something like that. Gabby?

She *had* been a talker. University of Miami, "the one in Ohio," she said, a vital point of distinction. Her program was out of Luxembourg. With a few fellow students, she'd traveled by train to Rome. This was to be her last night on the town before heading back to the States. Final chance for that foreign fling with the dark and handsome stranger. After all, what is that glorious semester abroad but a closet romantic's make-believe adventure? In reality, Europe is just one big museum, the display of a dead culture's former greatness, everything God left behind before he finally died, all prettily preserved for the tourists.

That's where I came in. Guide to the Eternal Museum by day, escort to the underground clubs at night. No dark and seductive Italian, perhaps, but good enough in a pinch, and probably safer, too. I made certain of that. Both of us could rest assured that nothing we did mattered. Aside from a hangover, our night of blithe abandon would be free of consequences. STDs. Pregnancy. Or God forbid, love.

Or even love-making, as it turned out. Yes, I *had* been that wasted. Waiting forever for her to return from the bathroom down the hall, I had fallen fast asleep.

I got dressed now quietly in the dark, careful not to wake her. Why go through the embarrassment? Why bother with goodbye? Would she remember *my* name? Even if she did, she'd probably feign to forget, laughing it off with the other young scholars swapping tales on the way to the airport, flaunting the newfound sophistication they were transporting back to Ohio.

But later, on the plane perhaps, sitting with her headphones on, gazing down at the sea, she might think of me a moment, conjure up my face, recall something I said—that joke about the gelded gladiator?—converting me into a reminiscence, an "experience" had in Europe, repeating my name one last time before filing me away for good.

Jack Duran. That derelict American I tried to hook up with

in Rome.

How quickly, I wondered, would *he* be forgotten?

[IN PERSIAN:]

"Vanitar. Wake up."

Arshan's voice startled me awake. I instinctively grabbed the steering wheel, then remembered the car was parked.

Arshan nodded out the windshield. "He's leaving," he said. "Alone."

Duran had stepped out the hotel door. He stopped under the streetlight and pulled out his cell. "Who do you think he's calling?" I asked.

"A taxi," Arshan muttered.

"How do you know that?"

"How do you think?"

"I have no idea."

"Look. What's he doing?"

"Standing there. Dialing."

"And what is it he's not *doing?"*

A thousand things, I thought.

"Walking and dialing," he said.

Duran held the phone up to his ear repeatedly.

"There's something wrong with his cell," I said.

"Yes. Something."

"Maybe the battery died."

Arshan watched in silence.

At last Duran pocketed the phone and started up the street. "If he was calling for a cab," I said, "looks like he's given up."

"Take us back to the hotel," Arshan said.

I started the car. "Don't you want to follow him?"

"He's going home," he said.

"How can you know that?"

Arshan watched the American slowly disappear into the dark. "I just know," he said.

2.
Maya

"I can't hear—are you there?"

The clock showed half past noon. I pushed open the shutters and squinted into the sunlight. "I am. ...Aren't I?" The grogginess still lingered.

"Hello?"

"Hello...hello...pronto—"

"There you are," she said. "For a second there I lost you."

"Sorry, it's my cell," I said. "Been acting funny lately."

"Have you complained to your provider?"

"No, why?"

"I just...wonder who's responsible."

"Responsible? Signora, this is Italy."

She laughed. In India, Maya is the goddess of illusion. In Rome, she was a tourist on the telephone.

She told me she worked in the city of Mumbai as a rep for a clothing company. Visiting Rome on business, she was leaving the following day. "I'm looking to hire a guide," she said. "I'd like a private tour of the Forum." She had found my travel site online and was calling me from her hotel room.

A professional woman, traveling alone, was not my typical client. Like my group of undergrads the previous day, my customers were usually students abroad, or American families on a budget. If they didn't want to hire an Italian guide, tourists of means preferred to call my competition, like the retired Australian classics professor, or the lesbian British historian, native English speakers with credentials and a license and connections to the major travel packagers. Why had Maya Rakshasi picked me?

After we hung up, I *Googled* her. No direct match turned up, but her surname drew a curious link. It turned out to be the name for the females of a race of Hindu-Buddhist demons known as the Rakshasas, warrior spirits that feed on human flesh and are shape-shifting masters of magic and illusion.

I looked forward to meeting her.

We rendezvoused at noon at the entry gate. She was easy to spot in the crowd. Striking, cinnamon-skinned, hair a lacquered black. On the phone her elegant voice had sounded smokily middle-aged, but in person she looked not much older than me, probably early thirties. She greeted me with a firm handshake and a penetrating gaze. While I might not describe her as a Bollywood beauty, she did have a provocative physicality about her, a barely veiled sexual presence. Something in her eyes seemed predatory, too—a dispassionate sort of cunning or curiosity. Definitely more cat than kitten, I thought. Her mother might have mated with a panther.

Late that evening, after the tour, we met at a restaurant in Trastevere. It was just a few blocks from the rooms I rented and a stone's throw away from the Tiber. An old man at the back played a violin, and the waiters spoke only Italian. I wore my weathered, ivory-colored jacket with its epaulet straps and button-flap pockets, playing up my image as "safari guide" to Rome. Maya sat across from me with her back against the wall, bare-shouldered in a gauzy summer sari. Her face looked dark in the candlelight, but her amber eyes shone bright. When she asked me to translate the menu, I slid into the seat beside her. Maya seemed to like the arrangement. After we ordered, I stayed.

We talked about India and various sites I had visited there several years before. Then we talked about Italy, the Italians, and Rome. This led to my mentioning the novel I was reading, the ribald classic of debauchery, *The Satyricon*, written in the days of Nero. It turned out Maya had read Petronius' tale, too, and we had both seen the film by Fellini. As so often occurs in that chronicle of excess, the two of us were soon swimming in wine. Wine was the point of our dinner, really, even if we didn't acknowledge it. We knew we had only one night together. There wasn't much time for romance.

When she asked if I often took lady clients out to dinner, I told her she was the first. She didn't even pretend to believe me.

After the meal we strolled out onto the Ponte Sisto bridge, now thoroughly defaced with graffiti like every other structure in Rome. An African immigrant in a Ché T-shirt was hawking wilted flowers. *"Rosone! Rosone!"* Halfway out we paused to gaze at the rippling moon on the water.

I asked Maya how she came to choose me out of all the tour guides in the city.

She grinned. "I'd be embarrassed to tell you." She spoke with a beguiling British accent, that enduring remnant of the Raj.

"Tell me," I insisted, nudging her.

Laughter lit up her face—"I can't!"

"I need to know," I told her. "For professional reasons."

Maya, smiling, looked away. "Well, if that's the case…" Stretching her arms to the rim of the bridge, she coyly turned her eyes on me. "The truth is, Jack…I liked your picture."

"Ha!" I scoffed.

But her eyes stayed with mine, and her smile faded away.

It's remarkable how willingly you can fall for an illusion, especially one that caters to your vanity and lust. I lifted Maya's hand off the rail and gently pulled her toward me. "You're beautiful," I whispered.

As I started to kiss her, she turned away, glancing shyly around us. "Didn't you say you lived near here?"

"I didn't say. But I do."

[IN PERSIAN:]

"They're leaving."

"Your powers of observation are improving by the day."

"Shall I follow?" I asked.

"We know where they're going. The question is why they're

going there."

"What do you imagine? Sex? Drugs?"

"You're the expert, Vanitar. I didn't go to university."

"Sex and *drugs, then, I suspect."*

"Yes, he is *an American."*

"But the lady is a Hindi," I said.

"And to you this makes a difference? Must you constantly pick at that?"

"Must you smoke in the car?" I licked the cut above my lip. "The scab is finally coming off."

"Little boys nurse little wounds. Learn to wear yours proudly."

"Why? Because you put it there?"

"Because it improves your looks."

"We're going to lose them if we don't—"

"Not just yet."

"What is it?"

"How many times have I told you? Look more carefully. See."

"The cop?"I asked.

"Open your eyes, brother."

"I don't—"

"The roach. With the flowers."

"What about him?"

"He was there. This afternoon."

"At the ruins?"

"Look—now. What do you see?"

"He's...walking."

"And?"

"He's...turning down the next street."

"And?"

"Same direction?"

"And?"

"And... The flowers—he left them on the bridge!"

3.
The Garden

My intention was to deliver Maya directly to my bedroom, but when she heard my landlord had a garden on the roof, she insisted I take her up there for a drink. I grabbed two glasses and a bottle of grappa and led her up the twisting stairwell.

The townhouse, like so many habitations in the medieval neighborhood of Trastevere, was undergoing a seemingly perpetual renovation. The first two floors, vacated and barren, were occasionally visited by a seventy-year-old carpenter and his crew of Albanian plasterers, but my rooms on the third floor, behind the owner's apartment, had not been touched by trowel or brush in probably fifty years. Gaps in cracking plaster revealed darkly rotting brick, the ancient floorboards sprouted deadly square-head iron nails, and the rickety staircase spiraled up the hall like an escape route out of Dante's Inferno.

The rooftop deck was another world entirely. My landlord's urban Eden was an ersatz jungle of potted citrus, bougainvillea, hibiscus and bamboo. *"Una parte piccolo di paradiso"* he called it—a little piece of paradise. He had left me to care for it over the summer while he attended to his dying mother in Palermo.

Maya's eyes were soon drawn to a green-glazed pot of water with a floating lotus flower. Its red and gold petals appeared to burn beneath the moon.

"I've never seen anything like it," she said.

I uncorked the bottle of grappa. "Signore Moscato grew it

from a seed."

She bent to caress the flower with her fingers. Her black hair shimmered as it fell around her face. "What is it called?" she asked.

I told her I didn't know.

She tucked her hair behind an ear, turning her bronze eyes on me. "Do you know where he found the seed?"

"My brother sent it," I said. I had told her he was traveling in Asia. "He knows about my landlord's amazing green thumb."

Maya stood upright. "Did he only send the one seed?"

"No, he sent a few." I poured her a glass. "But we were only able to get one of them to sprout."

"Did you keep the rest?"

"Keep them? No. Why would I do that?"

"Is there any way to contact him—your brother?"

"Dan is pretty much off the grid."

"Where did he send the seeds from?"

It took me a moment to remember; over a year had passed. "Srinagar, I think?"

"That's in northern India," she said. "Near Kashmir and Tibet." She crouched down to take another look at the plant. "I'm curious," she said. "My family's estate in India has a very old lotus garden. Been there for generations. Acres of ponds, many different species. I've never seen one as beautiful as this." She fingered the seed pod at the end of a stalk.

"Well, that calls for a toast." I set the bottle of grappa on the ledge of the roof, then turned and raised my glass to her. "To rare beauty," I said.

She rose and touched her glass to mine. Her eyes grinned as we sipped.

"This mysterious brother of yours. You really don't know where he is?"

I turned to rest my elbows on the ledge and gaze out over the rooftops. Leonard Cohen's *Bird on a Wire* droned from an open window. A glazed Mercedes idled on the narrow street below. "I don't hear from Dan," I said.

Maya hugged her purse, peering out at the ominous clouds

moving in from the east. “I read something about your… incident.”

“My what?”

“On the Greek island, Ogygia. With your brother. What did they call it? ‘Night of the—”

“Where did you read about that?”

“You can hardly avoid it,” she said, “—at least when *Googling* Jack Duran.”

“You *Googled* me?”

“Of course.” She looped her arm through mine. “A professional tour is one thing. An evening out is another.”

“I see. So you thought I might be Jack the Ripper. Was it something I said on the tour?”

Maya laughed and snuggled closer. “I *loved* the tour,” she said. “But a woman has to be cautious.”

We gazed out over the serpentine streets. Caution was certainly a requirement in Rome. “You’re right,” I said. “I’m surprised you agreed to dinner after finding out all that.”

“To the contrary,” she said. “It only piqued my interest.”

Nearly two years had passed since the “incident” occurred, and I had hoped it had all been forgotten. But having blazed its way across the digital globe, the “Night of the Furies,” as it came to be known, would never be more than a few key strokes away.

The story had been tailor-made for the tabloids. My brother Dan and I, and his Dutch girlfriend Phoebe, had stumbled on an ancient Dionysian cult, alive and secluded in the Cyclades. A friend of Dan’s, the heir to a Turkish shipping empire, quite literally lost his head. A violent, bacchanalian madness ensued. Many of the women in the cult were killed, a Byzantine church was nearly blown to kingdom come, and a long history of murder was uncovered, igniting an international uproar.

Although we were ultimately acquitted of any wrongdoing, an unwelcome notoriety hounded us. This was especially true with Dan. He had discovered the formula for the legendary elixir that inspired the Eleusinian Mysteries, the greatest religious rite of the ancient pagan world. Consequently besieged by reporters, Greek government officials, Big Pharma recruiters, chronically stoned "psychonauts" and pagan religious fanatics, he ended up running away to Nepal and trekking into the Himalayas.

I simply headed back to Rome. I'd been promised a job with an American travel packager, leading tours of the Vatican Museum, but given the incident with the Byzantine church, security objected, and the agency declined. Since then I'd been struggling to make a living on my own, working black market in the tour biz.

"My brother's the adventurous one," I said. "You've got nothing to worry about with me."

"Why haven't you returned to America?" Maya asked.

"I will," I said. "Eventually."

"What is it keeps you here?"

I sighed, then shrugged, "I like the food?"

Maya laughed. "I imagine there's something more to it than that." She considered me for a moment. "What happened to the Dutch woman? The archaeologist—what was her name?"

"Phoebe Auerbach." I sipped my glass of grappa. Had it really been nearly two years since I'd spoken her name out loud?

"Is she still with your brother?"

"Not that I know of."

Maya kept her eyes on me.

"Phoebe ran away, too," I said.

"From the press?"

"No." I thought of her scribbled note, that one-word exit line I chased in the god-blown winds of Dodona. "From love."

Maya eyed me a moment, then gazed back at the view. "Then that was her mistake," she said. "She was far too cautious."

"Unlike you?" I asked.

She continued peering out over the city. "When I decide to do something, I do it resolutely, with all my heart. In India we say the traveler who hesitates…'only raises dust on the road.'"Again she turned her eyes to me. Warm, gleaming amber. I moved close, took her hand, breathed in her perfume. The scent was so bewitching, it seemed to swirl around me. I thought it might just whisk away every trace of Phoebe.

A sudden shatter of glass startled us. I looked to see if we'd knocked the bottle of grappa off the ledge.

We hadn't. The noise had come from the rooms below.

Maya looked alarmed. "I thought the house was empty?"

Fear tickled the pit of my belly. "It was," I said as I headed for the stairs.

4.
Rakshasas

Maya followed behind me as we came out into the hall. The door to my rooms stood ajar. Someone lurked inside.

I started toward the door, then hesitated, debating if I should call the police or confront the intruder myself. Roman burglars were known to be brazen, but rarely carried weapons. Still, there was always the chance.

I groped my pockets for my cell.

"Wait here," Maya whispered, stepping out ahead of me. She extracted something from her purse.

"*Maya?*" I stared in stunned disbelief as she screwed a silencer onto a handgun. "*What are you—?*"

With a finger to her lips, she shushed me. Then she quietly lowered her purse to the floor, turned and slipped inside.

I clawed open my cell. My heart pounded, out of control. Thoughts sped up, then froze: Carabinieri? Polizia. Nine-one-one—no. One-one-two. No—one-one—

Maya cried out. The muffled pistol *cracked.*

A shock ran through me. I started toward the door. From behind me an arm slipped around my throat. I glimpsed a flare of steel.

"Drop the phone." The man's whisper at my ear smelled of cigarette smoke. He let me feel the edge of the blade. It brought an icy shiver.

My cell phone clattered on the floor. I could barely breathe.

"Please," I said. "Take my wallet. There's nothing here to steal."

He crushed the cell phone under his heel, then shoved me toward the door.

I turned. The only thing I saw at first was the long blade of the knife he held, curved for cutting throats.

"What do you want?" I asked.

He was a large man with a dark face, thick black brows and a short-clipped beard. A Romanian immigrant, I thought at first. They committed much of the city's crime and were much despised by the Romans. But this man wore a tailored suit, elegant and expensive. The haircut looked expensive, too, and the beard looked Middle-Eastern.

He bent to pick up Maya's purse and, moving forward with the knife, gestured toward the door.

I backed into the room.

The apartment lay in disarray, drawers dangling, a lamp shattered. In horror I spotted Maya lying twisted on the rug, her gauzy sari dark with blood. Beside her, a black man lay face down, bleeding from his ear. In his ragged hoodie and jeans, he looked like a bum off the street. Both of them appeared to be dead.

The man with the knife assessed them coolly. Seeing the gun in Maya's hand, he kicked it spinning across the floor. Then he rolled over the body of the dead man. The dead man wore a black Ché tee.

This was the immigrant we had seen selling roses on the bridge. He must have followed us home to rob us. But then who was this man in the suit?

I dropped to my knees beside Maya. The beggar's switchblade protruded from her chest. Had the blade reached her heart? Her eyes still held some feeble light; blood gurgled in her throat.

A panicky surge of hope filled me—*Maya was still alive*. I reached to withdraw the blade, then hesitated, envisioning a fountain of blood. My hand hung over her, trembling.

The big Middle-Eastern man searched through Maya's purse.

"I think she's still alive," I told him. "She needs an ambulance, fast."

He found her passport in the bag, briefly flipped through it, and slipped it into his jacket. Then his eyes alit on something else. He gingerly lifted it out of the purse.

The seed pod from the lotus plant.

He held it out to me. "Where did she get this?"

"I don't—" I stared at the wrinkly pod, confused. Had Maya actually filched it? Slipped it into her purse?

"Tell me where," he repeated. The man loomed over me, clenching the crooked dagger. The exotic blade looked menacing, as if designed for fright. Arcing from the hilt, the crescent straightened toward the tip, a piercing point for jabbing. Swirling patterns streaked the steel. The polished bone grip glimmered. The particular way the man held the knife—his thumb on the blunt edge of the blade—told me he knew very well how to use it.

"Upstairs," I answered, my voice shaking. "There's a garden on the roof."

"Show me."

I looked down at Maya. "She'll die if we don't get her help."

"Then you will be wise to—"

A humming noise interrupted him.

He looked down at the black man's corpse, then searched the man's pockets until he found the vibrating phone. He hit "answer" and raised it to his ear. "Your flower boy has stained the rug," he said. "Better call the housemaid."

I stared at him in confusion as he crunched the phone underfoot.

[IN PERSIAN:]

The third floor light went out. Shortly after, my cell vibrated. The caller ID showed the number from Ali Mahbood.

I hesitated. Arshan had asked me to stay off the phone. And I despised Mahbood. But he ran our intelligence and might have info on the Hindi. I answered in a whisper, said I couldn't talk for long.

"You tremble like a woman," he scoffed. He asked me to

describe the flower boy we had followed to Duran's.

"Deep black. Five-ten. One...sixty. I'd guess...early-20's?"

"Flowers, that's cute. My money he's Tunisian."

"Another dealer then?" I asked.

"North Africa's their Refah. Heard the news from Mali? They're not just chewing khat."

"Anything on the Hindi?"

"Mule for his brother, most likely."

"So you don't really know," I said.

"I told you, we're looking into it. Why are you so jumpy?"

"Arshan suspects the roach might be a floater for the RAW. Or even the CIA."

"What? *Why?"*

"He thinks Duran's phone got tapped by the woman he met last night."

Mahbood went silent. "You calling from the car?"

"He asked me to wait."

"Call back later—from elsewhere. They might've boxed the street." (Click.)

The man followed me as I scrambled up the stairwell to the roof. I stumbled, my mind racing faster than my feet. *Was the lotus the source of some illegal drug? Had I been caught in the middle of a gang war?* There had been nothing unusual about the seeds Dan had sent. And his note stated only that the plant was very rare. "See if your landlord can grow it," he wrote. "The lotus is truly divine."

Now I was standing with a knife at my back, pointing in terror at the plant. Its delicate red and yellow flower looked threatening, as if the little flame might engulf us. The seed pod, I noticed, had indeed been removed—Maya had surreptitiously snatched it off the stem.

The man with the knife approached the plant in awe, a modern bearded Moses before a miniature burning bush. He slowly lowered the blade to his side and stood there, silent and still. For a second I considered making a run for it: if I beat him down the stairs, I might lose him on the streets. He was big, but I figured I was faster.

The man turned and glared at me as if he'd read my thoughts. Grabbing a fistful of my hair, he hauled my head back and rested the edge of the blade against my windpipe. I could barely croak out a word. *"Please—"*

"Tell me where are the rest."

"No...more—"

"You lie. Where are the seeds?"

"Gone," I rasped.

"You lie again." He lowered his gaze to the blade at my throat. "I will ask you one last question. You will tell me the truth." His probing eyes fixed on mine. "Where," he asked, "is your brother?"

Staring into the slits of his eyes, I suddenly knew for certain he would kill me. Not because I didn't have an answer to his question, and not because I wouldn't be believed. The reason he would kill me was because of what I'd seen: the break-in, the bodies, the lotus, his face. Everything that had happened now inhabited my head. He could lop it off as easily as a flower.

"I don't know," I whispered.

He stretched my throat beneath the blade. I felt a sting and a trickle.

"You will tell me—"

Crack!

He gasped, arching his back in pain. A second shot blew a bolt of blood out of his neck. He staggered, turning, terrified.

Maya had crawled to the top of the stairs. She blasted one more bullet into his chest, then lowered the gun in her outstretched hands and collapsed on the floor in exhaustion.

The man, bleeding profusely, pulled out his cell and thumbed two keys. He gazed at me glassily, then toppled onto his clattering knife.

I scrambled over to Maya. She clung on, barely alive.

A phone was ringing. I glanced at the dying killer. But the sound was not coming from the cell in his fist; it was coming from down on the street.

I hurriedly peered over the edge of the roof. In the darkness below, a driver in a suit stepped out of the Mercedes, holding a cell to his ear. I could hear his voice crackle in the killer's phone behind me. He shut his cell and ran his eyes quickly up the building, where he spotted me staring down at him. For a moment we both stood frozen—until he broke it off and strode toward the door.

I stepped back, shaking, flooded with adrenalin. I ran over and crouched beside Maya. She had pulled the switchblade out of her chest, and blood now pulsed from the open wound. Slowly losing consciousness, she struggled desperately to breathe.

I slipped my arm under her shoulders and lifted her into my lap, trying to straighten her windpipe. She gagged.

"Maya—"

Words gurgled in her throat. *"Destroy...the lotus—"*

"What is it? Who are they?"

She strained with all her might to be heard. I lowered my ear to listen.

"They'll kill you," she whispered. *"Your brother, too."*

I watched in horror as her eyes went cold.

5.
See Jack Run

I could hear him spiraling up the stairs, leather soles on creaking wood. I yanked the lotus plant out of the pot, then ripped it up and tossed it over the side of the building. Then I went to the dead man, found the seed pod in his pocket and threw it over, too.

The door to the roof only locked from the inside. I hid behind the entryway. Barely had I gotten there when I heard his voice at the door.

"Arshan?"

Maya's corpse lay at the man's feet. He bent to examine her briefly, then he ventured into the garden. Spying him dimly through a shimmer of bamboo, I could just make out the dark figure of the man and the glint of his knife in the moonlight.

"Arshan!" he cried, suddenly racing forward and dropping to his knees.

I stepped out from behind the bamboo and slipped into the stairwell. The man turned abruptly as I shut and bolted the door. Seconds later, as I flew down the steps, the stairwell resounded with a violent battering. By the time I reached the bottom he had broken through the lock.

I ran for my life. The sound of the man's voice had sent a cold chill up my spine. Though he had spoken only a name, it was clear that "Arshan" had been more than a cohort or a friend. There had been blood in his voice.

Footsteps echoed in the alleyway behind me. I turned up the Via della Paglia and ran alongside the Santa Maria church.

It was late, but I hoped there would be people in the piazza. There were none. The moonlit fountain gushed in isolation. I dashed past it, sprinting to the far side. As I spun into an alley I caught a glimpse of my pursuer, pausing as he rushed into the square.

I turned and ran.

Except for solitary whores and drunks, the streets were largely vacant. I darted down the shadowy lanes, zigzagging corners at a full tilt, until by turn I stood before the Garibaldi bridge. No more footsteps clattered in my wake. If he followed, he ran without shoes. I sprinted over the Tiber.

That pained cry—*Arshan!*—still echoed in my ears. Surely he must have gone back, I thought. Returned to retrieve the body before the *polizia* arrived.

That is, if someone were to notify the police. Believe it or not, despite all the murder, I dreaded making that call. My stay permit had not been renewed, and my business was illegal—not to mention the lotus plant, which I now assumed had to be a drug my brother was smuggling.

I trotted up the side streets along Via Arenula. At Vittorio Emanuele I hailed a taxi cab, and ten minutes later, near the Esquiline hill, I was knocking on an apartment house's red-lacquered door.

After repeated banging, it finally cracked open, and a shrew wrapped in a shawl peered out, hair askew, eyes popping, looking almost comically unhinged. *"Tu?"* Spewing a stream of disparaging Italian, she started to shut the door.

I pushed in past her and leapt up the stairs. "I'll wait 'til he gets back," I declared in Italian, then barricaded myself in Vincenzo Accidi's room.

———

"Dead."

The word stunned Mahbood. "You're certain?"

I struggled to contain my swelling rage. "Yes. They killed *him."*

"Who?"

"The Hindi, she's dead. The American—"

"I'm having trouble hearing you...that noise—"

I moved away from the fountain. "Duran escaped."

"You gave chase?"

"Of course."

"You need to be careful. He may be armed—"

"My brother has been killed. You ask me to be careful?"

"I ask you to remain calm, think this through."

Calm. Like Arshan. The remembrance of Allah.

"Did you say something?"

"No." I started heading back.

"What happened to the African?"

"I don't know. I don't care."

"What about Duran? Any idea where he is?"

"No," I said. "But I'll find him."

"Listen to me. You must not return to his apartment—"

"I'm going back to the car."

"Leave it. We'll—"

I ended the call and shut off the phone. No more orders from Ali Mahbood. I knew what had to be done. And what I needed to do it.

6.
Rabbit Hole

Vincenzo was the closest I had to an actual friend in Rome. A 34-year-old Italian adolescent, he still lived under his mother's care in the same room he'd grown up in. Doting, disapproving, she cooked his meals and did his laundry, while he ran the travel business inherited from his father. That's how I had met him, through my work as a guide in Rome. He accounted for more than half of my referrals.

The imp was out, as I'd expected, but I knew he'd soon be back. Vincenzo would never submit himself to an entire night with a woman; he deemed anything more than a roll in the hay an unacceptable long-term commitment.

His computer glowed with a photograph of the current Italian heartthrob, the actress and singer Violante Placido. I sat down before this goddess and *Googled* "lotus, drug." This brought up a list of links to *Nymphaea caerulea,* the Blue Lotus, which apparently had been used by the ancient Egyptians to induce an ecstatic state, and was also a candidate for the addictive flower on the island of the 'Lotus Eaters' in Homer's *Odyssey*. But the plant had only very mild psychoactive properties, certainly not worth killing people over. In addition, the color was wrong, and it turns out the Blue Lotus is not a lotus at all, but rather a species of water lily, a different plant entirely.

After chasing these fuzzy lotus links down a few more rabbit holes, I searched for Maya Rakshasi again, skimming lists of sales reps at Indian textile companies. This got me nowhere, of course. If she was a traveling saleswoman, why would she carry a loaded semi-automatic? And even if she did actually carry it for protection, why would she also carry a silencer? Why, indeed, had she *used* the silencer?

The flower peddler was even more puzzling. Had he been looking for the lotus as well? Who had he been following, me or Maya? And had the men in the Mercedes been following us all?

Your flower boy, the man had said into the cell. Who had he been talking to?

I searched the Web for the kind of knife the two Middle-Easterners had brandished. An antique "Indo-Persian dagger" appeared the closest to it, while the swirling pattern I'd seen in the blade resembled "Damascus steel." The steel's secretive history intrigued me. The forging technique originated in ancient India, and in the Middle Ages was further refined in the Muslim Middle East, where the wavy-patterned, stormy steel took on its Syrian moniker. But it was the smelting process developed in Persia that created the most coveted "Damascene" blades. Swords and daggers of supreme sharpness and strength, they garnered an almost mythical reputation among the invading Crusaders.

Most curious of all was this: According to modern metalsmiths, the secret to producing this type of "true" Damascus steel was lost nearly 300 years ago. No one knows exactly how the deadly blades were made.

So what were these "Indo-Persian" knives—fabricated copies? Perhaps they were genuine antiques. Either way it spoke to the strangeness of these men, their odd anachronism, drawing Damascene daggers from beneath their Hugo Boss. But still it told me nothing of who the men were, or why they seemed so intent on the lotus.

I fell back on Vincenzo's bed and stared bug-eyed at the ceiling. My thoughts swirled like that stormy steel, my head awash in wine and dread. The rush of adrenaline had barely subsided, and my heart still rattled in my chest. I worried about what I should tell the police, and feared I'd be arrested when they found the link to Dan.

Over the years, my brother had compiled a lengthy criminal record. At least four different arrests in four different countries: once for attempting to smuggle *ayahuasca* out of the Amazon, once for possession of DMT snuff, once for selling fake antiquities in Mexico, and finally for suspicion of murder in Greece. Only in the latter case had he actually been acquitted.

Yet Dan could hardly be labeled an outright criminal. He was an eccentric, autodidact intellectual, a self-described "Dionysian libertarian" who disregarded laws he felt intruded on his freedom, in particular the freedom to explore his own psyche. His illegal "experiments" were conducted, he claimed, purely in the interests of science. They focused on the interface of consciousness and matter, the emergence of the disembodied mind from the brain. "Mapping the boundary of the human soul" is the way he grandly put it. Reality-altering chemicals were his primary tools of research, but in recent years his inquiries had turned more academic: historical and anthropological analyses, ethno-botanical pharmacology studies, readings on the origins of ancient religions, and experiential research into Eastern mysticism.

All of which I had hoped would finally keep him out of trouble.

After our last disaster—the aforementioned Night of the Furies—I myself had sworn off the use of anything illegal. Normal, everyday consciousness seemed plenty scary enough. I still indulged in wine, of course, to lull the inner autocrat and loosen inhibition, but even there I stayed within the bounds of moderation. "Nothing in excess"—words of caution carved on the Temple of Apollo, where we'd heedlessly embarked on our Furies misadventure. And *nothing,* of course, meant *everything*—not just drink and drugs, but food, money, lust, love, greed, hate, fear.

Fear.

I tried to calm myself. Too much fear befuddles. I needed clarity to think.

On the wall beside the bed hung a framed portrait of Jesus. Like me, Vincenzo had been raised Catholic, and like me, he no longer practiced. His mother had probably hung this picture to admonish her dissolute son. The image was a familiar one: the long, soft, flowing locks, the handsome, gentle countenance, the otherworldly halo hovering magically over his head. *The human face of God.* I'd seen essentially the same picture from the time I was a kid. There was something reassuring about it, even a bit entrancing, and for a moment, gazing into that all-forgiving face, I completely forgot myself.

Perhaps my situation wasn't really all that bad. At least not with the police. I knew in all likelihood they would slap me with a fine. Might even try to deport me. Or lock me up in jail. At the very worst I'd be implicated in murder. But surely the risk I faced with them was less than I faced with the drug gang. The gang had a man on the streets with a knife, a man determined to kill me. He was the real danger.

I had to go to the police. It was foolish to think I wouldn't. Except for failing to file some paperwork, I'd actually done nothing wrong. I decided I would tell the cops exactly what had happened. The minute Vincenzo returned I'd have him drive me down to the station.

I relaxed on the bed, breathing deep, repeating the same thought like a mantra: *I got away. It's all right now. I'm okay. I'm safe.* The adrenalin shock that had fuelled my run gradually subsided, and a heavy weight of exhaustion seemed to press me into the bed. Gentle raindrops ticked against the window. I turned and gazed at Jesus until my eyelids fluttered shut.

It was there. Under the passenger seat. Right where Arshan had stashed it less than half an hour before.

Barely half an hour! Alive, sitting beside me! Calm, unflappable, chain smoking cigarettes, dropping wry remarks. Now he lay on that roof in the rain—just there, above the street—dead, bleeding out his heart, no one there to mourn him.

I twisted off the silver cap and sniffed the musky scent. The odor evoked a vision. Rivers of milk and honey flowing beneath the Eternal Garden, where a drink from the bottomless spring drew one nearer to Allah. I quaffed from the goatskin in keen anticipation, eager for the blessings that would soon pour down upon me. Laying my head back, I closed my eyes, waiting for the words to come, the prayer Arshan would whisper.

"The gates of Paradise lie beneath the shade of swords. In the remembrance of Allah, the heart will find its rest."

The remembrance of Allah. His gift to us on earth. A taste of the sweet Paradise awaiting us hereafter.

Already I could feel it, descending like the rain. Suffusing me with certainty. Filling me with strength.

The killing of this American would be the start of bliss.

"Jack! Pronto!?"

I flicked the windshield wipers. Across the street a loudmouthed drunk banged on Duran's door. "E mio, Vincenzo!" *His call echoed down the street. The transom remained dark.*

Behind him loitered two spike-heeled raggaze, *impatiently tugging their earring hoops and brushing back rain-soaked hair.*

"Jack!"

I watched. And waited. It is not every day you see the hand of God at work.

7.
Loca

Leather soles on creaking wood.

I leapt from Vincenzo's bed. Someone was creeping up the stairwell. Had I fallen asleep? Had the killer tracked me down? My heart pounded frantically. I looked around for another way out. In the bathroom I knew there was a window. I wondered if I could jump.

Out in the hall, a woman giggled. It was cut off by a "shush" and a man's pleading whisper.

I snapped open the door.

One wore black mesh stockings. The other had raccoon eyes. They peered from behind Vincenzo, who gaped at me in surprise. "Jack!" he whispered. *"Lei é qui!"*

"Si," I sighed. "You woke me."

Vincenzo ushered the women inside and quietly shut the door. I noticed their hair and clothes were soused, and realized it must be raining.

"We look for you," he said in English, pushing back his damp locks and tossing down his keys. "I bring my friends to meet you."

"Look for me? Where?"

"Everywhere. *Accidenti, oy!"* He lifted my chin and winced at my throat. "You no use electric?"

"What time is it?" I asked.

He shrugged. "Two? Three?"

Dance music blared.

"No, piacere!" Vincenzo charged at the raccoon lady, who

had inserted her iPod into his dock and was trying to find the volume. He lowered it for her and—avoiding any mention of his mother—patiently reminded the girl not to awaken the *loca* (crazy woman) in the rooms below.

The girl pleaded. I interrupted. "Vinny. Did you go to my apartment?"

The raccoon defied him and turned up the juice.

"*Si,* you no answer your phone—"

"*Veeencenzo...*" The stockinged woman tugged him away, entwining herself in his arms.

"Did you see anyone there? Vincenzo?"

He turned as they danced. "Light was on. But door is locked. We are knocking, knocking, but no answer. So, I bring ladies here."

Raccoon Eyes had taken my hand and was dragging me onto the floor. Her hair a sopping mop.

"Did you see a man?" I asked her. "A man in a suit with a beard and moustache?"

She gazed at me without answering. Her dark eyes floated in pitch-black pools that bled down over her cheeks.

Vincenzo danced beside us. "She likes you, Jack!"

The ghoulish woman's drunken dance would frighten off the devil.

"Vinny, listen—"

He suddenly held up a hand to silence me, cocking his head to a sound. Then he reached over and turned off the music.

Someone was knocking at the door downstairs.

"Oh no," I whispered.

The stockinged woman asked if we had woken up the *loca.* Vincenzo shushed her and listened at the door.

I hurried to the window and scanned the cars below. Under a street lamp half a block away, falling rain splashed on a parked black Mercedes.

The pounding at the door grew insistent.

I grabbed the keys off the table. "Where'd you leave your car?"

His mother was answering the door downstairs. A man's voice calmly replied to her ravings.

Vincenzo flicked an accusing gaze at me. *"Polizia?"*

"Worse," I said. I locked the door to the stairwell. "Tell me where you parked your car."

"Around corner. On Capocci."

"*Grazie*."

"But you have no *patente*."

"*Non ti turba.* I know how to drive." I gripped his shoulder. "Do *not* tell him I was here. Understand?" I looked at the women. "You never saw me."

The man was coming up the stairs.

I scurried into the bathroom and shut the door. Vincenzo turned on the music. In the darkness I climbed into the claw-foot tub and closed the shower curtain. Rain battered the window. As I struggled to open it, I heard the man knock.

Vincenzo, gallantly delaying, called out over the music, asking who it was.

Seconds later, the women shrieked as the man busted open the door.

8.
Spider

They say it isn't the fall that kills you, it's the landing. The alley below was paved in stone. Dropping from the windowsill, I smacked down hard and rolled. My ankles survived, but my elbow was crushed. Cradling it, I hustled off, limping down the lane.

The black stone teemed with rain. In the rush I slipped and fell again, landing on the goddamn elbow. I struggled to my feet and hurried to the corner. Glancing back at the bathroom window, I saw the light had been turned on. I didn't catch him looking out, and worried that he'd already spotted me.

On Capocci I dashed right past Vinny's Alfa and had to double back. The Spider was jammed between two sedans and pressed up against the wall. My hands shook uncontrollably as I aimed the key in the door. It wasn't even locked—they'd been too rushed in the downpour.

The windows started fogging up the second I got in. I searched for the button to lock the doors. Listening for footsteps, all I could hear was my own frantic breathing and the clamorous patter on the canvas roof. The locks finally thumped in place. The radio blared when I turned the key, and the wipers rapidly swiped. As the windshield cleared, I glanced up the street.

Empty.

Unable to see out the back, I dropped the stick into reverse and proceeded to crinkle the bumper behind me. It set off a bleating alarm. Panicking, I shifted too fast and banged the fender in front. When I turned to back up once again, a shadow filled my window.

I gasped. Behind the fogged and rain-glazed glass, the blurry, bearded figure jerked my door handle. Then he struck the windowpane, and something metal cracked it. I shifted into gear. Shattering the taillight in front of me, I whirled out into the street.

The Spider fishtailed as I straightened the wheel, and the man leapt onto the hood. He hammered down his dagger, smashing the stock into the windshield. The butt of the handle busted through and lodged itself in the glass. In the rush I glimpsed its golden crown. It was shaped in the form of a lotus.

I swung the wheel, stomped the pedal, banked a corner hard. The man rolled twisting over the hood, but clung to the planted dagger. Climbing back, he grasped the wiper, inadvertently bending the blade. My view turned blearily liquid.

I slammed hard on the brakes, and the Spider shuddered to a sudden stop. The dagger popped loose, spraying glass, and the man flew onto the pavement. I jammed the stick back into reverse, then spun the wheel and floored ahead, barreling into the downpour. The spastic windshield wiper screeched. The street ahead looked empty.

In the rearview mirror, the shadow reappeared. It filled the oval window. Suddenly the Spider jolted. I held to the wheel and plowed ahead fast, wipers screeching madly. Then I heard a 'pop' in the canvas overhead and found myself staring at steel.

For a second I thought it was an optical illusion, a glint of reflected light from the rain or a crack in the fractured windshield. But suddenly I recognized the Damascene blade, its bold arc slicing canvas. The blade ripped toward me. I ducked my head aside as it razored past my ear.

The car careened. I held the wheel. The blade withdrew abruptly, then pierced the roof again, this time plunging inches from my face. I pressed my head back as it sawed another slot, angling in a "V" toward the first.

The cuts connected. The flap blew open. Thrusting down through it came the killer's clawing hand.

He grasped at my face. I ducked aside and spun the wheel, skidding a blind corner and pounding over a curb. Headlights swam, horns blaring. The man ripped still more canvas as he slid down over the side. Rain pelted my face. I squinted past the screeching wiper into a glare of headlights and a blaring wall of sound. My car had entered a thoroughfare on the wrong side of the street.

I swung across the center line. A taxi honked, veering off. A van swayed and skidded.

Speeding ahead, I scanned for the killer. Nothing showed in the windows. Distant sirens wailed.

Suddenly a hand grasped my hair—he was reaching down through the gap. Hauling back my head, he exposed my unguarded throat.

The dagger flared above me. I heard him shout to stop.

If he kills me now, I thought, he knows he'll kill us both.

At the corner of the roof I saw a release lever for the canvas top. I reached out and pulled it. The corner popped loose and vibrated in the wind. I reached for the lever on the passenger side, but he grabbed my wrist and held it back. Straining against him, I hit the gas. The sudden jolt broke his grip. I flipped the second lever.

The top flew up and caught the wind. Blowing back like a canvas catapult, it tossed him into the air. Something like a scream bellowed out of him. For a moment he completely disappeared.

Horns wailed. Tires screeched. I turned to see him crash and roll, headlights swerving to miss him.

Exhilarated, triumphant, I shook my fist at the wind.

Then quickly drew it back. In the opposite lane ahead of me, sirens whining, lights flashing, police cars barreled toward me.

For a moment I debated whether to run for it.

9.
Polizia

There are more cops in Italy than in any other country in Europe. In fact, hundreds of thousands, in no less than eight separate police forces. One of these is a branch of the military known as the *Carabinieri*, and it was an officer from these ranks who pulled alongside me in his blue-gumball-flashing Fiat. With a hand gesture like a Pope's blessing, he directed me to the curb.

Other branches of law enforcement soon arrived on the scene. Within minutes I was surrounded by a phalanx of policemen of every stripe and color. Questions and commands came in rapid barrages, and amid much manic gesticulation, I watched as a feud broke out. The cops seemed more concerned to prove who was in charge than to find out what had actually happened.

By the time they finally came around to looking for the killer, the cannon-balled madman had managed to slip away. We could find no trace of him on the rainy road behind us, and apparently none of the drivers who saw him had bothered to stick around. So with the cops all standing there, staring at me in the rain, I tried to explain what had happened—the Indian woman, the stabbings, the lotus plant, the chase—all of it spilling out of me in a torrent of garbled Italian. My nightmarish story began to sound absurd, even to myself. The men threw loaded glances at one another, or squinted at me incredulously, as if they had misheard. *Lotus plant? Daggers*?

Their initial assumption was gradually being confirmed: I

was just another confabulating, reckless-driving drunk.

A *Municipale* officer administered the breathalyzer. When the results showed I was under the half-milligram limit, they decided I must be on drugs. I was hauled to the local police station and ordered to take a blood test. When that proved *negativo*, too, the cops seemed disappointed.

"Three people were just killed in my apartment," I repeated. "Take me there, I'll show you. We're wasting time with this."

"You drove without a license."

"Without a *license*? I nearly drove without my head!"

Just after dawn, a patrolman from the *Polizia Municipale* shuttled me to a branch of the *Polizia di Stato*. A night-duty officer there took down my story, drowsily filling out some form on his computer. Despite the murder and mayhem I described, he seemed more concerned that my *Permesso di Soggiorno* (Permit to Stay) had expired six months previous and hadn't been renewed. I told him I'd been planning to head back to the States and simply hadn't bothered. He asked if I had ever had contact with the 'Ndrangheta, the southern Italian crime syndicate that in recent decades had taken over the illicit drug market in Rome. I replied by asking if he thought I looked insane. He then asked how I made my living in Rome without a worker's permit. I lied and told him my parents had died and left me a hefty inheritance.

The man scowled. I assumed he felt pity for my loss, or perhaps contempt for my gain. But then he swiveled his computer screen, revealing my *Jack's Tours of Rome* website, complete with its "safari" snap of the dashing young American guide.

After that they hustled me off to yet another police station, the Foreigner's Branch of the main Headquarters off Via Nazionale, where I was led into what appeared to be an interrogation room. Here I was asked to wait for a man being sent by the American embassy, a Special Agent in something called the DSS, the U.S. Diplomatic Security Service. They said he wanted to resolve certain questions regarding my history and background.

I had little doubt what that meant. Someone must have come across the incident in Greece and uncovered Dan's wide-ranging rap sheet. They probably figured we were smuggling Asian heroin into Rome, that 'Ndrangheta gang turf was consequently being defended, and that I'd been shaken down by one of their knife-happy goons. Given that I was small fry in the country that spawned the Mob, they must have decided to dump me off on the U.S. State Department.

I pleaded for release from this bureaucratic limbo, but instead they locked me in the horrid little room, and I waited, fuming under the bright fluorescent glare for what stretched into two interminable hours.

———

Above the red door, the windows of the apartment stared down darkly. Presumably the Italian had gone to the police—or squirreled off to hole up with his harlots. I limped to the Mercedes and climbed behind the wheel. My clothes sopped the seat, and for the first time I noticed my knees were bleeding. I drove off into the rain.

Though I still felt suffused with the presence of Allah, the night outside seemed tinged with evil. The wipers whispered, the tires hissed, and in the streets and alleyways I sensed an eerie silence. Fountains gleamed amid graffiti. Litter clung to temple steps. The wet city, bright black, seemed a sort of glinting hell—den of Western deviltry, yet touched and blessed by heaven. But whose heaven? Their pagan glories lay in ruins. Their churches echoed, empty. Why should God show mercy to a people who forgot Him? Their hearts will find no rest without submission to Allah.

I'd failed to kill the American, yet suffered no remorse. Only an abiding certitude. As if Duran's death had been divinely preordained, an unturned page of history, with vengeance for my brother's murder written there in blood.

———

Wearing an FBI look-alike suit, the dark, sleekly groomed American blew briskly into the room, saying "Good morning" and "How are you?" and "I'm Harry Grant" as he plopped a leather valise on the table and foraged through its contents. A woman sauntered in after him, a short-skirted, long-legged, dark-haired Italian I assumed must be the lucky man's assistant. She wore a pearl-colored blouse and a jade green choker that accentuated the color of her eyes. Grant introduced her simply as "Oriana."

I started to my feet.

"Please, don't get up," he said. He unpeeled his Eliot Ness jacket, revealing a shoulder-holstered pistol. Draping the jacket over the back of his chair, he asked me if I'd like more coffee, and began disgorging various articles from his bag: a crumpled dress shirt, a laptop, a yellow pad of paper and a clutch of manila files.

At this point I had soaked up so much espresso I could no longer stop my hands from shaking or still my bouncing knees. "No more coffee," I said.

My tone provoked a sudden scrutiny. "No, of course not." He eyed the soiled sleeve of my blazer, badly frayed at the elbow. "Your arm—is it all right?"

I had actually forgotten about the fall I had taken. "Yes."

"And…?" He stretched his neck and touched his throat.

"It's fine."

"Good. I'm sorry we kept you waiting. I've gone over the police report, but we have some questions I'd like—"

"No."

The woman lifted her gaze.

"Pardon me?" the Agent asked.

"No more questions," I said.

"I'm sorry," he said. "I know it's been a long—"

"No more questions until you take me to my apartment."

He glanced at Oriana. "Your apartment."

"Yeah. There's a woman there. A former model, from India. I'd very much like you to meet her."

Oriana threw him a glance, but Grant held steady on me. I noticed a sort of slightly jaded sparkle in his eye. He looked to Oriana.

In an intrinsically Italian version of the universal gesture, the lady shrugged, *Why not?*

10.
The Sayyid

The morning sun broke through the clouds, spreading its gloss on the wet cobblestones where the ebony Mercedes had been parked the night before. We stood on the spot and stared up at the roof as I recounted the moment when the driver caught sight of me. Then I led them around the corner to where I had tossed the lotus plant. The narrow street was devoid of pedestrians, but a stopped train of parked cars stood crammed along the curb.

I got down on all fours and searched beneath the vehicles. There was not a shred of the plant to be found. "Maybe it's under a wheel," I said. "Or maybe it landed on top of a car, and the car has driven away."

Harry Grant glanced up the street. "It's possible," he shrugged. Meaning that it was unlikely.

Oriana bent to peer in the window of a raindrop-dappled Fiat. Her hand rose toward her face as her mouth stretched wide in shock. For a second I thought she had discovered some horror, but she was merely using the tip of her finger to trim the edge of her lipstick.

We walked back around to the entrance.

Grant examined where the bolt had been shimmied. "This mortise lock is ancient."

"The landlord says replacing it would only advertise for thieves. I never worried about it. Nothing I own is worth stealing."

Oriana was perusing the graffiti. "These days the scum will

waste you for nothing."

It was the first time I had heard her speak. Her Italian slang had the inflection of the street; she sounded like a mafia moll.

"You can say that again," I replied. "They nearly cut my throat for a flower!"

We climbed the creaking stairs. The clip-clop of Oriana's heels made me think of Maya, the panther—her sandals had been nearly soundless. The house seemed ghostly quiet now. I dreaded confronting her corpse.

But first, the corpse in my apartment—the black street peddler-cum-murdering thief. We paused outside my door. A twinge caressed the cut on my throat. I nodded to the Agent. He gently nudged the door open and led us into the room.

I came to a stop and stared, dumbfounded.

The ransacked apartment had been neatly reassembled. The drawers had been shut, the table uprighted, the wood floor scrubbed to a sheen. I staggered to the place where the bodies had fallen. *"Impossible,"* I whispered.

The street peddler's corpse had vanished. There wasn't a drop of blood.

"What is it?" Grant asked. They were watching me with curiosity.

"He's gone," I said. Staring down at the bare oak floor, I realized something else was gone, too. "The rug. He died right here on the Oriental rug. It was soaked with blood." I looked at the upright end table. "And the porcelain lamp—it's gone, too. Maya and I heard it crash—"

A frightening realization came over me. I turned and raced out of the room.

Taking three steps at a time, I barreled up the stairwell to the roof. The door stood ajar, the lock still broken. I burst out into the garden.

"Maya—"

Her corpse was gone. Vanished. Along with the corpse of the man she shot.

The disposable pulsed in my pocket. Had I not turned it off? I pulled it out and saw that it was Arshan's cell, not mine. I had plucked the phone out of his lifeless hand, along with the Hindi's passport.

Bloody thumbprints fogged its glass. The ID showed no name.

"Alo, salam aleikom."

Silence. A ghostly presence on the other end of the line. Then: "You answer for your brother."

The voice elicited a shiver. It was the voice I had long imagined but never actually heard. Gentle, and elderly, yet sonorous and strong, its tone conveying experience and an intimidating intelligence. His formal Persian called to mind the fact he was a Sayyid, a black turban, a direct descendant of Mohammed, in whose pulsing veins coursed the holy blood of the Prophet.

Ordinarily I'd have felt too diffident to speak. But nothing seemed ordinary now. Everything that was happening had the blessing of Allah. I had nothing to fear.

"I am not worthy to answer for him. My brother is a martyr," I said.

Once more, a silence. Even deeper than the last.

Had Mahbood not told him what happened? Afraid of incurring his wrath? Had I incurred it now? I waited, wondering what questions he'd ask, how harshly he'd reprimand me. But no such reprimand occurred. The Old Man was only just absorbing his own grief. He said, "Please accept my deepest condolences for this most grievous loss."

"Forgive me," I replied. "I am unworthy, and you are too kind. Your loss is far greater than mine."

"We are all brothers in faith," he said. "But a brother in blood is twice a brother."

"He loved you like a father," I said. "And a son's love for his father is the strongest love of all."

"A love that will be sorely missed. The Prophet himself lost his three sons, and freely wept for each. But we as well shall follow them. Every soul must taste death. The life of this world is nothing but the enjoyment of illusion. Arshan fought as a warrior of God and drank the sweet syrup of martyrdom. He is

a shahid *now, and will rest in the Highest Gardens of Paradise."*

"The most excellent recompense," I said. "It is the will of Allah."

"Indeed. It also appears that the will of Allah is for you to remain here, with us."

I swallowed my guilt. I had lived. My brother had died. Surely I could have done something to save him.

All that was left for me now was revenge. "I am always ready to offer myself in sacrifice for Islam."

"Such a sacrifice at present I'm afraid would be too dear. The loss of your brother claws at my heart, and though I hunger for justice, I will not risk your life for it."

The words took me aback. "You may have reason to doubt my skills. But I have been trained by your finest warrior. With his death, God's desire for justice burns in me like a fire. And I am His obedient servant, just as I am yours."

"Your words bring honor to your brother's sacrifice. But I am given to understand your deeds proved less successful."

How had he found out so quickly? I had not reported to Mahbood. Interpol may have been alerted, I thought, and his contacts in intelligence picked up the dispatch. I knew the Old Man had eyes and ears everywhere. My brother always said he knew things about you before you knew about them yourself.

I knew only one thing: the American had to die. "May the Exceedingly Merciful grant me the chance to earn *His forgiveness."*

"Your repentance is unwarranted; your failure was no sin. Nothing happens to us except what God has decreed for us."

"The drug-dealing murderer of my brother still lives. Has that been decreed by God?"

The reckless words escaped my mouth before I could pull them back. Anger now darkened the Ayatollah's voice. "God brought us out from the wombs of our mothers; He will take us back when it pleases Him. Presently He requires that you finish your training. To kill the American is more lawful than rainwater, and you will be given your chance in time. For the moment, however, serious questions remain unresolved. Our very survival is threatened."

"Forgive me, I am your obedient servant, always. And you are so near to Allah. So tell me what is more urgent to God than the killing of this unbeliever."

A silence again. "The lotus," he said simply. "The lotus must be found."

Our plants had failed to propagate. Reserves of the pure drink were quickly running out. We had to find the source. "It's what my brother died for," I said. "Tell me what I must do."

"You must follow my instructions—and my instructions only. Trust no one but me.*"*

The tone of his voice sparked a shiver. "No one?" I asked. "Not even Mahbood?" Mahbood was second in command to my brother. Only these two were allowed to speak directly with the Old Man.

"Especially Mahbood," he said.

I thought of my call from the car. "But why?"

"Why?" *the Ayatollah roared. I'd finally awakened the much-feared anger Arshan had warned me about. "Who was this Hindi?! Who was this African?! Why do you think your brother was killed?!"*

I had no answer.

"We have been betrayed," he said. "An enemy of God lives among us."

11.
Queen of Hearts

The empty mirror of water in the green-glazed pot darkened with Harry Grant's shadow. "Maybe I could ask you those questions now?"

I lifted my gaze. His face eclipsed the rising sun, so I couldn't make out his expression. But the tone of his voice sounded vaguely sympathetic, as if, having caught me out in a lie, there was little he could do but pity me. Suddenly I realized why he'd agreed to bring me here. "You knew," I said.

"A patrol car was sent by early this morning. They found exactly what you see now."

Oriana, wandering the garden behind him, bent to sniff a scentless orchid. They both seemed to take my guilt for granted.

"You don't believe anything I've said."

The Agent frowned. "I believe someone chased you. The police confirmed it from the testimony of your friends."

"What about the people I saw killed here? You think I'm lying about that?"

"The police think you're lying."

On the deck where the killer had bled to death, there was nothing but puddles of water. "Somebody must have hosed off all the blood," I said.

"Or perhaps the rain just washed it away." His sympathy was slipping into sarcasm. "If what you say is true, why didn't you go directly to the police? Why did you hide at your friend's house?"

"I was scared," I said. "I wasn't thinking straight."

"Why would you be scared to go to the police?"

"Haven't they told you? I'm living here illegally. I haven't even got a driver's—"

"You say three people had just been killed in your apartment. And you were worried about your *papers*?"

"I told you. I wasn't thinking straight." He doesn't seem to know about Dan, I thought. I tried to change the subject. "Did the police say what time they came by this morning?"

"Around the time they transferred you," he said.

"That wasn't until seven, seven-thirty."

"You're about to tell me the driver who attacked you returned and tidied up."

"No," I said. "I think it was the housemaid."

The Agent cocked an eyebrow.

"The Middle-Eastern guy—Arshan—when he picked up the flower seller's phone, he told whoever was on the other end, 'Your flower boy's stained the rug. Better call the housemaid.'"

"In English?"

"Yes."

"So who do you imagine he was talking to?"

"I don't know. But whoever it was sent someone here to clean up after he was killed. What do they call them? Cleaners? Fixers?"

"Apparently they call them 'housemaids.'" He turned his gaze to Oriana. She was leaning out over the edge of the roof, exposing the dizzying heights of her thighs. "Your story raises an obvious question," he said. "Why would the people who sent this 'flower seller' want to clean up after his murder?"

He was right: It made no sense. Like Maya using a silencer. What had she been afraid of? Waking up the neighbors?

"That must be it," I said. "They want to keep it quiet. Away from the police and the media. They're afraid if word gets out, everyone will want it."

"The mysterious plant, you mean."

"The lotus. Maya was fascinated by it. The Middle-Eastern

guy was nearly drooling over the thing."

The Agent eyed me skeptically. "Why do you think that is?"

"I'm not sure," I said. "Maybe they're some kind of flower fanatics. Like those orchid hunters in the 19th century."

"Orchid hunters."

"You've heard of the tulip craze in Holland? The orchid craze was even crazier. Collectors would travel to the ends of the earth to discover some new variety, then sell them at auction in London for a fortune. Rich Victorian gentlemen became totally obsessed—they'd journey deep into the jungle and practically kill each other for them. They called it 'orchidelirium'—orchid madness."

The Agent squinted at me. "How is it you happen to know about this?"

I started to say, then stopped myself. "I read an article about it."

"I see," he said. "Is there any chance that article was authored by your brother?"

I stared at him, then looked away. "Part of his dissertation, actually."

"Yes. I understand your brother Daniel is quite a distinguished scholar. In fact, it's him I've been wanting to ask you about."

Here it comes, I thought. D. J.'s can of worms. Grant had been waiting all this time to crack it open. And sure enough, for the next twenty minutes, the Agent grilled me about him. He seemed to have studied in great detail Dan's so-called criminal record. And he knew all about the incident in Greece. Now this Sherlock was determined to discover what Professor Moriarty was up to. Why had Dan sent me the seeds? What was he doing in Asia? When had I last heard from him? Where did I think he was now? His questions reminded me of the questions from Maya—or the man with the knife, for that matter. They all seemed to be suffering from the same desperate need. I began to wonder what the Agent was really after. The killers? The lotus? Or Dan?

He gazed out over the rooftops. "What if you thought your

brother's life was in danger? How would you try to warn him?"

"That's a funny question."

"You said this man 'Arshan' almost killed you. You said he was after your brother."

I hadn't really considered the danger to Dan. "I wouldn't be able to warn him," I said. "I told you: I don't know where he is."

"No address. No email. No cell phone."

"No. He doesn't…we don't…communicate."

"Why?"

I hesitated. I didn't want to risk bringing Phoebe's name into it. "It's personal," I said.

The Agent glanced over his shoulder at Oriana, wandering among the pots of bamboo. He inched slightly closer. "By personal, you mean…?"

For a moment I considered answering him. Then I looked past him at Oriana as she crouched to caress a pink-flowered hibiscus. "Who is she?" I asked.

"Friend of mine," he shrugged.

"She in the DSS, too?"

"No," he said.

"Italian police?"

He hesitated. "No."

I waited for him to elaborate. He didn't. "Then I guess it must be personal," I said.

The Agent opened his mouth to answer, then seemed to take my point.

"Why are *you* here?" I asked. "Shouldn't you be taking a bullet for the Secretary of State or something?"

Oriana interrupted before the Agent could reply. "Someone's been playing hearts up here." She was sauntering toward us, and her comment, in accented English, was apparently directed at me.

I wasn't quite sure what she meant.

She handed me a playing card, soggy from the rain. The card looked familiar, though I couldn't remember why. I flipped it over.

Queen of Hearts.

The two of them seemed to be watching my reaction. "I found it between the slats of the deck there," Oriana said, nodding back toward the stairwell. "Maybe your friend was trying to tell you something."

"Maya?" I looked toward the entry to the stairs. The spot where the dissimulating Indian had died. Could she have dropped the card there? I didn't remember seeing her with it, but given how frightened I was at the time, I probably wouldn't have noticed.

Queen of Hearts. What could it mean?

12.
truth

"You believe I'm telling the truth."

Oriana briefly glanced at Harry Grant before she answered. "In the police report, you said this woman died in your arms."

I nodded, remembering with a shiver how the life had fled from of her eyes.

Again Oriana looked at Grant. "A man might lie about a lot of things, Harry. He wouldn't lie about that."

The Agent stared back at her. She seemed to be forcing his hand. He finally turned to face me with a look of resignation."I just flew in this morning through the air base in Aviano," he said. "I'm the Regional Security Officer for the U.S. embassy in Baghdad."

"Iraq?"

"We've been investigating a series of assassinations in the lead up to the Iraqi elections. The victims have been local politicians, mostly. But two weeks ago an attempt was made on the life of the U.S. ambassador."

I had heard about it in the news. The assailant had managed to infiltrate the highest levels of Iraqi security. But at the moment of attack he had been shot dead by an alert American bodyguard. I remembered they were surprised to discover he hadn't worn the obligatory bomb belt.

Again Grant and Oriana seemed to be studying me, looking for some kind of reaction.

I shrugged. "It's Iraq. What else is new?"

The Agent locked his eyes on me. "The assailant used a

dagger. Similar to the dagger you described to the police."

"Damascus steel?"

"An 800-year-old Damascene blade shaped in the form of a crescent."

I could barely contain myself. "What about the handle? Was there a lotus on the end?"

"Some sort of flower icon, yes."

"That's it!"

Grant didn't appear to share my enthusiasm. "There's more," he said.

I waited.

"Five days after the assassination attempt, investigators raided the office of a conservative Shiite political party in Baghdad. The police believed this office had links to a secretive group of Iranian ex-military. No one was apprehended, but a list of twelve names turned up on a confiscated laptop. One was Ali Ashiri, the Iranian assassin who tried to kill the Ambassador in Iraq. Another was the name of a man who'd been killed three months earlier in Damascus, after cutting the throat of a rebel leader suing for peace in Syria. And last but not least, the top name on the list, a former henchman of the Supreme Leader himself, a man believed to be their top commander in the field—a notorious assassin named Arshan Azad."

"Arshan!" I said. "He's the man Maya shot on the roof!"

"So you stated in the police report. That's what brought us here. The police ran the name through Interpol, and Interpol notified us."

The speed of the DSS response was nothing short of amazing. Grant must have wrangled a plane out of Baghdad in the middle of the night. "Who are these guys?" I asked.

"We believe they're fundamentalists recruited out of the Quds Force, the special forces branch of the Iranian Revolutionary Guard."

I had heard of the Quds Force. Iran's elite military commandoes. They received their orders directly from the "Supreme Leader" and reportedly sponsored terrorist groups all over the Middle East.

But if these men were truly the elite, where could they go from there? “You say ‘recruited.’ By whom?”

“We don’t really know for sure. But some think they may have been lured away by a Grand Ayatollah in the holy city of Qum.”

“I thought there was only one Grand Ayatollah.”

“Only one is appointed *Rahbar*—‘Supreme Leader,’ but there are a number of Grand Ayatollahs in Iran and several more residing in Iraq. Though they don’t often voice their differences in public, these senior clerics frequently disagree with one another—and sometimes come into conflict with the *Rahbar*. One of them, a radically hard-line cleric in his late seventies, appears to have had a serious falling out. He’s a paranoid recluse who grants no interviews and rarely ventures outside of his compound in Qum. But he has millions of followers, in Iran and around the world, and legions of supporters flood his treasury with donations. I’m talking easily over a hundred million dollars a year—which he invests in various ‘charitable’ and ‘educational’ projects.”

“Like buying his own private army, you mean.”

“A dozen men is hardly an army,” Grant said. “But twelve of the right men can do a lot of damage. And these seem to be stirring up as much trouble as they can—between reformers and hard-liners, Shi’as and Sunnis, Muslims and Christians, you name it.”

“I don’t get it,” I said. “What could they want with my brother?

Grant folded his arms across his chest. “According to you, they’re looking for a flower.”

Baiting me again with sarcasm. Despite the evidence Grant had found that clearly supported my story—same kind of knife, same name on the list—the agent remained suspicious. “Why is it you think I’m not telling the truth?” I asked.

Grant stared at me without answering. Oriana said, “Were you aware that your brother lived for a number of months in Iran?”

I scoffed. “That was years ago.”

“It was at the height of the Iraq War,” Grant said.

"Well…yeah?" I remembered a sketchbook Dan had filled with ink-wash drawings of Persian ruins. "Dan was a tourist, not a terrorist," I said. "It's probably just a typo in your report."

Grant was unamused. "We noticed he wrote a lot of commentary on various anti-war websites. Sounded a little angry."

"A lot of people were," I said. "It was not exactly a popular war."

Grant said, "It was not exactly popular with the Iranian regime, either."

"Look, I told you, Dan was a tourist. A visiting academic. Believe me, he's completely apolitical. He sees war as a neurological problem."

"Maybe it's not politics," Oriana said. "We understand he studied under a Sufi mystic in Qum."

How had they found out that? "Dan has studied under masters in every religion in the world," I said. "It's a basic part of his research."

Grant remained unconvinced. "So you know absolutely nothing about any connections he has in Iran?"

"No," I said. "And certainly not with some holy man's army."

The two of them continued eyeing me.

"So you've really got no info on this lotus?" I asked.

The Agent scowled and shook his head.

They apparently knew nothing about it. And maybe, I thought, they didn't even care. It seemed all they really wanted was Dan. "So *is* my brother in danger?"

"If he's involved with these people, yes."

I suddenly realized my heart was racing. "Is the danger from them, or from you?"

Again, the two exchanged a glance.

Grant uncapped a pen and scribbled figures on a calling card. "If you happen to remember anything," he said, "I urge you—for your brother's sake—to contact me immediately."

He waved the card to dry the ink and handed it over to me. *Special Agent Harold Grant, Deputy Regional Security*

Officer, United States Diplomatic Security Service, United States Embassy, Baghdad, Iraq. It showed the embassy website, along with a dot-gov email address and the Agent's scribbled phone number.

Grant looked to Oriana. Oriana nodded, and without another word, he headed for the stairs.

"Where's he going?" I asked.

"Back to Baghdad, I suppose."

"Baghdad? Why?"

"The ambassador likes to keep him around—he's proved to be very useful."

"You mean…Harry—?"

"Yeah. But he thinks he just got lucky. That's why he wants your help."

"He wants *my* help? What about helping me? I'm their next target!"

Oriana started to leave. "I don't think you need to worry," she said. She called back over her shoulder, "You'll be perfectly safe in jail."

I shouted after her: "Harry should tell the police what he told me!"

"He already has," she replied, and started down the stairs.

I stood there dumbfounded. Gears slowly turning. No wonder the Italian police don't trust me. They figure I'm either smuggling dope—or spying for the Ayatollah!

I ran to the stairwell and called down after them. "That nut is still out there—you can't just leave me here like this!"

"I'm sorry," Grant's voice echoed as they spiraled down the stairs. "Rome is a bit outside my jurisdiction."

They reached the entry and headed out. I raced down the stairwell after them.

Among the wetly glistening autos parked across the street sat their bone-dry, gem-blue BMW. Grant opened the door for Oriana. "Call me if you hear anything," he shouted. "I'll do what I can to help."

I stood numbly at the doorway as the Roadster pulled away. Shafts of slanting sunlight threw great shadows on the street. The low car neatly threaded through them, disappearing and reappearing again, until finally it turned a corner and vanished.

I scanned the street for the black Mercedes. He's sure to be coming, I thought. The shadows seemed to grow deeper. *He's probably already here.*

Two giggling schoolgirls flitted by as if nothing in the world was the matter. I backed inside and shut the door. Panic rippled through me as I stared at the broken lock.

13.
The Satyricon

I found my little backpack buried in my closet and tossed it onto the bed, then yanked out dresser drawers and threw a hasty selection of clothing at it. I didn't know where I was going, how hot or cold or wet it would be, even how long I'd be gone. I just knew I had to get out of Rome before the Iranian came to kill me.

I crammed the clothes into the pack, searched the desk for my passport, slipped it into a jacket pocket and started out of the room. At the doorway, I suddenly stopped and turned around.

Lying neatly at the center of the desktop—and not on the table where I'd left it—was the bawdy paperback book I'd been reading, an Oxford Classics edition of *The Satyricon*. Maya and I had discussed the book at dinner. I suddenly remembered the playing card Oriana had found on the roof.

The Queen of Hearts had been my bookmark!

I hurried back to the desk. Maya must have taken the bookmark with her when she made her bloody climb to the roof. *But why?*

Because only I would know where it came from. If the killer had somehow gotten hold of it, he wouldn't have had a clue. I grabbed the paperback and fanned through the pages. The fluttering stopped near the back of the book, where Maya had inserted a card of her own—a plastic, numberless, room key card from the Excelsior, an exclusive hotel in the Ludovisi Quarter, a few blocks from Piazza Barberini.

I closed the book with the card inside and stuffed it into my backpack. Out in the hallway, I stopped to listen. The coil of the stairwell seemed to reverberate with silence. I crept down the spiral to the landing and paused there, staring at the door to the street.

The quiet unnerved me.

Abruptly I turned and walked to the rear apartment. The workmen had left the door unlocked, and I stepped inside and found my way through darkness into the kitchen. The galley was gutted, draped with ghostly powdered canvas amid plaster-laden ladders. I unlocked the back door and peeked into the alley.

Except for the startled white cat on the step, the puddled lane was empty.

I slipped out quietly. The hungry cat meowed.

"Not today, Lily." It followed me briefly as I scurried down the lane. Alessandro Beronio emerged with his bicycle and gave me a curious look. I waved at the boy and trotted out to the street. For several blocks I hurried without a thought of where I was going, aiming only at getting away from the house and blending into the city. The morning traffic was already swelling, and a flurry of pedestrians coursed the narrow streets. I shouldered the pack, turned up my collar, and tried to merge in with the crowd.

Still I couldn't shake the sense the killer's eyes were on me. Grant had suggested the Iranian might be a member of the notorious Quds Force—special forces, highly trained, the elite of the Revolutionary Guard—hardly the sort you could hope to evade by sneaking out the back door and scurrying up the street. The night before, the man had tracked me to Vincenzo's place, hunted me down, and pounced on the Alfa like Spiderman. I could only imagine what he'd be capable of given the clear light of day.

I hurried on, glancing back, searching faces around me. The killer would blend in better than I. I, a Nordic Midwesterner—tall, blue-eyed, blond, a backpack over my shoulder, an American's loping gait. And I was still wearing my white safari jacket. Peering over the dark stream of stylish Roman businessmen, I felt like an albino alien.

Train station? Airport? The ferry to Sardinia? I'd been debating my escape route from the moment Grant had left—how best to clear out of the city, fast. But now I suddenly realized it wasn't the train station or the airport or the ferry I was heading toward. I was climbing into a taxi and telling the whiskered Albanian driver to take me halfway across the city to the Excelsior Hotel, probably the last place I should have been going if I wanted to avoid the Iranian. But Maya had taken a lot of trouble to provide me with her key, and considering she was halfway to dead at the time, it was probably for something important. Maybe something that could help me find out what the hell my brother was up to.

I looked out the back window as the taxi pulled away. No one appeared to be following me, either on foot or by car, and although I did spot a black Mercedes, it was driving in the opposite direction.

For the moment, it seemed I was safe.

I opened up my backpack and pulled out my dog-eared copy of *The Satyricon*. Something about it had bothered me.

Maya had inserted the card toward the back—not where I'd left off reading, but between pages 206-207 of the "*Index and Glossary of Names*." Though it may have been arbitrary, it appeared she had searched for this specific spot: several pages preceding it were smudged with bloody prints.

Why had she inserted the key card here?

It wasn't until later, inside the hotel, that I realized what she had done. I was trying to find out what room Maya had been staying in without revealing to the receptionist that I held the key card to it.

The man searched his computer for at least a full minute. "We have no record of a Maya Rakshasi. Are you sure you have the right hotel, sir?"

I asked him to check again, and again he came up blank.

"Maybe you saw her," I said. "Indian woman, early thirties, tall, black hair, nice looking?"

He shook his head. "Another clerk may have checked her in."

There were several now working behind the long granite counter, busily processing morning departures. A Japanese tour group had crowded into the lobby, assembling for the airport shuttle. Behind me, a long line had formed.

"Is there anything else I can do for you, sir?"

"*No, grazie.*" I withdrew. Maya had obviously used another name—which I now realized must have been why she left her card in the *Index and Glossary of Names.*

Rising from my morning prayer, I caught my reflection in the hotel room mirror.

The Old Man had said he could trust me. Me, and me alone, of all of them.

"You're the youngest, our newest recruit, and the purest of faith," he said. "Untouched by temptation, unblemished by corruption. The son of a shahid, now the brother of one, too. Intent to give your own life for Allah."

"You speak too highly of a lowly servant," I said. "But the last you said is true: I am not afraid to die."

Except for Ali Mahbood, whom I'd worked under at Kahrizak prison, the other men were unknown to me. All were fighters secretly recruited from el-Quds. The Old Man issued each his mission, communicating only through his commanders in the field—my brother and Mahbood. Yet now some devil among them had turned traitor to our cause. Even Mahbood himself was under suspicion.

"The other men have families," he said, "and some of them have relatives who live outside Iran. This leaves them more vulnerable to bribery or coercion, or the deceptions of the Israelis and the Americans."

"Not so for you," he said. "Your mother died in childbirth. Your father died in war. Arshan will join both of them in heaven."

"Insha' Allah," I said. "Arshan used to say I was the Revolution's orphan."

"You will be an orphan no longer," the Old Man said. "What about friends? Are you close to anyone?"

"I had a close friend," I said, thinking of Faraj. "But not anymore."

"What about students from your time at university?"

I remembered all the wealthy, dissolute young men, Westernized Tehranis, drinking, smoking shir'e, dancing with their whores. "They hid their sinfulness behind their Persian garden walls. I disliked their company. I left to study in Qum."

"Yes. The seminary. I'm told your brother boasted you'd come out an Ayatollah! What made you return to Tehran?"

"Allah knows all things," I said, "and Allah guides the way. He spoke to me one day through the words of the Rahbar, the Grand Ayatollah Khamenei. He said 'the expected justice, the justice of the Mahdi for the whole world, is not attained through admonition and preaching. Messengers of God preach to the people, but they also equip themselves with weapons.'"

"I remember the speech," the Old Man said. "Noble, but insufficient. Weapons alone are not enough. We need the courage to use them. Is this why you came back to work for Mahbood?"

"Yes. In Intelligence. Arshan arranged the position for me—Mahbood had been his friend from the old days on the streets."

"And you did well by him?"

"I went undercover," I said. "Infiltrating groups of suspected dissidents. Many were fellow students from my university days. I pretended to be one of them."

"God's lowly actor, strutting the devil's stage."

"I performed whatever role He required of me," I said.

"Sordid work, I'm sure. But don't indulge regret: The taqiyya doctrine gave you dispensation to deceive."

"I did what I had to do," I said. "What the Bringer of Death commanded. When the election protests broke out in the phony 'Green Revolution,' I went to work in the Ministry's interrogation section."

"Kahrizak," the Old Man said.

"The crucible of truth," I said. I remembered all the suffering we inflicted in that prison. Beatings. Rape. The singe of lash and blade. Even my bullheaded friend Faraj could not

withstand the torment; we beat the truth right out of him.

"Dividing truth from falsehood—a talent all too rare. This is one more reason that God calls upon you now. Our jihad requires only soldiers we can trust. We must work together now to purify our ranks."

"May the eyes of the cowards never sleep," I said.

"Help me cleanse my army, Vanitar. Help me do that, and I will take you as my own son."

The proposal stunned me into a momentary silence. "For such an honor," I said, "I will fight until my last drop of blood!"

"Then make ready your strength," the Old Man said. "Together we'll strike terror into the hearts of the enemies of God."

He gave me a number to call when I found out more information. "Destroy your phones," he ordered. "And unless I tell you different, do not call or meet Mahbood. I'll let them all continue on as if I've no suspicions. No one else will know that it is only you I trust, and you must trust in no one else but me."

When the call ended, I flushed my cell phones down the toilet. To discover who betrayed us, I would first need to find out who we'd been betrayed to. The flower-selling roach, the bare-shouldered Hindi—who did these devils work for?

I pulled out the Hindi's passport and examined her picture. Shameless worshipper of obscene gods. Hindus, worst of the infidels. And this one in particular. Indecent. Wanton. Lustful.

May The Watchful close my ears to the whisperings of evil.

I didn't know what gutter the roach had crawled out from, but I did have one lead with the Hindi. After we'd followed Duran to the ruins and watched her brazenly flirt with him, Arshan had tailed the woman back to her hotel.

The Excelsior.

14.
The Excelsior

In a well-upholstered lounge off the lobby, I found a vacant chair and once again opened *The Satryicon*. I scanned the two pages where the card was inserted in the *Index and Glossary of Names*. Barclay, Bargates, Battus, Bellona—all the way through to the 'G's: Gain, Ganymede, Gavilla, Giton. The two pages probably held at least a hundred names. But there was no indication as to which of them was hers. How could I ask the harried clerk to look up every one of them? I'd drive the poor man crazy.

As I stared at the milling crowd in the lobby and puzzled over Maya's intention, it gradually occurred to me that I didn't need her name; all I really needed was her room number. Suddenly the answer seemed obvious. Her room number could simply be the number of the page. She must have been in 206 or 207!

Excited, I quickly rose and crossed the lobby, winding through the throng of Japanese. Several Italian businessmen stood chatting at the elevator. The doors parted, and just as we started inside, I happened to glance back into the lobby.

A jolt of fear ripped through me.

I pushed in through the Italians and punched the second floor. The men, jabbering among themselves, crowded in behind me. My heart was racing madly as the doors began to close. Then, at the last second, one of the Italians saw someone coming and stuck his hand between the doors.

The doors stopped and glided open. Blood throbbed in my

ears. I turned away, trying to hide.

We waited for what seemed an eternity. Finally, with a clatter of heels, a small, round woman in a suit rushed in, carrying a clutch of canolli.

"*Grazie*," she smiled.

"*Prego*," the man replied. I watched in silent agony until the doors finally shut.

The Iranian must not have seen me. I had glimpsed the bearded man enter the lobby through the revolving door.

My pulse pounded as the elevator rose. He must have known Maya was staying here, I thought. Like me, he'd come to search her room!

I struggled to suppress the panic overtaking me, to calm down and try to think clearly. If he'd been going directly to her room, I thought, he would have easily made it into the elevator. He must have been going to the front desk first. Which means he also probably didn't have her room number. He'd have the same problem as I.

I wondered if I had enough time.

The doors opened to the second floor. The short, bulging lady in the suit stepped out and started down the hallway. I hurried past her, searching for the numbers Maya had bookmarked.

I found room 206 around the corner. No sound emanated from behind the closed door. I knocked. No answer. I slid the card in the slot.

Nothing happened.

I tried the card again. Just then the canolli lady came around the corner. When she saw me trying the key in the door, she gave me an indignant look. I backed off. She inserted her own key card in the door, and with a wary sideward glance at me, slipped inside the room.

I continued next door to 207. Again I heard no sound from within. But just as I raised my knuckles to knock, I noticed a sign on the doorknob: *"Non Disturbare."*

I hesitated. Maya had been gone since the previous evening. Why would there be a "Do Not Disturb" sign on the door? Perhaps my page-number theory was nonsense. Then again, I thought, maybe she had wanted to discourage the staff from nosing around in her room. I faced the door and knocked.

Silence.

I glanced up the corridor. The Iranian could be coming around the corner any second. I wondered if there was a way to escape at the other end of the hall.

Again I knocked, louder. No response. I slipped the card in the lock.

The door clicked! I opened it.

The curtains were shut, blocking all daylight. A bedside lamp revealed disheveled sheets, and a dim nightlight glowed in the bathroom.

"Hello?"

No answer. I glanced up the corridor one last time, then entered into the room. The door shut behind me. I bolted the lock and flipped on a light switch.

It was a formal room, befitting the Excelsior, with a soaring ceiling, elaborate drapes, an antique Empire desk and chairs, and a richly ornate bed. On the velvet stool at the foot of the bed sat a woman's pink-paisley suitcase.

I hurried over and opened it. The bag was a small, two-wheeled roller, the sort you could cram into an overhead bin. Most of her clothes had not been unpacked and were rolled up rather than folded. In a separate side pocket, a clear Ziploc bag held two fried samosas—the small, triangular, stuffed patty snacks I had practically lived on in India. Other than that, I found nothing else of interest in the bag. I started to close it, but stopped when I noticed how heavy the lid was. Something was stored inside it. On the outside I found a slim, button-strap pouch.

I opened it, peered inside and pulled out a wad of papers. Most of it appeared to be travel receipts—restaurants, hotels, taxis, rental cars—but among the stash I came across a color photograph.

A 4X5 snapshot of Phoebe, Dan and me.

For a moment, I stared at it, startled. The three of us stood side-by-side, posing against the low stone wall on the windy heights of the Acropolis, with the vast chalk-colored city of

Athens stretching to the horizon below us.

I liked your picture, Maya had said.

I had forgotten all about this photograph. Now I remembered: It had been taken by a passing tourist at Phoebe's request, using her Nikon 300. I had never seen it. Following the Furies blowup, we had all sworn to each other to keep our Greek jpegs off the Net.

How on earth had Maya got a hold of it?

15.
Knock-knock

I ruffled through the remaining papers and made another curious find: a tattered sheet of stationery with driving directions and a roughly drawn map. The starting point appeared to be a place called Ashkhabad.

Imprinted at the top of the stationery was a symbol of three lions on a pedestal, the front of which was adorned with a round sun or wheel symbol. A phrase written in an Eastern script was neatly imprinted beneath it.

I quickly folded the paper and slipped it into my pocket, along with the photograph. The suitcase lid still felt heavy, and I discovered another zippered pocket hidden on its underside. The zipper was fastened with a tiny brass lock.

I tried to tear it open, but the plasticized canvas was tough as shoe leather. Glancing around the room for something to cut it, I spotted on the desk blotter a ballpoint pen and a fancy letter opener. I grabbed the letter opener, then noticed beside it a hotel notepad on which had been scribbled a message:

Dr. Fiore 9:30 A.M. Orto Botanico, Largo Cristina di Svezia, 24.

The doctor's name rang a bell. After puzzling over it for a moment, I remembered a message on my answering machine I'd received the previous day. It had been left by a man whose first name was Felix and who pronounced his surname *fee-or'-ay.* He said he wanted to discuss a tour with me. I had cynically assumed from his elderly voice that he wanted to negotiate a senior discount. Strangely, he hadn't left a phone number, saying he would try me later. But at that point Maya Rakshasi called and I hadn't thought about the man since.

The address was on a cul-de-sac I knew very well, only blocks from my apartment in Trastevere. At the end of it lay *L' Orto Botanico di Roma,* a park-like botanical garden connected with the Sapienza University of Rome. I had often passed through it on my morning jogs, having found a hidden entry where I didn't have to pay. The views from its walkways were among the finest in the city. In my mind's eye, I now quickly jogged through its gardens and greenhouses, trying to recall if I'd ever seen a lotus plant on the grounds. I knew there were at least three ponds—

With bone-jarring intensity, the desktop telephone rang.

I stared at the ebony phone as if it had just fallen out of the sky. It rang loudly again. For the first time I noticed the message light was on. Someone had been trying to reach Maya.

RING!

I looked at my watch. It was 10:14 A.M.

Dr. Fiore 9:30 A.M.

I moved closer. The message light continued blinking.

RING!

I picked up the receiver. "Hello?"

There was a hesitant pause. Then a man's voice speaking in accented English. "Uh, yes. I am calling for Mayanda Ramanujan, please."

Ramanujan. Maya's real name. "She's not here right now," I said in Italian. "Is this Dr. Fiore?"

He ignored my Italian and continued in English. "This is Georgio, at the front desk. We have a gentleman here who has found Miss Ramanujan's passport. He would like to return it to her. Do you know where we can reach her?"

The passport. Arshan had taken it from Maya's purse. The other guy—

"Sir?"

"No. I mean..." My heart was pounding so hard that I could barely think. "I don't know where she is. She hasn't come back. Leave it at the desk, she can pick it up later."

"Sir. Of course. May I ask your name, please?"

I hesitated. "Tell you what. Ask the man to wait. I'll be right down." I hung up the phone.

Now I had to get the hell out of there fast. I hurried back to the suitcase and slashed the zippered pocket. The dull blade of the letter opener glanced off the hardened canvas. I stabbed it like a maniac. Still it wouldn't tear.

The phone rang. *Loud.*

Georgio from downstairs again? Or was it Dr. Fiore?

RING!

I jammed the point into the lock and tried to break it open. The letter opener broke instead.

RING!

Heck with this, I thought, I'll take the damn thing with me. Grabbing the suitcase, I started for the door, strewing clothes across the floor as I tried to zip it shut. My foot caught in the clothes and I tumbled to the floor.

"Christ Almighty!"

RING!

There was a light *tap-tap-tap* at the door.

RING!

I lay with the luggage, holding my breath.

A louder knock. "Hello?"

The phone stopped. Quietly I gathered the half-open suitcase and crept away from the door. I heard the tell-tale click of the lock as another key card was inserted.

The doorknob rattled. The deadbolt held. I heard a murmur of voices.

At that point I was clawing at the drapery, desperate for another way out.

"Security. Please open up!" I heard the unmistakable jingle of keys.

The heavy velvet drapes hid a pair of French doors. I threw the latch and stepped outside, onto the projecting balcony. Traffic coursed below on the Via Veneto, visible through the leafy crowns of trees. I suddenly remembered that the "second" floor of an Italian hotel is actually the third—above the "first" and the "ground" floor.

I was far too high up to jump.

Even the first floor balcony beneath me was too long of a drop, but the balcony of the room next door jutted close. Before I even thought about it, I had thrown Maya's open suitcase over to it and stepped up onto the balustrade.

Voices emerged from the room behind me.

I swallowed my fear and leapt.

If I hadn't looked down I might have landed on my feet. But a quick glimpse stolen in fright threw me off, and my back foot caught on the balustrade. I crashed onto Maya's suitcase and her scattered rolls of clothes, tumbling to a stop against the French doors.

The doors were partly open, but the heavy drapes were closed. I swatted through them and scuttled inside, dragging the suitcase with me.

As I got to my feet, clutching the bag, I saw them staring at me. Frozen in shock, on the bed in their underwear—the woman who'd been tardy to the elevator, and the man who had held the doors for her. I didn't have time to assess what they were doing—some form of canoodling with canolli—but a scene from *The Satyricon* flashed through my head as I scrambled from the bedroom through the doorway.

16.
Porsche or Audi

I peeked into the corridor. The Security people were still in Maya's room. Edging out quietly, I ducked around the corner and raced pell-mell down the hall. The stairwell was just past the elevator. As I flew down the steps with the pink suitcase in my arms, backpack swinging from my shoulder, I realized I'd be conspicuous if I dashed out through the lobby—the Iranian might be waiting there, too—so I continued on down the stairs to the basement, into what I assumed would be the bowels of the hotel.

It turned out to be the parking garage. I started running through it, looking for the exit, when suddenly a car came roaring from the side, screeching to a stop and nearly hitting me.

I froze before the black Mercedes.

The door opened.

A young Italian in a hotel uniform stepped out of the car and apologized. *"Mi dispiace."* Then he saw I was an American. "Are you okay, sir?"

I was backing away. "Yes...I...I'm looking for my car."

"*Mi dispiace molto.* We make you waiting too long. So busy. We are not normal so busy." He pried open his vest pocket and eyed a pair of tickets. "You are the Porsche or the Audi?"

I stopped backing away. "Uh...the Porsche?"

Scanning the garage, he spotted another valet trotting by and let out a piercing whistle. "Fredo, *porti la Porsche qui, pronto!*"

Fredo shouted back that he couldn't bring the Porsche pronto. Apparently he was busy, too.

I shot an anxious glance toward the stairwell. "Gosh. I'm in a real hurry," I said.

The valet reached into the Mercedes and shut off the engine. "Wait here," he said. "I bring for you." He sprinted off.

The Mercedes sat silent in front of me.

I glanced around. Aside from the two valets, there were no other people visible in the garage. The stairwell door remained shut. Security hadn't figured out where I was yet.

I stepped to the car, wondering if it really was the killer's. The rain-washed sedan gleamed like a jewel. Peering through the driver's window, I saw that the valet had left the key in the ignition. The leather seats were empty—no trash, no coffee mug, no briefcase, no luggage. I quickly scanned the garage again, then opened the car door, tossed in my suitcase and backpack, and climbed in behind the wheel.

Shutting the door encased me in silence. I noticed the scent of cigarette smoke, and remembered that moment with the dagger at my throat. My hand and arm trembled as I reached for the ignition. The engine purred, and as I shifted into gear, I caught sight of something moving on the ceiling of the garage.

A rotating security camera.

Up ahead a man in a dark suit was running up the aisle toward me. Through the passenger window, I glimpsed the bearded Iranian killer charging out of the stairwell.

I slammed the gas. The tires screamed. I aimed full on at the man coming toward me. Reaching under his coat—presumably for a gun—he leapt aside as the car flew past, rolling onto the trunk of a parked limousine. I screeched around the end of the aisle and raced toward the daylight at the top of the exit ramp.

In the rearview mirror, the Iranian appeared, sprinting full out after me. Up ahead a car suddenly backed into the lane—the valet retrieving the Porsche Carrera. I jerked the wheel and swerved away. The Porsche struck my passenger door and scraped all the way to the fender, sending the Mercedes into a tailspin.

As I fought the wheel I caught a glimpse of the Iranian. *My God,* I thought—*he's going to jump the car again!* The wheels straightened and I slammed on the gas, soaring into the brightness at the top of the ramp. A woman in a chef's smock screamed and leapt away as I bounded out onto the pavement. The garage had disgorged me at the rear of the hotel. I turned hard, squealing into the one-way street. Expelling cigarette smoke, kitchen workers cursed. A butcher's delivery van half-blocked the lane, its rear doors spread open, exposing frozen shanks. I swerved to avoid the van, but clipped a door and struck a row of parked motorbikes. They tumbled like dominoes.

I screeched out onto Via Veneto, cutting ahead of a bus—an open double-decker—eliciting a collective gasp from the tourists up on top. Flicking glances at the rear-view mirror, I wove through the lanes and tried to vanish into the traffic, but the freshly scraped and dented Mercedes hardly blended in. Although the Iranian was no longer chasing me, I was certain the security man must have made a call to the cops. They would all be descending on Via Veneto. I had to get off onto side streets.

How could this be happening? Was I really now fleeing the police?

Somewhere, a siren wailed. I wheeled off just ahead of Piazza Barberini and jogged a couple blocks onto Via Sistina. I took that a few blocks and turned off into an alley. Then I started zigzagging through the center of the city, tacking my way toward Trastevere.

In the pocket of my jacket was the note from Maya's room. My watch showed 10:23 A.M. In a mere seven minutes I would be an hour late. I prayed that the doctor would still be there.

17.
Safari

Across the Tiber, several blocks away from the entrance to the garden, I pulled over in a back lane and parked the battered Mercedes. It wasn't a legal spot, of course—that would have taken time—but at this point nothing I was doing was legal, and I felt a terrible urgency to rid myself of the car.

A helmeted girl buzzed by on a moped. I glanced around for pedestrians; it appeared I was alone.

In the glove compartment, I found the *Europcar* rental contract. Unfolding the document, I searched for the renter's name.

Vanitar Azad.

Just as I had feared! This maniac and Arshan Azad were obviously related. Father-son? Brothers? I was good as dead. Blood revenge fuelled his rage. I nervously stuffed the rental paper back in the glove compartment.

With the sleeve of my jacket, I wiped the steering wheel and the shifter handle. Did it make any sense to be cleaning off my fingerprints? Probably not, but at this point I was paranoid and scared out of my wits; I knew I wasn't thinking clearly and didn't want to take any chances. So I climbed out and wiped the door handle, too. Then I strapped on my backpack and hauled out Maya's suitcase.

The remote on the car key popped the trunk. I saw there was nothing inside. Apparently these minions of the Ayatollah traveled with only the clothes on their back. After shutting the trunk with my elbow, I glanced around and hurried off, bouncing the pink-paisley roller up the lane.

Several minutes later, as I scurried along Via della Scala, I tossed the car key through the grate of a drain.

———

The security man led the way back to her room, all the while jabbering into his cell phone. Though I couldn't understand his non-stop Italian, it was clear he was consulting with the police. I knew they'd soon connect me with the incident the previous night. It didn't leave much time.

Discreetly I buttoned my suit jacket, adjusting it over the dagger. The fabric, still damp from the rain, clung too close to my body. I wondered how long it would take them to see it, or to notice the stains on my knees.

The door to her room had been propped open, the curtains pulled aside. On the edge of the bed sat another security man—also on his phone. He eyed me suspiciously as I followed his partner inside.

Several dresses and women's underclothes lay strewn across the floor. As the man I'd followed ended his call, he turned to see me staring down at them. "He steal her suitcase," the man explained in English. "Look like he left the best stuff behind."

I didn't bother to hide my scowl. The grin on the man's face faded.

I slowly scanned the desk and the bed. In my head I heard an echo of Arshan's voice: Look more closely. See.

The Italian on the bed closed his phone and told his partner something.

The partner turned to me. "The camera. In the garage. We have his picture. Not to worry, you will get back your car."

I nodded.

The man on the bed stood up and gently waved the Hindi's passport. "Police want to see this. They saying something happened." His eyes stayed on mine, then drifted down my dampened suit and narrowed at my knees.

"You fall down? In the rain?"

I looked at him. "The phone," I said.

"Scusi?"

"There, on the desk."

The two men turned. The message light was blinking.

When I asked if she knew of a Dr. Fiore, the Gypsy in the booth at the entry gate furled her bushy brows. I repeated the name, "Fiore."

Memory struck and lit up her face. *"Il Professore!"* She told me I must hurry, and urged me up the path to *"la serra tropicale."* This was a large and decrepit greenhouse I often passed on my morning jog. It was not too far from where I was standing, so I quickly marched off, suitcase in tow, and hastened up the path.

In all the many times I had jogged through the gardens, I'd hardly given a thought to the greenhouse. Now, as I approached, its age and general state of decay struck me as oddly enchanting. It appeared to have been a fixture for centuries.

A sign on the access door read *Chiuso*, but when I tried the knob, it opened.

The canopy of fogged and leaf-littered glass enclosed an Amazonian jungle. Small birds flitted past, disturbing humid air awash with the sound of trickling water. I followed a winding walkway, dodging banana leaves and dangling branches, dragging my squeaky-wheeled suitcase. In spite of its sunlit expanse, the green-tangled interior felt somehow claustrophobic, and the thickness of the air quickly put me in a sweat.

I ascended an elevated walkway. It snaked over a tranquil, percolating pond, and my eyes went immediately to searching its surface, as if it might hold the treasured lotus.

"May we help you, sir?"

Behind me, in a clearing below, framed by the glutted foliage, a group of young Italians with clipboards and notepads stood staring up at me in amusement. A severe-looking woman with black-framed glasses stepped out from among them. "I am sorry, but the conservatory is closed," she said. "This lecture is restricted to the students."

Several of the future botanists snickered, and I suddenly realized how silly I looked, white safari jacket and pink suitcase, lost in a counterfeit jungle.

One of the young women giggled out loud.

"I'm looking for Dr. Fiore," I said.

The older woman shook her head. "There is no one here by that name."

"Felix Fiore? A professor, maybe?"

"I'm afraid I'm the only professor today. Now, please, if you will excuse us." She turned back to her students and resumed her lecture.

I stood there a moment, dumbly, then turned and began to retrace my steps. *Fiore. Professore.* The Romanian at the entry gate must have made a phonetic mistake, and thought I was a student running late for this woman's lecture.

What the heck was I doing? Forget this goddamn doctor. There was only one thing I *ought* to be doing—getting the hell out of Rome!

I blasted out the greenhouse door and started down the lawn.

"Perdoni!"

I turned.

A young woman stood in the greenhouse doorway. She called out to me in English. "A man was here, before."

I walked back up to her. It was the girl from the lecture who had giggled. She was pretty, with friendly eyes. "I think he is maybe your friend," she said.

"Did he tell you his name?"

She shook her head, "no."

"Why do you think he was my friend?"

She smiled. "He wears the white. Like you."

I wasn't sure I understood. I pinched the collar of my jacket. "Like this?"

She nodded happily, *"Si."*

"When was he here?" I asked.

She shrugged. "I think…an hour, before?"

"Did he say where he was going?"

"He ask me for where to find *l'Orto dei Semplici.*"

"The Garden of...Simples?"

"*Si.* Up there, behind the wall." She pointed through the trees up the slope. "Where they grow the herbs for the medicine."

I knew the place she was talking about. The plants there all had labels.

"Grazie," I said. *"Tante grazie."*

"Prego," she said.

I watched her go back inside.

My wristwatch read 11:28 A.M. I peered through the trees toward the Garden of Simples.

He wears the white?

18.
The Walled Garden

The garden lay hidden behind ivy-covered walls. Inside, a geometric labyrinth of raised planter beds concealed a central, circular pond. The waist-high brick planters formed odd-angled shapes and sprouted all manner of plant life, from delicate sprays of herbs and flowers to thorny thickets of shrubs and vines. Profuse growth had overwhelmed the initial attempt at order, and despite identification labels, there appeared no discernible pattern to the plantings, so that now even the geometric layout seemed obscure. The design, I decided, as I wound my way through it, could only be divined from above.

At first it appeared I was the only one there. But when I finally reached the plant-filled pool, I was startled to find a white suit jacket draped over its stony rim, with a pair of white-and-tan saddle shoes neatly arranged beside it. Out in the pond, behind a thicket of swaying papyrus, a man with a full white beard and a surging mane of snowy white hair waded knee-deep in the water.

Slowly, I circled the pond, trying to get a clearer view of exactly what he was doing. The old man seemed entirely preoccupied and paid me no attention. His white vest was buttoned, but he had rolled up his white suit trousers and sleeves, and was bent over, reaching toward the water. His reflection shone brightly on the jade-green surface; I watched him swipe his palm across it, as if peering into the depths.

I thought at once of the lotus. There were numerous lily

pads in the pond; a few even sprouted flowers and seed pods. But where he was standing there were no water plants, just a shimmering film of green at the surface. He cupped some of the green stuff in the joined palms of his hands and, trudging slowly back through the water, carried it to the edge of the pool.

I walked over to meet him.

Digging into the folds of his jettisoned jacket, the man fished out a powder-blue handkerchief and carefully placed what he had collected into it. As I approached, he stood upright, and a grin spread across the cloud of his beard.

"Find something interesting?" I asked in Italian.

He held out the hankie on the palm of his hand, squinting at it in the sunlight. On it was a collection of tiny green leaves, some sort of aquatic clover.

"Lemna gibba," he said. "A species of *Lemaceae*—more commonly known as duckweed." He spoke precisely in accented English, his voice soft and delicate, each syllable exquisitely pronounced. "Perhaps the simplest specimen in this marvelous Garden of Simples." The grin seemed a permanent part of his expression. His squinting eyes sparkled like Santa Claus.

I reached out to shake his hand. "I'm Jack Duran. Are you Dr. Fiore?"

"I am indeed." His grip was unexpectedly strong, his eyes a welcoming cool pale blue. He turned and sat on the flat stone rim with his feet still submerged in the water. Wet gray mud discolored his calves, but his rolled up pants were immaculate. Again he examined the duckweed. "*Lemna* reproduces quite rapidly. Very useful in the lab. But if it continues growing here, I fear it will choke out all the life in the pond."

"You don't work here, do you?" I asked.

"Heaven's no. I'm Swiss."

"Swiss?" He had said it as if it explained everything.

"I was born in the mountains of the Bernese Oberland, in good old Helvetia, which I love."

I sat down beside him. "Then why is this a concern of yours?"

He began carefully rinsing the pond mud from his feet. "Plants are my passion," he said. "Medicinal plants in particular."

I started to ask him about the lotus, but decided to be patient and wait. Old Father Saturn was running on a slower clock. He had a kind of reverential aura about him, a peaceful composure that felt vaguely religious. Even the methodical washing of his feet seemed curiously ritualistic.

"A garden like this is a sanctuary," he continued. "An oasis of the soul. Like the courtyard gardens of the medieval monasteries. Or the Mughal gardens of India. Even the garden of the Vestal Virgins, the pagan priestesses of ancient Rome."

That last one I knew well: a weedy patch in the ruins of a colonnaded courtyard, a highlight of my scandal-mongering Roman Forum tour.

He reached out for help and I took his hand as he carefully climbed from the pond. The man was quite old, but neither thin nor frail, and he moved with a dignified, slow-motion grace, like a sloth slowly moving through a tree.

He sat down again to don his silk socks and shoes. "These enclosed gardens descend from the walled gardens of ancient Persia, sanctuaries of beauty and a link with the divine. It's where we derive the word 'paradise,' from the Persian words *pairi*—'around,' and *daeza,* or *diz*—'wall.' Paradise, a place apart, separate from the world yet wondrously within it."

We glanced around us. The garden was indeed a wondrous thing, and it struck me suddenly how strange it was: to be sitting in this peaceful place, listening to this peculiar man, his voice as transparent and mysterious as glass, while outside, beyond the looming wall, the world, as I had known it, had gone completely insane.

The refuge he was talking about was just another illusion. I thought of my landlord's rooftop garden—his *"piccolo parte di paradiso"*—its walls had clearly been insufficient to keep out the modern-day Persians.

"You left a phone message for me," I said. "And you arranged to meet here with Maya Ramanujan."

"Yes. In fact I just left her another message not half an hour ago."

I pulled out the piece of stationery with Maya's directions and the hand-drawn map. "I found this in her hotel room."

The doctor looked at me, and I could see from his eyes he knew something was wrong. He gently took the note and examined it on his lap.

"Last night," I said, "a man broke into my apartment, and Maya was killed."

His shoulders subsided. He continued staring at the note in silence.

"Did you know her?" I asked.

"We never met," he said. He traced the lion symbol with his fingertips, as if he could feel its impression on the page.

सत्यमेव जयते

"Do you know what that is?" I asked. "Or what that writing means?"

"'Truth alone triumphs,'" he quoted. "It's Sanskrit. This is the Lion Capital of Ashoka. It stood atop an ancient pillar erected by the Indian emperor, Ashoka the Great. The pillar marked the spot where the Buddha first proclaimed his truth to the four corners of the earth."

"That circle beneath it looks familiar," I said.

"The Ashoka chakra—the chariot wheel, known as the Wheel of Dharma. It is probably Buddhism's most ancient symbol."

"How do you know all this?" I asked.

"I've been a student of Buddhism for nearly forty years," he said.

"Are you a Buddhist?"

"I'm on the path."

"Was Maya?"

"I don't know," he said. "It's possible. But the vast majority of Indians are Hindu. Most likely, this is just government stationery. The Ashoka capital is the emblem of the state."

I remembered now where I had seen that wheel: on the center of the Indian flag. "So she worked for the Indian government."

Fiore neatly refolded the note. "Miss Ramanujan was employed by the intelligence service in Delhi."

Maya was a spook. That made sense of the gun. "Why were you trying to meet her?" I asked. "Why did you telephone me?"

He lifted his eyes to mine. "By now you must know why," he said.

I stared back at him without replying.

"Listen to me carefully," he said. "This morning, near your apartment, I found parts of the lotus plant scattered on the street. As you have seen, there are people willing to kill for this lotus. It is vitally important we safeguard it from them. So please tell me truthfully: Are you in possession of any more of these plants or seeds?"

"No. Maya was dying—she told me to destroy it. How did you—?"

"Are you certain? I assure you I am willing to pay handsomely—"

"I told you: That one plant was all I had."

"Very well," he said. "I believe you."

"Then tell me what you're doing here. What is this all about?"

Fiore handed back Maya's note. "Those are directions to an archaeological dig site in the desert of Turkmenistan. An earthenware jar recently uncovered there contained some 3000-year-old lotus seeds. The species was known in ancient India but has long been thought extinct. Many believe this lotus offers psychoactive properties that could make it extremely valuable. Five days ago the seeds were stolen, and the Indian government became involved in trying to track them down. That's why Miss Ramanujan sought you out in Rome."

"Why me?"

He gazed calmly into my eyes. "Because they believe the lotus seeds were stolen by your brother."

Dan. Again. "Knowing my brother," I said, "I wouldn't put it past him. But believe me, Dan's no killer. And you said they were stolen five days ago? The seeds I grew that plant from he sent me over a *year* ago."

"Yes," he said. "And unlike those found in the desert, his seeds were fresh and able to sprout—they were taken from living plants."

His point slowly came home to me. "Which means...the lotus is *not* extinct."

"Your brother has found it growing somewhere, a source that's long been hidden. Unfortunately these people are aware of that now."

"You mean...the Iranians."

"Them, and others." He stood up and worked himself into his jacket. "We must get you out of Rome immediately," he said. "It won't be safe for you here."

He started through the labyrinth. I walked along beside him, still trying to figure out exactly what had happened. "Is that why you were meeting Maya?" I asked. "To buy the lotus if she got it from me?"

"She may not have agreed to selling it. But I had hoped to give it a try."

"Someone removed her corpse," I said. "And cleaned up the blood in my apartment."

"That would have been the Americans, I would think."

"The Americans?"

"When the Iranians are involved, they're usually not far behind."

"But why would they clean up after her murder?"

"You might want to ask your friend," he said. "The fellow with the pretty lady."

"Harry Grant? You saw him?" The old man seemed omniscient.

"I was waiting in my car near your apartment when the three of you arrived. Had you been alone, I would have introduced myself."

I wondered what the doctor had to fear from Harry Grant. And how he knew who I was. "You must know my brother."

"One does not soon forget him. Daniel and I met at a monastery in India. I discovered he shares a similar interest in the origins of religion." His tone seemed tinged with irony.

"Do you know where he is now?" I asked.

We had reached the exit through the wall of the garden. The doctor looked out, then turned to face me. In his sunlit suit, with his blinding hair and shock of beard, he looked like a parody of God the Father—that, or a dissimulating devil.

I waited for his answer.

"You must return home to America," he said. "You'll be safer there."

"Where is Dan?" I demanded.

Fiore hesitated.

I thought again of Harry Grant. "You know I won't turn him in," I said. "Dan's my only brother."

"Yes," he said. "I understand. The problem is I don't know where Daniel is—I'm looking for him myself."

"Why?"

Again he hesitated. "Because I am afraid of what will happen if others find him first."

I stared at him, uncertain. "Afraid of what'll happen to the lotus—or what'll happen to Dan?"

Distant voices came over the wall. Fiore peered out the doorway, then drew quickly back. "It's the police," he said.

I peeked out. Two uniformed cops and the hotel security man were heading up through the trees.

"They must have found your message on the hotel voicemail," I said. "I stole the Iranian's car and—"

"Go, quickly," he said, gesturing back through the garden. "You can exit through the other side. I will delay them here as long as I can."

"Where will you—?"

"I'll contact you later," he said. "When I find your brother."

"But I don't even know where I'm go—"

"You're going *home*," he insisted.

I looked at him a moment, then grabbed Maya's suitcase and ran.

19.
Running Scared

A quarter of an hour later, a pair of eyes silently queried me from the rearview mirror of a taxi.

"Fiumicino," I told the driver. "T-5, *per favore*." At the Aeroporto Leonardo da Vinci di Fiumicino, Terminal 5 was the point of departure for all U.S. carrier flights to the States.

It was obvious Fiore was right. I had to get out of Italy as quickly as I could, and certainly flying home to America offered the safest bet. The Roman police, now acutely aware that my stay was illegal, suspected me of having drug ties to the mob and connections with assassins in Iran. I had been the last person seen with an Indian businesswoman who had been murdered the very same night. If that wasn't enough, I had broken into her hotel room, made off with her luggage and escaped in a stolen Mercedes.

Earlier, Oriana had predicted I'd end up in the clink. I seemed to be doing all I could to prove her right.

And yet the police were the least of my worries.

I turned and scanned the traffic behind, wondering if somehow the Iranian had followed me. He had not accompanied the two cops and the hotel security man. Had the involvement of the police made him nervous? Perhaps he had split off to pursue me on his own.

They'll kill you, Maya had whispered. *Your brother, too.*

I recalled the Iranian's cry—*Arshan!*—and his maniacal, spider-like attack on the car.

He'll hunt me down, I thought. Facing forward I focused on

the crowded road ahead, trying to think things through. What if Iranian intelligence had access to passenger lists? If I made a seat reservation, how quickly would they know? And if they discovered I was heading to the States, what would stop them from following me?

"May I borrow your cell?" I asked in Italian. The driver made a face in the mirror until I offered to pay him something. He wearily shrugged and handed over the phone.

I dialed the number scribbled on Harry Grant's card. After two failed attempts at a connection, I finally made it through to the Agent's voicemail. I told him the name on the Mercedes rental contract, Vanitar Azad, said he was the guy trying to kill me. Then I asked if he could find out anything about an aging doctor from Switzerland named Felix Fiore. Finally, I told him I would call him back later, though I couldn't say exactly when.

Next I called Vincenzo Accidi. He had just arrived at his travel office, and the second he heard my voice on the line, he launched into a tirade of Italian obscenities. It turned out he had spent his morning at the central police station, trying to convince the *Carabinieri* to please release his car. They refused, saying the damaged Spider was potential evidence in a missing person's case, involving burglary, auto theft, possibly even murder.

Vincenzo now demanded to know what the hell was going on.

"I can't explain right now," I told him. "But Vinny…I need another favor. I want you to book me immediately on the next flight out to the States."

This brought a brief, astonished laugh. Then my friend hung up.

Three cars ahead, next lane over, Duran put down his phone. I pulled out a long stretch of the seatbelt and furtively sawed it with my knife.

The cabbie eyed me in the rearview mirror. "Tell me. This man we follow. He trying to steal your wife?"

"I have no wife," I said.

"You are lucky. My wife, she cheating on me. More than once."

I thought of my childhood friend Faraj and the unspeakable lies he later told about my parents. Fidelity in friendship and marriage is inviolable; the breaking of such bonds unforgivable. Faraj had earned the beatings we administered in prison. His mendacity was a betrayal to Islam.

"What will you do about your wife?" I asked the cabbie.

"' Divorzio all'Italiana.*' You ever see this movie?"*

"Marcello Mastroianni. Are you saying you'll murder your wife?"

"No," he said. "Not yet anyway. I only dreaming about it."

I finished cutting and rolled up the strap, stuffing it into my pocket. "When my father married my mother, she was the most beautiful girl in his village. She was fifteen years old. He was fifty-three. But he never once had to question her fidelity. In his village, if a wife betrayed her husband...she'd be buried alive up to her neck and stoned to death."

"Mamma mia!"

"That's 'Divorce, Iranian *Style.'"*

The cabbie smiled uncertainly, then stared ahead, unblinking. I could see him struggling to hide his fear. When again he caught my stare in the mirror he quickly looked away. Never would he dare to look into my eyes again.

———

"Why are you running away?" Vinny asked when I finally got him back on the phone.

For a moment I couldn't respond. I thought of that girl in the hostel I had abandoned the previous night. Then I thought of Phoebe running away, and Dan disappearing into Asia, and me now getting the hell out of Rome—

"Jack?"

"It's not safe for me here anymore," I said. I didn't even try to explain what happened, and made no mention of Dr. Fiore, or Harry Grant and Oriana. The less Vinny knew, the better, I thought. I made him promise not to tell the police or anyone else where I was going. Grudgingly he agreed to check the airline schedules and call me back with a flight.

I shut the cell and stared out the window. The traffic to the airport had slowed and thickened. A growing anxiety gnawed at me.

Why are you running away?

It reminded me of something Phoebe said she used to argue about with her father. A research physiologist at the University of Amsterdam, Professor Auerbach had made his career studying the physiology of fear and anxiety. He believed that pain—or more commonly, the *fear* of pain or death—was the elemental stimulus that provokes a person to act. Hunger and thirst were the most obvious examples, but he believed the idea expanded to include virtually every form of human endeavor. Fear was the great motivator: fear of not having the thing we desire, or of losing a thing that we have.

His daughter abhorred this dispiriting notion. She argued there was too much it failed to explain: the love between two people, for example, or the human ambition for accomplishment and greatness, or more altruistic aspirations, like compassion, generosity, and the spiritual longing for God. All these, she believed, were attempts to fulfill a deeper craving, a quest toward expansion and cosmic unity—the dream of transcending physicality and death.

Love was the true motivator.

Another triumph of hope over experience, I thought as I anxiously glanced out the back. Her father's view was a little too gloomy for me, too, but I couldn't find a way to disagree with it. Pain is a reality we all know too well, and while Phoebe's more romantic notions seemed a bit abstract, I had no problem understanding fear. In fact, at that very moment, trapped inside that taxi cab creeping toward the airport, I could feel the tight whorl of fear uncoiling in my belly, wriggling like some hairy worm birthed inside my gut.

Why was I running away? Because I was scared to death, that's why.

20.
Fractured Fairy Tale

On the taxi's radio, Violante Placido, in her sexy, guileless little girl voice, was singing her love song, *With U*. It was a favorite of Vinny's and reminded me of my dream, the one of Phoebe waiting under the oak tree.

I searched my pack for the photograph I had found in Maya's bag—Dan and me with Phoebe on the Acropolis. We'd all agreed to keep our Furies photos off the Net, and having searched out every image of Phoebe in existence, I knew this shot had never been uploaded. Maya could only have obtained the print from her.

Somehow Phoebe was caught up in all this; I felt certain of it.

In truth I really shouldn't have been surprised. The captivating rose had its complement of thorns. Although she could be tender and sweetly softhearted, Phoebe was high-spirited and stubbornly strong-willed. Likewise, though a keen intellect and coolly analytic, she readily let loose with a fiery frankness, and her judgments could be scathing and dogmatic. This volatile combination of compassion and will often drew the Dutch damsel into trouble, and I had to wonder now if she had put her life in danger, and if she might be on the run with Dan.

I studied the photograph. Phoebe stood between Dan and me, her waist bared and slender, her boyish, blond hair tousled in the wind, her smiling eyes blue as the sky. My brother had not yet shaved off his long, shaggy locks; with one hand he was pulling windblown strands from his face while his other hand rested on the crook of Phoebe's hip. I had an arm around her shoulders, and she had both her arms around us. At the moment the photo was taken, Phoebe and I were looking into the lens of the camera. Dan was looking at her.

Like me, Dan had been infatuated from the start; unlike me, he'd gotten to her first. They had met on a beach on the island of Crete, where Phoebe was in residence with an excavation team. By the time I caught up with them at Dan's place in Athens, they'd been visiting each other, back and forth, over the spring and summer. A relatively brief term of courtship, you might think, but long enough apparently for Dan. Right in the middle of the media frenzy that followed the Furies blow-up, he asked the archaeologist to marry him.

I wondered now exactly why he'd been in such a hurry. Dan was only twenty-eight years old at the time. Phoebe was twenty-four. He'd never had a long-term relationship with anyone. No girl had lasted more than a few weeks.

Phoebe wasn't pregnant; that I knew for sure. I knew it because I knew she hadn't slept with him. Phoebe had never slept with any man.

She told me so herself. The revelation followed one of her arguments with Dan, who simply could not comprehend her chastity. She wasn't old-fashioned, or frigid, or religious, and she certainly wasn't prudish—far from it. Shapely, slender, athletic, she found pleasure in the dressing and display of her body, carried herself with considerable style and aplomb, and the way she flirted clearly showed she had no fear of men; she took a provocative pride in her purity.

So was she just a lofty and unconquerable tease, the Duran brothers' Everest of Desire?

The truth is Phoebe's self-restraint was touchingly sincere. Sex, she believed, had lost its mystery, and sexiness gone dead. She rejected wholeheartedly the hookup culture and its casual disdain for devotion and marriage. In a reversion to more chivalrous times, she conceived of matrimony as a noble undertaking, and making love as something close to sacred. She had resolved to give herself to only one man: the man she loved above them all, who proved himself most worthy. A man she could commit to unreservedly for life. The one whose heart she knew for sure was true.

She recognized the fairy tale quality of her quest. The anachronistic, countercultural quaintness. I suspect it was in rebellion to her father's cynicism, his stonyhearted view that all we do is out of fear. For Phoebe self-control was the key to self-respect; she found a sense of dignity through freedom. Not the freedom to indulge every passion and pleasure, but a truer, deeper freedom—unchained from the mind's addictions and the tyrannies of the flesh. She believed that she was more than brain and body.

Spirit, self-sacrifice, nobility, true love—antiquated notions from another world, perhaps, but that was the kind of world the willful Dutch girl wanted to live in. That was the kind of woman she chose to be.

With the traffic moving sluggishly, I considered exiting my taxicab and striding up to Duran's. I could easily haul him out the door and kill him on the highway. Show my reluctant driver how it's done.

Like my brother, in his youth. Arshan would have demonstrated precisely how it's done.

Arshan alone had raised me on the streets of South Tehran. Faraj and I—both fatherless—grew to worship him. A laat *who lived by fist and knife, Arshan would slash his chest before a fight to show his fearlessness. Inspired by my father, whom God honored with martyrdom against Saddam's Iraq, Arshan joined the Basij, then later advanced up through the Guard until the Quds Force took him. Soon enough his knife became the Rahbar's brightest weapon—until the Old Man in Qum called him to lead his bold jihad.*

As now he called on me.

This was not the time or place to take Arshan's revenge. It would bring too much attention. Hordes of policemen hunting me down, helicopters, TV crews, cries of terrorism. The Old Man had requested that I find out who betrayed us, and to put off Allah's justice until that task was done.

"Hold yourself in patience," the noble Quran counsels, "'til Allah doth decide."

But still murderous thoughts returned, tempting me like the devil...

Awaiting the callback from Vinny, I warily scanned the surrounding cars as the traffic continued its crawl. Drivers were growing increasingly frantic, afraid of missing departing flights or dreading the wrath of arrivals. Exhaust fumes clogged the idling air and tensions seemed to crackle. Horns blared. The cabbie cursed. The shriek of a white-lining moped shook me.

We're all running scared, I thought. All of us, all the time, from one damn thing or another. And of course the Biggest Damn Thing of All could take you out any moment.

Maya had said these men would kill us. Fiore seemed to imply that was the least that they would do. If Dan really knew where this lotus plant grew, I began to wonder now if they wouldn't torture him to find it.

That terrible thought gave rise to another: What on earth would I tell my mother when I finally arrived back home? That I was safe, she didn't have to worry, but Dan was still out there on his own?

Years before, when Dan had disappeared without a word in Mexico, my mother grew sick with worry and sent me down to find him. As things eventually turned out, it was Dan who rescued me—bravely risking his life in the bargain.

I loved my brother for that. Owed him for it, too. And now I felt I owed him even more for something else.

I peered again at the picture: Dan looking sidelong at Phoebe, unable to pry his eyes away, while she and I gleefully smile for the camera. He had believed with all his heart that he was the prince of her dreams. He was the man most worthy of her. He was her one true love. Then his brother entered the picture and shattered the fairy tale.

Why had Dan popped the question so quick? The answer

was clear as day. I had fallen in love with his girlfriend. She was falling in love with me. Dan was afraid he was losing her, afraid I would steal her away.

Shamefully, I attempted just that, prodding and cajoling her to follow me to Rome. But Phoebe, unable to choose between us, ended up choosing the one thing she knew: her freedom.

She ran away.

How else could such a doomed triangle have ended? Phoebe had seen it coming first and fled to her family in Holland. Dan in despair then vanished into Asia, and I in my misery soon lost myself in Rome.

We had all run away. From love, from pain. From fear.

I turned to stare again at the anonymous traffic, fingering the feathery slit on my throat.

Dan is my only brother, I thought. How can I run from that?

The ring of the cell phone jarred me. "Hello?"

"There's a United flight to New York," Vinny said. "Departs out of Gate 3 in one—"

"Forget it," I said.

"Scusi?"

"Change of plan." I pulled out the map of directions from Maya. "I need you to get me to a place called...

21.
Ashkhabad

"Why in God's name," Vinny cried over the phone, "would anyone want to go to Ashkhabad?"

The answer, I knew, was complicated, but what I told my friend very simply was this: I wanted to find my brother. A dig site in the desert near Ashkhabad was the last place he had been seen. Dan was in some kind of trouble, I said. I feared he was in danger of losing his life. And Phoebe might well be with him.

A quick check revealed no direct flights to Ashkhabad—or to any other city in Turkmenistan. "You'll have to make a connection through Moscow," Vinny said. "Aeroflot #76 leaves Rome at 23:00."

"I can't wait that long," I told him. The police would be all over me, not to mention the Iranian. "Just get me somewhere in the region."

He called back a few minutes later. "How soon will you be at Fiumicino?"

"Fifteen minutes?"

"Head to Terminal 3, just past Alitalia," he said. "Turkish Airlines has a flight to Baku through Istanbul, leaves at 13:50."

I looked at my watch. The flight left in 83 minutes. "Where the hell is Baku?"

"Azerbaijan, in the Caucasus. From Baku you can hop over the Caspian to Turkmenistan."

All of it sounded the same to me—like the dark side of the moon. "Get me on it," I said.

"Already done," he said. Then he told me I would need a visa to enter Turkmenistan. I asked if he could arrange it. "*Dubioso*," he said. "Visa there could take you weeks. Worse than North Korea."

"I'll have to deal with it in Baku," I said. The main thing now was to get out of Rome.

I thanked Vincenzo for his help. "I owe you big-time, *amico*."

"You owe me a car," he said.

When the call ended, I asked the driver to take me to Terminal 3—but to Arrivals, not Departures, in case the Iranians or the police were lying in wait. Then I opened Maya's suitcase and took another look inside.

Most of her clothes had fallen out in the course of my escape. In the inner side pocket, I found the Ziploc bag with the pair of fried somosas. I gave the patties a sniff, then gave one a nibble. Onions, chilies, peas, potatoes. I hadn't realized how famished I was. Suddenly it felt like days had passed since having that meal with Maya.

I scarfed down the two samosas.

Again I examined the brass lock sealing the outer pocket. These suitcase locks had always seemed so chintzy and useless to me, but this was a stubborn little devil, actually quite well-made. Without the combination or a bolt-cutter, there was no way I could open it.

Scars streaked the canvas where I had stabbed it with the letter opener.

I asked the driver, "Do you by any chance have a pocket knife?"

In the mirror, he eyed me warily, then slowly shook his head, "no." I realized he had probably just overheard my cell phone call with Vinny.

The airport appeared ahead. I quickly decided to consolidate luggage; there wouldn't be time to check Maya's bag. After emptying out her remaining clothes, I crammed my little backpack inside her roller. It took a mighty effort to zipper the suitcase shut.

The cabbie headed to the lower level Arrivals in Terminal

3. It may have been my paranoia, but several times I caught the driver glancing in the mirror at me, as if he were memorizing my face. At the sign for Turkish Airlines, he pulled the taxi over.

"Thanks for the phone," I told him cheerily. I added a ten euro tip to the fare, hoping to assuage his suspicions.

Scooping up the pile of Maya's clothes, I extracted myself from the taxi. A quick scan revealed no Middle-Eastern maniac charging at me with a knife, and aside from a single traffic cop, there were no other policemen around. I dragged out the pink paisley roller and headed across to the doors. Slipping through the crowd of outpouring arrivals, I entered the building and dumped Maya's clothes into the first available trash container. Then I found the escalator and started upstairs to Departures.

My heart banged like a drum. If Vanitar Azad was in the terminal, awaiting my arrival, it was more than likely he'd be waiting up here, keeping an eye on the street. I stripped off my jacket and folded it under my arm. Stepping up past some teenagers, I stopped behind an obese couple. When the escalator deposited us, I followed closely behind them.

The Turkish Airlines ticket booth was halfway across the concourse. Keeping my head down, I split off toward it, stealing anxious glances through the crowd.

There's safety in numbers, I told myself. Surely it would be too risky to try to attack me here. The airport probably had more security personnel than any other place in Rome. I continued to reassure myself, and after waiting several minutes in the ticket line, searching among the bored faces of the many travelers around me, my anxiety began to dissipate, and my heartbeat settled into a tolerable clip.

It would take them a while, if they could, to trace my reservation. Less than half an hour had passed since Vincenzo had called it in. The flight was leaving in just over an hour—not much time to find me. The quick departure seemed to insure I would get off the ground alive.

I bought the ticket with a credit card, and ten minutes later I was checking my pack through security and stepping through the metal detector. By this point I had convinced myself there wouldn't be any problem. I had been too paranoid. The Roman police hadn't called out the dogs; they hadn't even flagged my reservation. I began to doubt the Iranian would have bothered with it either. For all I knew, he may have already fled the country himself. Surely by now he had realized that I didn't have what he wanted.

Other than revenge...

"Pardone, Signore." The female baggage inspector had her white-gloved hands on Maya's suitcase. "Is this yours?"

A sinking feeling came over me. "Yes."

The woman hauled it up onto an examination table and began to unzip the lid. Maya's hidden object had been spotted in the x-ray machine. Suddenly it occurred to me: If the Indian spy had kept a pistol in her purse, she may have kept another weapon in her bag.

I glanced back the way I came and considered making a run for it.

22.
The Object

Bucharest. Istanbul. Athens. Sydney. Prague. Cairo. Six departures from Terminal 3 within the next two hours. All of them heading east.

Allah be praised—Duran was not returning to America! Whatever he had found in the Hindi's suitcase, he was taking it now to his brother.

But where?

I will make him tell me when I kill him, I thought. Right now I just need to get inside the terminal.

"Bucharest. Coach. One-way."

"I...believe that flight is full, Signore." The clerk checked his computer. "Si, I'm sorry. The next—"

"Istanbul, then."

He eyed me quizzically.

I smiled. "Family on the Black Sea," I said. "I can drive from either city."

His gaze lingered a moment. He looked at his computer. "You have luggage?"

"Nothing to check."

Another curious glance. "May I see your passport, please?"

I handed it over, wondering if the devil Duran had already made it through.

Following a struggle with the zipper, the inspector had finally opened the suitcase and was now lifting out my compacted backpack, eyeing it curiously. She opened it and pawed through my tangle of clothes, and when she found nothing hidden among them, inspected the outer pockets. Uncovering no dangerous items there, she turned her attention to Maya's roller. It didn't take her long to locate the pocket under the lid. She asked me politely to open the lock.

"I forgot the combination," I said.

"We must open," she said. "You cannot open?"

"I told you, I don't know the combination. I don't even know what's in—"The woman looked away from me and called her supervisor. She asked for something in Italian I didn't understand, but moments later, a portly, balding uniformed official came over with a steel-jawed bolt cutter.

The two of them studied the x-ray monitor. Then the man examined the zippered pocket and the tiny brass lock. Finally he held up the cutters and declared, "You can leave luggage behind, or"—he clipped the air in demonstration.

I glanced between the two of them and the bulging suitcase pocket, trying to make up my mind. What had they seen in the x-ray? A knife? A gun? Why had Maya taken the trouble to lock it in her bag?

It had to be something important. Maybe something she'd brought along to help her track down Dan. Had I dragged the suitcase all this way to give up finding it now?

Curiosity overruled fear. "Go ahead, cut it," I said.

The supervisor grinned with perverse satisfaction. He leaned in with the metal shears and snapped the bar of the lock.

The woman stepped forward and opened the pocket.

The first thing she pulled out was a leather-bound sketchbook. My heart soared. I recognized it at once as belonging to Dan—he had kept one just like it when he lived in Mexico. The woman set it down on the table, then reached again into the pocket and pulled out a tall, narrow book bound with a green cloth cover. The book was very old, the binding frayed and loose. She laid the volume down atop the leather sketchbook. The gold lettering on the green cover looked similar to the writing beneath the lions on Maya's stationery—what Dr. Fiore had said was Sanskrit.

Finally, the woman reached into the pocket and pulled out a heavy, hard-edged object, wrapped in a cotton T-shirt.

This is it, I thought. I'm done for.

She unwrapped the object and held it up in puzzlement. It wasn't a gun, and it wasn't a knife. In fact it wasn't like anything I'd ever seen before.

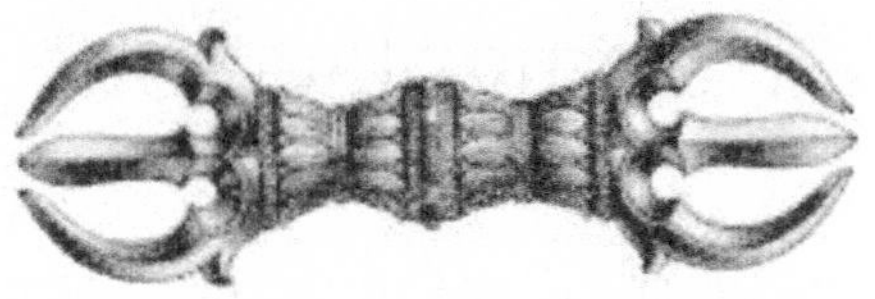

It was a small bronze antique of some sort, a kind of symbol or scepter. The thing looked as if it were designed to be gripped, a handle with four pointed prongs at each end, curved to form a pair of hollow spheres.

The portly supervisor examined it closely and asked me what it was.

"I don't know," I said, scrambling. "It's just…a good luck charm, I think. My girlfriend brought it from India. She must have forgotten to unpack it."

The female inspector eyed me skeptically.

With his fingertip, the supervisor poked the converging, pointed prongs. The way they were neatly pinched together rendered them perfectly harmless. "I think…is okay," he said, handing it over to me.

I thanked him and hurriedly inserted the object into my backpack, along with the old text and the sketchbook. "Would you mind just getting rid of that suitcase for me? She doesn't really need it anymore."

They took it without a word of comment, as if giving away perfectly good luggage were routine. I hurried off to catch my flight, wondering what the hell I had just discovered in Maya's bag.

23.
Someplace Safe

The gate was near the end of the main corridor. As I came within sight of it, I moved out of the streaming crowd to hide behind a phone kiosk and survey the waiting area. A boarding announcement was being read for the flight to Istanbul, stirring the rows of ticketholders slumped in their plastic seats. Most appeared to be Indians who would continue on to New Delhi. The rest were mostly Turkish and mixed-race Asian businessmen, along with some American and European tourists and a group of university students.

My eyes searched among them for the beard and the Hugo Boss, but no one fit the description. A quick scan of the surrounding areas also came up nil.

What if he changed his clothes? I wondered. What if he shaved off his beard?

I ventured closer.

A line had begun to form at the gate, businessmen and government officials assembling for encampment in the First Class seats. Walking along the wall of windows, I circumvented a Turkish family occupying an entire aisle. The father, a humongous man, stood bellowing into his cell phone, his sons sprawled at his feet over a laptop, his wife and daughters in chic head scarves and big, inscrutable sunglasses, whispering among one another in their seats. Beyond them, the group of Italian students laughingly joked and flirted, while restive tourists gathered their bags, maneuvering toward the line.

Everything looked perfectly normal—or as normal as you could expect on a flight to Istanbul. I stepped into line myself and tried to blend in with the others. Safety in numbers. Another announcement came over the speaker and more people got into line. I glanced down the corridor. No beard, no Hugo Boss, no panting policemen hot on my trail. I was only minutes away now from finally escaping Rome.

The First Class passengers finished boarding, and the line continued slowly moving forward toward the gate. Outside the windows, awash in sunlight, the massive Turkish Airbus loomed. A wind-swept flower logo streaming across its silver hull struck me as a cosmic joke. It may have been a tulip, or possibly a lily, but to me it looked exactly like a lotus.

I almost laughed out loud. But just then I glanced down the corridor again, and the grin on my face went slack.

There was no mistaking the Iranian. Even a long way off. He was wearing the same dark suit and open-collared shirt I had seen him in at the Excelsior that morning. And no, he hadn't bothered shaving off his beard. If he had any concerns about the police or security, it didn't show at all in his manner. He was pushing through the crowd with a keen determination—not quite like a madman ravenous for murder, but intently, like a hungry lion tracking down its prey.

I left the line immediately and briskly walked away. Not that I had any idea where I was going. Foolishly, I had made no plan for what to do if he showed up. My only hope was that he hadn't spotted me.

I nearly sprinted up the corridor, not daring to look back. If he knew what flight I was on, I figured it would take him only a minute to discover I was not at the gate. Then he would continue looking for me, or lie in wait until the plane departed to make sure I didn't board it. All I had to do was to keep out of sight until finally he gave up and left.

But where could I hide?

The crowd in the corridor was thinning out; I had reached the end of the terminal. Two of the final gates were empty. I spun around, searching for someplace safe.

The Men's Room. I crossed the hall and ducked inside.

A young Italian father was leading his little boy to the sink. Two other men stood at the urinals. Beyond them in the corner was a bucket and mop with a folding yellow janitor's sign, and beside me, near the sinks, an overflowing trashcan and a diaper-changing table.

There was only one place to hide. I locked myself in a toilet stall.

To make my concealment convincing—and because I suddenly realized I actually had to pee—I lowered my pants, sat down, and after struggling for a minute to calm my nerves, finally relieved myself. Then I simply sat there, listening.

"Molto bene," the father said, turning off the tap. The howl of a blowing hand dryer filled the lavatory. *"Andiamo,"* he called, and I heard the little boy's feet scurry out the door.

The two other men followed suit at the sinks. Then each took a turn at the hand dryers, which continued to blow well after they left. I sat in silence then for what seemed like several minutes, wondering what the Iranian would do when he couldn't find me at the gates.

The door burst open again and several men came in, including three chattering college students I assumed were with the group bound for Istanbul. One of them entered the stall beside me and stood before the toilet, continuing to converse with his unseen friends over the deafening plash of his piss. Finally, he lifted his sneaker to flush.

The boys left. The other men soon after followed them out, rolling their rumbling carry-ons across the grouted tiles. The Men's Room door swung shut. I was left in an echoing silence.

A final boarding call for the flight to Istanbul came muffled over the transom. I imagined the Iranian standing near the gate, watching to see if I'd show—and the frustration he would feel when I didn't.

A few stalls away, the sudden flush of a toilet startled me—I had assumed I was alone. The metal lock unlatched and the door creaked open, then loudly clattered shut. Water ran in a sink. The man crossed by and the hand blower howled.

I waited, listening for the sound of the door as he left.

The blow dryer stopped. The man had not gone out.

Instead, he walked leisurely past my stall.

It sent a shudder through me.

24.
The Grip

I heard the rattle of the metal bucket, then a *clap* as the man closed the folding janitor's sign. He headed back toward the entrance with them.

Thank God—the janitor. I breathed a sigh of relief.

My watch read 1:39 P.M. In eleven minutes, the Turkish Airbus would pull away from the gate. Vanitar Azad would leave to look for me elsewhere. I could finally emerge and find another way out of Rome.

The Men's Room door opened and closed, swallowing a rush of noise from the hall. In the silence that ensued, I assumed the janitor had left. His approaching footsteps alarmed me. What had he done? Put out the sign?

He walked directly to my stall and stood before the door. "Excuse me, please," he said in accented English. "Be so kind. The bathroom must be cleaned, Signore."

A sudden rush of awareness overcame me. My eyes were locked on the sagging cuffs of the man's damp dress pants, breaking over highly polished, black leather shoes.

"I'll…be out in a minute," I uttered. My voice choked with fear.

The Iranian didn't move. He abandoned the feigned politeness. "You must come out now," he said.

My mouth opened, as if to reply, but couldn't seem to form any words. My jaw began to quiver. The fear bottled up in my gut was spilling out into my body. I sat frozen on the toilet seat, staring at the door in front of me. The harrowing rush of awareness narrowed my focus into a beam. The enameled door had been nervously scratched, leaving scars like the claw marks of an animal. The box I had hidden in was nothing but a trap. All I could think of was the Damascene dagger. And all that kept me from it was this flimsy metal door.

"Open," he demanded.

Time stopped. My thoughts became oddly detached and distinct, like another man's voice coolly whispering in my head. *Of course I don't have my dagger, you fool—how could I have passed through security? But I am a trained assassin. I will take your life using my hands. That's why I put out the janitor's sign—to make sure we won't be interrupted. Your murder is going to take time.*

Azad shouted something I couldn't understand. A coiled strap dropped to the floor. At the top of the door, his fingers appeared. He shook the door violently, rattling the lock.

The strap lay coiled on the floor like a snake.

I was about to be strangled to death.

The stark realization paralyzed me. I found it impossible to breathe.

The 'grip' is what Phoebe's father called it. The brain freeze of fear. The panic that takes hold of the mind as the body prepares to defend itself. I felt myself succumbing to it, reflexively giving way, unable to keep control of my will, or even my bodily functions. Energy was moving to where it was needed. Blood roared out of my pounding heart to the muscles of my abdomen and limbs. The stimulated muscles started trembling. A sick feeling of queasiness spiraled up my belly—the immune system engaging. The digestive system—useless in a fight—was rapidly shutting down. Salivation stopped; my mouth went dry. The contents of my stomach suddenly surged up into my throat.

I vomited.

The half-digested somosas spewed out over the tile floor and splattered the Iranian's shoes.

He stepped back quickly and cursed.

His foot flew up in a sudden rage and slammed the metal door. The impact shook the row of stalls. Again he shouted something. Then he took a step back and prepared to kick again.

I could see the brace that held the lock had loosened in the door. Another battering would break it. He would burst into my cell.

"Vanitar!" I shouted.

The man hesitated.

At that moment the Men's Room door banged open. In walked a pair of clicking high heels.

The assassin spouted angrily, "Lady, is for men—"

The heels marched up to him. An odd, electronic *bzzzzzp* sound suddenly cut him short.

The Iranian collapsed. His knees buckled and he dropped to the floor, smacking face-down in the vomit.

The heels turned toward me, pausing for a moment. Cherry red leather topped with tiny black bows. Tanned, slender ankles. The heels quickly pivoted and strode off toward the exit. The door swung open and shut.

Again the room fell into silence. The assassin lay utterly still.

The fear that had rendered me so wretchedly helpless finally released its grip. Nauseous and numb, I buckled my pants, grabbed my pack and opened the loosened lock.

Sprawled on the floor outside the stall, Vanitar Azad lay prone with his head turned slightly, exposing a portion of his bearded face. Blood flowed into the puddle of puke. His eye was closed, his mouth partly open. I noticed a thin, pink scar above his lip. He didn't appear to be breathing.

I carefully stepped over him, avoiding the vomit and blood. For a moment I stared down at his body, wondering if he truly was dead. There wasn't the slightest flicker of life. In the side pocket of his suit jacket, I spotted his boarding pass. I reached down and slipped it out.

Flight 33, Istanbul. Passenger: Vanitar Azad.

The door to the Men's Room opened. I turned toward it, startled. An elderly little munchkin in a threadbare suit carried in a beat-up suitcase. He looked up and suddenly stopped in his tracks when he saw me standing over the body.

For a moment he simply stood there, grimacing slightly at the smell in the room. His whiskered, weathered face looked Turkish. He squinted at me and said something I didn't understand.

I gave him a knowing grin, and tilting back my head, made a drinking gesture with my thumb and fist. "Whiskey," I said.

It may have been the only English word he understood. He shrugged with the customary frown of the worldly: *What can you do?* The man trudged past me toward the urinals.

I hurried outside. Quickly surveying the various women in the hall, I searched their faces for some sign of recognition, and checked their feet for the black-bowed shoes. But the woman who had saved me was nowhere in sight. Whoever she was, she was gone.

The flight to Istanbul was set to leave in seven minutes. I tore up the assassin's boarding pass and dropped it into the trash, then raced back toward the gate.

25.
Gods and Beasts

It wasn't until the Airbus lifted off the ground that I finally began to breathe again like a normal human being. Relief unleashed a mountain of fatigue. From the moment of the break-in the night before, I'd been running on adrenalin and hounded by fear. More than once I'd come within an inch of being murdered. Finally, in the Men's Room, the tension turned into panic and I froze.

Withered, really. And a woman in heels had saved me?

I tried to make sense of it, but the fog of exhaustion befuddled me. It's the lack of sleep, I decided. I'd gone nearly thirty hours without rest. As I settled down now in my aisle seat—beside a Turkish teenager lost in the tin din of his iPod—I quickly disappeared into an obliterating sleep.

An hour or so later I was awakened by the boy. He had to get by me to make his way to the bathroom. I stood up groggily and allowed him to pass. Across and up one row sat the boy's loud-talking father—the Turkish tycoon I had seen earlier at the gate. The remainder of his family sitting alongside him took up the entire row.

I stood there in the aisle for a moment, eyeing the overhead bin. As drowsy as I was, I couldn't restrain my curiosity any longer. I unlocked the bin, reached into my backpack, and took out the old text and the leather sketchbook Maya had hidden in her suitcase.

The first I examined was the sketchbook. It was about an inch thick, maybe 100 pages. Dan had filled it with pen and ink drawings of various Eastern religious subjects: enlightened bodhisattvas, horrifying demons, multi-armed deities, meditating monks. The figures were set amid landscape features like mountain ranges and winding rivers, with caves, villages, temples and the like. The sketches appeared to be freely drawn copies of original Asian paintings. Though each was unique, a certain similarity of style suggested the work of a single artist. I couldn't say for sure: Dan had left no accompanying captions or notes of explanation.

Many of the pictures were startling. One human demon had a reptilian head, with terrifying jagged teeth and claws. Another, with bulging eyes, wore a hideous chain of human skulls. More docile deities, both males and females, airily reposed on puffy white clouds, while cross-legged yogis, firmly rooted on the ground, exuded a benevolent serenity.

One yogi sat with a woman facing him on his lap, the two of them locked in a sexual embrace.

I noticed several holy men sat on thrones of lotus petals, and toward the middle of the book I came across a drawing of the Buddha himself with a lotus. He sat cross-legged in a large, empty space, holding the flower in his upraised hand. The image looked simpler, more iconic than the rest, and felt somehow central to the book. But as much as I wanted to make something of it, I had to remind myself: The lotus flower is a basic motif of Hindu and Buddhist religious art. In India, I had seen it everywhere—in paintings, sculptures, temple decorations, incense holders and oil lamps. It was easily as common as the cross was to Christians.

The boy with the earphones appeared beside me, waiting to retake his seat. I got up to let him past.

When I sat down again I took up the tall, narrow book with the frayed, green cloth cover. Gold Sanskrit lettering crossed the cover lengthwise. Inside, the writing on the pages was the same, as if the old book had been printed sideways.

On a number of pages, Dan had inscribed lightly in pencil various words and phrases, presumably bits of translation: *Exhilarating. Invigorating. Swifter than thought. The pure. The purifier. Destroyer of enemies. Chief of the gods. Terrible as a lion.* Several fully translated lines were jarringly odd and obscure: *The dripping juice brought by the falcon has increased in the waters*, or *When you penetrate inside, you will know no limits, and you will avert the wrath of the gods.* Other lines suggested a vision of heaven: *Where there are joys and pleasures, gladness and delight, where the desires of desire are fulfilled, there make me immortal.* Still more lines, equally evocative, exhibited a martial character: *Let loose with a shout by ceremony, as a horse is let loose by the finger in a battle of chariots.*

The text seemed primarily concerned with invoking a powerful god named *Soma.* Soma was apparently the god of the moon, and connected somehow with a nectar or drink. He appeared to be an oddly paradoxical deity, representing both happiness and war. Here's one of the longer passages, crammed into the margin in Dan's tiny script:

> *Flow forth, O conqueror of thousands, who conquers and is not conquered, and attacking slays his foes. Pure-dropping, bounteous nectar, welcome the gods at our rite, overcome the demons and make us happy.*

Another passage continued the militaristic tone:

> *Flow thou who hast a host of warriors, who has all the heroes, full of strength, victorious, the giver of riches, sharp-weaponed, rapid bowman, irresistible in battle, overthrowing the enemy arrayed in hostile armies.*

The poetry, however obscure, was curiously stimulating. Descriptions of the heavenly utopia enchanted, while warlike passages quickened the blood. It was clear you would want to have this god *Soma* on your side, but I found no mention of the lotus plant, and the text offered no clue as to the whereabouts of Dan.

I continued pouring over the sketchbook and the text until drowsiness overcame me again and I drifted back into sleep. The poetry and pictures comingled in my dreams, along with the loud voice of the dad across the aisle, until finally I conflated the talkative Turk with the taciturn Buddha from the sketchbook. The Buddha held out the lotus flower, imploring me to take it. "Please. Sir. Please."

I awoke to find the Turk proffering what looked like a half-eaten Danish, wanting to share it with his son. After passing it between them, I went promptly back to sleep. An hour later I woke up again as the plane touched down in Istanbul. My fog of exhaustion had lifted, leaving a single thought perfectly clear.

I needed to call the DSS agent, Harry Grant, at once.

26.
Istanbul

The flight had arrived early but we were forced to wait for a gate. By the time we finally deplaned, I had less than thirty minutes to make my connecting flight to Baku.

I hurried through the terminal, throwing anxious glances back to see if I was being followed. If the Iranians had found my name on the flight list, they had to be aware of the connection, and I thought it very possible they might try to intercept me. Istanbul, after all, was the gateway to the East. They might well have an agent in the city.

I prayed they hadn't yet discovered what went down at the airport in Rome.

As it turned out, the departure gate was not too far away; I reached it as the line was just forming. My cell phone had been smashed by the assassin in Rome. With a few minutes to spare, I stopped at a credit card phone kiosk and made a call to Harry Grant.

This time I got him.

"It's me," I said.

"Jack. Where are you?"

I didn't want to say. "Is Oriana with you?" I asked.

"No. Why?"

"I'd like to know why she followed me to the airport in Rome."

He sounded surprised: "Oriana wasn't following you."

"You mean she just happened to be there when the Iranian tried to kill me?"

"What happened? Are you all right?"

"Yes, thanks to her. But why was she following me?"

"She wasn't following you," he repeated. "She was following *him*."

"Vanitar?"

"Vanitar Azad used to be an Iranian intelligence agent. He's the younger brother of Arshan Azad."

The brother. Somehow it seemed fitting. While I was trying to save my brother, he was trying to avenge his own. I felt relieved the two Iranians were dead. "Another name to cross off your list," I said.

"Vanitar wasn't on the list. We believe he may have been in training as an assassin under Arshan."

In training—with knives. I thought of the pink scar above his mouth. "How did you manage to find him in Rome?"

"We got a tip on his hotel. Oriana spotted him leaving and followed him to the Excelsior."

I realized she must have been there when I made my getaway. And followed him to the airport, too. How could a woman so attractive have made herself so invisible? I wondered again who she worked for. "Who gave you the tip?" I asked.

Grant seemed put off by my asking. "I work for the U.S. government, Jack. We have a lot of resources."

"Like housemaids to mop up a murder?"

"That story was yours."

"And now you know it's true," I said. "That Swiss doctor I asked you about? He seemed to think that you would know who cleaned up after the killings."

"I can tell you DS had nothing to do with it."

"Who was it then? Who sent that flower peddler to my apartment?"

"I'm not sure I would believe everything Dr. Fiore tells you."

"He didn't tell me," I said.

"Did he offer you money?"

I hesitated to answer.

"I'm not surprised," the agent said. "Felix Fiore is a very

rich man. Before he retired, he ran one of the largest pharmaceutical companies in Europe. My guess is he's after your lotus for himself."

"This morning you told me you didn't know anything about the lotus."

"I didn't," he said. "I still don't. All I know is that a lot of people seem to want to get their hands on it."

"Do those people include any friends of yours? Those 'resources' you were talking about?"

"We have sixteen separate intelligence agencies—"

"Just give me an answer," I said. The boarding line was dwindling; I was running out of time. "Does Oriana work for the CIA?"

"No," he said.

"But they did the clean-up, right? They sent the flower peddler. They killed Maya."

"It's possible, Jack. Rumor is they're trying to get a man inside. Our people in Iraq think that's why the assassins tried to kill our ambassador—as a warning."

"Wow. And you saved his life. Still they won't tell you what's going on?"

"I'm too far down the food chain."

"I thought you people were all supposed to be working together now. Connecting dots."

"Believe me, I'm trying. This one's wrapped up tight."

I sensed genuine frustration in his voice. But I still wasn't sure I could trust him. "I've got to go," I said.

"Where is it you're going?"

"I can't tell you that."

"Why?"

"Because I don't want you following me." I started to hang up the phone.

Grant stopped me with a question: "Did the doctor have any idea where your brother Dan might be?"

"No," I said.

I answered too quickly; Grant sensed I was lying. "You should be clear about something, Jack: You have nothing to fear from us."

“Fiore didn’t seem to think so.”

“I’ve been doing a little research on your doctor friend,” he said. “He’s fluent in seven languages and one of them is Persian. He learned it during the years he worked at the corporate office in Tehran, back in the days of the Shah. Seems he took a great deal of interest in their religion. There were rumors he’d ‘gone native’ and converted to Islam.”

“They’re just that—rumors,” I said. “Fiore is a Buddhist; he told me so himself.” But even as I said this, I couldn’t help recalling his talk of Persian gardens. “He lived in Tehran what—40 years ago?”

“Closer to 50. Still, if your brother has someone to worry about, I’d suggest it isn’t me.”

“Then why are you so intent on tracking him down?”

“It’s simple,” he said. “Your brother is the one the assassins are looking for. If I can find him, I can find them.”

“Then what?”

“Then…I’ll kill them. I swear I’ll kill every last one of them.”

27.
Madness

Grant's grim tone as he made that pledge reminded me of the rage of Vanitar Azad. While I doubted it was blood revenge that motivated Harry, his smoldering animosity sounded very much the same. Someone had been murdered, probably someone close. In a way it didn't matter who or why. Whatever drove him now, whatever fanned the flames—fear, guilt, righteousness, anger—the agent had a debt to pay and a bunch of men to kill. I felt like I had wandered into his own private war.

Our jet rose over Istanbul like a modern magic carpet, soaring above the sunlit domes, the maze of souks and skyscrapers, the gash of water glistening between opposing thumbs of land. We were crossing from Europe into Asia, passing officially from the West into the East. Below I spotted the silver bubble of the Hagia Sophia, for a thousand years the largest Christian cathedral in the world, until the Ottoman Turks captured the city and converted it into a mosque. Today, of course, it's a tourist museum. Ogling it now from 10,000 feet, I thought of the jet-setting Turkish tycoon with his fashionably modest daughters and his tech-savvy sons, schizoid descendants of that fuddy-duddy empire, who for over five centuries now had called the bisected city their home.

I had visited Istanbul several years before, after journeying up from India on my trek around the world. That trip had taken me from east to west, stopping first in the South Pacific and ending a year later in that barren room in Rome. Although I had always imagined I would continue the journey home, now I found myself heading in the opposite direction, crossing back over the Bosporus again, following the gentle arc of the earth into the deepening night, as if I had left something behind in the dark, a forgotten dream or memory, a lesson still unlearned. It reminded me of a remark made by an elderly British gentleman I had come across in India, a self-proclaimed seeker-after-the-truth. "The further you go towards the East," he said, "the further you go away from the West." At the time I had thought the tautology was some sort of British joke, an example of their peculiar humor. But watching the hordes of Hindu holy men bathe on the *ghats* of the Ganges, I realized it was a perfect description of the mystic's mode of life: the gradual shedding of the assertive Western ego while pursuing the so-called "inner peace" of the transcendental East.

There was only one problem with going in that direction, as the teeming mass of money-hungry Indians will attest. The danger was plainly demonstrated by the Englishman himself. The former Royal Marine, wading naked in the filthy river with a cockamamie grin on his face, appeared to all the world to have gone completely off his gourd.

Like Harry Grant's obsession and Vanitar's revenge, the old limey's quest for "truth" seemed just another form of madness.

I studied Dan's Buddha sketchbook until I fell asleep. Daydreams strain like hackneyed prose, but night dreams wax poetic. In my dream, Vanitar appeared in the form of Dan's bulb-eyed Tibetan demon. But I was sleeping lightly, and because some wary portion of my brain remained awake, the vision of this deadly assassin, who only a few hours before had come close to strangling me to death, now completely failed to frighten. With the hideous chain of grinning skulls slung around his neck, he struck me as more of a curiosity, a Saturday morning cartoon cliché of a Middle Eastern villain. Then, in the unexplainably fluid way that dreams often unfold,

I realized the demon had morphed into the yogi—the one locked in sexual union with the consort. I couldn't see the woman's face, only her sinuous back, but the awestruck face of the yogi, I realized, looked shockingly like my own.

I woke up. Night had fallen, the cabin was dark, and an Indian movie was playing on the monitors overhead—veiled women, flashing eyes, swirls of shimmering silk. The man beside me had fallen asleep, earphones buzzing like trapped flies. For a while I stared at the movie trying to figure out what it was—comedy? art-house? romance? adventure?—until a woman suddenly appeared in the aisle as if she'd stepped right out of the screen. She was wearing a headscarf and big sunglasses like an old-fashioned Hollywood star, apparently oblivious to the fact that it was dark. I recognized her immediately as one of the Turkish tycoon's daughters. Hadn't they gotten off in Istanbul? As she strutted her way up the aisle, many a male head slowly craned up for a view. She had bundled herself in a cashmere wrap, and her elegant black Capri slacks revealed slender calves. Wasn't exposed flesh verboten? Just before she reached my row, she seemed to lose her footing. Clutching at a seatback, she fumbled her large, gold-spangled handbag, which dropped to the floor with a plop.

Three men, including me, frantically reached to retrieve it. That's when I noticed the heels she was wearing.

Cherry red leather. Tiny black bows.

I handed her the bag. She took it from me and continued on without so much as a nod, as if she had done *me* the favor. I turned and watched as she sauntered away, then quickly got up and followed her.

A climactic sword fight on a moonlit dune flashed like a strobe on the monitors, and as I made my way down the flickering aisle, rapt passengers tilted to maintain their line of sight. I reached the woman just as she stepped into the bathroom. When she turned to close the door, I abruptly straight-armed it open.

"*It was you,*" I whispered.

She stared from behind her impenetrable shades, frowning

at me in confusion.

"In the Men's Room? The airport in Rome?"

A look of disgust distorted her mouth. She shouted some foreign curse at me and thrust me back with the butt of her hand.

The door slammed shut and locked.

I glanced around, embarrassed. Several passengers stared at me. A young stewardess unpacking a drink cart poked her head out from behind it. "Everything all right, sir?"

"Fine," I said, straightening my collar. I backed away from the door.

Could this possibly be another woman wearing identical high-heeled shoes?

28.
Hazel

It didn't take me long to arrive at an answer. I waited for her to unlock the door, and the moment she did, I shoved it open and forced my way into the tiny room, quickly locking the door behind me before she could get out a word.

But the lady did not protest. Backed against the sink, she eyed me impassively from behind the inky shades.

"What are you doing here?" I whispered.

"Brushing my teeth."

With her face only inches from mine, I could actually detect the minty scent on her breath. "Why are you following me?" I asked.

Oriana lifted the glasses and propped them on her head. Cool as an Italian cucumber. "Shouldn't I be asking *you*?"

Hazel. Her eyes. Light brown with a tinge of green. I don't know why it mattered, but for some reason, at that moment, I could think of nothing else.

Then I did. "You killed that man at the airport."

She exhaled a weary little chuckle.

"I don't think it's funny," I said.

"No," she said. "But I thought you would be grateful." Pouting, she loosened her cashmere wrap, exposing the plunging neck of her blouse and the chain of jade at her throat.

"I am grateful," I said.

"Strange way to show it."

I nodded toward the headscarf and glasses. "What's with the getup? Why were you hiding with that Turkish family?"

"Hiding? I just happen to sit beside them." She spoke calmly, very matter-of-fact, like a wife who was lying to her husband, and who knew that he knew she was lying.

"Before, outside, why did you shout, push me away?"

She glanced around the little room. "Isn't it obvious?"

The calmness of her voice irritated me. We were standing so close I could feel her chest heaving, sense her every breath on my cheek. Wisps of her hair had escaped from her scarf. Her cashmere gave off the scent of lilac.

"Look, Oriana: You killed a man. You probably saved my life. But if you don't tell me who you are, who it is you're working for, I swear I'll turn you in to the police."

Someone rattled the door. We stared at it in silence, then looked back at each other.

"I could turn *you* in," Oriana said, "for forcing your way in here."

"You let me in. Why?"

She shrugged, demurely, again looking away.

"What do you want from me?" I asked.

She turned her eyes to mine and this time didn't look away. "Do I have to spell it out for you?"

My mouth fell open. *Holy Christ.*

Now there was a *tap-tap-tap* at the door. The movie had apparently ended, and a line was forming outside.

"Just a minute!" I shouted.

Oriana continued watching me, waiting for the uptight, dimwit Yank to finally make his move.

It wasn't much of a move to make. A slow lean forward, a slight tilting of the head. Oriana rose up off the sink and slid her arms over my shoulders. Her chest lifted and pressed against me. I peered into those green-tinged hazelnut eyes, imagining the fresh-mint flavor of her mouth. But just as her lips barely brushed against mine, she paused there, hypnotically, holding off the kiss.

"Forgive me, *amore.*"

I felt something cold at the base of my neck. In the mirror behind her, I saw that she held an electric toothbrush in her hand.

"No—"

The electric *bzzzzzp* sound vibrated in my ears, and suddenly my entire body reverberated with it, humming like a smacked crazy bone. I stiffened, utterly benumbed with pain. The shock seemed to freeze me corpse-like in time, and as I glimpsed my aghast reflection in the mirror, I realized I looked like the yogi in my dream, now embraced by the wily Oriana.

The vibration stopped. My muscles gave out. I collapsed into Oriana's arms. She carefully lowered my body to the floor. I was conscious, but utterly disabled.

"As you've noticed," she said, "the shock didn't kill you. Unfortunately, the same is true of Vanitar Azad." She stuffed the toothbrush Taser into her purse. "He must have contacted his superiors—which is why they had another agent waiting for you in Istanbul."

Another agent?

"He's sitting in coach, three rows behind you. Though by now I suspect he's joined the line outside this door."

Knuckles rapped the door again. This time the young stewardess: *"Are you all right in there?"*

Oriana turned to the sink and ran the tap. "He won't be the only one," she said. "There'll be more at the airport in Baku."

"Open, please." Another stewardess, older, more authoritative. She knocked firmly on the door. *"You must return to your seat. We are preparing for descent."*

I wanted to see what Oriana was doing at the sink, but could barely lift my eyelids.

"With the stress of the shock," she said, "your blood sugar's turned into lactic acid. Your muscles have nothing to power them. Not to worry: I hit you with a shorter cycle. In about ten minutes you'll begin to recover." She crouched down and checked my pulse, pressing two fingers to my throat. "But if you want to get out of this alive, you'd better not recover too quickly." Lifting my lids, she examined my eyes. "I need you to play along—understand?"

No, I did not understand. Oriana had removed her headscarf, disheveled her hair, and splashed her eyes with water. Smeared makeup ran like tears down her cheeks. She looked crazier than Vincenzo's mother.

I peered groggily back at her, unable to respond. She rose up and opened the door.

Two stewardesses stood before a line of scowling passengers.

"Help—please!" Oriana cried. "My husband is having heart attack!"

29.
The Help of Allah

Why? I wondered.

If nothing happens to us except what the Giver of Life has decreed, then why had I again been thwarted, again humiliated?

Was I being tested? Had I misunderstood? Or had I not entirely submitted to His will?

Allah created human beings in strife and struggle. We all suffer for our ignorance, and are given to see things only in part. The Almighty does not speak to us except by inspiration, or from behind a veil. But for those who believe with certainty, the signs are always clear.

This thwarting then must be a sign. This defeat must have some meaning.

I rinsed the stink from my face and peered at my reflection.

"Look," Arshan had urged me. "Look more carefully. See.*"*

The face might be Faraj's, I thought. We'd always looked like brothers. And now I saw in my eyes the same shame I'd seen in his, bleeding on that prison floor in the stench of his own vomit.

This was no coincidence. The parallel was clear. We had both lost face.

Allah was granting me a peek into His grand design. But what exactly did it mean? What was His grand design?

Look more carefully. See.

See the path of Allah, and where Faraj had gone astray.

What was it that had lured my friend so far away from

God? The opium? His uncle? The drivel of the Sufis? Perhaps too much exposure to the toxins of the West. The movies that he dragged me to. The music that he loved. The dream of fake democracy unfettered by Islam.

Even his detention in the Kahrizak prison had failed to tear the veil from his eyes. All the beatings, all the torture, all the pain we had inflicted. Was it only willful pride that kept him from submitting? Where did he find his strength? How was it he endured? Despite his talk of Persia and the glories of the past, without the peace of Islam, how could he have survived?

The answer was...he couldn't.

Like all who stray from Allah's path, Faraj lived in illusion. So God had deemed to test him as He now was testing me—"to show the truthful in their sincerity and expose the liars in their falsehood."

Truthfulness. Falsehood. Look more carefully. See.

See how I had strayed from the guidance of my master. I had been far too impatient for revenge.

It wasn't until I spoke with the Grand Ayatollah that my path forward suddenly came clear. Instead of reprimanding me, he thanked Allah the Exalted One for allowing Duran to escape. The American was flying to Azerbaijan and the city of Baku, he said. A private jet was being fueled to take me there from Rome. "I put my trust in you," he said. "You must find the American and follow where he goes. Insha'Allah, he will lead us to his brother—and the source of the lotus seeds!"

I stood at the phone in the airport terminal, stunned in mute astonishment, a vision of God's intention suddenly forming in my head.

The city of Baku was the Caspian port of Faraj's old smuggling route! I remembered the connection he had there, an oily old Azeri named Pashazadeh. That double-dealing crook might very easily be bought.

This was it, no question—the grand design of Allah! Faraj would be the secret snare through which I'd catch Duran!

The Old Man mistakenly took my silence as regret for my defeat. "God is divine and Islam is our guide," he said. He quoted the blessed Quran: "Or do ye think that ye shall enter the Garden of Bliss without such trials as came to those who passed away before you? They encountered suffering and adversity, and were so shaken in spirit that even the Noble Messenger and those of faith who were with him cried: 'When will come the help of Allah?—'"

I finished the verse for him, my heart bursting with joy: "Ah! Verily, the help of Allah is always near!"

The Caspian

30.
Opera Buffa

I played along.

Not that I had any choice at first. I could neither move nor speak. It took three stewardesses to drag me from the bathroom and prop me up in my seat, all the while trying to get Oriana to calm down and answer their questions about my medical history and drugs I might have taken and what exactly it was we had been doing in there so long. I marveled at Oriana's performance: the hysterical Italian wife, fretting away in fractured English, tearing at her chest in grief-stricken anguish, mopping up her tap-water tears. She told them we had had some terrible row and she'd refused to sit beside me on the plane. But I was still angry and wouldn't leave her alone and had tried to confront her in the bathroom. She had told me again how much she wanted to have children, but I insisted I wasn't ready, and she couldn't believe I loved her, and—she went on and on like this, revealing tawdry details of our operatic marriage, until eventually the stewardesses were no longer listening to her. They were too busy forcing blood-thinning aspirin down my throat and trying to secure the cabin for landing and calling ahead for an ambulance to meet us on the ground.

Oriana's wacky plan was based on a kind of paradoxical logic. Having already been tailed from the airport in Istanbul, she knew I had no chance of slipping into Baku unnoticed. So rather than continuing to protect me incognito, she decided to draw as much attention to us as she could.

It worked.

I was carried off the plane the moment the engines were shut down and before any other passengers were allowed to leave their seats. Even though by that point I had recovered much of my strength, I felt painfully achy and nauseous, reinforcing my inclination to continue the pretense. Paramedics dropped me in a wheelchair and rolled me across the tarmac to a waiting ambulance. My hysterical spouse accompanied me. Shouldering my backpack, she scrambled into the hold with me along with one of the medics. "Please hurry!" she cried, glancing back at the parked plane's disembarking passengers.

An aging paramedic strapped me with an oxygen mask and asked me to try to breathe normally. He began taking my vital signs as the ambulance pulled away.

Our passports were inspected at the airfield gate by a dour-faced security official wielding a nightstick flashlight. He asked the paramedic questions in a language I assumed must be Azeri. Oriana grew anxious with the time it was taking and her pleadings brought the flashlight beam to her face. She was tying down her headscarf and tucking in her hair.

The officer eyed her a moment, then made some request in Azeri. The paramedic ominously turned to Oriana: "He say he need to speak to you. Inside."

Oriana protested: There wasn't time! "Can't you see my husband is dying?"

The officer held the light on her, repeating his demand, then disappeared into the gatehouse with our passports.

Oriana reached for her oversize purse, apparently her only piece of luggage. I wondered if she thought she'd have to pay the man a bribe—or if she was expecting something worse. When I tried to ask her through the oxygen mask, the diva shushed me, caressing my cheek. "Please don't worry your little head, *caro mio*."

I watched her climb out and head inside.

The paramedic donned his stethoscope and once again checked my heart. An old man in a young man's job, I thought. With his sagging jowls and watery eyes, he looked like a human bloodhound. "Is normal," he said reassuringly. He removed my oxygen mask. "You breathing easy?"

I took a deep breath and nodded.

"I no think you have heart attack." He noticed the bruise at the base of my neck, the mark from Maya's Taser. "What happen here? Two red marks. Very tender."

"My wife's a vampire," I said. I nodded toward the gatehouse. "What does he want from her?"

The old man shrugged, averting his gaze.

I craned my neck for a view outside. Suddenly the barrier lifted.

Oriana exited, passports in hand, scurrying back to the ambulance. "Please hurry," she ordered the driver.

He leaned forward, searching the gatehouse. The dour-faced guard was nowhere to be seen.

"Go!" she shouted.

The driver threw her a grudging glance and shifted into gear.

Oriana watched out the rear window as the ambulance drove away. She turned to find me studying her.

"Brighten his smile?" I asked.

"He seemed *shocked* to find out I was telling the truth."

Whether or not they believed I had suffered a heart attack, the paramedics took full advantage of their emergency right-of-way and sped with siren blaring toward the hospital. Headlight beams flared across Oriana's face as she made several phone calls on her cell. She spoke hurriedly in a guttural language I didn't recognize.

The hospital lay within sight of the harbor—my first glimpse ever of the Caspian. The night sea looked black as oil. I was unloaded and quickly rolled in through the Emergency entrance. Oriana carried my backpack, continuing her wifely charade. I could see her searching for an opportunity to spirit me away, but with the paramedics and all the staff around she couldn't afford the risk. The admissions nurse insisted she fill out paperwork, and a male orderly with a pirate earring briskly wheeled me away.

I continued my malingering, wondering what they'd do with us when they finally discovered the truth. The orderly deposited me in a large waiting room overflowing with a cast of unfortunates. A few women patients appeared to be sick, but most were men who had been injured. One large man in overalls cradled an arm that must have been broken. Another burly worker with a bandaged hand appeared to have lost a finger. Still another had injured his foot. Baku was a bustling oil port city, and this hospital was probably the nearest to the docks. My guess was these men were oil derrick workers or cargo stevedores; they looked rough and strong and seemed familiar with pain. Their grubby, solemn dignity put my silent deception to shame.

A wall of windows reinforced with wire mesh separated the waiting room from the busy admissions area. I looked for Oriana among the crowd and spotted her again on her cell phone, holding her hand over an ear to block the surrounding chatter. Who was she talking to? I wondered. Harry Grant? The Italians? Her boss at the CIA?

She froze suddenly, staring toward the entrance. Two men in dark suits had walked in through the door. One was heavy-set, the other small and wiry. Both sported clipped beards similar to the Iranians. Their eyes searched widely as they moved into the room. They walked directly to the head of the line and began to question the nurse.

I looked back for Oriana, but she had already fled. Turning, I found her standing over me, peering down through her shades. "Can you walk?" she asked.

"I don't know."

I struggled out of the wheelchair like Lazarus out of his grave. My tingly legs wobbled.

"Hurry," Oriana said. She took my hand and pulled, hauling me stumbling after her. The injured dockworkers stared.

As we entered the hallway to the examination rooms, I threw a glance back through the window toward the admissions line. The heavy-set Iranian was talking on his cell.

The wiry one had vanished. We hurried up the hall, turned the corner, and spotted him walking toward us.

His eyes locked on ours.

31.
Beatrice

Oriana hauled me sideways through a set of double-doors. A nurse shouted, waving her arms. Oriana blasted past her through a second set of doors. Emerging on the other side, we crashed into a gurney. The patient's IV toppled, clattering to the floor. Three attendants in surgical garb glared at us over their masks. We ran on past the OR's and through another set of doors. A surgeon scrubbing at a line of sinks shouted for us to stop.

Oriana momentarily froze.

I yanked her through a doorway into the doctors' changing room. A naked man stood gaping. We barreled down a passageway of steamy shower stalls, through a room of benches and lockers, and finally out the surgeon's entrance into the main corridor.

Hospital visitors streamed left and right. We plunged in among them, scurrying down the hall. A glance back at the door revealed no sign of the agent who had spotted us. Could we have actually lost him?

None of the signs in the hallway were in English, so we followed the general flow of the crowd. Eventually we found our way to the entrance lobby and hurried out the automatic doors.

"There!" Oriana said.

Beyond a row of idling cars a single taxi waited. The bald, bearded driver watched us hustle into the back. Both of us turned in tandem to check the hospital entrance—still no sign of the Iranians.

Oriana gave the driver an address, shouting over the Azeri pop tune blaring on his radio. In English, she asked him to drive as quickly as he could. “Understand?”

The man turned down his radio and looked in the mirror at me. “You lucky man,” he said. “My wife always say I driving too fast!” He shifted the taxi into gear and peeled out onto the street.

“Where are we going?” I asked.

Oriana was still peering out the back. “Away from *him*,” she said.

I turned. The wiry Iranian had finally emerged. He walked to the curb and stood there, watching his quarry speed away.

“Doesn’t seem in any hurry to catch us,” I said.

“No,” she said. “Maybe they don’t want to catch us.”

“What do you mean?”

She turned and stared ahead through the windshield, finally removing her shades. “They want to find your brother. Perhaps they think you’ll lead them to him.”

“Me?” I turned again and looked out the back. The street behind us was empty. “Then why isn’t anyone following us?”

“Good question,” she said. “And why were there only two of them here?”

“You were expecting more?”

“We’re less than an hour’s flight from Iran. Harry’s list had twelve names. One was killed in Syria. Harry killed one in Iraq. Your friend killed Arshan Azad in Rome. Since then, little brother’s joined in the fun. Do the math.”

“Twelve minus three, plus one, equals ten.”

“And that only counts the assassins,” she said. “I doubt that includes the man who got on our plane in Budapest. And the Grand Ayatollah is sure to have contacts all over the Caspian basin. Now that he knows you’re in Baku, they’ll all be looking for you.”

She worriedly fingered her jade necklace and turned to gaze at the streets. We had entered a more desolate part of the city. Shops were closed and gated for the night, and the streets and sidewalks were empty.

They'll all be looking for you.

The hairy worm inside my gut again uncoiled itself. My chest tightened, my heart raced, a sweating chill crept over me. I rolled down the window and let the hot breeze dry my neck. Only one thing seemed to calm the worm: this woman who was guiding me like Dante's Beatrice. I wondered why she was doing it.

"Is that why you followed me here?" I asked. "You hoped I would lead you to Dan?"

She looked at me directly. "These men may be going after your brother. But we're going after them."

Just like Harry, I thought. And I was glad to hear it. Especially now I knew Vanitar Azad was still alive. "It's Vanitar worries me most," I said.

"You have good reason to worry."

"What do you know about him?"

"Vanitar was a spy in the intelligence ministry under a sadistic thug named Ali Mahbood. During the Green Revolution, Mahbood led interrogations at the Kahrizak Detention Center. Vanitar worked under him. It was worse than Evin Prison. Lot of people went in there never came out."

"Great. A spook who likes to torture people thinks I murdered his brother."

"It's odd," she said. "Vanitar was quite well educated. He reportedly studied for years in Qum, preparing to become an imam. Yet sometime during the Green Revolution, he turned into a fanatic."

"What do you think happened?"

"I don't really know. Radicalization often occurs with an identity crisis of some sort. I suspect something pushed him over the edge in that prison."

"Maybe Mahbood pushed him over," I said.

"If he did, he's likely still pushing. Mahbood's name is second on the list of assassins. Right under Vanitar's brother."

I gave her a look. "Thanks for that. Just when I thought things couldn't get worse."

"Things can always get worse," she said.

I squinted into the breeze through my window. "Speaking

of that, where is it we're going?" The taxi was passing every car on the street.

"We need visas for Turkmenistan. I have a friend who can get us them quickly."

I turned to her, startled. "What makes you think I want to go to Turkmenistan?"

"Why else would you have flown to Baku?" she said. Lowering her cashmere wrap, she retrieved a note from inside her blouse and handed it over to me.

Unfolding it, I saw it was the stationery with the lion symbol—Maya's handwritten directions to the archeological site. At some point during the flight, while I was incapacitated, Oriana had apparently rifled through my pack.

I glanced at her ample chest. "You hiding my brother's books in there, too?"

She grinned. "I'm afraid it's too—" The taxi screeched around a corner. As Oriana reached to steady herself, her hand touched down on my thigh. I glanced at her. She looked at the driver. "You needn't go *that* fast," she said.

I smiled to myself. That was the moment I made the decision I wouldn't try to keep her from joining me. I probably couldn't have, anyway. And really, it only made sense. Whoever she was, she had saved my life, and was likely to save it again.

I looked at Maya's hand-drawn map. It started out from Ashkhabad, a city in southern Turkmenistan. "So how do we get there?" I asked. "I was told to fly over the Caspian."

"Too risky to return to the airport," she said.

"What do you recommend? Rent a car?"

"It would take a week to cross the deserts to the north—that is, if you get past the Russian border."

"What about the southern shore?"

"You want to pay a visit to the mullahs on the way?"

Of course. Iran. I'd forgotten my geography. "Probably not a good idea," I said. "What about a boat? Isn't there a ferry?"

"There's an overnight ferry to Türkmenbashy, but the Iranians will be watching the harbor."

The breeze blew Maya's map off my lap, sending it to

Oriana's feet. She reached to the floor and retrieved it. For a long moment she stared at the page, as if she saw something written there she had not previously noticed.

"What is it?" I asked.

She looked at me without speaking. Then she glanced up the street and called for the driver to pull over.

"Oriana, what's wrong?"

She spoke a little louder so the driver could hear. "The address. I'm afraid I gave the wrong address."

The driver talked to the rearview mirror. "Wrong address?"

I didn't understand what her friend's address had to do with Maya's desert directions. "I thought your friend was at the embassy."

"No," she said, now searching in her purse. "He doesn't work for the embassy."

The cabbie pulled to a stop at the curb. The moment he did, Oriana extracted her toothbrush Taser and slammed it into his neck.

Bzzzzzp!

The driver's bald head slumped to his chest.

"What the hell?" I glared at her in disbelief.

She coolly climbed out of the cab and opened the driver's door. The man sat slumped and didn't move. She quickly checked his eyes, then searched his seat and the floor beneath him.

The radio kept playing.

"What are you doing?" I frantically scanned the street—for the moment it was empty.

When she rose up, Oriana had a semi-automatic in her hand. She had apparently found it on the floor. Like Maya's gun, the barrel had been extended with a tubular sound suppressor. Oriana checked the magazine, then slammed it back in place. She leaned in over the driver and pulled the keys from the ignition. The radio went off. Then she took the keys and the gun and headed toward the back of the car.

"Oriana?"

Headlights flared off the outside mirror. A vacant, illuminated city bus noisily rattled by. When it had passed,

Oriana used the driver's key to open up the trunk. As I turned to climb out of the cab, my hand touched down on Maya's stationery. It felt wet. I picked it up and saw to my shock that a corner was soaked with blood.

"What the fu—?" I looked down at the floor. Blood was seeping out across it from somewhere behind the seat.

I turned to look out the back. Oriana stood staring into the trunk. She slammed it shut and walked back to the driver. Without a word she raised the pistol and shot the man through the head.

32.
Fake

The clatter of her cherry heels echoed off the walls. Oriana was scurrying up an alley a few blocks down from the abandoned cab, cutting across to a parallel street, with me trotting close behind her, still struggling to shake the shock. Just like Arshan Azad, another man had been shot in the head a few feet in front of my face. The bullet had blown out his forehead, knocking him onto the steering wheel and spraying his brain on the glass. In the frenzied moments that followed, Oriana shouted orders at me, and unable to think at all for myself I simply did what she said. My consciousness seemed to split off in time, with the splattering red eruption repeating in my mind, while Oriana helped me on with my backpack and urgently prodded me away from the cab.

After finding the real taxi driver stuffed inside the trunk, his throat cut ear to ear, she had felt no compunction about killing the assassin. I thought it quite possible she'd have killed him anyway, given that he may have overheard our conversation. Then again she might have killed him for the fact of who he was, or because she simply didn't like his driving. Oriana, I now realized, was capable of anything. For all I knew she might turn the gun on me.

Surveying the street from the end of the alley, she whispered that we hadn't much time; they would soon be looking for us. I assumed she meant the Iranians, but when she slipped the murder weapon into a restaurant dumpster, I realized she must have been referring to the police. She said the address of her friend, a man she referred to as "Steinberg," was not too far ahead, and if we hurried she was certain we could make it there on foot.

Every passing car sent a fresh shiver through me. The Iranians? The cops? We averted our faces from their headlights, and avoided the gaze of the few nighthawks still prowling the empty streets. Given the several time zones I'd been catapulted through, I didn't know exactly how much later it was than the ten o'clock hour on my watch. I guessed it was probably two in the morning when we finally reached our destination, what appeared to be a gallery or bookshop. My heartbeat was still raging as we walked up to the door.

Like every other storefront on the ill-lighted street, the window was dark, the door was bolted, and a security gate had been marched across the front. But Steinberg's old place had a certain flair about it, an air of refinement that seemed out of place in a neighborhood of sausage shops and pawnbrokers. The Cyrillic lettering on the unwashed window was indecipherable to me, and though the ancient, leather-bound books on display exhibited a variety of languages, I could not spot a single title in English. Above the books hung hand-colored antique maps; sepia photographs of rural peasants and 19th-Century townspeople; striking Japanese woodblock prints of sword-wielding samurai and red-lipped geishas; and several finely-rendered etchings of various characters out of the Bible, including an old engraved depiction of Christ, a distant forerunner of the picture that hung on the wall in Vincenzo's room.

Each item in the window was exquisite, but it was age more than artistry that linked them all together. Locked behind the steel grate and the foggy pane of glass, the whole array seemed to capture an atmosphere of timelessness, like a giant Joseph Cornell box or a ship inside a bottle. The simple act of looking at it seemed to calm me down.

Oriana rapped on the door with her knuckles. Headlights flared, and we pressed into the shadow of the doorway until the dark sedan had passed. She knocked again. Still nothing. Stretching up on her toes, she reached to the top of the doorframe. "He used to leave a key—"

A light came on in the window. "He's coming," I said. A moment later, the bolt unlocked. As the door pushed open, a cat darted out. The man reached down to grab it and missed. He was wearing pajamas and a bathrobe.

"Ach," the man groaned, rising from his slippers. He was heavy and balding with a whiskery beard, and his face was flushed and grimacing, as if he were out of breath. "Man and cat—like cat and mouse." He gestured inside. "Please." As we passed he stood against the door, appraising us from behind a pair of magnifying wire-rims, all the while noisily respiring through his nose.

He closed the door and bolted it, and turned to us once more. A single dangling bulb lit his face. I noticed that his magnified eyes were slightly disproportioned, the left one wide with an open stare, the right more squinty and discerning. Both eyes softened as they fell on Oriana. She was pulling off her headscarf and shaking out her hair.

"Bubbilleh," he said wistfully. "I hardly recognize you without your M-16."

"They carry the Tavor now," she said. "Made in Israel." She extended her hand. "Shalom."

He took her hand in both of his and hugged it to his heart. "Too long, Bubbi. Too long."

Oriana introduced me in English as "the American, Jack Duran," then spoke to Steinberg in the same guttural language I had heard her use on the phone. I realized now it was Hebrew. She was telling him what happened in the cab.

When she finished, he asked several questions. She responded to the last with what sounded like an apology.

Steinberg waved it off. "It was the only thing to do," he said, speaking now in English. "But it makes our situation more difficult." Reaching up with both hands, rasping with the effort, he gingerly unscrewed the dangling bulb until the glowing filament went out. "Please, follow me," he said.

He padded off into the darkness beneath towering shelves of books. Oriana indicated I should follow him.

I stood where I was. "You never told me your surname."

"You never asked."

"I'm asking now. What is your name?"

"My name is Oriana Shahar. Would you like to check my driver's license?"

"You're an Israeli," I said.

"You make that sound like an accusation." She headed off after Steinberg.

I followed. "Why did you pretend to be Italian?"

"I was in Rome. You know what they say."

"Sure—when in Rome, pretend you're not Israeli."

"It wasn't that much of a stretch," she said.

"Oriana's mother was Italian." We turned to see Steinberg resting halfway down an aisle, a dim pear-shape in the darkness. "She was a great beauty, too," he said. "And an even better shot than Oriana. This way, please."

The asthmatic shuffled off, wheezing his way through the black labyrinth. We followed more by sound than by sight.

I asked Oriana if she was still with the Israeli army.

"Not anymore," she said.

"Then who are you with? Mossad?"

"At the moment, I'm with you."

"Yeah, that's what I'm afraid of. You're Israeli. They're Iranian. I've stepped into the middle of a dogfight."

"You're an American, Jack. You were already in the middle of it whether you recognized it or not."

"One moment, please." Steinberg reached into the shelf on his right and triggered some latch or lever. The shelf swiveled open, revealing a hidden doorway. He waved us through and pulled the shelf shut behind us. Fluorescent tube lights flickered on, revealing a white-walled workroom. "We should be safe in here for the time being, but if anyone decides to pay us a visit," he nodded toward a heavily bolted door at the back, "that exit leads into the alley."

I made a mental note of all the locks to be undone, hoping we wouldn't be in too much of a hurry.

The room was humid and windowless. Steinberg tugged the chain of an ancient ceiling fan, and its sluggish blades groaned into a whir. Around us lay a clutter of old furniture and equipment: a mahogany writing desk stacked with prints and paperwork, a pair of battered library tables splotched with paint and ink, a collection of vintage typewriters, manual and electric, an adjustable overhead photography apparatus, and a slew of printmaking and copying equipment, from an antique pantographic etching machine to a large-format, inkjet digital printer, a type I had seen used to make Giclée.

On the table before me was a landscape etching. The style of the drawing looked strikingly familiar. As I picked it up for closer inspection, I spotted the signature: *Rembrandt*.

"Mr. Steinberg—this print, the others in your window, are they pulled from the original plates?"

He removed his glasses to rub them on his robe, blinking at me like a turtle. "Oriana didn't mention you were an artist."

"I'm not," I said. "But I used to give tours in the Vatican Pinacoteca."

"Wonderful," he said. "Then you tell me: What do you think?"

"I'm no expert," I said.

"Good. I don't trust experts. I want your opinion. Have I wasted my money?"

I brought the paper close. The plate had left an image no larger than my hand. It featured a wooden shack nestled beside a clump of trees. With Rembrandt's usual rich variety of strokes, the sunlit hut had been crisply rendered, but the darkly shadowed trees appeared velvety and diffuse.

"It's actually not an etching; it's drypoint," I said. "You can tell with the trees, especially these tall ones on the left. With drypoint you scratch lines directly into the plate, and it throws up residual metal in a burr on either side. That's why the lines bleed out when they're inked, and give you this velvety sort of watercolor effect. But the burr wears off slightly with each impression, so the effect is lost in later prints. So this must be a first state, which means…"

I stopped myself and lowered the picture.

Steinberg snatched it, donning his glasses. "Means what?"

"Look, I don't know. I told you, I'm no expert."

He set the picture down and leaned over to examine it.

"What you mean to say is that if it were a life print, made by the artist himself, it would be hanging on the wall of a museum somewhere, not gathering dust in a bookshop in Baku."

"If that is a first-state print," I said, "then yeah, very likely, it's a fake."

Steinberg—to my horror—suddenly ripped the print in half. "You're right," he said. "In fact, it's actually a proof. But with another dozen impressions, I'll pull a print that looks as if it could still be on the market." He glanced between the two of us, gesturing impatiently. "Passports. Please."

Oriana immediately handed hers over. Steinberg looked to me, waiting.

"Oh. Yeah. Of course." Having thought of his shop as a refuge from the streets, I'd forgotten why we'd come here in the first place. Oriana had said her friend could get us travel visas quick. Steinberg, I now realized, was a forger.

"They're here, in Baku," I said.

The Old Man was silent. "How many?"

"Three, four. I'm not certain."

"But you're certain they're our men?"

"I'm told there was an incident at the hospital. Two bodies were later found in a taxi, one shot through the head. Police say the driver had his throat cut."

Again the line was silent as the Old Man ruminated. "The men are taking orders from Mahbood," he concluded. "I've not been able to reach him since your brother was killed in Rome."

"Mahbood? But why?" He'd grown up as a knife-puller on the streets with my brother, his viciousness barely tamed by his obeisance to Islam. When I'd worked under him at Kahrizak, he'd tested me repeatedly, questioning my loyalty, skeptical of what he derided as my "lofty, talky" faith. His growing impatience for the coming of the Mahdi fed a maniacal zeal.

"He was second to Arshan," the Ayatollah explained. "Now he takes his place. Ask yourself the question why your brother was betrayed."

It was obvious. Orders from the Old Man went through his two appointed deputies. With Arshan out of the way, the men would now receive their orders only from Mahbood.

"There must be some way to go around him," I said. "They need to be told the truth."

"Their cell numbers, emails, everything's been changed. This devil misleads them, yet they believe they're guided right, even as he plunges them deeper into error."

"But how? Who could be funding him? The CIA? The Hindis?"

"I suspect there may well be another entity at work. We'll find out soon enough. Devils take many forms, but their intention remains the same. To lead us astray into the land of confusion. To drive us to the torment of the Fire."

"I'll give no ear to them," I promised.

"Seek refuge from their whisperings, hold fast to the Path of Allah."

"'He has adorned the near heaven with the stars,'" I quoted, "'to guard against every rebellious devil.'"

I sensed a smile in the Old Man's voice: "We shall bring them round Hell on their knees!"

33.
Tomb of Tomes

The whole process took Steinberg less than one hour to complete. He already had a rubber stamp with the state seal of Turkmenistan. It was pulled from a wooden box chock full of other stamps, seemingly from every country in the world. The real challenge for him was to create the visa stickers. In the bottom drawer of his desk, he pawed through a pile of passports. Eventually he found one with the most current Turkmenistan visa. He photocopied it several times, making various adjustments in the settings of his machine. Finally satisfied with a copy, he set to work removing the handwritten dates and signatures from the intricate, money-like background design intended to thwart counterfeiters. He used an ink-dissolving solution and a pointed razor blade. With a jeweler's magnifier pressed into his eye, the process was delicate and painstaking, and the intense concentration seemed to quiet down his breathing.

When I asked him where he had learned his trade, he told me from his father. A renowned Romanian illustrator, he had used his skills during the Second World War to help smuggle fellow Jews out of the country.

"I was one of them," Steinberg said. A baby during the war, he was taken by his mother to stay with her family in Azerbaijan. His father survived in Bucharest and joined them after the war. "He often reminded me," Steinberg said, "it was the art of deception that saved us."

Finally satisfied with the sticker, Steinberg made a copy for each of our passports, then forged the necessary signatures and dates. He glued one of the stickers into Orianna's passport, then began searching for an unstamped page in mine. "You've seen a lot of the world," he remarked.

I shrugged. "There's a couple of places I'd rather have missed."

"Sorry to tell you, but you're heading into another. And unfortunately, all these visas will only make you more suspect. The Turkmenistan authorities are notoriously mistrustful. Legacy of the Soviets."

He glued the sticker in place, then sealed it with the blue-inked rubber stamp and handed the passport back to me.

"Beautiful," I said. A blue band in the circular stamp contained the Islamic stars and crescent, while a blue circle at the center enclosed the tiny silhouette of a horse.

I told Steinberg I liked the horse.

"It ought to be a camel," he said. "That country is nothing but desert."

I pulled out Maya's map to the archeological site and asked him if he was familiar with the territory.

He stretched the sheet out on the table. "This main highway runs along the edge of the desert under the Kopet Dag range. The mountains form the border with Iran. Here it turns west toward the Murgab River. I'm not familiar with this road—it heads north into the desert. Be careful not to lose your way. Most of these side roads are little more than ruts, and dust storms can blow up in an instant."

I looked deadpan at Oriana. She ignored me and nodded toward my backpack. "Show him your brother's book," she said.

Steinberg was apparently very knowledgeable in languages. With a quick glance at the cover he identified the text. "It's a part of the *Rig Veda*," he said. "One of the oldest collections of religious verse in the world." He scanned several pages, running his finger across the lines. "That's strange…" He picked up the book and started toward the door, then remembered something and went to his desk. From a drawer he retrieved a flashlight and headed back into the shop.

Once again we found ourselves trailing him. The narrow beam of his flashlight turned the towering aisles into tunnels, and the palpable odor of dry rot grew thick. More than once we stepped up or down from one room into another. Each room seemed to represent a culture or a country, all of them long lost to the past. Wending through the twists and turns, I glimpsed random titles in English: *Zhuangzi, Book of Han, Commentaries of Zuo. Semonides of Amorgos. Great Hymn to the Aten. Code of Nesilim, Epic of Erra, Egyptian Book of the Dead. The Distichs of Cato, The City of God, Athenaeus—Banquet of the Learned.* The old shop, I realized, was a warren of multiple chambers, a cobbled together catacomb lined with dead or forgotten books.

And the Vedas, Steinberg was saying, were so old they were not even books.

"Not in the usual sense," he said. "They emerged from an ancient oral tradition, predating the written word. Memorized by Vedic priests, they were passed down from one generation to another in a highly metrical form of chanted poetry, with intricate, hypnotic melodies and precisely accented verses. That precise mnemonic metric was the key to their longevity. They're the oldest surviving poetry of the Indo-European languages."

I told him I had always thought that distinction belonged to the epics of Homer.

"The *Rig Veda* was composed a thousand years before Homer," he said. "It's the oldest of the Vedas, the Veda of Adoration. Over ten thousand verses, mostly adoring or adulating the gods. Many of the gods survive to this day, in one form or another. The Vedic worship of ancient India evolved into the world's oldest living religion."

"Hinduism," Oriana said.

"The *Rig Veda* was the fountainhead of Indian civilization."

I recalled the nearly unintelligible lines Dan had translated in the margin. "The stuff seems a little strange to build a civilization on."

"'The gods love the obscure,' they say." Steinberg ran his light up to a shelf of Indian titles. "Hence the profusion of translators."

Stretching up, rasping, he retrieved an elegant leather-bound volume embossed with Sanskrit lettering. He opened it to the first page of verses and compared it to the first page in Dan's book. "Yes. It's as I thought. Your brother's text employs a more archaic version of the ancient Sanskrit. The words are separated, not run together, which makes the original meter and rhythm more apparent. It should make for more accurate translation as well."

I knew meter and rhythm were essential to poetry, but I didn't understand how it could change the meaning of the words.

Steinberg explained. "In a way, the sound is more important than the meaning. It's believed the verses capture a kind of divine, elemental vibration. In fact, the ancient *rishis* who composed the Vedas believed the creation of the cosmos began with a subtle vibration of sound: *Aum*. 'By His utterance came the universe.'"

"In the beginning was the Word," I said. "Just like in the Bible."

"Exactly," Steinberg said. "'In the beginning was the Word, and the Word was with God, and the Word was God.' The cosmos emerges from a thought in God's mind. Thought is the subtlest form of sound. This is where the idea of the sacred sound, or *mantra*, is derived. It's a kind of tool for transcendence. A link to the divine. Transcending sounds are the pre-eminent means for attaining the state of enlightenment. 'By sound vibration one becomes liberated.'"

"Dan's translations didn't strike me as very enlightening," I said. "A lot of it seemed to be about war."

Steinberg aimed his light up at the book's empty slot on the shelf. It was near the end of a line of nearly identical, numbered volumes. "What you have here is the ninth book of the *Rig Veda,*" he said. "It contains some of the oldest hymns of them all. They praise a god known as Soma. Soma took the form of a sacred plant from which a divine elixir was derived, an intoxicating nectar, also called soma. Many of the hymns describe ritual celebrations in which the juice was pressed from the soma plant, filtered and mixed with milk and honey, and consumed by warriors before heading into battle. They believed it bestowed an invincible courage."

He paused to read a passage: *"Divine Soma, who art the beverage of the gods, flow at the sacrifice for their abundant food; urged on by thee may we overcome even mighty foes in battle; purified do thou render heaven and earth happy abodes for—"*

At this point I interrupted the scholarly Steinberg to ask him the obvious question.

"It may have been a lotus," he replied. "Many suspect it was, given the central place of the lotus plant in the history of Indian religion. But others think it was the mountain shrub containing the stimulant ephedra, or the hallucinatory fly-agaric mushroom, or the harmal perennial, Syrian Rue, even the common cannabis plant. In truth no one really knows the identity of the original soma. Descriptions of the plant seem to vary in the text, and translations are often contradictory. It's also quite possible—in fact, it's very likely—the plant may long ago have disappeared."

Disappeared, then reappeared again. It made more sense now why Maya had been involved, given the plant's historical relationship to India. But I couldn't understand the Iranians' obsession. Had they really believed the claims of some ancient Indian myth?

"The Iranians have their own mythology," Steinberg said. He led us around the corner, up a step into another room, and down another cavernous aisle. This time his light beam panned the lower shelves until it came to rest on a mauve-colored spine. He bent and tipped out the well-worn book. The cover featured a golden cauldron sprouting flames of fire, and above it, in Latin script, the one-word title, *Avesta*.

Steinberg licked his fingertips and leafed through the tawny pages. His flashlight beam threw a harsh glare at his face, flaring off his magnifying eyeglasses. "This is the sacred text of the ancient Persian religion that preceded Islam in Iran: Zoroastrianism. It emerged out of the prehistoric religion of the Indo-Iranians, and the verses were composed in a language remarkably similar to Vedic Sanskrit. For instance, the Vedic word for 'god,' *deva*, is *daeva*, 'demon,' in Avestan. And here"— his fingers stopped at a passage—"here's another word that should sound familiar to you: haoma. '*Haoma grows while he is praised, and the man who praises him is therewith more victorious. The lightest pressure of thee, Haoma, the slightest tasting of thy juice, avails to the thousand-smiting of the daevas.*'"

Steinberg lowered the book and the flashlight, but his eyes seemed to glimmer with their own internal light. "Soma. Haoma. They are both derived from the Indo-Iranian root word *sauma*, and no doubt refer to the very same—"

A sudden loud banging startled him into silence. He instantly clicked off his flashlight, and the three us listened breathlessly in the dark. Again the loud knocking rattled down the aisles.

Someone was pounding at the shop's front door.

34.
Cowboy

"I need to answer it," Steinberg said. "It may be the police."

"What if it's not?" Oriana whispered.

From the pocket of his bathrobe, Steinberg withdrew a small revolver. "You'll have to back me up." He offered the pistol to her.

She took it from him, gravely, and nodded in assent. The two of them turned to me.

Again the knocking broke the stillness.

"Wait in the workroom," Steinberg said. "If you hear any shooting, leave out the back."

I hesitated, heart pounding, wondering if somehow I couldn't help.

"Go," he ordered. I started off. "Other way," he said. I turned and headed in the opposite direction, and the two of them headed for the door.

I didn't get far before I realized I didn't know which way to proceed. Assuming that Steinberg would lead our way back, I hadn't paid attention to the route. Trying to retrace those steps in the dark now struck me as virtually impossible. Better to make myself useful, I thought. I turned around to follow them instead.

Hurrying as quickly as I could in the dark, I went back to where I had left them, then headed in the direction from which the knocking had come, hoping I could quickly catch up. But after only a couple of turns in the maze, I lost all sense of direction.

I paused a moment and listened. The knocking, I noticed, had stopped. The shop was completely quiet.

Whoever was at the door must have left, I thought. They assumed nobody was here.

I continued making my way down the aisle, listening for Steinberg and Oriana. Why don't I hear his wheezing? Why don't I hear her voice? The opaque air hung humid. A trickle of sweat crept down my neck.

Maybe it wasn't the cops at the door.

I pushed forward through the darkness until suddenly the floor fell away—the step into another room. Stumbling, I lost my balance and crashed face-down onto the carpet.

It took me a moment to recover. I strained to lift my head. On the bottom shelf beside me, barely visible in the dark, I noticed a shiny golden book title: *Shambhala.*

I was back in the South Asia section.

Shambhala. The cursive letters glimmered like a scraggy vein of gold. I started to reach for the book.

That's when I noticed the pair of cowboy boots. Pointed toes, snakeskin leather, caked with mud and dust. Mud-splattered jeans had been tucked neatly into them. A duffel bag hung from a pair of broad shoulders draped with a long, canvas duster. Though his face could barely be discerned in the dark, I was relieved to see he didn't have a beard. And wore a cowboy hat.

"Who are you?" I asked.

He pointed the barrel of a pistol at me. "Who are you?"

My eyes froze on the gun.

The beam of a flashlight found the man's chiseled face. Steinberg stood at the far end of the aisle. "Don't shoot!" he commanded.

The man raised his hand to block the light, squinting into the glare.

"Put down your gun," Oriana shouted.

He turned. Oriana stood at the other end of the aisle, aiming Steinberg's pistol.

The cowboy peered down at me while replacing his gun into his shoulder holster. "Looks like the Jews want to spare you," he said. "You must be the American."

I peered up at him, trying to place his accent. Uncombed, unwashed, unshaven, he looked like he'd just crossed the Caucasus Mountains in the pan of a pickup truck.

He offered me his hand.

"Jack Duran," I said.

He pulled me firmly to my feet. "Glad to meet you. I'm—"

"Sar!" Oriana rushed up and embraced him.

Steinberg approached with his flashlight. "You scared the daylights out of us!"

The bright glare of the workroom came as a shock to our dilated eyes. Steinberg hauled shut the bookshelf door. "I expected you at noon," he said. "I'd all but given up."

Sar dropped his hat and bag on the table. "I was in the Sinai. Came as quickly as I could." From his pocket he retrieved the front door key and handed it to Steinberg. "I was afraid they beat me here."

"Never got this far," Steinberg said. "Oriana made sure of that."

Sar lit up a cigarette as she told him what had happened—the two men at the hospital, a third killed in the cab.

"That leaves only the two then," Sar said.

"Three," Oriana said. "A man followed Jack on the flight from Istanbul."

"A Turk?"

"Possibly."

Squinting over the cigarette clamped between his teeth, Sar pulled a passport out of his coat pocket and tossed it across the table to her. "This fellow greeted my flight from Ben Gurion."

The passport's cover, embossed with Turkish crescent and star, was splotched with what looked like a wine stain. Oriana opened it to the photo, then stared in surprise at Sar. "That's him," she said.

"Then we only need to worry about the two," he said.

Her stare stayed on him. He coolly exhaled a stream of smoke.

Steinberg took the passport and thumbed through its visas. "Awful lot of trips to Iran," he said. He held it up, looking to Sar. "May I?"

Sar nodded.

Steinberg bent to open the bottom drawer of his desk and deposit the passport with the others. I wondered now how many had blood on them.

"So what's the plan?" Sar asked.

Steinberg rose up, red-faced, wheezing. "They make the crossing tonight," he said. "Pashazadeh has offered to take them."

"Pashazadeh? How generous. Are there no Caspian sturgeon left for him to poach?"

"The man owes me a favor."

"Whatever he owes you won't be enough." Sar turned to me. "You have dollars?"

"I've got about 500 euros, cash."

"Don't pay him more than 200. And don't let his manner fool you—he's nothing more than a thief."

"I'll deal with him," Oriana said.

Steinberg assured her, "He won't be a problem."

"Good," Sar said. "Because Jack will be making the crossing on his own. Oriana and I will take passage on the ferry."

She stared at him; it was an order. I wondered why she didn't object. "Didn't you say they'd be watching the harbor?"

She shifted her gaze to me but didn't respond.

"They *will* be watching the harbor," Sar said. He stepped up close, appraising me. "What are you—six-one? One-eighty-five?"

"*Huh?* No—180."

"What size are those sneakers?"

"Ten and a half."

"Excellent." He inspected my jacket. "I assume you wore this on the plane?"

"Yeah?"

"Give it to me. Please. The shoes and trousers, too."

"I beg your pardon?"

He was taking off his duster. "These men haven't had a good look at your face. All they know for sure is you're traveling with her."

I looked at Oriana. She still said nothing. Steinberg gazed down at his feet.

"You're going to try to *bait* them?" I asked.

"Something like that," Sar said.

"You'll get yourselves killed," I said.

Sar sat down to remove his boots. "Let us worry about that. For now, just give me your clothes. And the backpack, too. You can use this." He shoved his bag across the table.

I turned, gaping, to Steinberg and Oriana. "Who *is* this guy?"

The two exchanged a glance. Oriana helped herself to one of Sar's cigarettes. "Sar is my cousin. We work together. Please, Jack, just do as he says." She lit up, nervously.

Sar said something to her in Hebrew. Oriana nodded, then glanced again at Steinberg. Steinberg shrugged.

I looked at Sar, struggling to pull off his snakeskin boot. As weary as he was, he seemed driven, with a plucky sort of vigor he could barely contain. He was strong, fit, handsome, confident—a charismatic, yiddisher kop cowboy. I realized suddenly I envied him, but at the same time I feared he would get Oriana killed. And I, for one, didn't want to lose her.

"Are you with Mossad?" I asked.

"Me?" Finally, he unplugged his foot. "I work for Proctor and Gamble."

I stared at him blankly. "Is that some kind of joke?"

He yanked off the other boot and looked at me. "It would be really good of you," he said, "if you would please give me your jacket."

"It would be better if we just got the hell out of here," I said. But even as I said it, I began to remove my coat.

Steinberg helped me out of it. "Jack may have a point," he said. "There's plenty of room on Pashazadeh's trawler."

Sar looked aghast. "I didn't come here to go *fishing*."

Steinberg handed him my jacket. "I'm only suggesting you consider the alternatives."

"He's right," I said. "There's no reason to confront these people if you don't have to."

The suggestion brought a look of disgust. "There's a very good reason to confront them. These men are our *enemies*."

It struck me as anachronistic, his use of that word, as if he'd just returned from battling Nazis in the middle of the previous century. "They're not *my* enemies," I said. "They're just…I don't know, misinformed?"

Oriana crushed out her cigarette after having barely smoked it. "They tried to kill you, Jack."

"I know," I said. "I got the message."

"Apparently the wrong message," Sar said.

I asked him what he meant. He stepped close and looked in my eyes. "I mean they didn't try to kill you."

"The hell they didn't." I showed him my throat. "I came this close—"

Sar slapped me, knocking my head to the side. "Wake up."

I glared at him, stunned.

The Israeli spoke through a clenched jaw, his face only inches from mine. "You need to be clear about something. These men are trained assassins. They've murdered over two hundred people in the last three years. Two hundred that we know of. In Iran, Iraq, Syria, Lebanon, Egypt, Yemen, Saudi. Reformers, mostly. Moderates. Politicians, police officers, businessmen, reporters. Their throats slashed, their bodies dumped, gutted like butchered animals." He looked off briefly, wincing at some memory, then turned his burning eyes back on me. "These men are not fools. And they don't like being made to look like fools. If they had wanted to kill you, believe me, you'd be dead. The only reason you're not is because they think you hold information. They want you to reveal it to them. If not, they'll have to extract it from you. When that happens—and it will happen—you won't be able to run away. You'll be *forced* to confront them. On their terms, not ours."

I swallowed a lump of fear—and thought of my brother and Phoebe.

Sar turned to Steinberg. "If it's all right with you, Oriana and I'll cross on the ferry. We'll leave the fishing to Jack."

35.
The Hidden Imam

Steinberg got dressed and drove me to the harbor. Wearing a light overcoat and a wide-brimmed Fedora that covered his head to his brow, the old man appeared both morose and perturbed, and kept to himself on the ride. He seemed to be brooding over the fate of Oriana. Later that morning, she and Sar would purchase tickets for the Caspian ferry, and that evening depart for Turkmenistan. The Iranians weren't the only ones who needed information. Sar, posing as me, hoped to lure the two assassins aboard and turn the tables on them. He planned to conduct his own interrogation, intent on uncovering the whereabouts of the seven other assassins still remaining from the list.

I wondered how far he would take it. What would he do—slap them? Or use the very same methods he claimed the assassins would use on me? And what would happen if that didn't work? Given my experience with Oriana, I assumed he would fit his gun with a silencer, blast a hole in each of their heads and dump them into the sea. Then the charming cousins could continue their cruise and rendezvous with me at the dig site.

That was the plan at least, as far as I could tell. Sar was not all that forthcoming.

Steinberg didn't seem to care much for the swashbuckling Israeli, but he clearly was fond of Oriana. I wanted to ask him more about her, about whether she really did work for Mossad, and why she took orders from Sar, but he didn't give the

…n he was in the mood for a chat, and I thought he …ave resented me for all the trouble I had caused. I …ed not to disturb him.

But Steinberg disturbed me. Hunched over the wheel of his aging Volvo, staring out ahead into the dark, he began to speak in a quiet voice, as if he were thinking aloud to himself, mulling over some ominous vision.

"It's chaos they want," he said. "The Ayatollah in Qum. These men obsessed with killing. They're *Hojjatieh*. Proofers. They want to light the fires of the final conflagration, the anarchy that brings about the return of the Twelfth Imam. The last successor of the Prophet, the Hidden Imam lived in seclusion in ninth-century Iraq, and the Shi'a Muslims believe this leader never suffered death. For over a thousand years he's been their hope and their messiah, the promised savior of mankind. They call him the *Mahdi*, the 'Guided One,' or the *Hojjat*, the 'Proof.' Out of chaos he'll return to lead the righteous against evil, first in the Middle East, and eventually across the world. He'll end all doubt and shatter all illusion, restoring at last the political power and the true purity of Islam."

I listened, enraptured; Steinberg stared ahead. "There's no more dangerous illusion," he said, "than the fancies by which people try to avoid illusion."

My head was spinning. "This Hidden Imam—the Mahdi. They really believe that's true?"

"True?" He glanced at me with his squinty eye. "Take it from a forger. Few men want to know what's true. Most just want to confirm that *what they believe* is true."

The city had gone to sleep, and the seedy warehouse dock district appeared to be all but abandoned. At the waterfront, Steinberg peered around an unlit corner and steered us into an alley. He maneuvered among potholes—or tried to—until he came to stop at a padlocked gate, beyond which a number of cars were parked in the lot of a old brick fish house.

The forger beeped his horn.

We waited. The building was dark, save for a dim light over the entrance. He beeped again. I noticed two large cargo vans parked at the loading dock. Beside them was a car that stood out from the rest: a gleaming-wet, ivory-white Lexus.

A young boy burst out the warehouse door and ran past the cars to the gate. As he entered the flare of our headlights, I saw he was wearing a Muslim prayer cap and a stylish Levi jacket. He was probably seven years old. Without so much as a glance at us, he undid the lock and swung the gate wide.

Steinberg drove through and parked near the door. "Pashazadeh doesn't speak English," he said. "You'll have to let me do the talking."

The boy led us inside. We followed him down a narrow hall and through another door into a large, well-lighted processing room. The stench of fish and disinfectant mingled in the air. Somewhere a cheap radio blared a now familiar tune, the same one we had heard in the taxi. The boy led us past a long granite table lined with workers outfitted for surgery: white boots, smocks, caps, masks, and dark-stained rubber gloves. They were collecting gobs of black roe from the split-open bellies of sturgeon. Further down, several workers sieved the roe and rinsed the eggs in steel sinks. Their eyes scrutinized us from behind their paper masks.

Steinberg spoke to me quietly. "These men risk incarceration for less than ten manat a night. Pashazadeh smuggles the caviar to Europe and sells it at 1000 euros a pound."

It set my mind to calculating. "Does this go on 24 hours a day?"

Steinberg shook his head. "All will be cleared out by sunrise. He has a legal fishing business that operates during the day."

A worker beside us carried a stainless steel bowl of roe through a doorway, and the boy led us in after him. The room was smaller and colder. Here workers were weighing the roe, kneading it with salt and sealing it in tins.

At the back, two men conferred at the open door of a large refrigerator. One was dressed in the surgical garb, but the other wore a dark gray suit, with his silver-bearded face uncovered, and a brimless gray wool cap on his head. The boy went straight to him and took hold of his hand. I noticed a chunky Rolex on the boy's little wrist.

Pashazadeh looked up, saw Steinberg and smiled. They shook hands, exchanging greetings in Azeri.

Steinberg introduced me as "the American" again. Pashazadeh said something to him that sounded derogatory, then reached out, grinning, to me. His handshake was regal and effeminate, but I caught a steely glint in his eye. The hard look took in the clothes I was wearing—Sar's snakeskin boots, muddy jeans, duffel bag, long, frayed canvas duster, battered hat in hand. Still grinning tightly, he asked Steinberg a question.

I waited for Steinberg's translation. "He's wondering if you parked your horse in the lot."

"Oh," I said. "Yeah. Tell him, when we left, it was relieving itself on a Lexus."

It turned out Steinberg didn't have to translate: I could see he understood from the look on his face. But as quickly as the scowl appeared, Pashazadeh laughed. "Please, come, is waiting," he said as he walked off chuckling hand-in-hand with the boy.

Steinberg gave me a look. "Do let me handle it from here," he whispered.

We followed them back toward the doorway to the docks.

"You tell me three passengers," Pashazadeh said.

Steinberg hesitated. "Couldn't afford your rates, I'm afraid."

"Ah. The ferry then." Pashazadeh seemed displeased. Though he remained polite and soft-spoken, he again conversed with Steinberg in Azeri.

Steinberg grew argumentative. By the time we reached the trawler, he broke off in disgust. "He says two Iranian 'officials' have been murdered. One was found near the airport, the other in a taxi cab. He claims the Iranian Navy's been put on alert. They're looking for an American. If you're caught, his boat will be confiscated. To cover the risk, he wants 1000 euros."

"I can't do that," I said. "I told you—"

"I know. He's insisting. I'm sorry."

I looked at Pashazadeh. His son was playfully tugging his hand. "I can't pay you that much," I said. "I can only afford 200 euros."

Pashazadeh responded in Azeri to Steinberg. Steinberg said, "He's advising you to wait."

"How long?"

"A few days, maybe a week. When the patrols get back to normal, he can offer a better price."

I thought of the Iranians hunting me, along with the city police. "I can't wait that long," I said. "It might not be safe on the water, but for me it's a lot more dangerous here." I pulled the rest of the cash from my pocket. "Here's five hundred and…twelve euros. That's everything I've got."

Pashazadeh held up his hands and shrugged. "Impossible," he said.

"Take a credit card." I pulled it from my wallet. "American Express?"

He grinned tightly. "This isn't Bloomingdales." The boy hugged his father's leg.

"Please." I was pleading now. "Those men were not 'officials.' They were assassins trying to track down my brother. If I don't get to him first, I'm afraid they're going to kill him. I have to leave here tonight or—"

"Excuse me."

I turned. A man approached from behind me. He was one of three crewmen who had been waiting on the trawler. "We'll take you," he said to me calmly.

Pashazadeh objected.

The man responded. I couldn't understand what he was saying, but he seemed to be arguing my case. The fellow wore a knit cap over close-cropped hair, had large brown fearless eyes set in a solemn face, and unlike the others, was beardless. Although I doubted he was younger than me, he was dressed in jeans and Adidas like an American college student.

As they talked, Steinberg caught my eye and nodded:

apparently they were working out a deal. When Pashazadeh finally acquiesced, the sailor offered him a cigarette. Pashazadeh waved it off. The man lit one for himself, picked up my duffel bag and headed for the trawler. "Give him your money," he said.

Fearing Pashazadeh might change his mind, I thrust the wad of cash into his hand. "You'll get your boat back," I said.

He eyed me with disdain and passed the cash off to his son, who set about immediately counting it. "*Insha'Allah,*" he mumbled, and together with the boy headed back into the plant.

I asked Steinberg what he said.

"*Insha'Allah.* 'If God wills it.'"

"Well that goes without saying."

"Not to a Muslim it doesn't."

We walked toward the trawler. On its deck, the sailor and his crew were preparing to depart. "Who is he?" I asked.

"I'm told he works for Pashazadeh, running contraband. He's Iranian, goes by the name Faraj."

36.
The Source of Happiness

With the dark eyes and face and the five-o'clock shadow, I had thought the man might be Iranian. "Can we trust him?" I asked.

"He's the reason you're leaving tonight. He offered to give up his half of the 1000 euro charge."

"I don't understand," I said.

"According to Pashazadeh, Faraj escaped an Iranian prison. It seems he dislikes the rulers in Tehran even more than we do."

We reached the gangway to the trawler. Steinberg pulled out his own wad of cash and peeled off a bunch of bills. "You won't get far if you're broke," he said.

"Are you sure—?"

"Not to worry. That's only 80 manat—less than 100 dollars. I'll add it to my expense account."

"Who pays that? The Knesset?"

His squinty left eye twinkled. "Proctor and Gamble," he said.

As we pulled away from the dock into the inky harbor, I couldn't help feeling I was leaving something behind. Twice, my hand went to check for my wallet. It was there in my back pocket, stuffed with Steinberg's cash. My passport with the fake visa was in my duffel bag, along with Maya's directions to the archeological site. I checked and found the Rig Veda text and Dan's Buddha sketchbook, and the antique bronze object I had found in Maya's suitcase.

Everything appeared to be in its place, yet still something seemed to be missing.

The two grizzled crewmen coiled ropes and busied themselves on deck, while Faraj manned the wheel in the pilothouse and kept watch for the harbor police. I made my way to the stern to take in the widening view of the city. Beneath the slender blade of the moon, Baku gleamed like a shard of obsidian. Aside from Mr. Steinberg and his catacomb of books, all I would remember of the sunless city is what I had seen of it this night: the shadowy streets, the sturgeon surgeons, the assassin in the taxi with a hole blown through his head. Black-cloaked Death stalked through Baku with a dagger. As wary as I was of what was to come, I was relieved to be leaving this nightmare behind.

We exited the harbor. The boat's onboard lights switched off. From here on out, we'd be traveling in the dark.

I needed to get some sleep—it was nearly 3:00 in the morning. Reclining on the deck, I laid my head back on the "pillow" of Sar's duffel bag. The toes of his cowboy boots poked out from my duster. The duster reeked of cigarette smoke.

Perhaps the thing I kept missing was my famous safari jacket. Sar had promised to give it back when we met up again at the dig. *If* we met up again. Maybe that's what nagged at me: my guilt at leaving them behind to fight my battles for me, while I skulked away with that worm inside my gut.

Feeling suddenly weary, I pulled Sar's hat down over my eyes and soon drifted off into sleep.

I was out for a couple of hours. But just before I awoke, I was having a flying dream. I soared over the maze-like Garden of Simples, the botanical garden in Rome. Wading through the round green pond at the center was the pharmaceutical Santa Claus, Dr. Felix Fiore. The setting sun surrendered with a gorgeous, golden light, and as the white-haired doctor meandered through the duckweed, he left a golden trail of water in his wake. The trail seemed to spell out a word on the water, and when I awoke, the thing I'd been struggling so hard to remember now stood out clearly in my mind: a word scrawled in cursive like a scraggy vein of gold—the name of a long-lost paradise.

Shambhala.

It was the title of the book I had stumbled upon in the darkness of Steinberg's shop. When Sar appeared so suddenly, I completely forgot about it. Now I wished I'd taken another look.

My brother Dan had made a study of Tibetan Buddhism, and before I went to India often talked to me about it. He said Shambhala, a Sanskrit word that meant "the Source of Happiness," was the name of a legendary kingdom of Tibet, a sanctuary of mystics and sages. Lamas called it a "Pure Land," the only one on earth, a heavenly place meant only for those devoted to reaching nirvana. Dan said Shambhala was the basis for the novel and the Hollywood movie, *Lost Horizon*, which gave the utopian kingdom its more popular Western name: Shangri-la. But while the fictional Shangri-la was set in the mountains of Tibet, the Tibetans themselves believed the real Shambhala lay beyond the high Himalayas, somewhere out in the great land mass of Central Asia. Ancient guidebooks to the kingdom described a long and arduous journey over mountains, rivers, and deserts. But it was impossible to decipher where in fact Shambhala was; the accounts were too archaic and contradictory. Populated with obstructing demons and mysterious, magical deities, the texts seemed designed to thwart those seekers who might be deemed less than worthy.

As I now lay awake on the deck of the boat, staring up at the myriad of stars, I began to wonder whether Dan's Buddha sketchbook, with its depictions of gruesome demons and enlightened bodhisattvas, was itself some sort of guidebook—if not to Shambhala, then perhaps to the place where Dan had absconded with the seeds.

Across the deck, one of the crewmen sat cross-legged in the dark, laying down cards in a game of solitaire. I sat up and pulled out the sketchbook from my bag.

The answer has *got* to be in here, I thought.

37.
the Truth

For nearly an hour I ruminated over the drawings in Daniel's Buddha book, wondering if they might possibly hold the secret to his whereabouts. But nothing in particular struck me as a clue, and the continuous contemplation of all the mystifying images put me in a mild state of reverie. I watched the moon slowly slip into the sea, and with the ink-and-wash drawings now lit only by the stars, the depicted gods and demons seemed to dwindle into ghosts, and the mountains and rivers grew misty.

I found Maya's stationery note stuffed inside the sketchbook, and examined the Indian emblem again: *Truth alone triumphs.* Fiore had said it was from an ancient pillar erected by Ashoka the Great, marking the place where the Buddha first proclaimed his truth to the four corners of the earth. The wheel beneath the lions was the Wheel of Dharma—the oldest symbol of Buddhism, according to the doctor. Dharma, I recalled, referred to the Buddha's teachings and the duty of righteous action. It was the means of advancing down the path to enlightenment, the wheel on that royal road that led one to "the Truth."

Truth with that presumptuous capital "T." It was something I had never understood. How could anyone make the claim that they possess the ultimate truth? And what exactly is that exalted term referring to? The meaning of life? The sum of all knowledge? The ultimate reality? God?

I shuffled through the pages of his sketchbook until I found the picture of the lotus-holding Buddha. As I'd noticed before, it looked different from the rest. In the backgrounds of most of the drawings, curved lines arced across the sky like segments of a colorless rainbow. Landscape features filled out the frames. Only the image of the massive Buddha stood alone in empty space. As if he were separate and apart from everything...or that everything was contained within him.

Was that the Buddha's inscrutable Truth?

I lay back and gazed up at the night sky again. My intention was to contemplate the meaning of the image, but suddenly the spectacle of the heavens sucked my breath away. With the boat lights out and the moon gone down, the brilliance of the night nearly blinded me. In a flash my mind went blank. I felt myself transfixed. My eyes became entranced by what I had not seen before—beyond the bottomless black of space, beyond the vault of stars. What revealed itself was deeper, more mysterious and profound. It entered not just through my eyes, but seemed to strike my body—a blast of clear cognition, a stunning psychic blow. Everything at once and all together.

Terror. Awe.

It gripped me until I couldn't breathe.

The moment lasted only seconds. Then, as quickly as it arose, the wave of panic broke. In its wake came a froth of confusion and a swirling vertigo.

Words bubbled into my brain. *Planets. Stars. Galaxies. Space.*

I breathed. The vertigo settled. The stream of thought returned.

I sat up and looked around. The crewman was still plopping down his playing cards in the dark, while the other sailor scanned the sea with a giant pair of binocs. He lowered them and crossed the deck toward the ghostly pilothouse, where Faraj presumably still manned the wheel, steering our course through the night.

I peered up again at the sky.

What had I glimpsed in that fleeting moment? What had slipped into my mind? Everything seemed to have melded together. My mind had not broken it apart. Now all I saw were individual stars and the map-like constellations. The Big Dipper. The North Star. The three-studded Belt of Orion.

The terror was gone. All looked familiar. I was back in the world I knew, the world of language and labels, the world of thoughts and things. I could pick them all out—this part and that—and fit myself into the picture. I was on a boat on the Caspian Sea, on a search for my brother and Phoebe.

So what the hell had just happened? Perhaps nothing at all. Just some errant trick of the mind, some sort of synaptic misfire. The result of an hour of intense contemplation, puzzling over odd thoughts and images. The event already seemed strangely unreal, as if it had only been imagined.

And yet...

It hadn't been imagined. It had been felt. Perceived. Experienced. It had literally taken my breath away.

Infinity. The ungraspable. Not the transitory, dreamlike, dust-mote galaxies, but the unbounded, never-ending void that contained them. The eternal mystery of that—the cosmic, brain-busting *whole* of it—that was the "truth" that overwhelmed me.

My eyes fell again upon the Buddha book. Page after page of figures from a dream. And in the space around them, those gently arcing curves.

Bands of a rainbow. Segments of a circle. Portions or parts of…

The whole.

All at once I knew what lay hidden in the book. In a rush I started tearing out the pages.

38.
Mandala

At ten across, the first row was complete. The next ten pages filled the row below that. I continued on, page after page, following the order of their sequence in the book, until gradually the overall picture took shape. River segments joined, mountain ranges linked. The rainbow arches bridged across pages, forming perfect circles.

Gradually the various Buddhist entities settled themselves in the scheme. Beyond the farthest circle, the demons found their lair, while the empyreal gods and bodhisattvas alighted the inner rings. Halfway through the fifth row, I reached the massive Buddha. He would sit alone at the gravitational center, the light-giving sun in this sacred solar system. Encircled by a chain of snow-capped peaks, the Buddha held the lotus in his upraised hand while pointing down into the void with his other.

The secret of the book was not a secret at all; it had been right there before me all along. Ten rows down, ten rows across, the hundred separate sketches formed a mandala. I recalled now seeing these artworks in India. As inlaid mosaics, painted wall murals, or hanging paper scrolls, they were used by Hindus and Buddhists alike as objects of deep meditation. Tibetans, highly enamored of the art, developed the most complex and intricate designs. Their legendary sand mandalas, meticulously constructed by supremely patient monks, were ritually destroyed shortly after their completion, illustrating the impermanence of all things.

I kneeled now at the base of the assemblage to take in the picture as a whole. It was difficult to make out in the dim starlight, and under the constant current of air, the sheets stirred restlessly—I had to keep reaching out to realign them. Despite this disturbance, the configuration's overall symmetry and order, anchored to the firmly rooted Buddha in the center, generated a calming, almost sedative effect, and reminded me of the feeling I had at the window of Steinberg's shop.

For a long moment I stared at the pages, wondering what it all meant.

"You're an artist."

I turned to find Faraj standing behind me, along with the crewman who'd been playing solitaire. "I'm not," I said. "But you're the second person to tell me that tonight."

"If you are not artist," he said, "then you must be Buddhist."

"No. Not in this lifetime, at least." I stood up. "This was drawn by my brother Dan. He must have copied it from a temple or museum or something. I'm trying to figure out if it can tell me where he is."

A page at the edge blew askew. Faraj bent down to adjust it—the drawing of the yogi with the female partner on his lap. "I think is from Tibet," he said, gazing down at the mandala. "But this…this design is different."

He was right. Something about the layout did seem odd, but I couldn't put my finger on it. "What is it, do you think?"

"There are circles," he said. "Only circles. The ones I see, from Tibet, they have a square inside."

"Yeah…you're right." The mandala had no square at the center, just the inner ring of mountains. "I'm not sure what that means."

"It means…he is in paradise."

"Dan?"

"The Buddha."

A page blew. I nudged it back in place. "Buddhists don't believe in paradise, Faraj."

"Oh yes. They believe it. They believe it is inside, *here*." He pointed to his head.

I looked back at the drawing and at the demons in the outer circle. "It's an unusual paradise that has devils in it, too."

"No, no. The jinn cannot touch him. Inside, Buddha is safe."

"Safe?"

"Yes. See? He is safe from evil. Like inside a wall of mountains." He traced the circle of mountains around the Buddha.

I remembered what Dr. Fiore had said in the garden back in Rome: paradise—the "wall around." Separate from the world, yet within it.

"How do you know these things?" I asked.

He laid his hand over his heart. "I am Sufi Muslim. We believe the same. 'The Source is within you,' Rumi said. 'And this whole world is springing up from it.'"

"But how do you know about mandalas?"

"I trade Persian rugs—they have mandala, too. Made of flowers. And vines. With a beautiful garden in the center, like paradise."

I thought of my threadbare Oriental rug with its flowery central medallion—awash in Maya's blood. I nodded toward the Buddha. "Your garden has no wall to keep it safe."

Faraj smiled. "The wall must be in your mind," he said.

"Right."

Faraj gazed down at the mandala again. "To be honest, I prefer the Persian," he said. "Is more…pleasing. I tell my customers, is like you are buying a piece of—"

A shout from the pilothouse cut him short. Inside, the acting pilot pointed out to sea.

Faraj quickly scanned the horizon. The boat abruptly slowed.

"What is it?" I asked. I could see no ships or lights in any direction.

"The radar," Faraj said. He hurried off to the pilothouse with the deckhand at his heels.

I quickly gathered up the mandala pages and stuffed them into my pack. Before I finished, all three men emerged from the pilothouse and stepped to the forward deck. Faraj raised the pair of binoculars.

Though the eastern rim of the sea had lightened, dawn had not yet broke. I stepped up beside the men and scanned the faint horizon. A speck of light had appeared.

"Is coming fast," Faraj said.

"Iranian?" I asked.

He studied the gradually brightening point of light. "Yes. A patrol boat." He handed off the binoculars and turned to me. "We are approaching Türkmenbashy. The Iranian Navy is patrolling the coast. They spot us with their radar."

The tone of his voice unnerved me. "What do we do?" I asked.

He peered at the growing light. The form of the boat was taking shape—a prow riding high on the water.

Faraj looked at me with pity, then took Sar's cowboy hat off my head and wordlessly flung it overboard.

I bristled.

"I'm afraid you must sleep with the fishes," he said.

The three men held their gaze on me. I glanced from one pair of eyes to the next.

39.
I am the Buddha

"Jump," Faraj ordered.

I stood anxiously on the edge of the deck, battling the worm in my gut. "There must be another way," I insisted.

"There is," he said. He nodded over his shoulder at the oncoming cruiser. "They take you, they arrest us, they confiscate our boat."

The three men watched me and waited. I looked down into the glistening darkness, my heart crawling into my throat. Some fates are worse than death, I thought.

"Do it!" Faraj shouted.

A spotlight beam traversed the water.

"Now!"

The beam swept toward us. I jumped.

The drop was short and ended quick—not with a splash, but a whimper. The whimper came from me as I landed on the heap of gutted fish in the hold. The iced sturgeon, stripped of their eggs, were bound for markets in Turkmenistan. The plan was for me to "sleep" under them while the Iranians made their search of the boat.

The stench in the hold nearly gagged me. Ice shards filled my boots. I strained to see in the dimness, but when the hatch slammed shut above me, the hold went completely black.

If the Iranians boarded, they'd be sure to check the hold and I could be easily spotted. So following Faraj's orders, I started digging down into the fish. The carcasses were heavy and frozen, with knuckled, rocklike spines, and fins that cut like razors. Faraj had lent me his leather gloves, but hardly had I started when the left one slipped off. Searching for it in the dark, I snagged my thumb on pin-sharp teeth and cut my fingertips. Blood soon bathed my hand. I gave up on the glove.

The idling engine thumped nearby. Above its noise came shouting—calls, questions, commands. It spurred me to dig deeper. Chunks of ice slipped down my sleeves and up the legs of my trousers. I wriggled and squirmed, burrowing down, steeling myself against the cold and the stench. Finally I found myself so buried under sturgeon it became nearly impossible to breathe.

I stopped and listened. The shouting had ceased. Footsteps clattered back and forth across the deck. Wondering if my limbs and clothes were covered, I lay there, sucking in the suffocating air.

Minutes passed with agonizing slowness. I was now frantically gasping for breath. The darkness began to twinkle and glitter—consciousness seeping away. Then, from the cold or the mounting fear, my body started to shake. Within seconds it was uncontrollable.

The hatch cracked open and slammed to the deck. The sudden loud smack of it startled me. Voices poured down into the hold—unfamiliar voices. Then a light beam passed over the fishes above me, flaring through gaps and translucent fins.

I held my breath.

Only minutes before, up on deck, I'd been struck by the calming effect of the mandala. I thought of it now as I tried to steady the shivers of fear rippling through me: the Buddha sitting serenely at the center of the cosmos, safe inside his circle of snow-capped peaks, unthreatened by the demons, immune to the cold, free from every peril, even death.

A man spoke calmly, his voice far away. The light beam swept back over me.

I dared not breathe.

Around me, the darkness danced with glitter, and the voices faded into silence. Dangling over a black abyss, I clung in desperation to a fraying thread of thought: I am the Buddha, encircled by mountains, safe from every peril, even…

My eyes became transfixed by the glowing fissures above me. They seemed to grow brighter and brighter, until finally they merged with the twinkling glitter and bloomed into a blinding glare.

"Wake up!"

Awaken to the rustle of silk skirts, to the scent of jasmine oil on her wrist, to the clink of her coins in the alms bowl, to the young bride's whispered prayer.

I sit in the dust of the village road, grinning under closed lids despite the slashing sun. The wedding procession, the bride's scent, the hunger pains, the flies—all come and go like night and day. All things must pass—

"Wake up!"

Awaken to the creak of the wagon wheels, to the odor of the defecating horses, to the wife's farewell to her warrior, to the clatter of armor and swords.

I sit in the mud of the village road, grinning under closed lids despite the pouring rain. Though I live in every passing soldier, there's nothing I need do. Just sit in silent testament. Peace comes from with—

"Wake up!"

Awaken to the smoke of the funeral pyres, to the futile pleadings of the mourners, to the wail of the grief-stricken widow, to the chant of the senile priest.

I sit in the dark of the village road, grinning under closed lids despite the falling snow. Though demons circle, they pose no threat. Grief cannot devour me; the cold can only bite. I am the Buddha, and I am free. Free from want, free from fear, free from the bonds of birth and death. There is no joy like the joy of freedom!

"Wake up, Jack—you're safe."

The Karakum

40.
Camel Crossing

I awoke to a light so harsh and bright, it took a moment to realize I was staring at a scorpion. Its claws were raised and its tail was curled in the much feared pose of attack. The sight of it sent a little shiver through me. I was relieved to discover it was dead.

The critter was encased in the transparent globe of the gearshift knob in the truck. It amazed me that I hadn't even noticed it until now, but Faraj had been at the wheel ever since we'd left the coast, and despite his steady speed across the endless, flat terrain, his hand had rarely lifted off the stick.

Until now. Now he had left the truck at the side of the road and was walking off into the desert, past the triangular yield sign that displayed the silhouette of a camel. If there really were wild camels in this godforsaken desert, none had dared venture into view. The Karakum—the Black Desert—looked exactly the same here as it had three hours earlier, when I'd fallen asleep out of boredom: an infinite litter box of sand and scrub, bisected by a crumbling highway. At the Caspian the sun had been an orange beach ball and the air had been crisp and clear. Now I squinted achingly into a bright desert haze as I watched Faraj trudge across the sand.

What was he up to? I wondered.

Something about the Iranian still troubled me. I wasn't quite sure I could trust him. He seemed to be withholding some part of himself, some secret too dark to reveal.

We had spent the previous day in the slummy outskirts of

Türkmenbashy, where the family of the solitaire-playing crewman put us up. I scrubbed myself clean from my sleep with the fishes, and had to hand-soak Sar's stinking duster. We feasted on a homemade meal of something called *manty*, a kind of ravioli filled with goat meat. During the dinner I told Faraj my harrowing tale of the lotus, and of Sar's scheme to attract and catch the assassins on the ferry. He warned me the Iranians would not be easily deceived, and seemed genuinely concerned for my safety. When I told him we planned to meet up at the archeological site, some 300 miles southeast through the desert, he offered at once to drive me. He was heading that way with the shipment of sturgeon and some crates of black-market caviar. At the bazaar in Ashkhabad, he'd sell it all and pick up a load of his family's Persian rugs, which he then would take back to Azerbaijan to be sold through his patron, Pashazadeh.

I told him I didn't want him to go out of his way.

"The desert's a boring drive," he said. "The detour would be interesting."

"Hopefully that's all it'll be," I said.

He grinned. "I'll say my prayers."

Despite his assurances, it felt as if he were looking for an excuse to help me out. He'd already taken a heck of a risk, and forfeited his wages to boot. Now he was volunteering to drive me to a place that potentially could be very dangerous—the site where the coveted seeds had been found and the last place Dan had been seen. While Faraj seemed well-intentioned, I knew he had spent time in prison, and I woke up more than once that night wondering what exactly he was after.

We departed the next morning before dawn. As the sun bubbled up from the black Karakum, I asked Faraj to tell me his story. "Why is it you want to help me?"

His answer came as a shock. "This man who is after you. I know this man."

"Vanitar?"

"We were once great friends," he said.

I suddenly had the horrible feeling I'd made a grave mistake. "*Were* friends. Not anymore?"

Faraj fixed me with his dark brown eyes. “Vanitar Azad is the most evil man I know.”

I breathed in relief. “This may sound strange, but I’m glad to hear you say that.”

“It’s why Pashazadeh contacted me to take you over the Caspian. He knew about our past together, that I would jump at any chance to revenge myself on Vanitar.”

Vengeance. Again. The basic operating principle of the entire Middle East. I asked Faraj what happened between him and his former friend.

He pulled out his pack of cigarettes. “Do you mind?”

“No.”

He thumbed his lighter and lit one up. “Vanitar used to hate it when I smoke in the car. Believed it was *haram*—sinful.”

“I was told he’s some kind of fundamentalist.”

“He wasn’t always like that.” The two of them had grown up together, he said, in a rough neighborhood in South Tehran. Faraj was the youngest son of a rug merchant who was robbed and killed when Faraj was just a baby. Vanitar’s father was killed a year later in the horrendous Iran-Iraq war. Both boys fell under the influence of Vanitar’s older brother, the street fighter Arshan. Yet despite their rebellious and somewhat dissolute youth (opium smoking, petty crime, bootlegged American movies and music), the boys managed to score high in their *concours* exams and went off to attend university.

“That’s where our paths first parted,” Faraj said. “Vanitar started at university in Tehran, but eventually transferred to a seminary in Qum, where he studied Islamic religion and philosophy. I pursued the study of history in Isfahan, while working part-time for my uncle in the rug business.”

Although Faraj was involved in several protests at his school, it was this uncle—a spirited devotee of Sufism—who first got into serious trouble with the Iranian regime. In the Land of the Ayatollahs, followers of Islam’s inner mystical tradition are regarded with suspicion by the orthodox. Ruling clerics question the allegiance of those devoted to Sufi masters, and denounce Sufi practices as alien to the Koran. Strongly influenced by the traditions of the Hindus, Sufis believe the same truth lies at the core of all religions, and that the individual, through his own efforts, can achieve a kind of spiritual union with the divine.

Faraj grew intrigued with the Sufis' inner focus and his uncle's liberal view of religion. Though it clearly contradicted the Shi'a Islam of his youth, Faraj came to see it not as a betrayal of his faith, but a return, in a way, to its roots. He eventually decided to join his uncle's Sufi brotherhood.

"It was not long after that," Faraj said, "that everything got to hell. As if Allah were testing me."

"What happened?"

"The authorities decide to bulldoze a Sufi mosque in Isfahan. My uncle and I, and forty other Sufis, we stand arm in arm on the street, try to stop them. We are all arrested, thrown in jail. A Ministry of Intelligence official interrogated us. His name was Ali Mahbood. When we were released, my uncle complained that Mahbood had beaten him. For this, he was convicted of slander, flogged 74 times, and sentenced to a five-year prison term."

"This intelligence official—Mahbood," I said. "He's on the list of assassins. Oriana—the Israeli woman—she told me Vanitar worked under him."

"That came later," Faraj said.

"What happened to your uncle?" I asked.

"He died within a year of being jailed. A heart attack, they said. But they refused to perform an autopsy."

Faraj was devastated. His grief turned to anger and to politics, and he moved back to Tehran to pursue a degree in law. When the presidential election dispute occurred in the summer of 2009, he joined the growing Green Revolution, leading his fellow Sufis in demonstrations against the regime. Faraj was again arrested, and this time sent to Kahrizak, the notoriously squalid underground prison and the scene of that summer's worst horrors.

"That's where I encountered my old friend again," he said. "Vanitar was working for Mahbood, interrogating those who were arrested. Forcing them to give up the names of their friends—addresses, phone numbers, emails. To confess what they'd done. Tell everything they knew. Every secret. Every sin. Every last..." Faraj grew quiet and seemed to sicken of his cigarette. He tossed it half-smoked out the window, then chucked the whole pack out after it.

I remembered what I'd been told in Baku. "Oriana thought something must have happened to Vanitar during his stint at that prison. Something that pushed him over the edge. Some kind of 'identity crisis.' Turned him into a religious fanatic."

I looked at Faraj. He was staring intensely at the road ahead. I hesitated to ask him the obvious question. But I felt I was close to something, that darkness he seemed to be holding back.

"Did Vanitar interrogate *you*, Faraj?"

For a moment he didn't answer. He seemed to be struggling to contain his emotions. Then, suddenly, he erupted in anger. "This woman, your friend. She talks about a crisis. What does she know? Islam? Fanatic? She knows nothing. Nothing! Nothing but lies!"

I backed off; I'd struck a nerve. Exactly what it was, I couldn't be sure. But something had clearly happened between Faraj and his old friend. My question had disturbed him deeply.

41.
Saints & Sinners

I waited for Faraj to continue. After a long silence, he did.

"Every day, hundreds of protestors were taken into custody. The prison became extremely overcrowded and chaotic, with new inmates hauled in every hour as others were released. In the confusion, several of us managed to escape. I fled north across the border into Azerbaijan. I've lived there, in exile, ever since."

Faraj ran a rug-trading route through Central Asia, the same work he had done for his uncle. "Man's gotta do what a man's gotta do," he said with a joyless grin. But his self-reliant pride, while full of bravado, seemed haunted by an undertone of melancholy.

The prison must have changed Faraj, too, I thought. "It must have been a horrible experience," I said. "It's amazing that you managed to survive."

Faraj stared out at the onrushing road. "Others had it worse," he said. "I was only beaten."

"Only?"

He brushed it aside. "The body heals," he said. "No bones were broken."

I continued looking at him, waiting for more.

He kept his eyes on the road. "I never had men beat me before. They used sticks, and metal pipe. I couldn't… I had no strength to fight them. I felt…" He seemed to be searching for the right word—the one he had managed to forget.

"Humiliated," I said.

"Yes. You feel…less than a man."

I thought of myself trembling in that airport toilet stall. And shaking beneath the blade of Arshan Azad. "I know what you mean," I said. "Sometimes it's like…there's just nothing you can do."

"My uncle would have done something," he said. "He would fight back. Not run away. Not from his country. Not from God."

"But your uncle ended up dying in prison, Faraj."

"My uncle died for what he believed. Now I live. For what? For *this*? For to sell the Turkmen rugs and fishes?"

I peered ahead at the tapering road and the brilliant orange ball at the end of it. "To see the sun rise another day," I said.

Faraj shook his head. "Is not enough. Not for me."

This attitude of his unsettled me. I mulled it over now as I sat inside the truck, watching him walk out into the desert. Surely his uncle would be pleased that Faraj had escaped from the clutches of his jailers. A life lived in freedom was a form of revenge—even if that life were lived in exile. Not everyone is obliged to die fighting for their liberty or defending their unauthorized God. He had acted sensibly by fleeing when he could. Why should he feel remorseful about it?

Faraj abruptly stopped walking and dropped down to his knees. He appeared to be clearing off a space in the sand. I climbed out of the truck and headed toward him.

He pressed his hands firmly palm-down on the ground. Then, as I approached, he sat back calmly on his heels and began methodically wiping down his head and face and arms, as if he were washing himself.

I came to a stop. He was performing, I realized, a formal rite of ablution, the Muslim's ritual cleansing. In Turkey, I'd seen Muslims do this wash routine in preparation for prayer, but never without water. Here, in the desert, Faraj was using sand. And sure enough, when he was through, he stood and held his palms up, the start of his midday prayer. I watched him kneel and bow forward, touching his head to the ground.

Feeling intrusive, I walked away, and after crossing a respectable distance beyond him, stopped at a scrubby bush and peed.

I'm relieving myself, I thought, only I don't feel relieved. Perhaps I, too, need some form of ablution. Some ritual to wash away this cruddy feeling I have. This feeling that—what? That I was "less than a man?" Wasn't that why Faraj's discontent had so bothered me? Because I, too, felt useless and cowardly?

A glistening silver tank truck rolled down the highway. I zipped up and watched it rumble by. It was the first vehicle I'd seen since awakening in the truck. Even though the highway offered the only passage south, it had been surprisingly devoid of traffic—emblematic, I supposed, of the desert nation's cruel economy. According to Faraj, Turkmenistan was awash in gas and oil, but the billions it brought in were squandered by the state, leaving half the population unemployed.

A rusting van with a ruined muffler came belching after the tanker, its roof stacked precariously with luggage. Faraj, oblivious, continued with his prayer. As the noise faded and the dust settled, I noticed something through the haze I hadn't seen before. Beyond the road, far off in the distance, a faint silhouette of blue-gray mountains hovered just over the horizon. These ghostly peaks had not been there when I'd fallen asleep in the truck, back in the salty lowlands of the Caspian. I remembered now Steinberg's ink-stained finger pointing them out on the map. This was the Kopet Dag range, the mountainous border with Iran.

How strange, I thought, to be standing within sight of the one country that wants to kill me.

An ugly groan, like a injured lion's, came howling over the desert. I turned around. The horizon seemed to stretch into infinity. Shielding my eyes, I detected in the distance a traveling herd of beasts.

Wild camels. No men anywhere near them.

I watched them tramp slowly through rippling waves of heat. Six of them, maybe seven. It was hard to tell if they were moving toward me or if they were moving away. I wished I had Faraj's binoculars.

Again the growl erupted. Then, out of the silence came the

whining hum of a car. I turned and followed its approach from the north. The car was moving fast.

It was black. A Mercedes. And aside from the darkly tinted glass, virtually a duplicate of the rental back in Rome.

42.
Diplomacy

I dropped to the ground, scrambling behind the scrawny bush into which I had just finished peeing. Was I being paranoid? Sometimes a black Mercedes is just a black Mercedes. Among Turkmenistan's oil apparatchiks, it was probably a popular car.

I peeked over at Faraj. Having finished his invocations, he was trudging back toward the truck. The Mercedes blew right past him in a billowing cloud of dust. I watched it fly away.

Sighing in relief, I started to my feet. But just as I did, the Mercedes slowed to a stop. I quickly dropped back down on my belly.

The car made a U-turn and rolled back toward Faraj. I swore under my breath. Had they spotted me? The Mercedes pulled off the road and stopped a short distance from the truck. Its opaque windows concealed the interior. I struggled to calm my nerves.

Faraj seemed to only half-notice the car as he leaned in the open window of his truck. After a moment, he pulled out the jug of drinking water and gulped down a generous swig.

The driver of the Mercedes climbed out of his car. Heavy-set and slow-moving, he wore dark slacks and a white dress shirt with the sleeves rolled up above his elbows. Even from a distance, peering through the thistle, I could see the man clearly had a beard.

Faraj very casually glanced in my direction, then took another sip from his jug.

A second man exited the passenger door and flicked a

cigarette into the sand. Though similarly bearded, he was wiry and small. He wore dark dress pants just like the big man, but without the white shirt, just a wife-beater tee. I recognized him as the guy who pursued us through the hospital back in Baku. These were the two Iranian thugs sent out to track me down.

Sar and Oriana had failed to stop them.

Faraj screwed on the bottle cap as he watched the men approach. My heart seemed to pound against the hot sand beneath me.

The men exchanged greetings, and the large man asked Faraj a question. In a calm voice, Faraj replied. The man asked another question, scanning the desert around them. I lowered my head. Although I could barely hear what he said and had no idea what language he spoke, the affable tone of his voice sounded fake.

While the two of them continued talking, the guy in the T-shirt wandered over by the truck. He peered in the passenger window.

I thought of Sar's duffel bag lying on the floor. All my stuff inside it. Had I left something out that would tell them I was here? I'd been studying Dan's notes in the *Rig Veda* text just before I'd fallen asleep on the road.

Faraj noticed the guy peering into the truck and addressed him sharply. The man gave a curt reply. Just then a car appeared on the road—an old, dust-coated Russian Volga packed to the brim with a family.

The three men watched it pass. Then the nosy guy wandered behind the truck, moving completely out of view.

Faraj walked back to check on him. The big man followed, gazing in through the driver's side window as he passed. Then Faraj disappeared, and all I could see was the broad back of the big man standing at the rear.

I wondered what they were doing. Asking Faraj to open the back to see if I was hiding inside? For all I knew, at that very moment, they might have a knife at his throat.

The cargo doors swung open. The big man closed in for a look. All I could see was his hand on the door. Then his hand moved off.

A minute passed. Then another.

What the hell were they doing?

I raised my head above the bush, straining for a view. Just then a hand reappeared on the door and slammed it loudly shut. I ducked back down to hide. All three men—to my relief—emerged and walked up front. Faraj chatted with the exuberant Iranian, who was tucking a package under his arm. I had helped load the packages in the truck before we left—each was filled with several tins of caviar.

The Iranian agents seemed pleased with themselves. I watched through the bramble as they walked back to their car. Faraj was watching them, too, and stole a worried glance toward me.

The men reached the Mercedes and opened up the doors. As the big man started to climb inside, he happened to look my way.

He froze.

I ducked. He said something to his partner and nodded directly toward me. I pinned my nose to the ground, heart suddenly racing. The man spoke to Faraj; I heard Faraj respond. I lay there breathing into the sand, trying not to move. Afraid to lift my head to see them, I now heard their footsteps crunching toward me.

It was too late to make a run for it. There was nowhere I could hide.

A shadow fell over me. I heard his rasping breath. Slowly, I looked up.

The camel lowered its snorting nose and sniffed where I had peed. It raised its ugly head and groaned. Then it moved on casually, as if I wasn't there. Another camel followed, as enormous as the first. Then another a few yards farther off. And another beyond that.

There were seven camels in all. Single-humped behemoths, with mats of molting fur, and long drooping necks like deflated old giraffes. They leisurely ambled across the road as if they owned the desert. Right past the Mercedes. The big Iranian made some crack, holding out a tin of caviar. The animals ignored him. The wiry agent laughed.

Then the men, chuckling happily, climbed back into their car. They U-turned in front of Faraj and sped off down the road.

I waited until the Mercedes vanished, then started back toward Faraj. The camels appeared to be heading toward the foothills of the Kopet Dag and the mountain streams that bled into the desert. From the south a large semi grinded its way toward us, and I paused a moment at the roadside until it thundered past.

Faraj seemed disturbed, even angered. I asked who the men were and what they wanted.

"Iranians," he said. "They told me they are diplomats. They are looking for their American friend, want to know if I have seen him."

"What made them think you would know? Why did they stop?"

He nodded toward his truck. "They say their friend crossed the Caspian on a boat with a cargo of fish. They say he would come down this highway. That is why they stopped."

"I don't understand," I said. Only a few people knew our plan—Steinberg, Sar, Oriana. "Who could have told them? Pashazadeh?"

"No, he hates the Iranians. Their patrol boats always stop his fishing, force him to pay a bribe."

"Maybe he was pressured into telling them," I said.

Faraj peered down the sun-drenched road. "I can't say. I know only one thing. These men are devils. You can feel it, in their eyes. I wanted only for them to leave. Before they find you here."

"Is that why you gave them the caviar?"

"Yes. But I did not give it. I said they must pay, and they offered me this." He drew a necklace out of his pocket. A choker made of jade.

I stared at it in sudden despair. "They got Oriana," I said.

43.
Call of Duty

Something must have happened on the ferry. Sar's plan had gone horribly wrong.

"Do you think your friends, they are both of them dead?" Faraj was at the wheel again, speeding toward Ashkhabad.

"I don't know," I said. I didn't want to think about what happened to them. If they hadn't been killed, it was likely they'd been tortured; neither would have willingly divulged our plan. "If they're still alive," I said, "they may be in the backseat of that Mercedes."

"I'll never catch up to them," Faraj said. "They're driving much too fast." The empty road ahead appeared to stretch into infinity.

"They must know the plan is to meet up at the dig—that's got to be where they're heading."

"To find their 'American friend?'"

"They know I left earlier. They must figure I'm already there."

"What will they do when they find you are not?"

"They'll assume they were lied to," I said.

The two of us silently considered what that meant. If Sar and Oriana were somehow still alive, it was likely they wouldn't be for long.

"We must hurry," Faraj said.

I looked at him, then back at the road, then back at him again. "You've already done enough, Faraj. You don't have to take me there."

"It is my choice," he said. "I know these kind of men. I have seen what they can do."

"Just take me as far as Ashkhabad. I can rent a car."

"Rent a car? You are not a Turkmen. This will take too much time."

He was right. "But…you don't even know these Israelis," I said.

"Do you? Know them?"I recalled Oriana's near-kiss on the plane—and the paralyzing zap she administered. "No. Not really. But Oriana has rescued me twice from these men. If she's still alive, I have to try to help her."

"Yes. It is your duty as a man. But how is it you will do this?"

How indeed. Even the thought of confronting the Assassins started my stomach churning. If they had outmaneuvered Sar and Oriana, they were sure to make mincemeat of me. "The market you're going to in Ashkhabad—they sell guns?"

"They sell everything. What kind of gun you want?"

I thought about the last time I had used one. It had been the first time, too. "The only thing I ever fired was a pistol," I said. "And that was a long time ago."

"Did you kill the man you shot?"

I glanced at him. "It wasn't a man," I said.

"You shot a *woman?"*

"No. It was… In Mexico. It's a long story, Faraj."

"So you did not shoot a man to kill him."

"No," I said. "But…I actually did kill somebody there. I just didn't kill her with a gun."

He grimaced. "You should use a gun, it's quicker." He reached down under his seat and like magic whipped out a pistol. "It's a Makarov," he said, offering it. "Semi-automatic. Russian-made."

I looked it over, impressed, then turned to him with a sudden thought. "When the men drove up, is this what you got from the truck?" All I had seen him pull out was the water jug.

Faraj grinned. "You never know what to expect. Three times I was robbed in the desert. First time, I have no gun. Thief takes all my caviar. Second time, Afghan border, two

Tajiks steal a prize Persian rug. With the Makarov, I shoot one, but still they drive away. Twelve-thousand Euro—poof! Then, a few months ago, I am sleeping at Murgab bridge. Four Turkmen try to rob my truck. But I chase them off...with this—" Faraj reached his arm back behind the seat and pulled out a short-barreled shotgun.

"Holy smokes," I said. The compact weapon looked nasty and efficient—a mechanical black barracuda.

He handed it to me. "Is Russian, too. Riot gun. Pump-action, ten-gauge. One shell takes down three men."

I looked over the barracuda and compared it to the semi-automatic. The prospect of actually using either weapon brought an anxious lump to my throat. "Sounds like you recommend the shotgun, then?"

He aimed his steady gaze at me. "I recommend we use both."

We stopped in the outskirts of Ashkhabad to fill up the truck with diesel. Faraj seemed to know the owner of the station and acted very friendly with him, but the Turkman's dour, pitted face revealed not a hint of emotion. As one of his young sons filled up the tank, the man escorted Faraj to his office in the back, and minutes later the two emerged having agreed to a deal on the sturgeon. The man would sell the cargo of fish and caviar at Ashkhabad's weekend bazaar, set to open the following day. Faraj would stop on his return trip to collect his take and a shipment of rugs.

Three boys began unloading the truck. Faraj removed his two guns and led me into the field behind the station for an impromptu shooting lesson.

When he offered me first choice of weapon, I opted at once for the pistol. The shotgun had a powerful recoil, he'd warned, and the buckshot a very wide spread. The gun I had shot in Mexico had been a rickety old revolver, and that had worked out all right. Faraj's newer semi-automatic Makarov pistol looked to be a lot more effective.

He detached the magazine, filled it with eight rounds, and

slid it back into the handle. Then he showed me how to pull back the slide to charge it, and explained that I could carry the thing with the hammer down and the safety engaged. All I had to do when the time came to shoot was release the safety lever, aim at the target's head or chest, and gently squeeze the trigger. The trigger would cock the hammer and fire.

I watched him take several shots, targeting a pop can thirty yards away. He hit it on the fourth shot, and handed the gun to me.

After taking some instruction in the proper stance—two hand grip, one foot forward, trunk leaning in, sight down the barrel—I took careful aim at a second pop can and gently pulled back on the trigger.

Miraculously, the can disappeared—a bull's eye on my first shot! But with three more bullets and another full magazine, I failed to ever hit the can again.

Faraj decided not to fire his Russian riot gun—he said he had only a half a dozen shells left, that he had hoped to buy more at the bazaar. Also, he was afraid the shotgun was too loud and someone might call out the police. Still he gave a cursory lesson in how to load it and shoot—"in case I go down," he explained.

In case I go down. Sleep with the fishes. A man's gotta do what a man's gotta do. Faraj had boasted of reading Shakespeare in college, but he clearly had picked up his hard-boiled English from watching old Hollywood movies.

I was heading into battle with Bogart.

44.
Three Deaths

In less than half an hour we were back on the highway, cruising southeast along the looming Kopet Dag. Though distant, the Iranian snow peaks looked threatening, a white-capped tsunami wave rising over the desert. We drove beneath them for an hour in silence. I kept eyeing my Makarov pistol and staring ahead at the road, fingering Oriana's necklace like a string of worry beads. What would we find at the dig site, I wondered, the last place Dan had been seen? If the Iranians had already arrived there, they may have discovered where he went. And what about Sar and Oriana—was it possible they could still be alive? If I had to, could I shoot the Iranians? How would I feel if I actually killed one?

Just past the town of Dushak, the highway bent northward, away from the Kopet Dag and deeper into the desert. The heat swelled and a wind sprang up, slinging swirls of dust. Soon great gusts jostled the truck, and sand streamed across the road in low, scudding waves. The highway's contour shifted and blurred. Distance shriveled into fumes.

Amid this mist we glided by a string of shrouded women, lethargically sweeping the asphalt. Grim sisters of Sisyphus, they eyed our passing like hooded ghouls, a road crew out of hell.

Faraj drove on, unfazed. He said a sandstorm was raging somewhere north, deep in the core of the desert. "The wind there can lift a dune," he said. "In the old days of the Silk Road, whole caravans were buried."

It was wonderful to have a student of history guiding my trip into Hades. "Pleasant thought," I said. I asked if his phone was still in range.

"Not out here," he said. He glanced at me with a grin. "Why—you want to call your mother?"

"No," I said. "I'll want *you* to call her. Let her know where it is I'm buried."

He laughed. "I'll make sure to mark the spot with a cross."

"Thanks, Faraj. She'll appreciate that. What do I put over you—the crescent?"

"Sure," he said, still smiling. "But you must wash my body first and wrap it in clean white cloth. Like a proper Muslim burial." He turned his grinning gaze back on the road.

We passed another shrouded woman standing aside with her broom.

Faraj's grin slowly faded. He reached into his pocket, pulled out his cell, and after thumbing several buttons, handed me the phone.

The display showed a single word, *Madaar*, along with its corresponding number. I looked at him.

"Her name is Naseem," he said. "She lives with my sister's family in Tehran."

I stared at him a moment, then again at the word: *Madaar*. "Okay," I said. Then I started adding another number to his phone. "Faraj?"

He turned to me.

"My *madaar's* name is Ruth."

Faraj gripped the scorpion knob and grinded the truck down a gear. I noticed a tawny powder covered the hairs on the back of his hand. Although we had rolled the windows tight, dust and grit seeped into the truck, settling on every surface. Even the inside of the windshield was grimy. I tried to clear the glass with my sleeve.

"We should have seen it by now," I said.

"Perhaps your map is wrong."

"This map is all we've got."

Following Maya's hand-drawn directions, we had taken a double-rutted road off the highway and careered across the desert for an hour. The scrub had begun to thin into dunes, and all signs of humanity had vanished. Air dark with dust dimmed the sun to a milky stain. On the ground, rippled drifts lay thick across the ruts, muffling the sound of our tires and obscuring long tracts of the road.

Choking on the dust, it felt as though we were slowly being smothered. Once again I took a look at Maya's crumpled map. She had drawn three rivers that intersected with the road, but we had yet to encounter the first of them. I was beginning to wonder if they actually existed. "How can there be so many rivers in a desert?"

Faraj was leaning forward over the wheel as he drove, straining to see through the dust storm. "The Murgab River is born high in the Hindu Kush," he said, "but it dies down here in the desert." He extended his arm and spread his fingers. "One birth, many deaths."

"I think the English word for that is 'delta,'" I said. "But I never would have thought of finding—"

The truck plunged. Faraj hit the brakes and grabbed hold of the shifter. We were dropping into a gully. I reached to brace myself against the dash as we rolled headlong down the slope.

"The first death!" Faraj cried.

The truck swam down the sand embankment. At the bottom, we lurched to a stop.

Faraj took the truck out of gear. The wind was calmer; you could hear the tappets rattling as the hot diesel idled. We were sitting on a dry riverbed of stones and gravel partly hidden under rippling waves of sand.

"There's no water," I said.

"Only in Spring. And this far out, for many years, I think there comes no water at all." He turned to me. "But at least now we know where we are on your map."

I nodded; it *was* a relief—though my stomach still felt tickled from the drop. "Only two more to go," I said. My eyes roved up the opposite embankment. "That is, if you can climb out of this one."

It took some skillful driving, but Faraj soon had us up the slope and once again rumbling down the ruts. Quarter of an hour later, we crossed the river's "second death," and shortly after that, rolled to the rim of the third. Undoubtedly, it was the deepest.

Gusts whirled up from the gully. The two of us peered down through the smeared windshield. At the bottom of the ravine, rusted to tatters and stripped of its wheels, sat a long-abandoned VW van. We could barely see across to the opposite embankment, but the drop down the near side looked steep.

Faraj hesitated.

"Forget it," I said.

"I can make it," he said.

He was channeling the Bogie of *African Queen*. "No way," I said. "We'll just get stuck down there. And there's really no reason to." I showed him Maya's map. "Once you cross here, it's only a short ride down to the site." The road ran along the opposite rim for barely half a mile. "We can easily walk it," I said.

Faraj took the map and studied it.

"If we're on foot," I added, "they won't hear us coming."

He gazed out into the swirling dust. "We take water, guns, ammo."

I held up his cell phone. "Shall we leave this here for the one who comes back?"

He took it, eyeing me as he slipped it into his pocket. "We are both coming back."

"*Insha'Allah,*" I said.

"Yes. *Insha'Allah.*"

45.
Black Coffin

It seemed quieter down below in the shelter of the ravine. Blown sand skittered over the dry riverbed, while above us, gusts howled off the scarp. Having found no tire tracks on the windswept ridge, we were searching the calmer ground in the gully. I slowly circled the VW van, a half-century-old relic of the Sixties. The dazzling psychedelic paintjob had long faded into pale pastels, but love beads still swayed from its rearview mirror, and its shattered windows danced with ragged tie-die. I imagined a stoned tribe of expat hippies set out on the Ultimate Trip, lighting across Asia toward the promised land of India, seeking the permanent high of nirvana. Their quest had ended badly. Instead of reaching enlightenment, they had stumbled down into the trap of this gulch and likely wandered off to die or been waylaid.

Just another casualty on the road to Shangri-la.

Faraj called to me. I found him standing a short way down the riverbed, examining a set of tread marks in the sand. The wind was gradually erasing them.

"You think it's the Mercedes?" I asked.

"They come from over there," he said, pointing with his shotgun toward the far wall of the canyon. "I think they drive in, but cannot climb out."

The road up the canyon wall looked formidable. A four-wheel-drive jeep or sand buggy might have scaled it, but not a street sedan, not even a Mercedes.

I peered ahead in the direction of the tracks. "Looks like

they decided to drive through the canyon. They're heading the same way as the ridge road on the map."

"We follow the car then," Faraj said. He trudged off down the riverbed without a second thought.

For some reason I hesitated, and for a moment I turned to gaze back at the van. Veiled in a fog of dust, the rotting shell of shattered dreams struck me as a kind of warning, a ghostly reminder of evils unforeseen. I reached for reassurance into the pocket of my coat and felt the cold metal of the Makarov. The hell with peace and love, I thought. I'm going to make it out of here alive.

I plowed ahead into the wind. Faraj was barely visible less than fifty yards ahead. He strode with the shotgun ready in his hands like a Fed going after a mobster. His need to stop these killers seemed even stronger than my own. What was it drove him on? Rage over his torture in the Kahrizak prison? These men were not employed by the regime back in Tehran. They were working for some lone-wolf Ayatollah.

Perhaps his inner demons simply needed a ready target, and these two cutthroats conveniently fit the bill. Whatever it was that drove him, I was glad he'd come along. His intensity helped to bolster my own courage.

Despite the blowing sand, the tire tracks in the riverbed were fairly easy to follow, even over wide swaths of gravel and stone. Faraj's footprints marked a steady beat between them, like notes for the drummer in a military march. While his fresh prints, I noticed, were fairly faint and shallow, the fading tire tracks had been quite deep. It occurred to me there might be more weight in the sedan than just the two men and a crate of caviar.

We had walked less than fifteen minutes when Faraj came to a stop. He waited for me to catch up. I squinted into the wind.

The black Mercedes hovered like a shadow in the dust.

"It's not moving," Faraj whispered.

We stared at it in silence for a full minute. If the engine was running, we couldn't hear it in the wind.

"You think they wait for the storm to end?"

"I don't know," I said. "Maybe they got stuck."

Faraj started forward. "Only way to know."

"Wait," I said, grabbing him. "We're too easy a target. You come from that angle, over there. I'll come from over this way. We'll both converge on the car."

Faraj eyed me curiously, then nodded his okay. He lifted his shotgun and pressed the bolt button in the trigger guard. "Take the safety off your Mak," he said. "If the men are inside, we must shoot them."

I peered through the wind at the hazy black mirage. "Just make sure it's them you're shooting." Grappling my pistol, I struggled to work the safety lever down off the slide into the fire position. Then I pulled back the slide to charge the gun. My hands were sweaty and trembling. When I saw Faraj had noticed, I tried to cover up. "Don't walk too far to the side," I told him. "We need to approach from a 45-degree angle, or we'll end up shooting cross-wise and likely kill each other."

He gave me another sideways glance. "You say you have not done this before?"

I shrugged. "Call of Duty," I said.

Faraj squinted. "The *video* game?"

"Bit of an addict in college."

Faraj grinned. I tried to grin back but couldn't, and after one more anxious look at the car, the two of us split up. I snuck across the gully to the left. Faraj disappeared to the right. When I reached the edge of the riverbed, I started moving slowly toward the car. The contours of its ebony form gradually emerged. I was approaching the left taillight; Faraj would be approaching the right. The tinted rear window looked black as the trunk, with a thin, dull film coating all of it.

Nothing moved.

I crept closer, both hands gripping the Mak out in front of me. The gun was shaking absurdly. I tried to remember to breathe. Lifting a shoulder, I wiped the sting of grit from my eye. Sprawling thistle bushes scraped my feet. I kept glued to the doors of the car.

Faraj had yet to appear. I paused for a moment to wait for him and guardedly observe the Mercedes. Its nose had nestled in a steep sloping dune, the base of the wall of the gully. In the wind I could hear no idling engine, nor detect any exhaust fumes. Indentations in the sand around the car appeared to be recent footprints. I moved slowly closer, straining to see where they led.

A thick gust suddenly swept past the car, and like an apparition, Faraj appeared, approaching the Mercedes with his shotgun. He glanced at me briefly but kept on walking. Right up to the passenger door.

I started to call out to him.

Faraj threw open the door, aiming his gun inside. I sighted down my pistol barrel, finger on the trigger.

Nothing.

No assassins. No shots. No screams.

Faraj looked over at me and shook his head, "no." I lowered my gun with a sigh of relief, and walked on over to the car. Faraj was looking in the passenger side. I opened the driver's door.

The interior reeked of cigarette smoke, the ashtray erupting with butts. I noticed two empty cans of caviar on the dash, and between the two seats, bread crumbs on a flattened paper bag, and three drained bottles of soda.

The back seats were empty.

Faraj picked a sheet of paper up off the floor. "Your map," he said, handing it over. It was the same as Maya's, but in a different hand, copied on a blank sheet ripped from Dan's sketchbook. Oriana had made it when she pilfered the original from my backpack on the plane from Istanbul.

Faraj opened the rear passenger door. A man's white dress shirt had been tossed onto the floor. Faraj held it up to me, grimacing in disgust.

I shuddered. The front and sleeves were covered with blood.

It belongs to the one in the T-shirt, I thought. The smoker. The laugher. The wiry little runt.

The only question now: Who had he killed?

I peered warily into the blowing mist around us, wondering if he was out there. Footprints mottled the sand at my feet; I tried to discern a direction.

"Jack?"

Faraj stood at the back of the car, staring down grimly at something in the sand. Pulse pounding, I moved toward him, stepping through the mishmash of prints. On the ground below the bumper, upside down with its spike pointed skyward, lay a woman's high-heeled shoe. I squatted down and gently extracted it from the sand.

Cherry red leather, little black bow. Sand grains caked to the blood on it.

I looked up at Faraj. "Pop the trunk," I said.

He walked around to the driver's door. I rose up slowly, unable to breathe, waiting for the coffin lid to open.

46.
Lock and Load

As I struggled up the slope behind Faraj, I fought head-spinning nausea and a recurring urge to vomit. My legs bowed and wobbled like a circus clown on stilts. Blowing sand whipped my face. The sky seemed to have vanished.

So much blood.

The horror flooded back and blinded me. I stumbled to my knees.

Get up, keep going. Forget about it now.

But I could not forget. Curled inside a plastic sheet like some aborted fetus, the naked, bloody, gutted corpse kept floating into view. Disappearing. Reappearing. A corpse inside my head.

Think of something else.

I looked up at Faraj. Climbing in a frenzy. He was using his shotgun like a walking stick, gripping the muzzle of the metal barrel and jamming the stock into the sand. With every step he took I thought he'd blow his fucking head off.

"Have you put your safety on?"

He didn't seem to hear. His dogged steps sent slow cascades spilling down over my boots.

Throat slit clear through the windpipe. Intestines spilling from the lacerated belly. Shocked eyes frozen in terror.

Think of something else.

Think of Oriana—she might be alive.

Her shoe, we had decided, must have gotten knocked off when they hauled her out of the trunk. Only her cashmere wrap remained, soaking in the blood of the cadaver. Her clothes must have been awash in it; she'd lain in there for hours. Down below in the gully they had finally pulled her out. I imagined her blinking into the daylight, trying to wake from the nightmare of being locked in the dark with Sar.

Had he been dead when they drove off the ferry? Or had he expired en route? Judging from the lake of blood in the trunk and the viciousness of his wounds, if he had been alive in there, he hadn't been for long. His body was blue and putrefying. Given the stench and the suffocating heat, I wondered how Oriana could have survived.

Why had they locked her in there with him? Pay-back for the killing of their colleague back in Baku, the hole she had blasted through his head? Or was it for the shame she'd brought on Vanitar Azad, dropping him into my vomit outside that airport bathroom stall? An Israeli, a *woman* yet, guarding a son of Satan and allied with the vile Mossad. The assassins must have despised her. Or more deeply, must have *feared* her. How else to explain the savagery of Sar's brutal murder, and the disgusting nightmare they had forced her to endure.

It was a wonder she was still alive. What were they keeping her for?

We had found her bare footprint in the sand beside theirs, along with the spiked impression of her one remaining heel. The tracks led down the riverbed to where the canyon wall could be scaled. The shoe had finally fallen off halfway to the top; Faraj stumbled across it in the sand. From that point her two bare feet led up the steep incline, between two sets of shoeprints from the Iranians. It appeared the men were helping her—or forcing her—to climb, in some places even dragging her up the slope.

After cresting the bluff, the tracks continued on, heading away from the gully. "They're looking for the road," I said. According to the map, it ran along the rim. We found it roughly twenty yards ahead. The shoeprints turned and continued along the ruts, Oriana's bare footprints between them. Sand streamed over the fading tracks and lifted into the wind; ahead, the road vanished into oblivion.

I glanced again at the map, trembling in my hand, and peered once more into the dust. But all I could see there was the cadaver's empty stare—gaping into the void, or out from it. My voice cracked with trepidation, "Should be just ahead."

Faraj did not respond. I realized he hadn't spoken since we'd left the open trunk. The corpse festered in his head, too, a head overcrowded with other corpses—his murdered father's, his uncle's, his friends'—and with memories of the torture he himself had endured. The accumulation of outrages left no room for fear.

He turned to me, his brown eyes blazing. "We will send them both to hell," he said. He started up the road.

I fell in alongside him. "We need to be careful, Faraj. Keep our heads. Think this through."

He looked at me, almost sneering, and trudged on into the wind.

Alert to any movement, any sign or sound of the men, my fear concocted mirages. Gusts spun ghostly figures toward us. Whispers caught my ear. Icy blades slipped round my throat, eliciting sudden chills. We plowed ahead through these intangible tortures, advancing step-by-step as in a trance, until at last, barely visible in the dust, the mirage of a giant, heaving, camel-colored creature transformed into a billowing canvas tent.

We stopped.

Men's gruff voices floated on the wind. Snatches, indistinct, hostile.

I blindly tucked away my map while peering at the misted shelter. Faraj turned to me slowly, raising a finger to his lips. Taking up his shotgun, he nodded down at my coat pocket. I reached in and pulled out the Makarov. Nervously I struggled again to release the safety latch, which seemed even more resistant than before. Grit may have gummed the mechanism; my trembling fingers couldn't budge it. But finally the latch grinded into place, and I nodded to Faraj that I was ready.

He gestured off to the left of the road, indicating that I should approach from that side, that he would approach from the other, just as we had done with the Mercedes. I nodded agreement and moved off cautiously. Faraj faded off to the right.

Sand swept over the ground before me, veiling scrub and stone. With no more footprints or tire ruts to follow, I kept my eyes glued to the tent. It seemed to be stitched from sand and sky and given its form from the wind. When I'd wandered far enough to the side and started closing in toward it, the structure materialized out of the dust: a sagging sort of military field tent. Restrained by ropes and propped with poles, the canvas swelled and flapped in the gale like a pinned and prodded pterodactyl.

Scraps of voices fluttered by, louder, but still indistinct. It was hard to tell where they were coming from—inside the tent or behind it, or perhaps from somewhere else entirely. As I listened intently, drawing gradually closer, searching for a door or an opening in the tent, I suddenly stumbled to the ground.

My pistol went into the sand. I pulled it out and shook it off, then blew sharply at the hammer and the slide, trying to clear out the grit. The last thing I needed was the mechanism to jam.

I stood up—and was startled to discover that I'd tripped over a corpse.

47.
The Shot

The body belonged to a man, a policeman from the looks of it: his uniform had epaulets and a shield pinned to the pocket. His clothes and face were covered with a concealing film of sand; it dusted his open eyelashes and dulled each cornea's sheen. The pistol in his holster had never been unstrapped—the fellow had been taken by surprise. I figured he hadn't been there long, but I had no doubt he was dead. Blood still trickled from the gash across his throat. Like Sar, it had filled up his windpipe.

A painful cry tore through the wind. I spun around to the tent.

The canvas idly fluttered and snapped. Where, I wondered, was Faraj?

I crept up to the wall of the tent and paused a moment to listen. No sound emerged. I peered around the corner. Faraj was nowhere in sight, but the door of the tent hung partly open. I edged slowly toward it and peeped inside, holding my Mak at the ready.

A chicken drumstick on a sheet of newspaper lay half-eaten on a bench. A tripod stool beside it stood empty. Beneath the stool, a coffee mug lay on its side, its contents soaking the tarpaulin floor.

I listened, but still heard nothing. Sucking in an anxious breath, I peeled back the door flap.

A pair of trousers lay neatly folded on a sleeping cot in a corner, a duffel bag stuffed beneath it, along with stacks of books. At the back wall, several wooden crates surrounded a long, foldable table. On it rested a kerosene lamp, a blue enamel coffee pot over a canned-fuel cooker, and a steel-cased laptop, folded shut. Fragments of encrusted pottery and artifacts littered the rest of the tabletop, with various archeological tools scattered in among them—calipers, paint brushes, a trowel, dental picks. A collapsible director's chair had toppled to the ground, and several plastic-coated geological maps littered the floor around it, along with a floppy canvas hat and a smashed pair of aviator sunglasses.

There was no one inside the tent. The cry had come from outside.

I released the door flap and continued around the perimeter, past a water drum on a stand. A Land Rover sat parked nearby, thickly coated with dust. Beyond it, not too far off, I discerned what looked like a long, dark wall.

Faraj was nowhere to be seen.

The voices seemed to be coming from some place beyond the wall. I moved cautiously toward it. A single English word sailed over on the wind, a question delivered as a command: *"Understand?"*

Shifting the pistol to my left hand, I wiped the sweat from the palm of my right. Thoughts and second-thoughts bombarded my febrile brain. My heart pounded uncontrollably. I tried to focus by concentrating on how I would shoot the gun: two hand grip, one foot forward, trunk leaning in, sight down the barrel.

Aim for the head or chest, he'd said. Gently squeeze the trigger.

The wall turned out to be a wind-screen fence—green vinyl mesh stretched to block blowing sand. The mesh shivered and whistled in the gale. A deep drift had banked up against it. I crouched low and crawled to the rim. Raising my gaze above the blowing embankment, I peered through the weave of the mesh.

The gauzy view revealed a gaping excavation, like the pit for a swimming pool or the foundation for a house. At the bottom of the pit, beside the remains of a mud-brick wall, an empty wheelbarrow, and the ancient foundation of some circular structure, several figures clustered together. I pressed my face against the mesh to get a clearer view.

A man on his knees—burly, beardless, hands tied behind his back—was watching Oriana and the two Iranians. Oriana was kneeling between the two, wrists bound behind her, head hanging down, hair nearly touching the ground. At her back stood the hulking assassin, his sleeves rolled up above massive forearms, while in front of her the runt in the Dago-T gazed down on her, talking softly.

A fury rose inside me, tangled with dread and doubt. I feared if I tried to shoot the assassins I might miss them and kill Oriana.

The runt reached out with a crescent dagger and lifted her face to look at him. The man on his knees cried, "Leave her!"

The runt shouted something back at him. Again he spoke softly to Oriana. I strained to hear what he said.

Out of nowhere, Faraj suddenly plopped down beside me. Startled, I turned my gun on him. He opened his hand and urgently whispered, *"Give it to me."*

"What?"

"Your pistol. My shells spread wide—they're too close to her. I'm going down—"

Oriana groaned.

We peered through the fence. The big man had grabbed her hair and hauled back her head, exposing her throat to the guy with the knife.

"She said she told you all she know!" The protest came again from the kneeling man, whom I assumed was the site's archaeologist. The runt turned abruptly, and with a backhanded slap, nearly knocked the man to the ground.

Faraj yanked the Mak from me and thrust his shotgun into my arms. *"Stay here,"* he whispered. *"Second they clear, shoot them."*

I took his gun. *"But how—?"*

Faraj was gone, running crouched along the berm, heading to the other end of the pit where an earthen ramp led down below.

I looked at the Russian riot gun, trying to remember how to cock it and fire. Pump-action—push and pull. Three extra shells. Fourth in the barrel, ready to—

Oriana howled in agony. I peered down through the mesh. The runt had opened the top of her blouse and was carving bright lines on her chest.

The archaeologist hollered, "Stop!" and struggled to his feet. The runt turned and swiftly booted him.

Faraj had disappeared into the dust. I scrambled along the fence line to find some kind of break in the windscreen. A short ways down, a joint between panels left a narrow vertical slot. I crept to the top of the sand drift, eased the gun barrel through the slot, and peered down into the pit.

They were closer now, less than twenty yards away, yet still unaware that I was watching them. In fact the two men were so absorbed in their torture they didn't notice Faraj at first. He boldly marched down the earthen ramp with the pistol held out in front of him. At last the big lug saw him and called to the runt, who whirled around to face him with his dagger.

Faraj aimed and fired but the runt dove aside. The shot grazed the shoulder of the big guy. Clutching the wound, he released Oriana. She collapsed in a heap on the ground.

Faraj kept shooting but the pistol failed to fire. Again and again he clicked the trigger. Finally, he gawked at the useless weapon, and in frustration flung it at the runt.

Dodging it, the man started toward him, leading with his long, curving dagger. The big guy—bleeding, furious—followed him. Faraj started backing away.

Pulse racing, I rose up on my knees at the top of the drift and aimed through the slot in the windscreen. The assassins were too close to Oriana. I tracked them in the rifle's V-notch, my finger tight on the trigger, ready to fire the moment they were clear. But suddenly the archaeologist rose up from his knees and launched himself at the men. Barreling into their ankles, he toppled them both to the ground.

Faraj, emboldened, grabbed a spade from beside the wheelbarrow and charged at the fallen men. But before he reached them, the runt took a swipe at the archaeologist, slashing across his thigh. The man crumpled.

Faraj attacked the wiry Iranian, swinging the shovel at his head. Even in the wind I could hear the metallic *thwack*. The runt staggered. His nose ran red.

Faraj turned as the big Iranian stormed toward him. Again Faraj swung the spade, but the giant easily blocked his strike and grabbed the shovel away. Then he tossed the thing aside and drew out his knife, another gleaming Damascene blade.

The runt stepped up beside him, his face now streaming blood. The two Iranians started toward Faraj.

Faraj, backing away, turned tail and ran up the ramp. The men charged after him. Faraj hollered, "Jack!"

Up on my knees on the rim of the drift, arms now tight and trembling, I struggled to center the V-notch on the two men crossing the pit. The barrel pivoted, following them. *Aim for the head or*—suddenly the mesh obscured my view. I frantically squeezed the trigger.

The shell exploded and the recoil knocked me back.

I tumbled backwards down the drift. The shotgun fell from my hands. For a moment I lay at the bottom, stunned and disoriented, completely unable to hear. Then the sound of the wind came howling back—and in it, the moan of a man.

48.
God is Great

The giant lay sprawled against the mud brick wall, the side of his head riddled with buckshot, a shoulder and sleeve of his shirt bright red. Even at a distance, bounding down the ramp, I could tell at a glance he was dead.

The moaning had come from the runt. He lay bleeding in the sand nearby, reaching out feebly toward his knife. I stopped in front of it and pointed the shotgun at him. Up close, with his body stretched out, he no longer looked so small. As he raised his bloody face, the exhilaration I'd been feeling until then turned all at once into horror. His right eyeball had been obliterated and the skin of his cheek was gone.

"Leave it," I said, more a plea than a demand.

He continued groping toward the blade. I wondered how much buckshot had lodged in his brain, or if the problem was he simply couldn't hear me—the flesh of one ear had been destroyed. I called to Faraj, "This one's still alive."

Faraj had taken the other Iranian's knife and cut free the bound archaeologist. The man, bleeding from the knife wound to his thigh, now helped Faraj cut loose Oriana's ties and lift her gently back onto her feet.

I aimed again at the Iranian, still groveling in the sand. There was something fascinating in his stubborn refusal to die. A defiance, a willfulness, a curious lack of fear. I would have expected him to plead for mercy; instead he strained to reach his weapon, ignoring the gaze of my gun.

The others slowly made their way toward us. The wind

moaned high above, but an eerie silence pervaded the pit. The remains of the wall that had been uncovered looked as old as the Earth itself. Beyond it, the circle of ancient foundation stones gave off a numinous aura. Strange place to kill a man, I thought. In the sanctum of some lost civilization.

Faraj and the burly, limping archaeologist silently stepped up beside me. Oriana, unrecognizable, hung limply draped between them. The runt had carved a Star of David into the flesh of her chest. Haggard, hair wild, blouse drenched in blood, only her eyes seemed to show any life as she stared down upon her torturer.

The man's fingers curled around the handle of his dagger. As he dragged the weapon toward him, he seemed to come alive. We watched him slowly struggle to his knees and lift up his good eye to glare at us. The eye held a moment on his victim, Oriana, then drifted across and settled on me.

The runt seemed to recognize my face. I gulped, and leveled the shotgun at him. He noticed the barrel was shaking, and a smile creased his remaining cheek.

My finger tightened on the trigger.

He slowly lifted the blood-edged dagger. *"Allahu Akbar—"* he croaked, then toppled face-down in the sand, dead.

While bandaging her knife wounds in the shelter of the tent, we discovered Oriana had a serious gash, on her left side beneath the bottom rib. The assassins, back in Baku, had ambushed her and her cousin before they had even boarded the ferry. Someone—probably Pashazadeh—had tipped the Iranians off. They knew Sar was an imposter, and they tried to force him to reveal where I was headed. When he refused, they began to disembowel him—alive—in front of her. "I had to tell them everything," Oriana said. Still it didn't stop them from cutting Sar's throat and stuffing the two Israelis into the trunk. "They wanted to make sure I am telling the truth. When they see you are not here, they say that I am lying."

I told her how, at the camel crossing, they had come very close to finding me.

"I don't remember the car ever stopping," she said. She had been unconscious, apparently, for most of the ride, and had lost a lot of blood. Even now she verged on delirium.

"I'm afraid of infection," the archaeologist said, gently cleaning her puncture wound with an antiseptic solution. His name was Vladimir Karakov. "I don't want to close it. We must get you to a hospital."

"And you as well," Faraj said, nodding toward the burly Russian's bloody pant leg, where he'd hastily wrapped a strip of cloth around his wounded thigh.

"We leave when the storm pass," Karakov said, gazing up at the ceiling. The wind, thrashing the canvas, had reached a fevered pitch. Darkness had fallen, and the lantern's flickering light revealed a thick swirl of dust. Squatting on the stool beside Oriana's cot, Karakov pawed through his medical kit. Given his boldness in battle, I'd expected a much younger man; Karakov looked to be in his fifties. He pulled out several bandages and a fat roll of gauze, and threw a quick glance up at me. "You are Duran's brother, yes? The one they were looking for?"

"I'm sorry to have caused you so much trouble," I said.

"No, no," he said. "You save my life. This woman's, too, I'm sure." Pinching closed her puncture wound, he applied the first of the butterfly bandages.

Far from believing I had saved their lives, I knew it was I who had endangered them. If I'd followed the advice of Dr. Fiore back in Rome, I'd have been home safe in the States by now and none of these killings would have happened.

The road to hell, as they say. It had led me to nothing but guilt.

"Outside, the man they killed, was he with the police?"

Karakov nodded. "The authorities sent him out to guard this site, after the seeds were stolen."

"You mean…they thought you might find more?"

"I told them it is unlikely. I am more than thirty years digging in the Karakum. This is the only oasis site we find the lotus seeds. But many believe—or want to believe—more seeds might be found. And not just the Iranians. The last thugs to visit us were Taliban."

"Afghans? Here?"

"We are not far from the border. They control the poppy trade and the smuggling routes up into Russia. It didn't take long before they hear the rumors."

"What rumors?" I asked.

"Please, we must lift her," Karakov said. Faraj and I assisted him in sitting Oriana up on the cot. I held her shoulders as the Russian wrapped the gauze around her abdomen, covering the bandaged wound. Oriana seemed to be drifting in and out of consciousness. Still she managed to mumble "*Spasiba*," the Russian word for thanks.

"Eyn davar," Karakov replied.

"You speak Hebrew," she said.

"I attended your field school at Hazor," he said, then glanced up at me. "And for six years I teach American students—at the Cotsen Institute of Archaeology, UCLA."

He finished the wrapping, and we laid her back down on the cot. "Allow her to rest," he said. Handing me the lantern, he carried the stool across the floor and set it down near the table. Faraj brought him the medical kit, and the Russian went to work on his leg. With a scissors he cut the pant leg off just above the knife wound. Then he unwrapped the cloth around it, and for the first time I saw his cut.

It sent a cold shiver through me. The top layer of his thigh muscle had been neatly severed.

Karakov gestured to a nearby crate. "There, please, the Imperia." Faraj peered inside the crate and pulled out a crystalline bottle, its label in Cyrillic script. "I apologize," Karakov said. "But I have only two glasses." From the crate, Faraj retrieved a plastic drinking cup and a shot glass with the image of a monkey in a fez. He poured a jigger of vodka into each, then handed the shot to Karakov and the plastic cup to me.

"*Za Vas!*" the Russian growled, and tossed the contents down his throat.

I took a searing sip from mine and offered the cup to Faraj. He waved it aside. Karakov thrust out his empty glass and

Faraj carefully refilled it. Again the Russian slammed down the jigger. I took another sip.

"My razor," Karakov said. "Over there, by the basin."

I retrieved it, along with a can of Gillette shaving cream. "You mentioned rumors," I said.

Karakov set about shaving off the leg hair around his wound. "On the Asian plains, rumors spread like the wind. It has always been so. Men crave what they do not have, and everything on the known earth has passed along this way. That craving built the Silk Road."

I glanced over the table. "Is that what you've uncovered here? Relics of the Silk Road?"

"I've been digging at oasis sites for decades in this desert. But the fire temple we uncovered here came long before the silk routes. It was built by the Indo-Iranian people, better known as the Aryans."

Faraj said, "These are the people gave my country its name!"

"Yes," Karkakov said. "'Iran' comes from *Aryana:* 'Land of the Aryans—the Noble Ones.'"

I asked if they were the people who made the sacred drink from the lotus.

Karakov dragged the razor along the tender edge of his wound. "The Aryans were horse-herding nomads and warriors, the inventors of the chariot, who poured down out of the Eurasian steppe in the second millennium B.C. One wave swept over the Hindu Kush into the Indus Valley of India. They brought with them the beginnings of Vedic religion and the ritual drink called soma. Another wave descended on the Iranian plateau, bringing with them a similar polytheistic religion that included a drink called haoma. It's believed that both soma and haoma were derived from the same source, a plant whose identity has been lost to the mists of time."

"Until now," I said.

"We found the seeds buried in a sealed pot, underneath remnants of the fire altar."

"What made you think they were from the soma plant?" I asked.

"The things buried with them. A ritual pestle and mortar. Straining bowls and ceramic stands for processing a liquid. And cult vessels and bone tubes for drinking the libation."

Karakov doused his now shaven wound with the antiseptic solution. Faraj poured him another vodka, and the Russian continued his story. He said a lab at the University of Zurich determined the seeds were from an extinct species of lotus, and carbon-dated them to around 1500 B.C. Inquiries immediately poured into Karakov's office at the History Museum in Mari, and scientists from around the world came to visit the dig site and examine the seeds for themselves.

One was the noted paleoethnobotanist Daniel J. Duran.

"I felt honored to meet him," Karakov said. "He was the American professor who had discovered *kykeon*, the legendary elixir of ancient Greece, the secret of the Eleusinian Mysteries. He was coming, I assumed, to honor another legend, one that stretched back even deeper into the past."

But what Dan brought with him shocked the Russian to his core: *identical lotus seeds of his own.*

"I was astonished," Karakov said. "And highly skeptical. Unlike the ancient seeds found buried here, your brother's were fresh and viable—recently plucked from a living plant."

Dan was intent on confirming that his seeds were the same species as Karakov's. But before sending them off to the laboratory in Zurich, he insisted the seeds be sterilized. "He wanted to make certain they couldn't be used for propagation."

Ten days later, they received the results. The laboratory tests proved a positive match.

"It left no doubt," Karakov said. "The ancient soma lotus, lost for several thousand years, had not only been identified, it was alive and propagating somewhere on the planet. The question, of course, was where."

Dan refused to say; he feared the precious lotus plant would fall into the wrong hands. And sure enough, the following night, two Iranians showed up at Karakov's apartment, asking where Dan was, where he kept the plants, and threatening the Russian's life. But before the men could reach him, Dan managed to slip away, taking with him every last seed.

Though relieved that his American guest had escaped, Karakov clearly resented the fact that Dan had made off with his find. "I can understand why he took his own seeds," he said, "but he had no reason to take mine. I felt betrayed."

"Do you have any idea where he went?" I asked.

Karakov unfolded a packet from his medical kit. I noticed what looked like threads of dental floss. Then I saw they were attached to curved needles and realized they were stitches.

He downed another shot of vodka. "Did your brother ever mention a professor named Borzoo Baghestani?"

It wasn't the sort of name one would easily forget. I shook my head, no.

"He teaches archaeology at the University of Bukhara. Your brother told us that on his way here he paid the professor a visit. I have met Baghestani on several occasions. Interesting man, but I don't know him well. He has always seemed…a little reticent with me. He's Iranian, and in the past he has worked for the government in Tehran. I suspect that may be how they found out about your brother."

"Have you tried to contact him?"

"We leave many phone messages, but have not heard back. For now, he is our only link to finding your brother—and where he has taken our seeds. My colleague left here yesterday to look for him.

"How far is Bukhara?" I asked.

"Couple hundred miles to the northeast," Faraj said. "Across the border, in Uzbekistan."

"Have you heard back from your colleague?" I asked.

Karakov was carefully unpacking the kit: needles, sutures, scissors, clamps. The vodka seemed to be slowing him down. "She was supposed to call me last night. I tried to reach her this morning, before I left Mari. No answer. The guard tried her on his satellite phone. He couldn't get through." The Russian picked up a curved suture needle and contemplated the pointy crescent. I noticed both fear and a kind of wistfulness in his eyes, and realized it had been there all along. "I am worried," he said, a bit groggily. "This woman…I have grown quite fond of her, you see. She has worked at my side now for…over a year. It was she who convinced me to pursue this excavation."

I stared dumbstruck at Karakov as a realization came over me. "Is she the one who contacted my brother?"

He nodded despondently. "She told me they used to be friends."

Faraj noticed the look on my face. "What is wrong?"

"I know this woman," I said. "I used to be friends with her, too."

49.
Cipher

In the dream, as always, Phoebe sits on the grass under the giant oak at Dodona, looking exactly the same as she did that very last time I saw her. Her porcelain skin seems to glow in the shade. Her blonde bob ruffles in the breeze. Try as I might to read her thoughts, her face remains inscrutable, her cool eyes fixed on nothing. Gone is the ice-blue sapphire sparkle, the curl of a grin at the corner of her mouth, the peals of easy laughter and the quick-minded chatter, the teasing and flirtation that had captured me. She's been spirited away by the light-fingered wind, and all that remains before me is this stony-eyed veneer, this cold marble statue Aphrodite.

I didn't know it at the time, but Phoebe had already decided to leave me, well before that hour beneath the tree. At some point she had glimpsed, through my cavalier façade, the emptiness I'd hidden away, even from myself. She had seen the void of doubt, the lack of aspiration, the dilettante's desultory interest in art, the pathetic uselessness of my very minor talents. What, after all, did I really have to offer? A room in a broken down apartment house in Rome? A rich man's taste and a poor loser's pocketbook? The peripatetic life of a vagabond? A man needs something more than a cynic's sense of humor. I had found no real meaning, no purpose to pursue, no great passion or loyalty to sustain me. And indeed, I could barely make a living on my own. My very occupation was illegal. There was little I believed in, less that I could love, and nothing I could bring myself to fight for. Not even this comely Dutch girl who had made off with my heart. I had turned my sprightly Phoebe into stone.

Just as in Dodona, the wind woke me up. The tent canvas rippled like a battered battle flag, and the kerosene lamp threw wobbling shadows. I had fallen asleep on the floor beside the cot. Oriana was still out of it, and Faraj was snoozing soundly beside the drunken, snoring Russian, who had promptly keeled over after stitching up his leg.

I got up and searched for the gallon water jug, stepping over Karakov's upturned belly. The omnipresent dust had left my mouth and throat encrusted. I poured a half cup of water and drank.

It occurred to me the dryness may have triggered my stony dream, conjuring up Phoebe like a sphinx out of the sand. The riddle she posited troubled me. How had she managed to contact Dan? And how did she know the lotus seeds were likely to be found here?

The answer to both seemed suddenly obvious: *It must have been Dan who had contacted her.*

I took another sip of the lukewarm water. A story began to fall into place. My paleoethnobotanist brother had somehow figured that soma seeds were likely buried here. He got word to Phoebe, who would have been intrigued. As would any archaeologist—including the Russian expert she recruited to unearth them. Once the ancient seeds were found, Dan showed up to see if they matched the fresh seeds he'd discovered.

They did. He had proved his living lotus plant was the same as the ancient soma.

And now Phoebe had gone after him.

Gazing down at Karakov snoring on the floor, I realized the old Russian bear had fallen in love with her, too. Hell, it probably happened to every man she ever met. Even that old crackpot on Ogygia had been smitten.

I felt again that awful pang I hadn't felt since Athens. "Jealousy is a form of fear," Professor Auerbach would have told me. Fear of not having the thing you desire. While I had been pining away in Rome, Dan had been busy luring her back. How many times, I wondered, had the two of them gotten together? He'd just now spent nearly two weeks with her—long days and nights in the desert. Undoubtedly, she still had feelings for him. And Dan surely never stopped wanting her. I wondered if he'd renewed his marriage proposal. And if Phoebe had finally broken down and slept with him.

For a moment I just stood there, trying to summon the will to scrape my heart up off the floor. As I gazed unthinking over the pottery shards on the table, my eyes came to rest on a single artifact, an object both odd and familiar. It appeared to be made of bronze, like the shapely axe head beside it, but looked neither functional enough for a tool nor deadly enough for a weapon. On each end of its cylindrical handle, four pointed prongs sprang outward. They might have been eagle talons, or pointed, leaping flames.

I gauged its weight in my hand. Though it was larger and more crudely made, the basic design looked strikingly similar to the object I'd discovered in Maya's suitcase. I felt certain the two items were related.

Excited, I woke up Karkakov. Snorting and grunting, he came back to life, in the process waking Faraj. The two of them sat up, saucer-eyed.

I held out the artifact to Karakov. "Tell me what this is."

50.
Vajra

"A Vajra," he said. "That's the second recovered at this site. The first was what brought me here and got this whole thing started." He straightened his sutured leg and winced. "Could somebody please make some coffee?" He gestured toward a tin on the table, and Faraj set to work.

I helped the archaeologist up onto the stool. "I thought you said it was Phoebe convinced you to excavate this site."

"Phoebe had heard about the Vajra that was found here, uncovered after a flooding of the Murgab. I was digging in the foothills of the Kopet Dag at the time. She persuaded me that excavating here might be better rewarded."

"Why? What's a Vajra?"

"'Vajra' is a Sanskrit word meaning 'diamond thunderbolt.' The thunderbolt was the weapon of Indra, the great lord of heaven and the god of storms and war. For the ancient Aryans, the Vajra symbolized his power and strength—like the lightning hammer of the Norse god, Thor, or the thunderbolt of Zeus."

Faraj struck a match. We watched him light the canned fuel cooker under the coffee pot.

I picked up the decayed, verdigris thunderbolt. "What's it have to do with the soma lotus seeds?"

"It was the clue to finding them," he said. "The Vajra belongs to Indra, and Indra is described in the Rig Veda hymns as the foremost imbiber of soma. The divine drink invigorates and strengthens him. It allows him to rise above his fear and perform heroic action."

I thought back to something he'd said earlier. "That's what you meant, isn't it—about rumors and the Taliban? They think this legend is true—that soma will instill them with courage."

"The Taliban control the drug trade. They'll capitalize on whatever they can sell to fund their war, and kill whoever gets in their way. It's the Iranian obsession that I don't understand."

"But you said yourself: a tribe of the Aryans split off into Iran. It's a part of their Persian heritage."

"Believe me, the Ayatollahs of the Islamic Republic of Iran do not care a fig about their heretic ancestors."

"It's true," Faraj said. "The clerics discourage it. The Aryans have nothing to do with Islam. The religion of Mohammed comes out of Arabia—more than two thousand years later."

I looked to Karakov. "But didn't you say that archaeology professor worked for the Iranians?"

"Professor Baghestani is one of the few archaeologists the Islamic government in Tehran has ever hired—and that was for research into the history of Islam. Even that, they never allowed him to publish!"

"I want to talk to this professor," I said. "But tell me something. An Indian woman I met in Rome was killed while trying to track down the lotus. I found a thing in her suitcase that looked an awful lot like this Vajra. It's in my bag, back in the truck. Like this one, it's made of bronze, but the spikes at each end are curved inward, forming spheres."

Karakov stared at me. "This woman who was killed, what was her name?"

"Maya Ramanujan."

The Russian fell silent. He seemed to be assembling some puzzle in his head.

"You knew her?" I asked.

"She came here after the seeds were stolen. She worked for the Indian intelligence service."

"Yes! She also had Dan's sketchbook and his copy of the *Rig Veda* hymns."

"I know," he said. "Your brother fled in the middle of the

night when he found out the Iranians were searching for him. He left his pack in Phoebe's apartment. Inside we found the books and this Vajra you describe. We turned them over to Miss Ramanujan. She thought they might be helpful in trying to track him down."

"I see." But they obviously hadn't helped, I thought, or Maya wouldn't have bothered to seek me out in Rome. Still, given her desperate effort to guide me back to her suitcase, she must have hoped that I might finally make sense of them.

"Why does Dan's Vajra look different?" I asked.

"It is a much later version," Karakov said. "The Vajra described in the ancient *Rig Veda* is a notched battle club with a thousand prongs. By the time it passed down through the Vedic religion to the Hindus, and finally, the Buddhists, the weapon fundamentally transformed. Your brother's Vajra is a ritual instrument used by Tibetan monks. They say the Buddha bent its lethal prongs together into a peaceful sphere, turning Indra's weapon inward toward the conquest of oneself."

Faraj interrupted to say the coffee was ready. Karakov untwisted a thermos, and Faraj filled it with the steaming brew.

The Russian's account of the Buddhist Vajra reminded me of the chariot wheel, another creation of the war-making Aryans. According to Dr. Fiore, that wheel, too, became a sacred symbol of Buddhism, now peacefully residing at the heart of the Indian flag.

I asked Karakov if Dan had talked about the Vajra.

"Yes, of course. Your brother has a theory. But then he seems to have a theory about everything, does he not?"

Once again, the ire at losing Phoebe and the seeds. "What can I say? He's a know-it-all. Very irritating."

"He contends the spheres of the Buddhist Vajra represent the buds of the soma lotus. The unopened buds symbolize the un-awakened mind. To blossom, they need light. He believes the soma elixir really is a kind of thunderbolt—a lightning flash that illuminates the void and offers a glimpse of enlightenment."

Chemical nirvana? A drug-induced awakening? "I thought Buddhists frowned on the use of intoxicants."

"So do the Islamists," he said.

"Then his theory doesn't make any sense." Nor did it jive with the bellicose bluster I'd read in the Rig Veda text—*conqueror of thousands, irresistible in battle, attacking, slaying his foes.* These were not the mellow musings of a sage but the rallying cries of a warrior. "Soma must be some sort of stimulant," I said. "That is, if it's anything at all."

"Yes, if it is anything—" Karakov filled his thermos cup, eyeing the rich black blend—"it may be no more than this." He offered the thermos to Faraj. "The wine of Islam."

Faraj smiled and poured himself a cup. "It's true—Sufis were the first to brew coffee. Fifteenth century, in the monasteries of Yemen. They used it to keep awake in nighttime devotions. They called it 'the reviver from the sleep of heedlessness.'" Faraj's eyelids fell as he delicately sipped, savoring the flavor and aroma. "They say when you imbibe with prayerful intent, the drink becomes a bridge to paradise, a gateway to the hidden mysteries, to the great revelations, to the bliss and power of the Divine Presence."

"Wow," I said. "Monks jacked-up on Arabian Roast—who'd of thunk it?"

Faraj lowered the cup and grinned. "To be honest, doesn't do it for me. I drink to stay awake on the road."

I laughed and turned to Karakov. "Maybe the Islamists aren't such teetotalers after all. The Iranians certainly seem to believe the soma legend is true. There's got to be something to it."

Karakov shrugged. "Without access to the living plants, we have no way to find out."

"Did you try to sprout your seeds?"

"Your brother took them before we could. But I'm sure it doesn't matter. The oldest lotus seed ever germinated was found in a dry lake bed in China. It was some 1200 years old. The plant that grew from it didn't live long and it failed to reproduce. The soma seeds we found here in the desert are more than 2000 years *older* than the one found in China. It is extremely unlikely they are viable."

"Apparently Dan thought different," I said. "That's why he

stole your seeds."

Karakov bitterly sipped his coffee. "His fear distorts his reason."

I wondered if this were true. Dan surely knew more than we did. And after everything I'd just seen, paranoia made perfect sense.

"She's awake," Faraj said.

We turned to see him crouching at Oriana's side. He offered her a sip of water, holding the cup to her mouth. She managed to swallow, but it triggered a cough, and half a minute passed before she could speak.

"We must…leave here," she uttered.

"She's right," I said. "They'll be coming for us." Having not heard back from the two dead assassins, more would be sent out to find them. Vanitar Azad was very likely on his way. His brother and three of his cohorts had been killed; their commander would be in a rage.

Karakov eyed the ceiling of the tent, now brighter and ruffling lazily. "The storm has passed. The sun is coming up." I offered him a hand as he struggled up from the stool. "We must report what has happened to the police," he declared. "But first we need to take her to the hospital in Mari."

"No," Oriana said. "They will look for us there."

"We've got to get her out of the country," I said. "I just shot and killed two men. A policeman has been murdered. Neither she nor I have proper visas. We could be held for months here while they try to sort things out. Meanwhile the assassins will track down my brother. I need to get to him first."

Faraj rose up. "I'll drive you to Bukhara. I need to get out of here, too."

Karakov gazed down on Oriana, his brow furrowed in thought.

"Look," I said. "I don't want to get you in any more trouble. But please, just give us enough time to get across the border."

He continued staring off, as if at some regret.

"When I find Dan," I said, "I promise I'll get back your

seeds."

"It's not the seeds I'm worried about." He raised his gaze to mine.

"I'll find her," I told him. "I swear I'll do whatever I can to make sure Phoebe's safe."

His wistful eyes peered into mine as if he were reading my heart. "I know you will," he said.

I swallowed.

He glanced between Faraj and me. "The two of you were never here," he said. "The Iranians were shot by the Taliban."

51.
The Proof

"O you who believe! Do not take the Jews and the Christians for friends; they are friends of each other, and whoever amongst you takes them for a friend, then surely he is one of them; surely Allah does not guide the unjust people."

This is the truth from the book of the Prophet.

The Jews say the Christians do not follow anything good, and the Christians say the Jews do not follow anything good, while both recite the same book! Both mix truth with falsehood. They light wax candles in their empty stone traps as if to lure God there like a moth. But I have seen a moth with eyes painted on its wings, and butterflies that dazzle and deceive. False faith offers nothing but the comfort of illusion. Islam is the only true guidance.

Faraj knew the truth, yet he chose to ignore it. He revered the Sufi mystics with their ecstasy and longing—Ghazali gaping endlessly at the face of some young beauty, Rumi losing himself in the gaze of another's eyes. Faraj called it "the love that obliterates the lovers." But seeking only God's love, he brushed aside His law. And so he was disgraced in this world and will suffer a painful chastisement in the next.

My former friend had thought his lies would sow the seeds of doubt, hoped his gazing eyes would lure me in. But I defied the doubters. Reaffirmed my faith. No twisting of the truth left me uncertain.

The truth is Allah's alone, and the Mahdi will bring it forth: that is all I needed to remember. It was the reason why I joined the Old Man's secret war. To see his grand vision carried out into the world, to fan the flames of chaos throughout the Middle East, to draw the outer world into the great apocalypse that will bring about the coming of the Mahdi.

The Mahdi—the Shadow of God, the Master of Time, the Proof. Indisputable proof for all who doubt: the return of Islam's Messiah!

Bukhara

52.
Seven Good Reasons

The Uzbek guards at the border crossing couldn't fathom the combination: an Iranian, an American, and between the two, a Jew. They poured over our passports like Koranic scholars analyzing the books of the Hadith. Faraj explained that Oriana and I were vacationing together, attempting to retrace the old Silk Road route across the Stans into China. He was traveling to Bukhara on business and had picked us up on the way. His passport showed he had made the journey many times before; it looked to be fairly routine.

Still, the guards remained suspicious. We were entering yet another country invented by the Soviets, who seemed to have thoroughly inculcated their obsession with control. After ordering us out of the truck and searching Faraj and me, they turned their sights on Oriana. She wore a head scarf that Phoebe had left behind in the field tent, a NY Yankee's sweatshirt she had borrowed from Faraj, and a pair of jeans from my duffel bag. The jeans had been loosely rolled up into cuffs, revealing the infamous red-leather heels recovered from her desert death march. Although the borrowed clothes concealed her many bandaged wounds, she found it too painful to stand upright, and her face looked pale and sickly. Fearing a body search, I told them she'd contracted some rabid flu virus and might vomit profusely at any moment.

The men left her alone.

Faraj had buried his guns safely in the desert, so their search of the truck revealed nothing. But they did turn up an item from my bag.

"Problyema."

"That? It's nothing. They call it a Vajra. From Tibet."

"Antikvarnaya."

"Antique? Not really. It's a Buddhist thing. Spiritual. Like a thunderbolt, but harmless. Look. See how the prongs are—"

"No papers."

"I told you. It's nothing—"

Faraj interrupted with a carton of caviar. "Enough for everyone!" He ripped the box open and began passing out the tins.

Suddenly the guards were breaking into smiles. "*Nyet problyema.* Let them pass."

I helped Oriana climb back into the truck. Faraj winked at me as the men waved us through. We had entered into the Stan of the Uzbeks.

Despite many hours of sleep on the road, Oriana had weakened considerably. We had stopped only once in the middle of the desert to change the dressing on her wound, and the discoloration of the flesh around it suggested some kind of infection. As we entered the outskirts of Bukhara, Faraj headed directly for the hospital.

Oriana objected. She insisted I be taken to the university first and begin at once my tracking down of Dan. "You must find him before they do," she muttered. "Or all is…for nothing."

I knew she was referring to Sar. But I was afraid we'd lose her, too. "We've got to take care of you first," I said.

"No. Too much time."

Faraj shot a glance at me while navigating the traffic. "I can take her," he said. "It's not far from the university."

He looked bleary-eyed, hell-bent. He'd been driving nearly nonstop since we left the site at dawn. On a journey he'd never planned to make. With an American who'd just shot two men, and a woman he barely knew.

"Faraj?"

"Yeah?"

"Why are you doing this?"

He glanced at me as if annoyed by the question, and went back to battling the traffic. "How many assassins are left?"

I had to think. "The day before yesterday, there were ten. Oriana killed one in Baku. We just killed two more in the desert."

"That leaves seven," he said. "Seven coming for you and your brother. And for Oriana."

I swallowed. "That gives you seven good reasons to get out of here while you can."

"No," he said. "That gives me seven good reasons to stay."

They dropped me at a corner of the campus. It lay sprawled among several blocks near the edge of the Old City, the labyrinthine heart of Bukhara. I wandered over the grounds for several minutes before realizing I had no clue where to go. Although the signs and building plaques were written in Latin script, they were all in largely indecipherable Uzbek.

Students shrugged in response to my queries, but a few spoke English and pointed out the way. Eventually I found myself in a courtyard. Along one wall, beneath a series of domed arches, students were lounging on wooden divans, sipping hot drinks and smoking narghile at what must have been the campus teahouse. One of the students directed me to the archaeology department in a gray stone building across the courtyard.

I passed through the old building's entry door and started down a long, dusky, hallway. The clack of my boot heels echoed. Every office door was closed, and their indecipherable labels gave the corridor a Kafkaesque strangeness. I knocked on a door and tried the knob. It was locked.

The next was locked, too. And the next.

Hearing footsteps, I turned to see a man at the far end of the hall making his way toward an exit.

"Hello!" I shouted, hurrying toward him.

He slowed as I approached. At least a foot shorter than me,

and considerably wider, he peered up from a broad, dark-skinned face with the faded garnet smudge of a tilak on his forehead.

"I'm looking for Professor Baghestani," I said.

The man grinned and nodded, gesturing behind him toward a door at the end of the hall. I thanked him, and he ambled off, disappearing out the exit in a blinding burst of light.

I walked down the hallway and knocked on the door. To my surprise, it creaked open. "Hello?"

No answer. I pushed the door aside and ventured in.

53.
Borzoo Baghestani

Through the break between the drapes of a soaring window, a swath of sunlight sliced across a large and cluttered room. For a moment I thought I was back in Steinberg's shop. Books lay everywhere, crammed into the shelves that lined the high walls, piled in precarious towers on the carpets, and splayed like fallen, upturned doves on the massive antique desk.

There was no one in the room. The desk looked as if the professor had momentarily stepped away. A filigreed glass held the dregs of an espresso, and a fountain pen lay uncapped on a pile of scribbled notes.

A fountain pen—no computer. Positively medieval, I thought.

I looked around. The sliver of sunlight arced across a blue and amber globe, mounted on a stand beneath the window. On the wall beside it hung an antique map of Central Asia, and on the other side, the framed print of a 19th-century Orientalist painting, a Mongol warrior lording it over a captured, prostrate sultan. On the shelves I spotted a squat stone Buddha propping up a copy of the Koran, while two shelves higher stood the knuckled leather spine of an ancient *King James Bible*. Stepping back, I kicked over a slippery stack of *manga*, the comic books I had devoured while living in Japan.

This Borzoo Baghestani was an interesting fellow.

Across the room, nestled between two sea-green leather chairs, a carved-jade chess set darkly gleamed. Its peculiarity drew me closer. The chessboard, I realized, held extra rows and columns, with a single space jutting out like a thumb on either side. Many of the pieces struck me with their strangeness—elephants, giraffes, camels, princes. It was some exotic form of desert chess I'd never seen before.

A collection of framed photographs checkered the teal-colored wall above it. Stone ruins, dig sites, and workmen holding picks and shovels, posing with their finds. The same man appeared in nearly all of the shots: tall, dark-skinned, handsome, with aquiline features and vivid, intelligent eyes. I took him to be Baghestani. There were no photos of any women or children, so it appeared he was probably a bachelor. In one shot he stood beside a tweedy, pale, balding man with a handlebar moustache. I recognized the monument looming up behind them from pictures I'd seen of Tehran: the "Freedom Tower" they called it, though I'm sure Faraj would have—

A rap on the door flung me around.

A woman stood there, looking surprised, her arm around an empty cardboard box, a ring of keys in her hand. She said something to me in Uzbek.

"Do you speak English?" I asked.

"No English." She wore a babushka and the uniform of a maid.

"I'm looking for the Professor," I said. "Borzoo Baghestani?"

"Baghestani?" Again she spoke rapidly in Uzbek. Another uniformed woman came in, rolling a Stalin-era vacuum cleaner. She was taken aback when she spotted me. The two women conversed at breakneck speed while examining the lock on the door, upset, apparently, that the office had been opened, or had never been locked, or perhaps had been broken into—

I interrupted. "Please, just tell me: Where is Baghestani?"

They stopped. The first woman approached me with great earnestness and, pointing into the air behind her, began to elaborate detailed directions I couldn't begin to decipher. She walked two fingers across the palm of her hand, then tapped on the face of her watch. It seemed that wherever it was I was going, I had better hurry to get there. The Professor was leaving, or would be leaving, or maybe had already left.

The one place name the two women kept repeating sounded like "Bolo House." I pictured drunken Uzbek frat boys wearing shoestring neckties.

"Bolo House," I said. The women nodded excitedly. I thanked them both and ran out the door.

———

My destination, it turned out, was the furthest thing from a frat house. By asking "Bolo House?" to every person I passed, and racing off in the direction they pointed, I eventually left the campus altogether and entered the streets of the Old City. Cars were apparently not allowed, but there were plenty of tourists and locals on foot. I'd ask the way and then run off, tunneling between pale walls of clay, twisting out into clearings and then back into meandering lanes. Dripping with sweat, running out of breath, I finally arrived at a deep, green pool in a gorgeous, tree-lined plaza, the jewel-like setting of an extraordinary mosque.

The Bolo-Hauz mosque.

I paused to catch my breath.

The beauty of the scene struck me like a painting, some luscious Orientalist tableaux by Gérôme. Beneath the soaring columns of the mosque's elegant portico, a mixed congregation in blue and green prayer caps and multi-colored headscarves stood behind a white-turbaned mullah. Facing the grand entryway with upraised hands, he appeared to be conducting some ritual or ceremony, or waiting for some figure to emerge. I began to realize they must be part of a wedding ceremony and started looking for the bride and groom. The maids had been so afraid I'd be late, I wondered if it was the professor himself getting hitched.

Across the way, tourists waiting to enter the mosque loitered restlessly at the edge of the pond. Many busied themselves by taking pictures. As if warding off vampires, three Catholic nuns in light summer habits held up their cell phones like crosses.

Still, no bride and groom emerged.

I approached the prayerful congregation as discreetly as I could. Like the mullah, all were facing away from me toward the high-arching entry to the mosque. The group had arranged itself neatly into rows, with men standing in front, women in back, and children and young teens in between. Although I couldn't quite see their faces, many in the adult rows appeared to be college-age, and I assumed they must have come from the university.

The worshippers recited a short prayer together. Unlike Faraj in the desert, they didn't kneel or prostrate themselves, but they did end with "*Allahu Akbar.*"

Peering over the crowd toward the men at the front, I thought I caught a glimpse of Baghestani in a prayer cap.

The group intoned another prayer, and another "*Allahu Akbar.*" Then I heard a final "*Salaam alaikum,*" and the assembly began to disperse.

I moved through the departing crowd, seeking out the professor. Solemn faces eyed me warily; mothers safeguarded their kids. Maybe it was Sar's duster and the cowboy boots, or the lack of any covering on my sweat-soaked head. But their suspicion of a stranger seemed a little excessive; I wondered if I was breaking some taboo.

Finally I spotted the lanky man I'd thought was Baghestani. He was actually the guy with the handlebar moustache in that photo with Borzoo in Tehran.

"Excuse me, Sir? Sorry to bother you—I'm looking for Professor Baghestani?"

He scowled at me in disgust. "Is this some bloody joke?" Brushing past, he hurried off.

I watched him enter the street. When I turned back toward the portico, now largely clear of the crowd, I noticed a group of men remained in front of the entryway. They had assembled themselves around a bier draped with a Persian carpet, and were lifting up, in unison, a long, white-shrouded corpse.

Is this some bloody joke?

Shuffling along like a human centipede, the men bore the body toward the open arms of a hearse.

I looked back at the Persian rug. Garden of flowers and

vines.

Baghestani was gone all right—gone to paradise!

54.
Woolsey

The man with the moustache had covered two blocks before I finally caught up. He was walking at a fast clip. I strode up alongside him. "Sir, I'm sorry—"

"You'd best not follow me," he said. The accent was British, not Aussie.

"I just want to know what happened—"

"Ask the police." He glanced over his shoulder and picked up his pace.

I looked back and saw no one. Then had to rush to catch up. "I travelled a long way to meet the professor. I know you were his friend. If I could just—"

"I told you, it's not safe—"

"That's why I'm here. The professor met with my brother shortly before he disappeared. A friend came to find him, and now I'm afraid she's—"

He turned into an alley and stopped. "This friend of yours. Describe her to me."

"She's…blond. Late twenties. Attractive. Five foot…seven, maybe."

"American?"

"Dutch."

"Student?"

"Archaeologist. She—"

He put up his hand. Footsteps sounded. He looked to the corner. The steps grew louder until…

A squat, covered woman appeared, bearing a basket of

laundry. She passed the alley without a glance.

The Englishman turned back and looked me over. "I suggest you remove your coat," he said. "And here, take my *duppi*." He scraped off his embroidered prayer cap and handed it to me.

As I put on the cap and rolled up the duster, he peered around the corner. Suddenly he pulled back and started down the alley. "This way," he said. "Quickly." He resumed his rapid pace. "Professor Baghestani was murdered yesterday. Not far from here. Stabbed in broad daylight on a crowded street."

"My God."

"The murderer attempted to fight off the police until he was killed himself."

"Do they know why—"

"There's no motive as yet. The police are looking for a blond woman who fits the description of your friend. Yesterday morning she was seen entering Borzoo's office. She was the last person to talk to him. No one has seen or heard from her since."

Phoebe. I wondered if something had happened to her, or if she had fled the city.

We had entered a street of shops and stalls, thronged with tourists and locals. As the Englishman threaded his way through the crowd, I noticed him glancing behind us.

"What is it?" I asked.

"We're being followed," he said. "We've been followed ever since we left the Bolo-Hauz mosque."

The Englishman bellied up to a door lightly carved and studded with brass. As he flipped through his keys, I glanced back at the motley of citizens sauntering along the street. We had walked countless twisting blocks and I still hadn't spotted our tail.

"Do you think we lost him?" I asked.

"No. And there's more than one, I'm afraid." He twisted the key and the door swung open. We entered into the dark.

"They already knew where I lived," he said. "Now they know you're here, too."

Coming off the sundrenched street, I couldn't see a thing. I followed the clack of his footsteps down the pitch-black passageway. Another door was opened and we entered a bright courtyard of weathered wood, bougainvillea, and flaking walls of white-washed clay. A gnarled vine climbed a wriggled stairway to a balcony. We ascended to another door and entered his apartment.

As he crossed the room to the sunlit window, I heard him whistle the opening bars of *God Save the Queen*. He peered down from behind the curtain at the bustling street below. "Welcome to the last British outpost in Bukhara."

It was yet another book-lined bunker, with a writing desk, a sitting area with an old TV, and a tidy single bed in the corner. The casement windows looked out on a brick and stucco skyline punctuated with turquoise domes and a crown-topped minaret.

The Englishman swept the curtains shut and flipped on a shaded floor lamp. "Keep calm and carry on, as we say."

I heard the whistled bars again, and turned to see a green parrot inside a mosque-shaped cage. "So *you're* the whistler," I said. I raised an eyebrow to its owner. "Patriotic parrot?"

He nodded toward the television. "Cricket fan," he said. He fed the bird some seed. "With all this...espionage, I'm sure you'll be relieved to know that Darzee doesn't talk."

"Thank God for small favors."

"Thank Allah," he said. "Believe me, the bird's no Anglican."

As if on cue, the parrot whistled.

I smiled and reached for the Englishman's hand. "Jack Duran," I said.

"Pleasure to meet you, Jack. My name's Conrad Woolsey."

"Those men you saw following us—you say they already knew where you lived?"

"That's right."

"Who are they?" I asked.

"I'm not exactly sure."

"Have you told the police?"

"No. Not yet. I need to sort out a few things first. Once I go to the police I'll have to remain in their protection. And I can't be sure how safe that will be."

Two quick knocks at the door startled me. I turned to Woolsey in alarm.

"It's quite all right," he said. "You may come in, Rashid."

The door opened just enough for the young boy's face to show. He had the Mongoloid features of the Asian steppe I'd noticed of so many on the street. Woolsey asked if I'd like some tea, then spoke to the boy quickly in what I assumed must have been Uzbek. The kid nodded briskly and was gone.

"Landlord's grandson," the Englishman explained. He gestured to the pair of wingback chairs and asked me to take a seat. After all the walking I'd done, I was more than willing to oblige.

On a low table between the chairs sat an ivory and ebony chess set. The regular kind.

Woolsey noticed me looking. "That was a gift from Borzoo," he said. "We used to play on that very set every Friday afternoon at his office."

"I went by there," I said. "I saw the set he has there now. Very strange."

"Indeed. Borzoo was from Iran, and what you saw was a Persian variant called Tamerlane chess. It's named after the Mongol warrior king who supposedly invented it during the years he ruled over Persia. Borzoo is…was…writing a book on Tamerlane's mausoleum. He purchased that jade set on a recent trip to Samarkand. He was quite keen on it…" Woolsey gazed off forlornly. "In the last few weeks he'd been teaching me how to play."

The Englishman seemed to be struggling to grasp the reality of Baghestani's death. I asked how they had come to be friends.

"That was on account of quite another game," he said.

Conrad Woolsey held a senior professorship in history at Cambridge. A year ago he came to Bukhara on sabbatical to research a book on the so-called Great Game—the 19th-century rivalry between the British and Russian empires for supremacy in Central Asia. He met Baghestani while guest lecturing at the University of Bukhara. Along with their mutual passion for chess, both shared a deep interest in the history of the region and often traveled it together.

"Borzoo was Muslim, of course. I sometimes accompanied him to mosque on Fridays. And on those rare occasions when I could find a church, he would accompany me."

It occurred to me the two of them may have become more than simply friends. "I saw the picture of you together in Tehran."

"I met his sisters and brothers there," he said fondly. "All those lovely nieces and nephews. Of course, he didn't know it at the time, but as it turned out that was Borzoo's final trip home."

"Was it only to see his family?"

"Mostly. Why do you ask?"

"I was told he did some work for the Ayatollah's government."

"That was years ago. Borzoo was an expert on the history of the Ismailis, a minority branch of Shi'a Islam. He was hired to direct the excavations of their most famous landmark, the Alamut castle in northern Iran."

I remembered Dan's Iranian sketchbook, filled with drawings of ruins. "My brother lived for a time in Iran. I wonder if that's where they met?"

"It's possible. However, the important question now is why your brother met with him here."

"Yes, I'd like to know that myself."

Woolsey noticed something and slowly tilted toward me. "Forgive me for asking, but…I wonder if you could tell me how you acquired that nick on your throat."

I'd nearly forgotten the scar was still there. "Close shave," I said, wondering just how much he knew.

He eyed me shrewdly. "Much too close, I'd say."

"Did the professor ever talk to you about a sacred lotus plant?"

Woolsey looked intrigued. *"Sacred?"*

"It's called soma," I said.

The word brought a gradually tightening squint to his eyes, the historian's brain buzzing through a labyrinth of connections. Finally he emerged from it and returned his gaze to me. "I think it would be best, Jack, if you start at the beginning. I want you to tell me absolutely everything you know."

Sinking back into his armchair, he tented his fingers beneath his moustache and waited for me to begin.

55.
The Old Man

Following another double knock on the door, Rashid backed into the room, carrying by the handles a steaming samovar. I gathered up the mandala pages assembled on the floor, Woolsey removed the chess set from the table, and the boy set the copper contraption down and proceeded to prepare our tea. He worked silently, without a wasted move, and seemed barely aware of our presence. I watched with growing fascination his choreographed routine—un-stacking the teapot and the delicate china, heating the pot and then emptying it out, measuring the dry tea leaves and refilling again from the spout, finally setting it up to brew over the stack—until the boy, with a neat little nod of his head, vanished from the room without a whisper.

Woolsey had been pacing all the while in a fever, mulling over the story I had told him. When he noticed the boy was finally gone, he strode back to retake his seat.

"This group of Mahdists recruited from the Quds Force—I believe that Borzoo knew who they were."

I waited, watching as he filled our cups with tea.

"I told you that he was hired to direct the excavations at Alamut. In the 11th century, that mountain castle became the headquarters of the Ismailis, a minority sect of Shi'a Islam that felt under threat from the dominant Sunnis. Their charismatic leader was a brilliant Iranian scholar from Qum named Hasan-i Sabbah—'the Old Man of the Mountain.' Hasan was determined the Ismailis should not only survive under the

Sunnis, but should ultimately subvert them and rise up to rule. He believed they were destined to build the foundation for a new Islamic utopia.

"It was a seemingly unimaginable dream," Woolsey said. "The Old Man knew he could never accomplish it by preaching and conversion alone. At the time, Sunni Islam was the entrenched orthodoxy, enforced by the vast military empire of the Seljuk Turks. Open insurrection would quickly be crushed. Random acts of violence would be futile.

"So Hasan forged a new way, a more effective and efficient approach to what's now called 'asymmetrical warfare.' With years of careful indoctrination and training, he developed a small force of highly disciplined and dedicated commandos. Sent out in secret from Alamut and other mountain redoubts, they performed systematic, targeted killings. Sunni sovereigns and scholars, Turkish princes and ministers, Seljuk generals and politicians—none were immune to their knives. They raised the art of political murder to a level that had never been seen before. The force became known as the *Hashishin*—the name that gave us the word 'assassin.'

"Their method was deception, and their courage and daring were legendary. Sleeper *Hashishin* would covertly infiltrate the governments or the households of their enemies, living secretly among them, often for years, awaiting the call to execute a killing. They chose the most difficult and protected targets and, oddly, the most dangerous mode of attack. Although they had access to poisons, bows and crossbows, invariably their weapon of choice was the dagger."

"Up close and personal," I said.

"Precisely. The knife is more frightening. Which is also why they preferred to slay their victims in public. The killings had a ritual, almost sacramental quality, a mixture of cool planning and fanatical zeal. And no *Hashishin* could be taken alive—they would rather die fighting than submit to capture."

I remembered the runt I had shot in the pit, reaching for his dagger even as he died.

"The Old Man," Woolsey went on, "was the great-grandfather of terrorism. His Assassins' self-sacrificing mode of attack, showing no emotion in the face of death, struck such terror among potential victims that it often made their actual murder unnecessary. Fear itself became a method of persuasion. For example, a victim might wake one morning to find a *Hashishin* dagger lying on his pillow. This was a plain hint to the targeted individual that he was not safe anywhere, that perhaps even his most trusted servants had been turned, and that whatever had brought him into conflict with the Assassins would have to be stopped if he wanted to live."

Woolsey rose up anxiously and strode across to the window. He cracked open the curtains and peered down at the street. "What we're dealing with here, Jack, is the revival of a cult—a messianic cult practicing an age-old form of terror."

I slowly turned my gaze from him to the steaming samovar. As my hand drifted up to the scar on my throat, a question I'd asked before came to mind again: "Why did you say those men who followed us already knew where you lived?"

Woolsey released the curtain. He crossed to a trunk at the foot of his bed, lifted something from it and carried it over to me. It was wrapped in a pillow case.

"This morning, when I awoke, I found this lying beside me." He set it on my lap and drew back the covering.

With horror and fascination, I lifted the crescent dagger. The knife looked identical to the others I had seen—the arc that straightened as it narrowed toward the tip, the squiggly, storm-like Damascene steel, even the lotus blossom symbol cast in the handle's crown.

The grinning blade seemed to conjure up the face of death itself.

"You think your houseboy, Rashid…?"

"I don't know," he said. "It doesn't really matter. The fact is these Assassins have issued me a warning."

"But…why threaten *you*?"

"I assume because I was so close to Borzoo. He must have known something they feared he might have shared."

I contemplated the dagger and its golden lotus crown. "Karakov told us the professor never published his findings at the castle."

"It's true," Woolsey said. "Borzoo told me many stories about the Ismailis and the *Hashishin*, but he claimed he never found anything in the excavations at Alamut. He never wrote or spoke of it, to anyone as far as I know."

"Maybe they left a dagger on his pillow," I said.

"They may not have needed to." Woolsey paused a moment, stroking his moustache. "I always wondered... His family, his work, his life was in Tehran. He took the position here soon after completing the excavations. Bukhara, Uzbekistan—a waterhole in the desert! It seems clear to me now they must have forced him to leave Iran."

"To keep him quiet," I said.

"With his family in Iran as collateral."

"So why kill him now?" I asked.

Woolsey continued pacing. "I'm not entirely sure. But I think they must have found out about his meeting with your brother."

I watched as he walked back and retook his seat.

"The *Hashishin* was a secret society, built around a ritual of spiritual initiation. The rites have long been rumored to have included some trance-inducing herb. The very name *Hashishin* is derived from the Arabic word 'hashish.' Accounts by Marco Polo and western crusaders describe a hidden Garden of Paradise and drugged devotees. The mystical garden was said to offer a foretaste of the afterlife, the paradise that awaited the Assassin upon the completion of his mission."

The Persians and their gardens again. In this world, but out of it—literally. "Hash is basically cannabis resin," I said. "You'd be more likely to drown in a hot tub than try to murder somebody."

"Agreed. That's why most of these stories have been dismissed as fabrications—attempts by Christians to explain away the Assassins' fanatical devotion. Or rumors spread by their Sunni enemies to denigrate their daunting fearlessness. After all, neither the crusaders nor the Seljuks ever managed to conquer the castle. How could they have known what went on behind its walls?"

Woolsey slapped his knees and again rose to his feet,

unable to contain his excitement. "But your tale of the soma plant brings all this into question!

"Originally, the Arabic word *hashish* referred to herbaceous plants in general, especially their succulent or edible parts. Could it be possible the sacred *haoma* plant of ancient Persia had never been entirely lost? No one would have been in a better position to rediscover it than the brilliant Hasan-i Sabbah. His mountain fortress at Alamut was a great center of Islamic learning, visited by scholars, astronomers, alchemists, historians, scientists, and Sufi mystics. The Old Man lived as an ascetic there for thirty-five years until his death, never once coming down from the rock, all the while ensconced in one of the greatest libraries known to the medieval world."

The pacing Englishman came to a stop and gripped the wings of his chair. "What if Borzoo found the same lotus seeds in the ruins of Alamut that your Russian friend found buried in that ancient Aryan temple?"

"There'd be one crucial difference," I said. "The seeds Borzoo found might still be viable."

"And the *Hashishin* could again revive the rite that emboldened their legendary forebears."

We both fell silent for a moment. Woolsey's account seemed to fill in many blanks, but it still left crucial questions unanswered. What exactly had Dan discussed with Baghestani? Where had he gotten the seeds he showed to Vladimir Karakov? From Alamut—or somewhere else? Why were the Assassins hunting him down? And why had they murdered the professor?

"Because Borzoo failed to heed their warning," Woolsey suggested when I put the question to him. "They must have found out he told your brother what he knew."

"If that's true," I said, "they'll probably want to silence Dan as well."

"They will do whatever they have to do to keep the lotus secret. Secrecy and deception are the hallmarks of the *Hashishin,* derived from the Muslim doctrine of *taqiyya.* They call it the 'Holy Deception.' *Taqiyya* gives Shi'a Muslims religious dispensation to conceal and deceive in the service of their faith."

I wondered if there was a Catholic equivalent; it would have come in handy with the grammar school nuns.

"Everyone seems to want to keep it a secret," I said. "Maya with her silencer. The 'housemaid' in Rome. And now the Iranians—by killing off the archaeologist who rediscovered their seeds."

Woolsey nodded agreement. "What good is a drug that inspires bold action if your enemy employs it as well? Audacity is what gives the *Hashashin* their intimidating mystique."

"I thought Sharia law forbids drinking and drugs? How could this Ayatollah in Qum condone it?"

"He couldn't," Woolsey said. "Not publicly, anyway. The Assassins' daring demonstrates the power of their faith. But that faith, that sense of certainty, may intensify with soma. The transcendent experience provided by the drink may be seen as validation of their radical beliefs. They are soldiers fighting in the service of their God, who offers them a taste of the afterlife. There are in fact Koranic verses that describe just such a drink. In Paradise, where rivers of milk, honey, water and wine flow beneath the gardens, the righteous sip a 'pure drink,' sealed with musk, that cleanses them spiritually from forgetfulness of Allah, drawing them closer to Him. 'You will recognize in their faces the brightness of bliss.'"

I thought of Vanitar's intensity that night he chased me in Rome. He did seem in a state of bliss—not the bliss of mindlessness, but that of pure conviction.

"No fear. No doubt. How do you stop a man like that?"

Woolsey shook his head despairingly. "All men harbor fears and doubts. We struggle to overcome them. Fanaticism springs from the effort to *deny* them."

Once again we fell silent. The parrot clucked, rocking on its bar. Woolsey eyed it broodingly. "Nothing is true," he said. "Everything is permitted."

"What's that?" I asked.

"Supposedly Hasan-i Sabbah's last words, uttered on his

deathbed. Though Borzoo remained rather skeptical."

"I'm with the professor. Hardly sound like the words of a true believer."

"I wonder," Woolsey said. "Perhaps the Old Man grew disillusioned in the end. He'd failed to overturn the existing order. In fact, he never held a single city. His dream of an Islamic utopia ultimately came to naught."

Nothing is true. Everything is permitted. "Final decree of the devil," I said.

"I'm loathe to admit it, but it brings to mind the final words of Jesus on the cross. 'My God, my God, why hast thou forsaken me?'"

I'd always thought that last cry only proved that Christ was human. "His moment of doubt," I said.

"Indeed. Just as the old devil came to doubt the power of fear, it seems that Christ himself came to doubt the power of love."

I stared at the steaming samovar. The dagger lay beside it. "Maybe the Old Man was right: Nothing *is* true."

Woolsey's eyes drifted to his murdered friend's chess set. Their game had been abandoned in the midst of battle, like a pause to cart off the dead. "I refuse to believe that," he said. "I'll cast my lot with love any day. I'd be willing to die for it."

I thought of the dagger held at my throat, of Borzoo knifed in the street. "Dying is easy," I said. "Maybe the tougher question is...would you be willing to *kill* for it?"

Woolsey strolled to the window and pulled the curtain aside. "If these devils count the game worth the candle, then certainly we must as well."

I rose from my chair and stepped up beside him. The sunlight prompted a squint. On the crowded street below, shoppers stopped to peruse the stalls hung with jewelry and carpets, a gang of jubilant children raced past, and an Uzbek clad in a multi-colored coat promenaded among the throng like a sultan.

"Do you see the men who followed us?"

"No," Woolsey said. "But I *feel* them."

I knew exactly what he meant. Concealed inside the shiny

apple, the worm was gnawing away.

"I have to find my brother and Phoebe," I said. "I haven't a clue where to look."

Woolsey continued to gaze at the street. "I wish I could help you," he said.

Outside, the *azan*, the call to prayer of the muezzin, resounded hauntingly over the rooftops.

"Do you pray?" Woolsey asked.

"I used to," I said.

"Perhaps you remember the 23rd Psalm?"

Oddly enough, I did, in part. "Though I walk through the valley of the shadow of death, I will fear no evil, for thou art with me..." I paused, waiting for more to come. "I will dwell in the House of the Lord forever…" I glanced at the Englishman. "That's about all I remember."

"It's all you need to remember."

We listened as the muezzin's crooning continued. It was coming from the tall minaret in the distance, set amid sea-colored domes.

"The Kalon minaret," Woolsey said. "They call it the Tower of Death. The last emirs of Bukhara had criminals thrown from its summit."

"Long way to fall," I said.

"Indeed, over forty-five meters. Nine centuries ago the tower was a beacon to caravans crossing the desert at night. Even Genghis Khan was impressed. When he sacked the city in the year 1220, it was the only structure he left stan—"

Woolsey stopped, slowly turned, lowered himself to the sill.

"What is it?" I asked.

"Alamut," he said. "It was the Mongols who finally destroyed that, too. Slaughtered the *Hashishin* and burnt the castle to the ground."

I looked at him, waiting.

Woolsey stood up. "Tamerlane!"

He looked at the stack of mandala pages. "Borzoo was trying to solve a final problem with his manuscript. I think your brother may have given him the answer." He charged past the startled parrot, crossing the room to his desk. "I've got to hurry to his office before the Iranians get their hands on it."

"I think you're too late," I said. "I went by his office this morning: there was no computer or laptop there."

"They may have taken his laptop, but Borzoo wrote his manuscript longhand, in Persian. It's hidden in a compartment under the chessboard table." Woolsey grabbed a shoulder bag from the back of his chair and emptied it onto his desk.

"Let me go with you," I said.

"Too risky," he said, eyes darting in thought. "And it won't be safe for you here. I'll try to make them follow me out front; there's a route I can take to lose them. Wait a bit 'til after I've gone, then quietly slip out the back—you can exit across the courtyard, just past the trash containers."

He jotted down an address and a name. "Head left out the door, then right at the corner. Six blocks up you'll find this travel agency. The woman there knows me. Here." He pulled out a thick roll of Uzbek cash, peeled off a bunch of bills and jammed them into my hand. "Buy us two tickets for the night train to Samarkand. Then meet me in one hour at the Kalon minaret. If you wait in the gallery at the top, you'll be able to see if I'm being followed. Don't come down unless you're certain I'm alone. I'll explain everything to you there." He looped the empty satchel over his shoulder and headed for the door.

I called after him. "What about my friend? I can't leave here without her."

Woolsey wheeled in the doorway. "If I'm right," he said, "she's on her way to Samarkand and Tamerlane's tomb!"

With that the door shut and the Englishman was gone.

56.
A Not-so-tall Tail

God Save Our Gracious Queen. The whistling parrot rocked in his Kasbah, eyeing me as if *I* were the prisoner.

I walked to the window and drew the curtains shut, then peeked out, watching for Woolsey. The Kalon minaret? Samarkand? I wondered if he'd even make it as far as Baghestani's office. And if he did, and found the professor's manuscript, I wondered how it could possibly help me track down Phoebe and Dan.

Tamerlane's tomb? What was *that* about? How could a grave be connected to the lotus?

Whatever it was, it was all I had to go on. I was more convinced than ever that Dan was in terrible danger. No doubt Phoebe, too. To calm myself I parroted the parrot's British anthem, only the words that came were those of "My Country, 'Tis of Thee," the more familiar and reassuring American version of the tune. *Land where my fathers died, land of the pilgrims' pride—*

Woolsey appeared. He strolled off down the street at a leisurely pace, weaving through the crowd in his herringbone jacket, a tall, pale Englishman among the swarthy mob. The Iranians could tail him easily, if that was what they wanted. But from my lofty vantage I could spot no stalking shadows, and I began to wonder if maybe they only lived in Woolsey's head—ghost-mummies spun from the turning of the worm, cut loose by that dagger on his pillow.

Then I suddenly realized that whoever was out there could

be lying in wait for me.

I released the curtain and turned inside. Woolsey's deadly souvenir gleamed beside the samovar. I stepped before it and stared down at its copper-gold reflection, a crescent moon grinning through the kettle's steamy mist.

With barely a thought I swept the knife up and slipped it into my bag.

Then I went to the telephone that sat on Woolsey's desk, an ancient rotary dialer with a heavy, cradled handset. On the underside of my left forearm I'd written a number in ink. I dialed the digits and waited.

"How is she?" I asked when Faraj answered.

"Doctor say she should recover. But there is damage to her spleen. They need to make the cut wider, so to go in and repair. We are waiting for the operating room." Faraj lowered his voice to a whisper. "They are asking many questions, Jack. About the stab wound and the cutting. Who she is. Who I am. I am doing my best, but—"

"Hang in there, Faraj. Stay with her. I'm going to call someone to help, I'll get back to you late—"

"You find the professor?"

"Yes. I mean, no. I'm heading out now to meet a colleague of his at the big minaret—I'll call you later and explain everything. Please just make sure Oriana's okay."

"Don't worry, my friend. She is very strong, and very beautiful. I have promised I will stay with her until she is well, even longer if she likes, and that she will live a long life, *Insha'Allah.*"

"Yeah, *Insha'Allah.* Thank you for all your help, Faraj." I asked for the name of the hospital, then said goodbye and hung up.

I couldn't help but smile.

I pulled out Harry Grant's business card and dialed his cell phone number. Harry didn't answer, so I left a message with the name of the hospital, telling him Oriana had been wounded and was about to go into surgery, that he'd better send someone quick to straighten things out. I said there was an exiled Iranian Sufi friend staying by her side, adding, "I don't want to make you jealous, Harry, but I think the guy's falling in love!"

If there was anyone actually tailing me, they were doing one hell of a job. From the moment I entered the street behind Woolsey's place to the time I reached the travel agency, I never spotted anyone remotely suspicious.

The Englishman had apparently drawn them off. I wondered if he'd be able to shake them.

I bought the train tickets from the lady inside who, though she spoke only a very limited English, lit up when I said the name "Conrad Woolsey."

"No for Mr. Borzoo?" she asked in surprise.

She hadn't yet gotten word of his murder. "No," I said. "Just one for me and one for the professor."

"Going to see tomb again?"

Now I was surprised. "Yes...actually. At least, I think that's where we're going."

She seemed pleased. I wondered just how often Baghestani had made the trip.

Before stepping outside, I carefully scanned the street. A young woman ambled by with a toddler in tow, a T-shirted boy bicycled past, and across the way, by the open door of a tobacco shop, an old man sat smoking on a wicker chair.

These four were the only humans visible on the street. I headed for the Kalon minaret.

The travel agent's directions to the tower had been vague, but I got the general gist of it, and soon enough, as I entered a broader thoroughfare, I spotted the minaret above the rooftops.

The afternoon sun was low in the sky and the street was half-cast in shadow. Though devoid of cars, the pavement teemed with the citizenry of Bukhara, a veritable rush hour of foot traffic. Many congregated along a row of food stalls where blue smoke rose through slanting light, and stewpots simmered over fire-blackened bricks. I kept glancing behind me, scanning for stalkers, but no one held my eye for very long. Each person seemed preoccupied with his own separate troubles, lone sailors in a sea of anonymity.

Having not had a bite in what seemed like days, the scent of the street vendors' smoking kabobs snared me like a Mongol's lasso. I paid for a *shashlik* skewer of lamb and scarfed down the chewy meat like a mastiff. Then I paid for a bottle of flat, warm Coke and sipped it as I strolled on toward the tower. The twenty minutes remaining until my rendezvous with Woolsey seemed more than enough time for me to reach it.

I almost began to relax. Until, at some point—I couldn't say exactly when or why—a peculiar sensation at the edge of awareness began to assert itself, finally urging me to confront the suspicion I was secretly being observed. I stopped walking and abruptly turned around. Scanning the flock of faces, my eyes settled quickly on a small, dark man.

The man turned and perused a food stall. Inky-haired, beardless, he wore a tilted rug cap, along with a dark gray jacket and slacks, not unlike the Assassins. He gestured toward a cauldron and was served a mound of pilaf. I watched, and waited. Something about him intrigued me. His youth, his nonchalance, his air of haughty solitude. It all seemed dimly familiar, and I tried to recall if I'd glimpsed him at some earlier point in the day.

I couldn't say for sure; I'd seen a lot of faces. Yet something about this diminutive fellow seemed wrong to me, even sinister. Maybe it was only his resemblance to the runt, the sicko who had gutted Sar and tortured Oriana.

For a while I just stood there in the midst of the throng, waiting to see if he'd look at me. Waiting. Waiting.

Subtly, barely moving his head, he glanced in my direction.

The look sent a shiver through me. The man, I felt certain, was my tail.

As if to demonstrate indifference, he turned his back and gorged on the pilaf, shoveling it in with his fingers.

Slowly, I backed away, then turned and casually continued up the street. Blood pulsed as Woolsey's words echoed in my head: *Stabbed in broad daylight on a crowded street.*

I glanced back. The man's eyes were on me.

57.
Tower of Death

I swiftly made my way through the crowd, then ducked into a side street. The moment I was out of view I bolted. People stood aside, staring as I passed. A mongrel in a doorway started yapping. The narrow, twisting corridor eventually disgorged me, and I found myself on another crowded thoroughfare. Heading once again in the direction of the tower, I scurried past a strolling pack of European tourists. Then I tore off Woolsey's prayer cap and ran flat out for several blocks, duffel bag bouncing at my side. Finally, I came to an open plaza and paused in a doorway to rest.

The street curved away behind me; if my pursuer was there, he was hidden. Across the square stood an old brick mosque and a complex of religious buildings. A smattering of tourists strolled between them, while behind a closed gate, a caterpillar line of white-turbaned students were filing into a school, an Islamic madrasah. At the end of the plaza, looming above rows of violet-tiled arches and glistening turquoise domes, the golden-brown brick Kalon minaret muscled up into the sky.

I checked the street again, then hurried toward the tower.

The closer I came to it, the taller it seemed to grow. Forty-five meters, Woolsey had said; roughly 150 feet. I grew dizzy staring up at it. Horizontal bands of patterned brick, with intricate, ingenious variations, gave the simple, tapered column a dazzling complexity. The gallery at the top, with its crenulated crown, made the minaret appear both organic and ancient, like the stalk of a giant, budding plant petrified by the desert. You could see why it had survived the merciless gaze of Genghis Khan.

When I reached its massive base, I turned and scanned the plaza. There was still no sign of the stalker, and Woolsey was nowhere in sight.

Access to the minaret was through the adjacent mosque. I paid a small fee to the attendant inside, then climbed a staircase to the rooftop, where a brick bridge crossed to the tower's elevated entrance. Walking out across it, I suddenly felt exposed, and again experienced the unnerving sensation that I was being watched.

I paused to survey the courtyard. There were hundreds of archways, windows and doors—a honeycomb of impenetrable shadows.

———

"Open your eyes, Duran." Even looking directly toward me, still you cannot see!

And if he cannot see me, I thought, he had certainly missed the others. The sly, beardless Uzbek, now slipping off into the mosque. And over there, under the arch, the patient Hashishin.

Yes, he was one of us, of that I had no doubt. Not Mahbood, not as smart, but clearly an Assassin.

I had watched him follow the American; the Uzbek had followed him. Who was this rat-haired Mongol? Slinking through the shadows. A local floater, hired to kill? A Taliban connection? Perhaps a spy dispatched from Delhi to avenge their whore in Rome.

Duran was equally blind to them both, as he now was blind to me. I might cross the square in the light of God's sun and wonder if he would even notice. Americans must suppose all Middle-Eastern men look alike: dark, bearded, dour. And act alike as well: quarrelsome and dyspeptic—unlike the saintly Zionists they so worship and admire.

Here he comes, there he goes. Allah mocks him to wander blindly. No doubt he'll be sightless in the Hereafter as well, and even more astray from the Path!

———

The feeling wouldn't dissipate; the tension seemed to grow. Yet still I could see no one. I continued across the bridge. Stepping through the minaret's doorway, I started up the pitch-black stairwell.

A figure suddenly emerged from above. I drew back with a gasp.

"Forgive me if I frightened you," the old nun declared. She stepped down into the light. Giggling female voices followed. "Come along, dears."

It was the three cell-phone sisters I'd seen at the Bolo Hauz mosque. Judging from the accent, they were Irish. Some "interfaith cultural exchange" I imagined. The two following the mother superior looked to be barely in their twenties.

I pressed against the wall as they passed by like shadows. A phrase bubbled up from Sunday school. "Who walks in darkness and has no light," I said.

The last young nun looked back from the doorway. "Yet trusts in the name of the Lord and relies upon his God." She smiled sweetly. "Isaiah," she said. "The Muslims take him as a prophet as well."

"Hey," I shrugged, "whatever gets you down from the Tower of Death."

"That'd be 103 steps," she said.

I laughed. Mother superior called from the bridge. The nun grinned warmly and went out.

I headed up the stairs. Irish nuns. Where was I, Bukhara or Belfast?

The stairwell quickly faded into blackness. Shuffling up the spiraling steps, I grew disoriented, and kept a hand feeling along the constant curve of the wall. My eyes couldn't seem to adjust to the dark. The image of the nun in the bright, arched doorway had imprinted itself on my rods and cones, or my optic nerve, or the back of my brain—wherever it is visual stimuli linger before they're filed away or forgotten. My optic nun lingered in reverse silhouette, like a photographic negative or a cameo relief, a bright white angel in a black archway, hovering incessantly before me. I probably should have ignored it and thought about something else, or followed the sister's humble example and simply counted steps. But with all the anxiety I was feeling, I couldn't stop wondering if it wasn't some kind of a sign. A vision sent by Isaiah, as if the prophet were insisting I remember what he said through the mouthpiece of a Belfast nun.

After-image or God-sent vision? Transcendent or mundane? Maybe the two together, both sacred and profane?

These are the kind of thoughts one has while ascending the Tower of Death.

When finally I emerged into the rotunda at the top, bright beams of sunlight through the arches made me flinch and stagger. I steadied myself at the barrier wall and peered out over the city.

Every corner of Bukhara lay visible. Low-rise, flat-roofed structures stretched to the hazy edge of the desert. Below, the vast rooftops of the mosque and the madrasah, dotted with rows of structural domes and crowned with blue-green cupolas, bordered the open plaza I had entered from the street. A few scattered tourists cast long, sweeping shadows. The vantage would provide me, as Woolsey had predicted, a wide-ranging, unobstructed view of his approach.

It was only minutes 'til show time.

I heard some spoken French behind me, and turned to see a student couple heading down the stairs. Wind whisked through the vacant arches. I circled the gallery and discovered I was alone. For some reason, this increased my anxiety. Ever since my near fall from a church tower in Greece, I'd been afraid of heights. The gallery floor felt unsteady beneath me, and the slanting beams of sunlight made the room appear askew. Woolsey had mentioned that criminals used to be thrown to their deaths through these arches. Looking straight below now sent a tremor up my spine.

Death is always with us, just one small step away...

A bent mullah in a white turban, with a shadow stretching several times his height, shuffled with aching slowness in the direction of the madrasah. Opposite, beneath the glinting, violet-tiled entry to the mosque, the two young nuns posed before the upheld cell of their super. I studied each of the other tourists milling about in the plaza. None looked particularly sinister; for the moment it seemed I was safe.

"Okay, Woolsey—it's time." I wondered if he'd found the manuscript in Baghestani's office, and whether he'd make it to the minaret without being followed—or killed.

The French student couple finally exited below and crossed the little bridge to the mosque roof. One behind the other, they filed down the stairs.

Someone else was coming up. I squinted down in disbelief as he stepped out onto the roof. A piercing shock went through me. It was the beardless little man in the rug cap.

There was no mistaking him. As he walked across the bridge, he glanced up. I pulled back, instinctively, then realized at once there was no point in hiding: The man already knew where I was. Somehow he had managed to follow me and, without crossing the open terrain of the square, had slipped in through another door to the mosque.

They must have caught Woolsey, I thought. Forced him to tell what he knew, then killed him. Now they were coming for me.

58.
I am the Assassin

I looked down at the plaza in a panic. The plodding mullah, the Irish nuns, the tourists savoring the sights—for a second I thought about shouting for help. But if this man was a *Hashishin*, clearly nothing would deter him, and by the time any policeman arrived on the scene I would already be dead.

All I could think of was the knife at my throat. In Rome, I'd been helpless to stop it; I couldn't let that happen to me here. I dropped my duffel bag to the floor and pulled out Woolsey's dagger. The edge looked keen as a razor. Lifting it into the sunbeam, the blade appeared to ignite. I felt simultaneously empowered and absurd. Did I actually have the nerve to *stab* him?

I practiced slashing it through the air and thrusting it like a sword. My gestures seemed awkward and stiff. Fighting in the open, I wouldn't stand a chance. Surprise was my only advantage. Emerging from the pitch-dark stairwell, the assassin would be momentarily blinded by the sun. I propped up my duffel bag on the windowsill of an arch, hoping it would draw his attention. Then I hid behind the doorway, crouching low, and braced for the moment of attack.

What seemed like a full minute passed in silence. Nothing stirred but the breeze. My bent knees and ankles trembled. The knife started shaking in my hand.

Breathe. Breathe.

I am the assassin now. I am the assassin—

From the resonant stone of the stairwell came the faint echo of his steps. The sound grew louder, closer, quicker, the echo fading fast—

He was there.

Lunging from behind, I swung the dagger around his throat, knocked off his cap and grabbed his hair. The man yelped as I yanked his head back and brought the blade to bear. "Don't move or I'll cut—"

His elbow slammed hard into my gut. Gripping the fist that held the knife, he twisted me over his leg. I fell and tumbled onto my back. Before I could react, his boot slammed down full weight on the dagger, pinning my hand to the floor.

I looked up in a daze

His face contorted, upside down: *"You?"* The man wasn't holding any weapon. He lifted his foot off the knife. "And I thought you'd be glad to see me."

I rose up, stunned, gaping. My fingers stained black. *"Phoebe?"*

The former blonde's blue eyes sparkled. Her face had been darkened with make-up and her hair dyed a bluish black. "It's ink," she said, pinching a lock. "Try finding a colorist in Bukhara."

I stared at her, aghast. "I could've *killed* you!" I said.

"For a second there I was terrified they'd already killed you." She picked up the knife, admiring it. "Looks like you got to them first."

"Not exactly," I said. "That was left as a—*Why are you wearing those clothes?"*

She put on her prayer cap. "Flea market, vintage Uzbek. You don't like?"

Somehow she had managed to flatten her chest. "No, not really," I said, still barely able to speak. A simple stroke of eye-liner made her face look Asiatic.

"They're searching for a blond femme fatale," she said. "Why make it easy for them?" She looked over my boots and duster. "Where have you been, the Outback?"

"Something like that," I said. I could not get over the shock. "Phoebe—"

"I've *missed* you," she said.

She was looking up into my eyes. Her gem-cut blues were the one thing I could not fail to recognize. They had an uncanny effect on me, stirring that ache of longing I'd tried to bury in my heart. "I've missed *you,*" I said. "Every single day."

She lightly touched my hand. "I'm glad to hear you say that."

"You haven't changed a bit." I gently took her hand in mine.

"Just a little," she said. Her gaze fell to my lips.

My gaze fell to hers. "This would get us in a whole lot a trouble down on the street, Mister."

Our faces moved closer. "Is that why you lured me up here, cowboy?"

"Not exactly—oh my God." I'd forgotten. "Woolsey!"

I rushed to the railing and scanned the plaza.

"The man you met at the funeral?"

I turned to Phoebe. "You were *there?* Why didn't you—?"

"The two of you were being watched," she said. "I couldn't approach you without being seen." She stood behind a pier of the arch, gazing down into the plaza without exposing herself to view. "The same man followed you here."

Woolsey had said we had more than one tail; one of them had apparently been Phoebe. "Where is he?" I asked.

She nodded toward the mosque. "There, at the entrance."

I squinted down at the archway, the same place where moments before the nuns had been snapping pictures. At first I saw only an elderly Uzbek ambling past with a cane. But now, peering into the dark recess, I perceived the barest hint of a figure backing away from the light. "What's he look like?" I asked.

"Beard. Suit. Haven't seen much beyond that."

"The man is an Iranian Assassin," I said.

Phoebe peered down. "He's been waiting there since you arrived."

A flash of fear shot through me. Waiting? For what?

"There's your friend," Phoebe said.

Woolsey had reached the end of the street. Glancing about

like a paranoid, he padded across the open plaza toward the minaret, clutching the satchel to his chest.

"We've got to warn him!" I said. Leaning out, I waved my arms. Woolsey saw me and stopped.

The figure emerged from the archway. His shadow swept across the pavement as he headed straight for Woolsey.

The professor was searching for something in his bag. I shouted down to him, *"Run!"* He turned, saw the stalker approaching and frantically scurried away.

Around him, tourists were gawking up at the lunatic who'd just shouted from the tower. I pointed down at the *Hashishin*. "Stop that man—he's got a knife!"

Screams erupted. The Assassin drew out his dagger as he closed the gap on Woolsey. Startled tourists fled in panic. Phoebe gripped my arm. "Jack—!"

Woolsey cried out abortively as the men's long shadows merged. The killer's shining blade flamed upward, then abruptly plunged.

The professor, stumbling, collapsed.

Quickly disentangling Woolsey's satchel, the Assassin fled with it across the plaza and disappeared down the street.

59.
Silk Road Tea House

No reason to carry evidence of the killing he just committed.

The Assassin had discarded the shoulder bag, tossing it away as he raced up the street. I picked it up and saw that the leather was splattered with the victim's blood. There was nothing left inside. Whatever my colleague had been after, he had taken.

On the next block, I caught sight of him again, crossing at the corner. He was clasping a thick sheaf of papers against his chest. Careful to keep my distance, I followed him around another block. He appeared to be doubling back, his initial course having been a feint of misdirection. Finally he disappeared through a doorway off the street. A sign in English read "Silk Road Tea House." Looming overhead was the ubiquitous minaret, glowing with the last rays of sunlight. We were mere blocks from the scene of his crime. Police sirens wailed in the distance.

I sunk into the shadows. Let him relax a little, I thought, allow him to believe he'd shaken off any tail. At least five minutes would need to elapse before I could go inside.

I pulled out my disposable and dialed the Ayatollah. After describing to him the Assassin and the killing I had seen, he told me he believed the papers were a research manuscript, and the key to finding the source of the lotus seeds. "It is vital you obtain these papers for us as soon as you possibly can."

I peered at the door to the tea house. "Who is this Assassin?" I asked.

The Old Man considered a moment. "It is better for the task at hand if you know nothing about him. This brother has fallen under the sway of the devil. I fear you may be called upon to redeem him as a martyr."

By the time we made our way down from the tower, a large crowd had gathered around Woolsey. Gaping tourists strained for a view, while locals gibbered in break-neck Uzbek and hollered into their cells. Where had all these people come from? Neatly turbaned clerics from the mosque and madrasah, students, shopkeepers, sightseers—all had poured out from the surrounding buildings and converged on the site of the stabbing. I heard no English spoken, only the single word, "British." Over the clamorous din of the mob, sirens ululated; police and paramedics would shortly be arriving. If Woolsey was still alive, we'd have only seconds to talk with him.

Phoebe followed close behind as I pressed my way into the throng. Several onlookers eyed me warily—the American who'd yelled from the tower—but a man in loose clothes and a black-and-white turban, assuming we might be of help, urged the others to clear a path and eagerly guided us through.

Before we knew it we were staring down at Woolsey's lifeless corpse. It was clear to me at once he was dead. Lying twisted on his back, he did not move or breathe, and his eyes stayed frozen open. Bright blood flowed out over his buttoned shirt and jacket, pooling into a lake beneath him. The murder weapon was nowhere to be seen. After cleaving through his rib cage and apparently piercing his heart, the blade had been withdrawn by the *Hashishin* and carried off with Woolsey's satchel.

The encircling crowd hung back from the corpse as if it leaked some lethal contagion, a menace spreading toward them like the growing pool of blood. Even I stood back instinctively, grimacing, repulsed. This gentle scholar I'd been sharing tea with only an hour before, now looked like some horrifying harbinger from hell. I wanted to flee from the sight of him.

Phoebe, however, remained detached, and crouched to

examine the body. Dispassionate, focused—I'd seen this demeanor with her before. Bringing her expertise to bear. The others might have thought her a detective or mortician, some dark-suited, inky-haired, grim-faced public servant. To me she was simply the archaeologist inspecting a treasure of bones. She studied the corpse carefully, but did not move or touch it. Finally, she threw a glance my way that drew me down beside her.

"What is it?" I asked.

"His hand," she whispered, nodding toward the clenched fist half-buried under his thigh. I'd hardly noticed it before, but now I could see it was clutching something. Suddenly I remembered: when I'd called down to warn him, Woolsey had reached into his bag.

"Get it," I whispered. "I'll distract them."

I stood up and addressed the crowd. "He's dead," I announced, arousing a ripple of reaction. "Does anyone know who he was? Did anyone see the killer?" I continued throwing out questions, eliciting responses in Uzbek and English. Claims were quickly countered and arguments ensued. Stealing a glance at Phoebe, I saw her bending over the body. When I looked up again, a squad car was pulling into the plaza from the street.

"Here they are!" I said, pointing. The crowd turned to watch as the squad came to a stop and two uniformed policemen clambered out.

Phoebe popped up and nodded—she had it!

With all eyes focused on the approaching police, we made our way through the back of the crowd, slipping finally into a lane behind the mosque.

"He saw me," she said as we hurried away.

"The cop?" I asked.

Phoebe glanced back. "That man—he's following us."

I looked back and saw the bearded guy in the checkered turban who had guided us into the crowd. He wore a long dark vest over a knee-length white gown, with baggy white trousers and open leather sandals, Bible-era garb I'd seen little of in Bukhara.

We picked up our pace. "He was at the funeral this morning," Phoebe said.

Woolsey had said more than one man followed us. I'd assumed the second "man" was Phoebe, but now realized there may have been three. "He must have followed Woolsey when he left the apartment," I said. The other man—and Phoebe—had waited to follow me. "We better lose him."

Without another word, we took off running, and several blocks later hustled into a cab.

"Train station," I commanded the driver. As he pulled away, we peered out the back. The man ran out onto the street and watched us speed away. I felt a familiar thrill. It was *déjà vu* all over again, exactly as happened in Baku.

"Forgot to wear his Armani," I said.

"That man is not Iranian," Phoebe said. "From the looks of him, I'd say Pashtun."

Pashtun. Afghanistan, Pakistan, the Hindu Kush. "Don't tell me."

"I think I've seen him before," she said. "He came with another Pashtun to the dig site in Turkistan. Vladimir was convinced they were Taliban."

It's rare to find a man alone in a tea house, drinking the stuff by himself. In this one there were two of us: him at one end of the high-vaulted room and me far off at the other.

Between us the tables bristled with men, alive with convivial chatter. They tasted sweets, sipped spiced tea, and inhaled smoke from hookah pipes while samovars steamed and simmered. No one seemed aware that a few blocks away a man had just been murdered. I peered through the crowd of bobbing heads, catching glimpses of the unnamed killer. Leafing through the pages he had pilfered, the man appeared completely absorbed in his reading and never seemed to notice I was watching.

I sipped my tea and waited. A blurry TV against the wall showed news footage of riot police and clouds of tear gas in the streets. Waiters crisscrossed in front of it, transporting trays of cakes and cookies. At a chessboard nearby, a big Uzbek in a three-piece suit stoked a fat cigar, watching the beady-eyed hunchback in front of him take out his bishop with a knight.

Nearly half an hour passed. Finally the Assassin made some inquiry of his server, who pointed off as if giving directions, then exchanged some coins and bills. I watched the killer gather up his papers and depart. After waiting a half a minute, I followed him outside.

The sun had gone down behind the buildings. I spotted him a block away, facing a wall with his back to me. As I approached, I realized he was talking on a payphone. I kept my head down and walked past him.

He was probably talking to Mahbood. But why a payphone? I wondered. Afraid cell calls were being monitored? I ducked into a doorway and waited in the dark, silently unsheathing my dagger.

Women's voices caught my ear. A block away, three nuns in habits scrambled into a taxi. I moved the blade behind my back. The taxi glided by.

A steel point pricked my throat. I froze.

"Enjoy your tea, Vanitar?"

60.
Black Camel

I could not turn my head. The Assassin was nothing but a blade and a voice.

"You look more like a talib than a Hashishin," he said. "Too many years in the seminary?"

"I studied as I serve," I said, "at the good pleasure of Allah."

He poked the knife deeper, pinning me to the door. "You serve Christians and Hindus, fench. And maybe the Pashtun who tail you like a dog."

"I serve Islam. You dishonor my name and the name of my bro—"

He slammed my head against the door and held it there, hissing: "Do not speak of your brother's name. He was a warrior, now a shahid. You are his betrayer and will burn in God's Hell."

A trickle of blood ran the rim of my clavicle. "My brother was betrayed. But not by me."

"The Old Man begs to differ," he said, pressing the dagger still deeper.

I strained for a glimpse of his face. To show him the truth in my eyes. "The devil Mahbood deceives you—"

"Enough—" I stumbled back suddenly as the door behind me opened inward. The Assassin, startled, raised his dagger. I quickly slashed his belly. White pages floated to the ground. As he folded forward, I brought the dagger down, severing the tendons of his shoulder.

He fell. Alive.

I plunged the knife through the ribs of his back, down through his left lung and into his heart. Drawing the blade back out again, I staggered for a second, then turned.

A white-eyed boy in his teens stood gaping at me from the door. He wore a stained apron and held a dishrag. Steam billowed from the piled sink behind him.

We stared, for a moment, into each other's eyes. Then his eyes lifted to my dagger rising overhead.

I prayed to the Exalted One to accept another martyr—

The train station lay 30 kilometers east of Bukhara in a suburban town called Kagan. As our cab wound its way out of the city, Phoebe asked where we were going.

"I've got two tickets to Samarkand," I said. When she asked me why, I told her I wasn't sure. "What did you find in Woolsey's hand?"

"A camel," she said, reaching into her pocket. I thought she meant the cigarette, but what she lifted before her eyes was a small, black stone carving. "A two-humped Bactrian camel, to be exact." She handed it to me.

On closer inspection, I could see the inky stone had a deep emerald tinge. "It's jade," I said. "This is from a chess set in Baghestani's office. He supposedly kept his manuscript in the table underneath it."

I handed it back and she studied it. "How curious," she said. "Why do you suppose Woolsey grabbed it?"

"He must have wanted to tell us something." I related what Woolsey had mentioned about Tamerlane chess, and Baghestani's research on the Mongol's mausoleum. "He assumed when you met the professor you must have talked to him about it. He thought you'd be on your way to Samarkand and Tamerlane's tomb."

"The *tomb?* Why?"

"I don't know," I said. "The answer is in that manuscript. Baghestani never mentioned it?"

"I went to his office to ask him about Dan. He wouldn't

talk, said it was dangerous for me to be there. He didn't even trust his own cell phone—and warned me not to trust mine. Finally he agreed to meet in the evening at a coffeehouse near his home."

"What happened?"

"I waited there for hours. He never showed up. It wasn't until this morning that I found out he had been murdered."

"So you dyed your hair and…" I glanced over her attire. "Went to his funeral."

She adjusted her hat and fussed with her jacket, appraising her Uzbek disguise. "I didn't have much time—Muslims always rush to bury their dead. I was hoping to find some friend of his there, someone who might be able to help me. Your man Woolsey was the only European. I noticed the Pashtun in the turban watching him. Then I saw you."

As Phoebe told her story, I found her dissemblance fascinating: the beguiling face of the Dutch blonde kept morphing into the visage of an Asiatic man. She seemed like a character from a dream I must have had, or some mutating goddess from Dan's Buddha book. The duplicity aroused and confounded me. Her clothes, the makeup, the ink in her hair—I longed to strip them all away and *see* her.

"Something wrong?"

I'd been staring. "You were with Dan for two weeks in Turkmenistan."

"Ten days, actually."

I nodded. "Ten days. In the desert."

She cocked her head. "Yes?"

"Did he… Did he ever talk to you about any of this?"

"Not about Tamerlane. I had no idea."

"Did he say why he met with Baghestani?"

"He wanted to show him the seeds he'd found. Dan knew Baghestani from that summer he spent in Iran. The professor was working on an excavation there—"

"Alamut," I interjected. "The castle of the *Hashishin*."

Phoebe looked impressed. "Well. Somebody's done their homework."

I related Woolsey's conjecture, and she confirmed it was

true. Beneath the ruins at Alamut, in a sealed chamber carved into the bedrock under the castle, Baghestani had found a cache of Damascene daggers, a large bronze cauldron, a number of ritual drinking vessels, and a crock containing the seeds of a lotus thought to be extinct.

"Soma," I said.

"That's what Dan suspected, but at the time, the professor wouldn't say. A commander from the Quds Force had confiscated everything and forced him to sign an oath to never speak of them again. To do so would have put his family in danger."

"Then why did Baghestani tell Dan about it now?"

"To warn him. He said if the *Hashishin* knew he had viable seeds, they were sure to come after him with their knives out."

The professor told him they had managed to sprout a number of Alamut's 800-year-old seeds, but the lotuses they produced were stunted and deformed, and failed to grow seed pods and propagate. Consequently, only a limited amount of soma was extracted from the plants—enough to prove the potion still delivered.

"As in 'full of strength, irresistible in battle?'"

Phoebe arched her "Asian" brows. "You *have* been doing your homework."

I told her how I'd come into possession of Dan's *Rig Veda* text in Rome. She was shocked to hear of Maya's murder.

"A lot of people have been killed," I said. I told her about the two Iranians I shot to death in the desert. "And now Baghestani and Woolsey have been murdered. I don't see how the loss of life could possibly be worth it."

Phoebe explained that, without the sacred soma, the central rite of the *Hashishin* could not be consummated. "The Ayatollah in Qum seems determined to find another source," she said. "When the news hit about our find in the desert, his agents were the first to pay a visit."

But the ancient Aryan seeds proved useless. It wasn't until later, when word got out that fresh seeds had been tested at the lab in Zurich, that the Iranians returned to Turkistan, bent on finding out who had sent them.

Dan had foolishly disregarded Baghestani's warning. I asked Phoebe why.

"For the same reason he urged us to dig at the place where the Aryan Vajra was found. Dan wanted to know the truth. He wanted to know if the lotus seeds he found were from the same sacred soma plant treasured by the ancients."

"Where *did* he find his seeds?" I asked. It seemed the critical question.

"He wouldn't tell me," Phoebe said. "He wouldn't even let me tell Karakov what Baghestani had said."

"Why?"

"To keep the source a secret. He's determined to keep the soma safe from those who would misuse it."

The Iranians, the Indians, the Taliban—and Dan would undoubtedly add the Americans to the list. "That must be why he didn't tell you about Tamerlane," I said. "He didn't want you or anyone to know what Baghestani had discovered." I squinted at the blood-red sun setting behind the passing trees. "Now the *Hashishin* have his research on the tomb, and we're left groping in the dark."

"We do have this," Phoebe said, holding up the black jade camel.

I took it from her and examined it again. "What did you call it—Bactrian?"

"Yes. As opposed to the one-humped dromedary, the Arabian camel. Bactria was the ancient Greek name for this region of Central Asia."

I eyed the double humps. "From which the ancient Aryans emerged, splitting off into Persia and India?"

"Yes," Phoebe said. "The Persian word for the region was *Bakhtar*—derived from the Pashto word, *Pakhtar*."

"Pashto?"

"Language of the Pashtun."

The Taliban again. Zealots. Warriors. Throat-cutters. "Haven't we got enough trouble with the Iranians?" I asked.

Phoebe took back the camel—some quality of the jade seemed to make you want to clutch it. She said, "The fact is, the Pashtun may be the most direct descendants of the Aryans.

You could say they have a greater claim to the soma lotus than anyone."

———

In the reflecting pool of the Bolo Hauz mosque, the molten orange sky shimmered. I sat cross-legged at the rim of the pond, the finished pages piled before me. My eyes had grown bleary and the twilight had dimmed, but the title, in Persian, still read boldly:

"The Sultan's Dream of Paradise"
by Borzoo Baghestani

It hadn't taken long to find the secret I had sought. I'd skipped ahead to the ending. Where else should one expect a Muslim king to find his dream? And sure enough, there it was, in a fabled city of dreams—the source of the lotus of the Hashishin!

I peered across the pond in wonder. The epigraph to Tamerlane's tale, four lines in Persian verse from his grandson, Ulug Beg, voiced itself within me as I gazed out on the mosque:

His yearning, born in the womb,
Still sought with his last breath,
Now lay above his silent tomb,
Unconquered yet in death.

By the grace of Allah, I prayed, I shall fulfill the Sultan's quest!

61.
Heaven on Earth

As the taxi approached the train station, we noticed a squad car parked out front, just like the one at the Kalon minaret. My pulse began to race again.

But it wasn't just the cops that worried Phoebe. "After you left the travel office," she said, "the man who was following you went inside. When he came out, I saw him make a call on his cell."

She looked at me and I grasped her implication: The man had forced the travel agent to tell him where I was going.

I scanned the people entering and exiting the station. "So you think it's likely they've sent someone here."

"Here...or to Samarkand."

We had half an hour before our train was to depart. No sense parading ourselves in front of the police—or any *Hashishin* who might be looking for us. I directed the cab to drop us off at a street of shops nearby.

Baghestani's reported visits to the Samarkand tomb had long piqued the Ayatollah's curiosity. Now at last the reason for those many trips was clear.

"Allah be praised!" he said, his voice betraying a rare excitement. "You're sure of what you've read?"

One hand on the wheel, the other on the phone, I answered, "Yes, it's true, I'm certain."

"There is only one Truth with certainty," he cautioned.

"Insha' Allah, you'll see it with certainty of sight. Such is the power of the pure drink of Paradise."

"May you see the lotus of the Hashishin grow once again in your garden in Qum," I said. "Could there be any greater proof that you are God's instrument on earth?"

The Ayatollah answered humbly. "If the believer submits to His will, Allah empowers the believer."

"May He empower us to defeat evil and carry the flag of Islam to the Mahdi!"

"The will of Allah will always prevail."

The Old Man said he would have me booked on a direct flight out of Karshi. The Assassin who had made the payphone call had surely informed Mahbood, which put me in a race now to beat him to the site. We said our goodbyes and ended the call.

Moments later, I pulled up in front of the hospital. Duran, I assumed, would be arriving any moment. Although I had told the Ayatollah I'd leave for Karshi at once, I could no longer resist the command of Allah to avenge my brother's death.

Having left her overnight bag at a hotel back in Bukhara, Phoebe popped into a women's apparel shop to buy a change of clothes and shoes for the trip. She was planning to transform herself back into a woman once we got ourselves clear of the city.

While waiting for her on the street outside, I used her cell to call Faraj.

Oriana, he said, was in surgery. "Last thing she ask before she went in is whether you talked to Professor Baghestani."

"No," I said. "We were too late. And now his friend has been murdered as well."

"I warned you about these men," he said. "There is only one way you stop them."

"That's going to be harder now. The Iranians are way ahead of us." I told him what had happened, and that I'd found Phoebe, and that we were about to board the train to Samarkand.

"Samarkand?" he asked. "But...are you not coming to the hospital?"

His disappointment was palpable and added to the guilt I felt. "I'm afraid not. We have—"

"But you must!" he said. "You must!"

His insistence surprised me. Was he upset that I wouldn't be there, or that he wouldn't be coming with us? "I'm sorry, Faraj. There isn't time. We have to catch this train and find my brother before the Assassins get to him. I'm counting on you to take care of Oriana until Harry Grant shows up. I hope you understand."

A long silence followed on the other end of the line. I thought again of the darkness he seemed always to be hiding from me, and wondered, after everything, if he really could be trusted.

"Faraj?"

"Yes. I understand." His voice was flat, emotionless. "I would very much like to go with you, to fight and kill these men. But it is best now I stay with Oriana."

"I'm so glad you're there, that she's not alone. I can't tell you how much I appreciate it."

"It is my great honor to serve her," he said.

He hadn't heard yet from Harry Grant; I told him he was probably en route. When I hung up and tried to call Harry myself, all I got was his recording again. I left Phoebe's cell phone number.

———

Night had descended without my even noticing. As Phoebe and I walked together back to Kagan station, we found ourselves once again puzzling over the chess piece and Tamerlane's possible connection to soma.

Woolsey had said the Mongols sacked the castle at Alamut. I asked Phoebe if she knew whether Tamerlane led the charge.

"Alamut fell to the Great Khan Möngke in the 13th Century," she said. "Tamerlane didn't come to power until more than a hundred years later. Besides, I doubt the *Hashishin* would have allowed their secret to fall into their enemy's hands. Dan said the cache Baghestani discovered was concealed deep under the castle's foundation."

"Then how could Tamerlane have known about the lotus?"

We passed by a cluster of men waiting at a bus stop, none of whom paid us any mind. I'd almost forgotten about Phoebe's disguise; normally, the wolves would have ogled her.

"There is one connection I can think of," Phoebe said. "Woolsey's mention of Tamerlane's tomb reminded me of another mausoleum. I toured it last year in the city of Turkistan. It was built to house the remains of a famous 12th-century Turkic poet, a Sufi mystic named Ahmed Yasawi."

Yasawi, she explained, was a highly influential philosopher and theologian, and helped spread Sufism throughout central Asia. His focus on the religion's inner, mystical dimension allowed Islam to sustain itself amid waves of Mongol invaders, gradually resulting in their adoption of the faith.

Phoebe continued: "Now it just so happens that Yasawi lived during the glory years of Alamut and the *Hashishin*. He traveled widely, and it's not inconceivable he might have visited the castle—the scholarly Old Man would have gladly welcomed him. Remember the bronze cauldron Baghestani found at Alamut?"

A bearded, flat-faced man in a prayer cap walked past us in the opposite direction. Phoebe waited until he was out of earshot before she went on.

"Under the massive dome of Yasawi's mausoleum—the largest dome in all of central Asia—the builders installed a giant, two-ton bronze cauldron, six feet in diameter, its brim the height of a man's mouth. It has eight bronze handles in the shape of lotus blossoms."

She paused to let that fact sink in; then, with a wary glance around us, continued: "The mausoleum was erected as a tribute to Yasawi more than two hundred years after his death. Guess who commissioned it?"

"Tamerlane," I said.

"The Scourge of God himself. It was the last monument he ever built."

"Must have been quite a fan," I said.

"More than that," she said. "Tamerlane was barbaric in his passion for conquest, but he had an insatiable craving for knowledge. Whenever he conquered a city, his army would bring back scores of captive scholars and theologians. He built renowned academies and vast libraries. I can't help wondering if he learned about soma from the writings of the Sufi master."

I asked her if there was a similar cauldron at Tamerlane's tomb in Samarkand.

She shook her head briskly, no. "There's only his coffin," she said. "Made out of jade."

I fingered the chess piece in my pocket, pondering a possible connection.

"The mausoleum is exquisite," she said. "In fact, the old city itself is quite beautiful. Samarkand was the capital of Tamerlane's empire. Along with those captured scholars, he brought back as slaves architects and artisans, stone masons and marble carvers, metal workers and craftsmen. All were set to work building mosques, palaces, gardens, fountains—his jeweled imperial paradise in the desert."

"Sounds like another heaven on—"

"Look," Phoebe said. We had come within sight of the train station; the squad car was no longer there.

"Keep your fingers crossed," I said as we made our way toward the station.

That Duran would not be coming to the hospital galled me. God's desire for justice had been hindered once again.

I peered down at the unconscious Oriana. Pale without her face paint, her eyes drugged shut, she gave off the scent of a soulless corpse already commencing to rot. But above her the monitor annoyingly beeped, as if all that remained was her greedy heart clinging to life out of fear.

Beep, beep, beep.

The Jews are the greediest of mankind for life. Everyone of them wishes she could live a thousand years. If you think that you are the favorites of Allah to the exclusion of other people, then invoke death *if you are truthful—unless you fear the fire of God and His Hell—*

"You're back."

I turned.

The nurse walked briskly to Oriana's side and began a routine check of her vitals. "Enjoy your dinner?" *she asked in English.*

"I went for tea instead," *I said.*

"Ah—you like your sweets." *She eyed me conspiratorially.*

I grinned back at her warmly. "You read me like a book."

I waited until she left the room, then quietly closed the door.

No need for the knife this time, I thought. Too much unwanted attention. I glanced around the room. The closet door hung open.

A wire coat hanger would do the trick—and buy me precious time. I pulled one down and untwisted it.

Beneath the bandage I found her wound, stitched like Frankenstein. In contrast to her clumsy surgeon, the Assassin had cut with skill. Though his dagger could easily have sliced through her spleen, he'd followed a delicate technique of his training and only nicked the organ, assuring that death would arrive more slowly.

It had been useful to keep her alive, but I could see no reason any longer.

Still, I hesitated. Her angelic, bloodless face seemed to taunt me. Beep, beep, beep. *Was it true that her heart only beat out of fear? Or might it be pounding for me?*

Might she be dreaming *of me?*

Slowly, I lowered my face to hers...and wet her lips with a kiss.

To my surprise, as I withdrew, her eyes suddenly fluttered open. "Faraj," *she murmured sweetly.*

"No!" *I backed away, flush with shame, casting off the devil.*

"What is wrong, Faraj?"

I eyed the Jewess coldly. "You will no longer call me Faraj," *I said.* "Faraj was an apostate and a sinner." *Wiping the demon's kiss from my mouth, I smeared off the powder that had covered up my scar, the 'veil' that concealed my true identity.*

Her eyes flared. "You're Vanitar!" *she gasped.*

The terror in her voice as she uttered my name incited a libidinous thrill. "All this time together," *I said.* "You failed to see the truth." *I moved in, staring down at her.* "You should have looked more carefully—"

"Hel—!"

I clamped my hand down to stop her scream and took up the quivering wire.

Samarkand

62.
Caravan on Wheels

Despite our trepidation, Phoebe and I boarded the train without incident, and half an hour later, ensconced in sweat-stained, second-class seats, we were rolling over a vast expanse of desiccated cotton fields, pale wastes in the moonlight, tracing the ancient Silk Road east en route to the city of Samarkand. Caravanning by camel might have been more accommodating. The train was dirty, noisy, and crowded, the air ripe with body odors, the stench of food and urine, and hot, dry, dusty gusts belching in off the flats. In front of us, a bantering gaggle of men played cards, while down the aisle, young mothers with wailing babies lined up for the lavatory. Across the way, a potbellied man in a sheepskin hat gnawed a scraggly chicken bone. Other passengers roamed about, from seat to seat and car to car, often with multiple children in tow. The train was a traveling village.

Wearisome as it was, I felt a great relief. We had escaped from Bukhara's Byzantine streets, where eyes had peered from every corner and footsteps trailed every turn. Luck had left my throat intact and kept me out of jail, and being on the move again stoked my optimism. Though two innocent academics had been savagely murdered, it appeared that Oriana was likely to survive, Faraj remained hale and hearty, and my brother Dan, despite the odds, had apparently not yet been captured or killed—we still had a good chance to find him.

In the meantime, it seemed a miracle that I was together again with Phoebe. Two years had passed since we'd seen each other last, and my memory of her had dimmed into a dream-dwelling ghost. Now she was sitting there vividly beside me, whispering furtive observations, flashing her diamond blues, brushing her leg and arm against mine without even seeming to notice. Her near-perfect English still retained odd remnants of accent, with her r's softly slurred into w's, her s's rendered silky and precise. Her boy-like locks were still clipped close—shorter even than my own. Dark bronze powder concealed the freckles on her cheeks, but the corners of her mouth still hinted at a grin, and her overbite, endearingly, still plumped her upper lip.

I had to keep restraining myself from staring at her too long. Despite the blackened hair and brows, the tawny complexion and the man's suit of clothes, the Dutch girl appeared as enchanting to me as ever. In truth the manly ruse she used only made her more alluring, paradoxically enhancing what she'd tried so hard to hide: her essential, undeniable, irresistible femininity.

Growing aware of my gaze, she turned to ponder the moonlit wastes slung with frayed power lines and ancient telegraph poles. "The Soviets ruined this region," she said. "All in the name of cotton. 'White gold,' they called it. Forced workers into state-run farms, poisoned the land with pesticides, bled the rivers dry. Up north the ancient Aral Sea was drained into a salt pit."

The road to hell, I thought again. Central planners dreaming of a workers' paradise. "Dan always said it was crazy how they thought they could change the world, when most of us can't even change our own minds."

Phoebe asked what I'd been doing in Rome. I gave her an offhanded answer, cavalierly glossing over my pathetic tour guide biz, before hastily turning the question back to her. She said that after returning to her family in Amsterdam, she applied for several teaching positions. But before she heard back from any faculty recruiter, she received an urgent phone call from Dan.

"He'd heard about the ancient Vajra found in the sands of the Murgab delta. Dan felt certain the initial dating was correct—that the relic was from a 2nd Millennium BC Aryan site." He urged Phoebe to contact Karakov and persuade him to initiate an excavation. The Russian had strong connections inside the government of Turkmenistan; for over three decades he'd been digging up their desert.

I asked her why Dan didn't call Karakov himself.

"He did," Phoebe said. "Vladimir declined—he was busy digging in the Kopet Dag. But Dan knew I'd worked as his TA for several quarters at UCLA. He thought I'd be able to convince him."

Now I knew why Karakov was so miserable. "You did more than convince him—that poor man is head over heels."

"I feel badly about that," she said. "But I never led him on. Men fall in love too easily."

True enough, I thought. Especially with her. I cast my eyes over her manly attire. "Does that mean now's my chance?"

She laughed, then looked away, her reflection faint in the glass. In the darkness the passing wasteland appeared as remote as the face of the moon. "I suppose I should tell you I'm sorry," she said.

"For what?"

She looked at me. "For leaving the way I did."

I thought of Dan and me at Dodona, waking up under the oak of Zeus and discovering Phoebe was gone. "We put you in a tough position," I said. "I can't blame you for leaving."

"No, it wasn't right. I just didn't know what else to do."

She'd left a note on the car's windshield: the Greek word for *freedom*. "We understood what you wanted. What else was there to say?"

She turned her gaze away.

I asked, "Isn't it what you wanted?"

She continued peering out through the glass. "I thought I wanted to marry your brother. Then I fell in love with you." She turned to look at me.

It took a moment to register the words she had just spoken. "You never told me," I said.

"How could I?" she asked. She turned back to peer into the dark. "You think it's going to be simple. You think it will all be clear. But it's not. It's messy and complicated. It seems there's no good choice. That no matter what you do, someone will get hurt."

I stared at her ghostly reflection in the glass. Phoebe had not wanted to be free of us, as I had always cynically assumed. She had wanted to minimize our misery. It was true, she had abandoned the both of us, but if she had gone back to Athens with Dan, she knew I'd be alone and devastated; and if she had gone on to Italy with me, she knew Dan would have suffered the same. The choice she made to abandon us both was intended to diminish our pain.

Phoebe had been thinking less about herself and more about keeping two brothers together.

The fairy tale lives on, I thought. "Do you know what it is you want now?"

For a moment she seemed unable to say. "I just...want to make sure Dan is okay." Her eyes came back to mine. "And to be with you...for a while?"

I held her gaze, entranced.

A small man in a uniform came by to collect our tickets. Despite the hubbub around us, I'd been so absorbed with Phoebe I'd almost forgotten about the train. As I fished out the tickets and handed them over, I noticed the conductor seemed to be scrutinizing Phoebe. Up close, her gender appeared ambiguous at best, and I worried he would see through her disguise. The scrutiny shifted to me. After a moment's appraisal, he seemed to arrive at some unpleasant conclusion. He huffily tore off the stubs and moved on.

Phoebe leaned back and smirked at me. "Maybe it's those fancy boots, cowboy."

I affected my best Brokeback twang. "To the contrary. I believe it is on account of my present travelin' companion. You are ruinin' my reputation, Slim."

"I hope I'm not leading you on."

I stared into those eyes of hers. "You know how men are," I said.

"Tell me," she said. "How are they?"

Black feather lashes, faint fog of freckles, pouty, open-mouthed overbite. "Easy," I whispered.

Her gaze fell to my mouth. "How easy?" she asked.

Our faces floated closer. "Like fallin' off a horse."

"Does that mean now's my chance?" she asked.

We tilted toward each other. "Our chance," I said.

Our lips were nearly touching. Phoebe's eyes began to close...then fluttered open suddenly as her gaze climbed quickly upward.

A bearded man loomed over us, glaring down in disgust. At first I didn't recognize his black-checkered turban, but then I noticed the dark vest and the long white gown, the baggy white trousers and the sandals.

A shock of adrenalin ripped through me. Phoebe and I disentangled.

"Salaam," I offered lamely.

The Pashtun grimaced in disgust. *"Kafirs,"* he snarled. With a swoop he grabbed my duffel bag and charged off down the aisle.

63.
Kafirs

I called to Phoebe. “What does it mean?”

“Infidels,” she shouted back.

We were struggling through the crowded train, searching after the bandit. Pushing through from car to car, calling out for help, I began to think we were the only human beings on the train. No one seemed to pay us any mind. Thievery was either too common an occurrence, or accosting a Taliban too dangerous a risk. Not a soul came to our aid. Having apparently finished his walk-through and collected his quota of tickets, the conductor had conveniently vanished. No security guards appeared. Even the army officers gambling in the dining car sucked their cigarettes and ignored us.

Reaching at last the tail of the train, we entered a first-class sleeping car lined on one side with two-berth compartments. We peered into each, sliding open every unopened door we passed. Nearly half of the cubicles were empty. The rest contained travelers stacked like corpses in their bunks, with arms and feet projecting from under crumpled ivory sheets. In one compartment, a dot-headed Indian in frayed socks lay reading an ancient Kindle with a penlight. In another, two young Chinese men brooded over a Go board littered with black and white stones.

Just as we were about to give up our search, an open door in the last compartment revealed the pilfering Pashtun. Perched on the edge of the bottom bunk, he was rifling through my duffel bag on the floor between his feet.

"Hey—what the hell!"

He glanced up at me, growled some Pashto epithet and went back to digging through my bag.

"We're not carrying any drugs," I said. "Nothing. No soma. No seeds. Understand?"

The man ignored me and continued his search, tossing out a pair of cargo shorts and examining the contents of my First Aid kit.

I turned to Phoebe. "Go find the conductor, will you?"

She turned to leave and came face-to-face with another black-bearded Taliban. A black turban hovered like a storm cloud on his head. He blocked the narrow corridor.

"Excuse me," Phoebe said.

The man stood firm.

"Out of my way," she demanded in her most muscular, masculine voice.

The man's eyes narrowed. A smile cracked open the forest of his beard, revealing grim shards of rotted teeth.

Phoebe backed away. I saw it was more than his teeth that deterred her: at her belly the cretin poked a wedge-shaped dagger. He forced her back into the room.

I followed behind him. "Leave my friend alone. He's got nothing to do with—"

The man swung around and pinned the dagger under my chin. I went cold with sudden fear—then hot with sudden anger. "What is it with you people and your knives?"

"Jack—"

The man's smile tightened as he raised the dagger's tip, lifting my chin. To avoid being cut I had to rise up on my toes. He held me there, throat stretched, trembling, completely unable to move.

"Point…taken," I muttered.

The tip poked through my skin.

"Please, stop it!" Phoebe cried, her true voice cracking through. She turned to the beard on the bunk. "Make him stop, please."

The man was browsing the stack of pages from Dan's dismembered Buddha book. He barked out something in

Pashto, and the dagger man lowered his knife. Another command sent him out of the room, sliding the door shut behind him.

Phoebe and I glanced at one another. "He's bleeding," she said to the Pashtun.

I used the back of my hand to stem it. The man continued his search.

Phoebe dug into my medical kit. She unwrapped a Band-Aid and applied it under my chin. As she did, she gave me a look that said, *Get ready to take this bastard.* I subtly nodded agreement, though I had no idea just how we'd take him, given his friend outside the door was standing guard with a knife.

The Pashtun had finished with the Buddha book and was leafing through Dan's *Rig Veda* text. He paused when he discovered Maya's stationery note. After scanning the dig site map directions, he glared at us, as if the note confirmed his worst suspicions.

"There was nothing there," I told him. "The seeds have all been stolen."

Phoebe glared back at him. "He's been there," she said. "He knows that."

With a smirk he tossed the note aside and shut the Vedic text. Again he searched the duffel bag, this time extracting the "spiritual lightning bolt," the bronze, two-sphere, Buddhist Vajra. Cryptic, occult, probably a form of idol worship, or worse, Satanism, it was further evidence, he must have assumed, of our sinful infidelity to Islam. But the object didn't appear to be what he'd seen us take from Woolsey, so he set the thing aside and delved again into the bag.

Next he pulled out Woolsey's *Hashishin* dagger. I had wrapped it in a T-shirt and buried it near the bottom. As he unwound the shirt and his eyes fell on the blade, he glanced at us again suspiciously. But the beauty of the knife provoked his admiration. No doubt we had stolen this shining crescent of Islam. He set the knife down solemnly beside him.

I exchanged a furtive glance with Phoebe: *The knife might be our chance.* But Phoebe's eyes evinced a more immediate concern: The Pashtun was pulling out her bag of recent purchases.

He peered into the bag, then eyed us once again, his suspicion now shadowed with confusion. Reaching in he drew out a pair of leather pumps, a white cotton nightshirt and a black satin blouse. Then, plucking delicately, he lifted by its spaghetti strap a black-lace, demi-cup brassiere.

His baffled gaze shifted to us, then zeroed in on Phoebe.

Phoebe snatched the bra from him and stuffed it back in the bag. "Gifts for my wife," she declared. "Unless you continue to insult your faith by stealing these as well." She huffily re-bagged the blouse and shoes.

If I had harbored any doubts about his comprehension of English, the jihadi's look of loathing made them vanish in a flash. He slowly rose to his feet. Standing just in front of her, he towered over Phoebe.

She lifted her gaze and gulped. "I hope you don't exp—"

He brushed the cap off her head. Phoebe tried to strike him but he knocked her arm away. Violently, with both hands, he clawed open her shirt.

I went for the knife. Grabbing it off the bunk, I turned to drive him back—and froze.

The jihadi was standing with his back to the door, aiming a revolver at us.

Outside, the dagger man called to him. The gunman shouted back, some word or phrase in Pashto. Then he made some other comment and the man in the corridor laughed.

I looked to Phoebe. Beneath her open shirt, a wide band of stretched cloth tightly wrapped her chest.

The gunman smirked, nodding toward my dagger. "What with you people and your *knifes, Kafir?"*

I had no answer for him. He wagged the gun at the dagger and angrily spat a gruff command.

I glanced at Phoebe in defeat. Knife at a gunfight, nothing we could do. I set the blade back down on the bunk.

He eyed me with contempt. "She—like man," he said. "You? Like woman."

I stared at him in frustration, voiceless.

The jihadi took a step toward Phoebe. Aiming the revolver

at her, he patted her various pockets, finding her passport, sunglasses, some cash. None of it interested him. An object in the pocket of her suit jacket intrigued him, until he discovered it was her cell phone and threw it aside.

Next he stuck the gun in my chest and started patting me down. He extracted my wallet and passport, and when he felt the lump in my right pants pocket, he backed off and gestured for me to empty it.

Out came the black jade camel.

A glimmer lit his eyes. He made some remark in Pashto and snatched the camel away. But looking it over, he grew perturbed and swung the gun between us. "What is?" he asked.

Phoebe glanced at me before giving him an answer. "It's a chess piece," she said. "From a game named after Tamerlane."

He frowned, still puzzled, then peered at us again. "Why the dead man give you?"

Phoebe shook her head. "We don't know," she said.

The man continued turning it over in his hand, growing increasingly upset. He jabbed the revolver at me. "You say. Why he give?"

"I don't know," I said.

He pressed the muzzle to my forehead. "Tell me why!" he shouted.

I clamped my eyes shut. The cold steel barrel seemed to suck the life right out of me. "Please. I told you. I don't—"

A cry from the corridor interrupted me. Someone thumped the door.

With the muzzle still pressed to my forehead, the jihadi called to his companion. No answer came. He slowly backed away toward the door, training the gun on the two of us. Again he called to his friend. Again no answer came. He swung the pistol toward the door and slowly slid it open.

A body lay slumped on the floor. The jihadi, moving carefully, pointed his revolver through the opening.

In a flash, a hand grabbed the gun, and the door slammed shut on the jihadi's wrist. He cried out. The door flew open.

A portly, middle-aged, dark-skinned Indian now held the pistol and aimed it at the Pashtun. The red smudge of a Hindu tilak faintly marked his brow. I recognized the man as the fellow down the hall who'd been reading alone in his compartment. He was standing shoeless in frayed, floppy socks. He had a bald pate and multiple chins, bulbous eyes in an impish face, with a grin baring nicotine-stained incisors.

The jihadi backed away, still clutching the jade camel.

In a calm, high voice, the Indian spoke reassuringly to him, holding out his hand for the stolen merchandise while leveling the revolver at the Pashtun's heart. I assumed the language was Pashto, for the jihadi had no problem understanding what he said, and in fact tried to argue with him, pointing a finger at us.

The Indian wasn't buying. He continued to address him in his high, lilting voice, every other word accented with a cheery, upward swing, until finally, after much back and forth, the Pashtun acquiesced. He handed over the chess piece, and the Indian passed it back to us.

I thought that would be the end of it. But the Hindu wasn't done.

He ordered the jihadi out of the compartment and prodded him toward the back of the train. Stepping over the body of his fallen companion, Phoebe and I followed at their heels. Behind us, passengers withdrew into their quarters. The two Chinese men in the next compartment quietly shut their door.

The Indian forced the Pashtun to open the rear hatch.

A gust blew in, and the clatter of the wheels on the rails made a roar. Out in the darkness, the pale, stubbly farm fields swiftly receded, while the moon hung unmoving in the sky. The Indian, pointing the gun at the Pashtun, ordered the jihadi to jump.

Phoebe called out, "Please, don't!"

"I'm not sure about a bullet," the Indian said. "But he'll survive the jump just fine."

The man pleaded with him in Pashto. The Indian responded with a bobble-head shrug and targeted the pistol at his crotch.

With that, the jihadi made his exit. We watched him tumble headlong down the slope to the side, a ghostly white pinwheel of pajama limbs.

The Indian brushed past us, but not without noticing the

look on our faces. "Much the kindest thing to do, I assure you." Crouching beside the man on the floor, he lightly slapped his face. "Wake up!" he said. "Wake up!"

Blood brimmed the Pashtun's nostrils. His eyes remained a blank.

"You think he's dead?" I asked.

"Good heavens, no," the Indian said. "I merely broke his nose." Taking hold of the Pashtun's ankles, he dragged him toward the hatch. "We don't need to kill the man, just get him off the train."

Phoebe looked appalled. "Shouldn't we wait for the police?"

The Indian paused to catch his breath. "Trust me," he said in his high-pitched voice. "I am quite familiar with the Uzbek police. Far better we dispatch of him ourselves." Again he started hauling.

Phoebe and I looked at each other. Long way to Samarkand—why wait until he wakes?

"I beg your pardon, would you be so kind?" Standing at the doorway, the Hindu needed help.

I looked again at Phoebe.

"We really are *kafirs*," she said.

All three together, we jettisoned the jihadi.

64.
Delhi Man

The Indian was actually of Nepalese descent. His name was Anand Pandava. Staring at the faint red tilak on his brow, I remembered that I'd seen him at the university that morning. "You're the guy who directed me to Baghestani's office!"

He was lifting fried dumplings from a brown paper bag and distributing them individually to our plates. "I hope you like the *samsa,*" he said, ignoring my remark. "Lacks the spices of our Indian *samosa,* but exhibits some remarkable flavors of its own."

The Uzbek version looked close enough to Maya's to remind me that I'd thrown them up in that toilet stall in Rome.

Anand noticed the expression on my face. "Perhaps it's the scent that deters you," he said. "The nose is always on guard with unfamiliar grub."

"In my case," I said, "the grub's all too familiar." I downed another swallow of Shiraz.

The truth was, I still felt much too shaken up to eat. Just half an hour earlier I'd had a dagger at my throat. Like Phoebe, who seemed hyper, I was gulping down the wine.

"I'll take his *samsa,*" Phoebe said, directing them to her plate. She had changed unbound into her black silk blouse and heels and was now engaged in a devastating impression of a woman. "Forgive me, but I'm starving and I absolutely *love* these little devils."

Anand forked over the dumplings, looking very pleased. "Love is a word quite properly applied to your delight."

His high, lilting accent tickled Phoebe. "Spoken like a true gourmand, Anand." The unintended rhyme—or the wine—made her giggle. She raised her glass. "To love and delight!"

The three of us happily clinked.

Our host had picked up the food and wine before leaving the station in Kagan. It was more than enough to feed us all, which made me suspect that Anand Pandava must have planned our little picnic all along.

Guffaws erupted at a table behind us—the disheveled army officers merrily gambling away their wages. Our booth in the smoke-filled dining car seemed set amid every race and tribe in Asia: Uzbeks, Turkmen, Mongols, Tajiks, Afghans, Chinese, Koreans. Most were working-age men and migrants—farmers, pickers, laborers, traders—but several elderly Chinese women shuffled mahjong tiles, a clique of drunken college students loitered by the door, and packs of shrieking children ran repeatedly down the aisle. At the far end of the car, a duet of male peasants plucked some sort of long-necked lutes. Their song was consumed by the babble. Even we had to shout to be heard.

"On the other hand," Anand was saying, "I much prefer their garlic *plov* to our saffron *pilao*." He began dishing out the rice concoction. "This was stewed with the mutton for several hours, I was told."

I considered eating it despite my lack of appetite.

Phoebe saw my hesitation. "It's just a form of pilaf, Jack. Pilaf probably originated here. Alexander ate it when he conquered Bactria."

Anand piped in: "And betrothed himself to Roxana, the Bactrian princess."

"By all means then, let's have it," I said. The wine had begun to take.

Anand filled my plate. "The discovery of a new dish does more for human happiness than the discovery of a new star."

"I couldn't agree more," Phoebe said. She helped herself to the wine. "You could say the same thing about this."

The two of them fell into a discussion of Shiraz.

I pecked at the *plov* and thought about Anand. He must

have picked the door lock to Baghestani's office: he was leaving and the door stood ajar when I arrived. I wondered if he'd followed me from that point on—Baghestani's funeral, Woolsey's apartment, the travel agent, the minaret, the killing, the camel. He probably saw the Taliban were tailing me as well. On the train, he had taken the compartment right beside theirs, then waited until the very last second to finally intervene.

At the moment, he and Phoebe were debating the quality of viticulture in Central Asia following the departure of the Soviets.

I interrupted. "Anand? Excuse me, but… Who is it you work for?"

He chased down his mutton with a mouthful of wine and dabbed his double chin. "I am a humble servant of the government of India."

"What department?" Phoebe asked.

"Research and Analysis," he said.

"Good one," I said. "Tell me: What you just did to the jihadi—was that research or analysis?"

"Jack—"

"What happened was unfortunate, but necessary," he said.

"And probably saved my life, which I do appreciate. So why not just tell us who you really work—"

Phoebe cut in. "He works for the RAW, Jack—the Research and Analysis Wing. India's version of the CIA."

"Oh," I said. "I see."

Phoebe asked, "Did you know Maya Ramanujan? She came to our dig site in Turkmenistan. Jack said she was killed in Rome."

Anand leveled a sober gaze. "Maya's death was most unfortunate. And quite unnecessary." He looked at me. "A tragic lack of coordination between your country's intelligence service and mine."

"So the flower peddler *was* CIA," I said. "Have you been sent to avenge Maya?"

"My efforts are in counter-terrorism and the collection of intelligence. Vengeance, I have found, is extremely unproductive."

"Are you looking for my brother?"

"I am looking for the lotus plant, a legacy of my country."

"Is that why you broke into Baghestani's office?"

He sipped his wine. "I wonder if you would be so kind as to allow me a look at the chess piece in your pocket."

I glanced at Phoebe. She shrugged.

"Of course," I said, retrieving it.

He turned the piece in his hand, curious.

"Are you familiar with Tamerlane chess?" Phoebe asked.

"A bit," he said. He set the piece down on the table. "If I remember correctly, the camel moves two spaces diagonally and two spaces straight."

He demonstrated: two diagonally, two straight.

What the hell could that mean? We ate our *plov*, staring mutely at the camel.

"That damn thing almost got me killed," I said.

"Many Afghans as well," Anand said. "When the Taliban ruled their country, along with music and dancing, playing chess was strictly forbidden."

"Amazing," I said. "Who knew chess was the gateway to sex and rock 'n' roll?"

Our eyes fell again on the camel. Anand asked, "Why do you suppose your friend wanted you to have it?"

"I don't know," I said. "Baghestani was researching a book on Tamerlane. Woolsey seemed to think the connection with soma had something to do with his tomb."

"His tomb," Anand repeated. "That's why you're traveling to Samarkand."

"Yes," I said. "It's all we've got to go on."

Anand sipped his wine, contemplating the camel. "I was born near Kathmandu, in the mountains of Nepal," he said, "but in my youth I became a soldier in India, and for most of my life my home has been in Delhi. The terror of Tamerlane is well-remembered there. And the date: December 17, 1398. That was the day his army of 70 thousand soldiers approached the city gates. Twenty thousand had frozen to death crossing the Hindu Kush. The Conqueror of the World had come to teach the Sultan of Delhi a lesson. The Muslim sultan, he asserted, had been too tolerant of his Hindu subjects. Tamerlane would show no such mercy.

"The Sultan of Delhi knew the threat he faced. All across Asia, Tamerlane had left the cities that resisted him piled high with corpses and cemented towers of skulls. On his march across the Punjab toward Delhi, he put whole cities and towns to the sword, burning them to the ground, driving all before him, leaving behind a vast swath of death and destruction. Those who fled were captured and beaten. A hundred thousand Hindus taken in chains were mercilessly slaughtered to hasten his march. When finally the Scourge of God reached Delhi—the ancient treasure house of the Indian empire—he set up his encampment and prepared to take the prize.

"In response, the Sultan assembled his army: 10,000 horses, and at the forefront of his massive infantry, 120 war elephants. Armored in mail and metal plate, their tusks lashed with poisoned scimitars, with flame-throwers and crossbowmen mounted in castle-like turrets on their backs, the war elephants struck fear in Tamerlane's men—they'd never seen anything like it."

I thought of the elephant chess piece I'd seen on the board in Baghestani's office. No doubt the sight of those exotic beasts had been Tamerlane's inspiration.

Anand picked up the camel chess piece. "Tamerlane had only his camels. Skittish and unruly, they were clearly no match for the mighty war elephants. But Tamerlane knew the one thing to which even the most powerful beasts on earth were not immune: fear. And so he turned his cowering camels into instruments of terror.

"He had his men load the camels with bales of hay and set the hay on fire. Roaring in pain, the camels raced frantically toward the advancing Indian army. Facing the strange spectacle of flaming camels charging toward them, the elephants panicked and turned to flee, sparking a thunderous stampede and trampling the Sultan's soldiers. The Indian army was quickly routed.

"Tamerlane entered the city, and three days of the bloodiest of massacres began—soldiers, old men, women, children—with tens of thousands more forced into slavery. Delhi was sacked and left in ruins. Ninety captured elephants were loaded with treasures and set off on a great procession back toward Samarkand."

Anand lowered the camel chess piece back down on the table. "It took more than a hundred years for Delhi to recover."

Holding our empty forks in hand, Phoebe and I had stopped eating. The sphinx-like camel seemed somehow different now, its darkly impenetrable jade imbued with a kind of malevolent power.

The power, I thought, of *fear*.

I asked if there was any more wine.

65.
The Flower Sermon

By the time we finished our second bottle, the dining car had quieted some and a number of tables had emptied. The soldiers' raucous poker game had grown dull and somber with drink, streams of children no longer terrorized the aisle, and we could finally hear the crooning of the hayseed minstrels plucking their gourd-like lutes.

Anand opened a dessert wine labeled *A Thousand and One Nights*, which he said had been produced at a winery in Bukhara. Phoebe expressed some doubt about this and the two began another wine debate. As this wound on, I retrieved from my pack Dan's Buddha Book drawings and laid them out in rows on the table for Anand.

He recognized them immediately as a mandala. "Tibetan, I would think. But unusual," he said. "The remarkable profusion of figures. And the central core is usually a square fortress, not a circle."

"Someone else told me that, too," I said.

He picked up the drawing of the Buddha and studied it. "Also, this combination of gestures is unusual."

"How so?" I asked.

"These ritual gestures are called *mudras*. Each one has a specific symbolic meaning. You are perhaps familiar with the Namasté *mudra?*"

"Oh. Sure." I pressed my hands together, palms touching, fingers pointing skyward as in prayer. Bowing slightly to him, I said, "Namasté." It was the standard formal greeting in India and much of the Hindu and Buddhist world.

"The word Namasté is derived from the Sanskrit," Anand said. "It translates roughly as 'I bow to you.' Together with the *mudra,* it means: I honor the place within you where, when you are in that place in you, and I am in that place in me, there is only one of us."

Phoebe lowered her wine. "It's beautiful," she said.

"Or delusional," I said. "But maybe it's just me—I mean you. I mean us."

"Yes," Anand laughed. "But which is the delusion?" He held out his glass: "To the one of us!"

We clinked. As one. And drank as three.

Anand set the drawing down for all of us to see. The Buddha was holding up the lotus flower while reaching down with his right hand to touch his fingers to the ground. Anand pointed to the right hand. "This is the *Bhumisparsha mudra.* It shows the Buddha at the moment of his awakening, summoning the earth to witness his enlightenment. The gesture represents his unshakable nature."

"It's as if he's in heaven," Phoebe said, "but still living here, in touch with the earth."

"Wonderfully put," Anand said. He pointed to the Buddha's left hand. "Here, the upraised palm is held outwards, with the thumb and index finger forming a circle—what Westerners call the 'OK' sign. With the Buddha the circle means 'giving refuge.' It's closely related to the *Abhaya mudra,* which may be the oldest gesture of all: the open hand held up at the level of the heart in a sign of greeting or friendship. Usually it's the right hand, the weapon-bearing hand. The gesture is meant to dispel fear."

"But here the fingers hold up the lotus," I said.

"The implication seems clear," Phoebe said. "The lotus bestows fearlessness."

"'Divine Soma,'" I quoted from the *Rig Veda.* "'Urged on by thee may we overcome even mighty foes in battle.'"

"Yes, refuge from fear," Anand said. "But there is also another possible meaning, one that complements the enlightenment gesture of the right hand. Depictions of the

Buddha holding a lotus flower are often ascribed to a teaching of the Awakened One known as the Flower Sermon."

"I've heard of this," Phoebe said. "Isn't it called 'the wordless sermon?' In China and Japan, they claim it's the origin of Zen."

"It is perhaps only a legend," Anand said. "But it is said that one day, toward the end of his long life, the Buddha arose before his assembled throng of disciples and held up a lotus flower. He spoke no words; the flower itself transmitted the essence of his wisdom. Enlightenment came, not through scripture or philosophy, but through a direct experience—a deep realization—of the miracle of existence."

"Tathata," Phoebe said. "In English it's translated as 'suchness' or 'thatness.' It's the transcendent reality that shines through the ordinary world of appearances."

"Zen aims to awaken this awareness," Anand said. "It's not about thinking the right thoughts or gaining some knowledge beyond us. It is simply experiencing the miracle of what is right in front of our eyes."

As he spoke, I was staring into my amber glass of *A Thousand and One Nights,* contemplating the miracle, the "suchness" of the wine. It just so happens it truly was a remarkable thing to behold. The clear glass goblet, with its myriad reflections, was itself a visual spectacle and a marvel of lucid design. It seemed the perfect instrument to display what lay inside: an enclosed, miniature, sunset world, a windless ocean of wine; a crumb of cork floating like a microscopic ship; one translucent, planet-like bubble orbiting the sea's round edge; and finally, the hue of the sea itself, a luscious honey-yellow, glowing with a radiance all its own, as if the crushing of the dusty, vine-ripened grapes had set free captured sunlight.

This is what the old Dutch masters observed when painting their gorgeous still lives, what art lovers flock to museums to see, crowding in close for a view.

A golden drink in a glass on a table.

"It looks so *real,"* we say—that is, so replete with "suchness." The painted wineglass taunts the eye. It seems to contain some mystery. *Look closely,* it says. *Look carefully.* If your eyes can pierce the veil of *maya,* you might just glimpse the truth.

This put me in mind of that other golden drink and those venerating verses in the *Rig Veda*—hymns of praise for the sacred soma juice, elixir of the Aryan gods. If a drunk like me could glimpse the eternal in a glass of fermented grape juice, then surely those horse-herding cowboy warriors could have gleaned it from the "suchness" of soma.

Exhilarating, intoxicating, the mighty, golden-hued showerer of blessings. Pleasant to the taste, dripping with milk, thou flowest like horses let loose in battle without reins, without chariots, unharnessed. Flow for us, o conqueror of cattle, of chariots, of gold, of heaven, of water, of thousand-fold wealth, who the gods have made for their drinking, most sweet-flavored, invigorating, dripping, honeyed, causing happiness—

These were more than drinking songs to buck up soldiers' courage. Soma was the Aryans' Holy Hooch, their version of the Lamb of God bleeding into the Grail. One inspired the *Rig Veda* hymns; the other—three millennia later—inspired the *St. Mathew Passion.* Though clearly incomparable in musical terms, both compositions were a means of transportation, vehicles designed to enchant and enthrall, to carry one out of one's limited self, to penetrate the veil of sound and reach beyond the reach of thought into the realm of silence.

Silence.

"Jack?"

It was Phoebe.

I had lost myself in the glass of wine—a glass I'd apparently emptied.

Anand lifted the bottle. "More?"

"Please."

He filled my glass and offered a toast. *"Tat tvam asi."*

We clinked and sipped. I had no idea what he had just said; at that point I didn't really care. Call me a drunk or call me a sage, or call me a drunken sage, but in that delirious moment, sipping wine on a train with the woman I loved and this spy who expounded like a guru, the fellow known as Jack Duran had temporarily vanished, levitating up from the dining car toward some cloudland paradise, a place where bald-headed bodhisattvas floated by on lotus thrones, and soma flowed in golden streams that ran like wild horses. Beyond the wastes of Bactria, beyond Tamerlane's teetering towers of skulls and Stalin's dried-up cotton fields, this hidden paradise had appeared out of nowhere—a breezy green oasis, faint as a mirage. Long ago, those horse-herding Aryans had stumbled on this bottomless watering hole and found themselves invigorated. I'd caught only a glimpse of it, but now I felt determined to find out if it was real.

"More?"

"Please."

Anand grinned and poured, and the three of us once again clinked our golden goblets, a silent toast of camaraderie. Phoebe and I were unaware at the time that the Indian intelligence agent, while happily replenishing our glasses, was not really doing any drinking himself. Cheery as he was, he was sober.

I have little memory of what happened after that, though I do recall Anand raking winnings off the poker table, and Phoebe and I singing *Suspicious Minds* with the two lute pluckers from Urgut. At some point the charming agent kindly offered us his sleeping compartment, and before long I found myself wobbling after Phoebe down the long, snaking aisles of the train. My hands kept inadvertently touching down on shoulders, waking wrathful travelers from their sleep. Phoebe tossed several giddy glances back at me while stumbling in her stiff new pair of pumps. My gaze began to linger on the nape of her neck and the slit down the back of her blouse. To me it appeared like a crack in her shell, a glimpse into the mystery of her body. At the top of the slit, a single pearl button held the carapace in place; I could barely keep my fingers from undoing it.

Enlightenment? "Suchness?" The ultimate Truth? With all the talk of oneness I could think of just one thing: how badly I wanted Miss Chastity to merge with me.

66.
In Your Dreams

The light in the sleeper was out. Phoebe kept flipping the switch. I looked around for the penlight I'd seen Anand using earlier for reading. But he had left nothing behind. His bag and possessions were gone. Even his bed was made. Just as our dinner had appeared prearranged, so did this bequest of his quarters.

The train relentlessly rumbled on with a clock-like *clickety-clack*. A plane of air skimmed in through the barely open window. Beyond it, a faintly flowing blackness framed the ever-present moon.

Phoebe pulled the cotton nightshirt out of her shopping bag. I sat down beside it as she laid it out on the bed. "I doubt that'll fit me," I said.

She laughed. "Don't you cowboys sleep in your clothes?"

I yanked off a snakeskin boot. "Depends on the cowgirl," I said. I pulled off the other boot and looked back up at Phoebe.

She was reaching back, elbows up, unfastening the pivotal pearl. "Which do you prefer: top or bottom?"

It took me a second to realize she was asking about the bunks. "Top," I said.

"Good. I like the bottom."

"Naturally." I stood up. "Need a hand with that?"

She smiled, still straining. "That's sweet, but no, thank you. Would you mind turning around?"

"Would you mind if I didn't?"

"Jack, please?"

Reluctantly I turned and faced the window. "You're not going to try to take advantage of me, are you?"

"In your dreams," she laughed. "I need to get some sleep."

I stared at the moon in the blackness and began to unbutton my shirt. "You must be dreaming if you think I'll let you sleep."

Phoebe didn't respond. Amid the click and rattle of the gently rocking train, I discerned the delicious swishing sound of the black satin blouse softly sliding off over her head. Miraculously her milky figure suddenly appeared in the glass. I shifted for a better view. The reflection was uncanny. Though her face remained in shadow, the moonbeam through the tinted window colored her body blue. Her pale breasts lay cradled in the black demi bra, and her black slacks tapered into darkness. She reached back to an upraised heel to remove an invisible shoe, first one foot, then—with a stumble—the other. Still unaware of me watching, she bent slowly forward, peeling off her pants, hips rocking gently left and right. She was chattering about something, a nervous sort of chatter, but I was so absorbed with her mirror-like reflection I couldn't spare a brain cell to listen.

The blue-skinned Dutch girl in her lace bra and thong was now tilting her head to unpin a pearl earring, dipping the rim of her face into the moonbeam, talking nonstop all the while. Her pincer-like fingers then pinched off her other earring, and as she placed them both carefully into her shopping bag on the bed, my gaze fell to the spider-black lace around her hips, its web narrowing neatly into the cleft between her cheeks. Like butterflies her dexterous hands reached up behind her back and with unthinking expertise unhooked her bra. She brushed the ribbon-like straps off her shoulders and released the crescent cups from her breasts. A spasm of delight coursed through me, trailed by a tender tug of guilt. As she bent over the bed to retrieve her lifeless nightshirt, her breasts swelled into a shape that seemed to cry out for my touch. Finally she straightened and faced me again, preparing to don the gown.

Clickety-clack, clickety-clack, clickety-clack.

Phoebe had stopped talking. She'd noticed I wasn't

listening. And suddenly she saw the reason why.

She froze. Silent. Staring at me in the glass. Realizing I'd been watching all along. For several long seconds, neither of us spoke, and she made no effort to conceal herself. Phoebe seemed to be spellbound by the pull of her own desire, even while refusing to give in to it.

I thrust open the window, erasing the reflection, and in the swirling rush of air, turned around and faced her.

She clutched the gown to her chest. Though her face was veiled in shadow, her eyes mere hints of light, I sensed her nervous tension like an aura.

I pulled off my shirt and dropped it to the floor. "I'm just a man, Phoebe. What is it you're afraid of?" I waited for her to respond, but nothing came out of the dark. "Please don't tell me it's Dan," I said. "I won't believe you."

She looked away, then looked back. Hesitant to answer. Her chest gently rose and fell with every breath she took. I moved closer, trying to see her face, until at last her gleaming eyes came clear. Though fraught with apprehension, they seemed filled with desperate longing. A struggle raging deep inside her heart.

"How do you *know?*" she asked.

I looked at her, uncomprehending.

"How do you know for sure that I'm the one?"

For a moment, I fell silent. Wondering what she meant. Then the emotion I saw in her eyes seemed to find its way into mine. The fear. The desire. The naked longing for love. To fall in love, to be in love, to stay in love forever.

"You have to trust the feeling," I said. "You have to take a chance."

Her gaze fell to my chest. "You mean...have sex."

"No. I mean yes. I mean... I want more than that. I want..." I didn't know how to say it without sounding like a fool. I looked her in the eye. "I want to do what neither of us has ever done before. I want us to make *love*."

The word brought a sigh, as if she truly wanted to believe me.

The train rumbled on, the night swimming past, air

breezing in from all of Asia. "I've been dreaming about this night," I said, "ever since we met."

Her eyelids closed a moment. Soft, feathery lashes. When she opened them again, it seemed she'd made up her mind. "I've been dreaming about it all my life."

I felt a sudden pang for her, an ache deep inside. "Phoebe..."

She reached out slowly and touched my stubbly cheek. As if to feel if it was real, that I was no reflection, that this was not a dream. I gently laid my hand on hers and brought it to my beating heart. To let her feel it throbbing.

Her other hand released the nightshirt she'd been tightly clutching. The shirt fell to her feet. Taking my free hand in hers, she laid my palm against her breast. A sharp breath escaped her.

I caressed her gently. Phoebe started trembling.

The scent of soap on soft white shoulders. Tousled, blue-black hair. Sun-bleached down on sun-dark forearms. Pink, unpolished nails.

I gathered her beauty into my arms. The night air whirled around us. She raised her yearning face to mine and whispered, "I'm yours."

67.
Conqueror of the World

Some hours later, in the middle of the night, the train hissed to a stop in the Samarkand station. Awakened from a blissful sleep, Phoebe and I reluctantly disentangled our limbs and dragged ourselves out of bed. We dressed and exited to the platform where we searched among the disembarking passengers for Anand. When we failed to find him there, we searched back through the train, then through the entire station, and finally, out into the street.

He was nowhere to be seen. The Delhi snake charmer, after luring us into our lovemaking, had inexplicably vanished.

Samarkand looked better in the daylight. The night before, the dark streets and alleys had looked sordid and confining; we withdrew to sleep in the station until morning. Now, as our bus edged down a tree-lined boulevard toward the city's center, turquoise domes blossomed from the red-tiled, green-leaved skyline, and a haze of snowless mountain peaks tinged the air beyond.

We were on our way to the *Gur-e Amir*, Samarkand's "Tomb of the King."

I was eager at the prospect. Despite the fact we had no idea how it might lead us to Dan, the tomb had been the subject of the stolen manuscript, and Woolsey had been convinced we had to travel there. A thin thread, perhaps, but it offered us some hope, and with Phoebe finally at my side, I needed little else.

I took her hand in mine. "I know I probably shouldn't be, but I have to say, for the first time in a very long time...I'm happy."

She squeezed my hand. "I'm happy, too." But her smile seemed less certain. She turned to gaze pensively at the passing line of trees. "If we do find Dan...what will we tell him?"

I wondered if Dan still loved her. It was clear that Phoebe still cared for him. "We'll have to tell him the truth," I said.

Phoebe seemed reluctant. "It would be a shame to finally find him, only to lose him again."

I put my arm around her, and she leaned back snug against me. "We'll take it one step at a time," I said. "Right now, we just need to find him."

Morning sunbeams flared through the trees, searing our bleary eyes. We averted our gaze to the street life, observing local habits and attire. The citizens of Samarkand seemed more secular than Bukhara's. Along with the usual peddlers in prayer caps and tweed were cell-phone chatting commuters in tieless business suits, book-lugging university students in jeans and miniskirts, construction workers in hardhats cueing up for cups of latte, and loitering clusters of unemployed youths playing hip-hop, texting, and hawking Blu-rays.

Perhaps it was a legacy of the cosmopolitan Tamerlane. Phoebe said the continent-conquering psychopath was celebrated as a national hero in Uzbekistan. When freed of Soviet rule, Uzbeks had enlisted him as a patriotic icon to rally their struggling young nationhood. On her weekend visit here the previous summer, Phoebe had watched newlyweds pose for wedding pictures at the ogre-king's monumental statue in the park. As we exited the bus and headed toward the mausoleum, I asked her to tell me what she knew about him.

"He's known here as Timur," she said. "He was born the son of a petty Mongol chief in some small town south of the city. In his youth he was little more than a bandit and mercenary. Early on he was wounded in battle, and walked for the rest of his life with a limp, giving rise to the nickname

"Timur the Lame." In the West it became Tamburlaine, or Tamerlane."

"*Tamburlaine the Great,*" I said. "I remember now—my Shakespeare class at Grinnell. It was a play written by the Bard's contemporary, Christopher Marlowe. First big hit of the London stage—audiences found it shocking."

"For good reason," Phoebe said. "Timur was the worst of the worst."

The steppes of Central Asia, she explained, had long been a womb of terror—2000 years of pillaging and slaughter borne on the back of the horse. First came the marauding Scythians, fierce descendants of the Aryans. Then came Attila and his Huns, then the Mongols led by Genghis Khan. Finally, the Turkic-Mongol Timur emerged, Central Asia's last and most terrifying conqueror.

The "Earth Shaker" marched his massive armies into Persia, the Caucasus, Russia, India, the Middle East, and the Ottoman empire. Renowned for his bravery, the indomitable Timur—unlike Genghis Khan—led his military campaigns in person. His ruthlessness and brutality were calculated to terrorize. Resistance meant annihilation. In a rebellious city south of Herat, Afghanistan, two thousand captives were piled upon each other and cemented alive into a tower. A tax revolt in the Persian city of Isfahan led to the massacre of 70,000 citizens, piling 28 towers, each with 1500 heads. In the ruins of Baghdad, his men stacked 120 towers out of 90,000 skulls. His invasion of India left five million dead.

Listening to Tamerlane's catalog of horrors, I thought of the grinning Buddha and his frail little flower. Fearlessness, courage? The idea seemed absurd. Who could dwell in the miracle of "suchness" while facing an army like Timur's? If "truth alone triumphs," I thought, then truth clearly stood with the butchers.

"The ultimate head-lopper," I said. "Doesn't sound like the kind of guy who'd stop to smell the lotuses."

"Yes, he was a monster," she said. "But he was a brilliant monster. Uneducated but highly intelligent, with a ravenous curiosity and a passion for learning. He had a strong interest in history and in the practical disciplines—mathematics, astronomy, medicine—particularly as applied to war. If Tamerlane heard of a plant that might infuse his soldiers with courage, believe me, he would have been interested."

"Wouldn't it go against the tenets of Islam?" I asked.

"His approach to religion was entirely pragmatic. He fought in the name of Islam and used it to extend his power, but he also invoked shamanism, omens, astrology and ritual to serve his military ambitions. The religious rites of the *Hashishin* would have been fantastically intriguing."

We left the street and headed through a park toward the aquamarine dome we had spotted from across the city. It looked unlike any other—ribbed and swollen like a cantaloupe and crowned with a golden stem. The dome was flanked on either side by two slender minarets, and before it lay a courtyard walled off by a monumental entrance portal.

We passed through the portal under a blaze of blue and golden tiles. In the courtyard garden, a pair of toothless crones wearing dresses over pajama pants, and babushkas on their heads, were hacking overgrown hedges with short-bladed scythes. One of them muttered something to Phoebe.

It was too early, Phoebe told me as we approached the mausoleum. The building wouldn't open for at least another hour. Which explained the fact that no tourists had arrived, and why, in the nearby parking lot, there was only a single car.

I gazed up at the dome. It was set atop a high drum of blue, green, and golden tiles blazed with an inscription in huge Arabic letters.

"'God is Immortal,'" Phoebe translated.

"Thank God Tamerlane wasn't," I said. "Since when do you read Arabic?"

"I don't," she said, still scanning the façade. "That's what I was told the last time I was here. But I have to say I didn't notice *that*." She nodded toward a pattern of flower tendrils and a lotus motif woven into the intricate mosaics.

"You often don't see a thing until you're looking for it," I said.

"Then you wonder how you ever could have missed it."

We walked under the entrance arch and tried the wooden door. As expected, it was locked.

I pounded it in frustration. The door remained resolutely shut.

"We can wait in the garden," Phoebe suggested.

I stood with her and stared across the courtyard at the crones, heading off with stuffed sacks of clippings. "We don't even know why we're here," I said.

"Wild goose chase," Phoebe said.

"Wild camel chase, you mean." I pulled it from my pocket.

"I can't look at that now," she said, "without imagining a bale of hay burning on its back."

"Camels on fire, hell of a distraction." I pondered the jade piece. "Maybe Anand's Delhi story was nothing more than that—a distraction, along with the dinner and that wine. I'd sure love to know what he's up to."

"Research and analysis," Phoebe said. "I just hope nothing bad has happened to him."

"I wouldn't be surprised if—"

The door creaked open behind us. A figure boded forth from the darkness.

68.
Moonbeam

No, not Anand, it turned out, but a thin, bearded man in an ill-fitting jacket and tattered skullcap, holding a wicker broom like a staff.

"You're open!" I exclaimed.

"I am only the caretaker," he said. "I am working in the cellar and hear banging. *Gur-e Amir* opens in one—"

"I'm sorry," I said. "I know we're a little early, but it's very import—"

The man started closing the door, waving us way. Phoebe pleaded with him but the door kept moving.

I held it open.

"Last night a friend of ours was killed," I said. "He gave us something we think might be related to the tomb. We have to find out why—what he was trying to tell us. Please, I beg you."

His scowl appeared to slacken. The man looked carefully at Phoebe, then carefully studied me. We certainly didn't *look* like grave robbers. After glancing around the grounds to be sure we were alone, he stepped aside and waved us in.

"You're very kind," I said.

We followed him down a cool, dim passageway with a vaulted ceiling, our eyes slowly adjusting from the bright sunlight. At the end of it we emerged into the cavernous central chamber, far larger and more impressive than I'd imagined from outside.

"Wow…"

We had entered the heart of a jewel. Every surface glimmered. High above, sunbeams shone through latticed windows across the gilded dome, effusing a soft, luxurious shimmer on all that lay below. The four vast walls, each inset with elaborate bays, were lined with an astonishing array of tiles and patterns, from hexagonal onyx in the lower sections, to circling streams of Koranic inscriptions in flowing gold and jasper, to mosaics laced with golden flowers and iridescent stars.

I immediately began searching for lotuses or camels, craning my neck and whirling, but no telltale image declared itself in the interlacing matrix, and the sheer dazzling complexity of it all put my head in a spin. It was as if the entire cosmos had been condensed into a puzzle. The futile attempt to decipher it left me visually overwhelmed.

I steadied myself against a balustrade. The marble railing fenced off the central part of the chamber, directly beneath the dome, where the graves of the mighty were gathered. There were six rectangular blocks of pale marble and alabaster, and in the middle of them, where Phoebe was pointing, a six-foot carved monolith of near-black jade, set atop a marble plinth.

"That's Tamerlane's," she said. "He lies at the foot of his spiritual advisor, a Sufi imam. The others are Tamerlane's sons and grandsons."

The imam's grave was larger, and others were more ornate, yet Tamerlane's simple stone stood out, dark amid their pallor. It appeared to be the same black jade as the chess piece. I moved to get a better view of it.

The caretaker watched with casual interest, hands folded atop his broomstick. "Is carved from a single stone," he said. "The largest block of jade in the world."

"It was placed here by his grandson," Phoebe added. "The astronomer sultan Ulug Beg. He lies buried at Tamerlane's feet."

His was a small block of flesh-colored marble, devoid of any inscription. In contrast, the entire perimeter of Tamerlane's block seethed with a slashing Arabic. I asked the caretaker if he knew what it said.

"Is listing of Timur's ancestors," he replied. "From Genghis Khan all the way back to the Commander of the Faithful, Caliph Ali. It say he appeared in the form of a moonbeam, to make pregnant Tamerlane's virgin mother, Alangoa."

Phoebe glanced askance at him as she stepped up beside me. "It was propaganda perpetrated by his grandson, Ulug Beg, to unite the history of the Mongols with the heritage of Islam. Timur was a megalomaniac, but he never claimed descent from such noble ancestors."

The caretaker grinned wryly, as if in pity of Phoebe's pettiness. "Greatness gives birth to great legends," he said.

"Yes, even virgin births," Phoebe said.

"Insha'Allah," he replied. "It is written that truth, even if it were painful, delighted Timur." Scowling, he took up his broom and poked at the floor.

I looked at Phoebe. "Interesting about the moonbeam."

She cocked an eyebrow. "Don't get any ideas," she said.

I laughed. "Seriously." Turning away from the caretaker, I lowered my voice so he couldn't hear. "Soma was regarded as the moon, remember? Dan made note of it in his *Rig Veda* text."

"You're right. The crescent moon was the cup that contained the soma drink for the gods. It waned when they drank it, and waxed when the Soma god replenished himself."

"And soma is described as enhancing the virility of the men and gods who consumed it."

Phoebe eyed Ulug Beg's gravestone. "I wonder…"

"If Timur's grandson knew about soma?"

Phoebe sighed. "I don't know," she said.

We were grasping at straws. Our gaze fell dispiritedly on Tamerlane's jade.

Black jade, I thought. A Bactrian camel. Beast of burden on the famous Silk Road. What did it say about soma or Tamerlane?

Staring down into the inky block, I tried to imagine the shrunken monster rotting for centuries beneath it. After all I had heard about the Conqueror of the World, it seemed somehow impossible that he'd be reduced to this.

"He's not there," Phoebe said as if she'd read my thoughts.

"What do you mean?"

"It's a memorial, a cenotaph. The actual grave is in the crypt below. Isn't it?" she asked the caretaker.

He looked up from his sweeping and saw at once where this was heading. "The crypt is closed to visitors, madam."

Phoebe dug into her wallet. "Last time I was here, the guide took us down for a two dollar fee."

"But I am not a guide."

"I'll pay you twenty," she said, holding out the bill.

He eyed it suspiciously. "Why do you offer this? The crypt is only a shadow of the glory you see here. What is it you seek?"

Phoebe glanced at me, hesitant to answer.

"We're not exactly sure," I said. "We just don't think we've found it yet."

He eyed me as if deciding if I was a liar or just a fool. The latter, it seemed from his bemused shrug. He waved aside Phoebe's cash. "I will take no barter in the presence of the dead. Please, follow me."

The man led us across to a corner of the chamber where a hidden stairwell descended steeply into the dark. He gestured for us to proceed him.

I paused at the top of the stairs, overcome with a sense of foreboding.

69.
The Crypt

Phoebe and I cautiously made our way down the shadowy steps. At the bottom we passed through a doorway into a glacial, echoing blackness. Phoebe hugged her arms. I tried to peer beyond her but couldn't see a thing, until finally, behind us, the caretaker flipped a switch.

The light fixture hung from a sweeping vault of bare brick and stone. Though smaller and drably unadorned, the crypt mirrored the layout of the great chamber above us, with deep, arched, inset bays tapering off into darkness.

In the pool of light at the center of the room lay seven flat, rectangular graveslabs.

"They're arranged exactly the same as the cenotaphs upstairs," Phoebe said.

I moved among them. "Then this one would be his," I said. I crouched down beside the emperor's slab. It was not made of jade, but of plain, pale stone, split clean across in two places. Its entire surface was lightly inscribed with the same seething script as the cenotaph.

"The genealogy again," Phoebe said. "Lest anyone forget."

The caretaker stepped beside us. "Also it holds a warning: 'Anyone who violates my stillness in this life or the next will be subjected to inevitable punishment and misery.'"

"Fitting epitaph for a terrorist tyrant," I said. "Still issuing threats from the grave."

The caretaker eyed the slab somberly. "It was said that for a year after Timur's internment, people heard him howling from the earth."

"My goodness," Phoebe said. We gazed around the chamber. The darkness felt palpable, the air cold and still. "It's awfully quiet down here now," she said.

The silence was unnerving. I stared at the broken graveslab, trying again to imagine the corpse crumbling to dust beneath it. What secrets had the tyrant taken with him to the grave? I asked the caretaker if—despite Timur's warning not to "violate his stillness"—the tomb had ever been opened.

"Yes," he answered. "In 1941. Russian anthropologists opened the coffin. They found the skeleton of a big man, lame on his right side—just as the stories told." The caretaker's eyes crinkled knowingly. "A few hours later, the news arrive that Hitler is invading Mother Russia."

I squinted skeptically.

"It's true," Phoebe said. "And when the body was re-interred in 1942, the battle of Stalingrad began—the turning point of the war."

"I'll be damned," I said.

The remark drew a glare from the caretaker. "Fear the fire," he admonished, "and fear Allah wherever you may be."

"Of course," I said. "And fear Tamerlane's ghost, too, apparently."

"When they opened the grave," Phoebe asked, "do you know if they found anything else buried with him?"

"What else, Miss?"

"Like flowers, maybe, or perhaps flower seeds?"

He looked at her curiously. "I have not heard of this. Why do you ask such a question?"

Phoebe and I exchanged a glance. So much had been revealed, why hold back now? I turned to face the caretaker. "Did you ever hear of a professor from Bukhara named Borzoo Baghestani?"

His hand flew over his heart. "May peace be upon him. I hear of his terrible murder. A very kind and learned man. He visit the tomb here many times."

Again I glanced at Phoebe, then pulled out the camel chess piece. "Another man was killed last night—a friend of the professor. He thought this would help us find something, some secret in this tomb. Do you have any idea what he meant?"

The man took the piece from me. He seemed intensely curious about it, and held it up under the light. The dark camel gleamed with its sinister allure. "Yes," he said slowly. *"Yes."* He turned to us, beaming. *"The secret is right before your eyes!"*

He reached under his jacket.

BLAM! BLAM! White-hot gunshots pierced the dark.

The earsplitting blasts stunned me. I turned in fright to Phoebe to see if she'd been hit. A startled look had frozen on her face.

She was gaping at the caretaker. He stared back vaguely into the empty space between them. Then he staggered forward and crumpled to his knees. He opened up his right hand and gazed down at the camel, then he looked back up at us and tumbled over, dead.

Two bullet holes bled out his back, just behind his heart.

We peered into the darkness beyond him. Out from the shadows stepped the stout figure of Anand. His eyes were on the caretaker, his hands clamping the revolver he had seized on the train.

Phoebe gawked in horror. *"Anand—what have you done!"* She rolled the caretaker onto his back and checked his throat for a pulse. Grimacing in bewilderment, she glared up at Anand. "He's *dead*."

"Save your pity," he said. He reached down and pulled aside the caretaker's jacket, revealing a Damascene dagger in a sheath.

"An *Assassin?"* I said.

"Yes, though not the one who killed Professor Woolsey, I suspect." He nodded toward the darkness behind him. "The real janitor lies back there."

I ventured in that direction with Phoebe. A man's body appeared like a shadow on the floor. Stripped of his jacket, he lay beside a puddle of blood from a slit across his throat.

The Assassin had apparently murdered the janitor, then donned the dead man's jacket and cap when he heard our knock at the door.

Anand walked up to the body, wiping the revolver with his handkerchief. He placed the gun in the caretaker's hand and pointed it toward the Assassin. "Perhaps the poor fellow was not quite dead when the Iranian walked away from him."

Phoebe and I stood gaping at Anand in amazement. I realized that once again he wasn't wearing shoes. No wonder we hadn't heard him. He bent down to pick up the Assassin's own suit jacket, neatly folded on the floor nearby—alongside an iron crowbar. Pulling a passport out of the jacket, he read the owner's name: "Mowwafak Mousavian." Anand placed the passport back in the suit pocket, then fished out the Iranian's car keys—"Don't think he'll be needing these—" and slipped them into his pocket.

His nonchalance irritated Phoebe. "This is *crazy*," she said. "We have to inform the police."

Anand addressed her calmly in his lilting intonation. "I told you how I feel about the Uzbek police. But of course I will leave that to you. I'd appreciate it, however, if you delayed a few minutes"—he picked up the crowbar, appraising it—"long enough to find out what he was looking for in that grave."

70.
Grave Robbers

The night before, Anand had come straight from the train station to Tamerlane's mausoleum. Finding the building securely locked and no one answering the door, he decided to set up a stakeout and await the Iranian's arrival. It wouldn't be long, he thought. An Assassin had murdered Woolsey for Baghestani's research, and according to Woolsey that research would direct him to the tomb.

The answer to Tamerlane's soma secret lay in the mausoleum. With nothing more than a chess piece to go on, Anand felt he had little choice but to wait.

What he didn't know was that another Assassin was already inside.

"How did he get here so quick?" I asked.

"The call outside the travel agent's office," Phoebe said. "They must have sent him here immediately when they found out where you were going."

"He forced his way in with the janitor," Anand said, "then killed him here in the crypt."

"So he was in here all night by himself?" Phoebe asked.

"It wasn't until you two showed up that he finally came to the door."

"He must have been waiting for us," I said. "To find out what we knew."

"And to kill us," Phoebe said.

I bent down to retrieve the jade camel from the corpse. Though rigor mortis had not yet set in, the cold, curled fingers seemed to cling to it. I bolted upright. "You sure that guy is dead?"

"He doesn't have a pulse," Phoebe said, then glanced around the dark. "But down here, who knows?"

I raised the chess piece up into the light, just as the Assassin had. "Right before your eyes," I quoted, wondering what he had meant. The black jade seemed to devour the light and exude a kind of darker luminescence of its own—vividly present, yet negative and cold, like some sinister inversion of "suchness."

Anand lowered my hand. "Right before your eyes," he said.

I looked down. We were standing before Tamerlane's graveslab.

"Whatever it is that's in that grave," he said, "it mustn't be left for the *Hashishin.*"

I stared at the ominous Arabic inscription. "I'm not sure I can take any more punishment and misery."

"Let's just hope we don't start another war," Phoebe said.

Two cracks split the 600-year-old slab into three separate segments. Anand began tapping each one with the crowbar, gauging their relative size and weight. "We haven't much time," he said. "The tail segment seems the smallest and lightest. I would suggest—"

A thumping sound interrupted him.

The three of us fell silent, listening.

The sound came again—a muffled double thud. We stared down at the grave.

"Oh my God," I said.

Again, another thump, with a barely-audible shout, as if Tamerlane were howling to be let out of his tomb.

"Quickly!" Anand said. He stepped between us and slipped the tip of the crowbar under the stone. Applying the full force of his weight against the bar, he levered the tail segment, shifting it over half a foot, opening up the crack.

Phoebe and I peered inside and detected a shadowy movement. "He's alive!" I shouted.

"Pull the stone!" Anand commanded. We slipped our fingers into the crack and hauled the block as he levered. One final strenuous tug slid it completely off.

The air thickened with a ghastly odor. Our heads came together as we gaped into the grave. Two pairs of feet lay side-by-side, one completely wrapped in linen, the other clad in hiking boots, ankles lashed with rope.

"Get him out!" Phoebe cried. Anand and I grabbed the bound ankles and hauled them out the gap. Blood stained the trouser legs. An open shirt revealed the man's bare chest, streaked with bleeding wounds. His wrists were tied behind his back. Phoebe grabbed his shoulders as at last his head appeared: long, scraggly blondish hair, dark with blood and sweat; a gag stretched across his mouth, a cut across his throat.

The whiskered face looked so battered I failed to recognize it. Not until we set him down and Phoebe fell upon him.

"Daniel, my God! What have they done to you?"

I dropped down beside him, so shocked I couldn't speak. Like Oriana's Jewish star, a bloody Christian cross had been carved into his chest.

Anand took up the Assassin's blade and reached to cut loose the gag. Dan jerked back, terrified.

"It's all right," I said. "Anand is a friend."

The agent handed the blade to me. I gently sliced the gag.

"Water," Dan whispered.

I grabbed a bottle from my pack. Lifting his head, we let him drink. It brought him slowly back to life. "I must have passed out," he said.

"Not much air through those cracks," Anand said. "The gunshot and my tapping probably roused you."

"You're okay now, brother." I rolled him onto his side and cut his hands free. Phoebe took the blade from me and sawed the rope from his feet. "Can you stand?" she asked. We helped him up.

Anand wiped our prints from the dagger's handle, then carefully reinserted the knife back into the Assassin's sheath.

Standing unsteadily between Phoebe and me, Dan stared down at the killer's corpse, unable to look away. The blood on my brother's face, I noticed, was streaked with tracks from tears.

"He can't hurt you anymore," Phoebe said.

Dan looked more depleted than resentful. "He thought I was holding out."

"You did hold out," Phoebe assured him.

"I don't have that much courage," he said. "I told him everything I knew."

"He's dead," I said. "It doesn't matter."

Dan remained disconsolate. "It matters," he said, "to me."

"You live to be brave another day," Anand said. He was busy prying open the head end of the grave. "Lend me a hand here, Jack. We're running out of time."

I helped him slide the stone aside.

"There's nothing there," Dan said. "Only Timur's bones."

"Afraid you're right," Anand said, withdrawing his head from the hollow. He tore open the top of the burial sheet. A puff of dust settled as we peered into the slit. I glimpsed a patch of sallow skull, scraps of skin still clinging to it, and clumps of russet beard.

"Conqueror of the World," I said.

Anand turned to Dan. "It was you then, I take it, opened the grave?"

"I came in with the tourists," he said. "Concealed that crowbar in my pants leg, and hid down here when the building closed." He nodded toward the sarcophagus. "I was struggling with that gravestone when he struck me from behind."

Anand eyed the Assassin's corpse. "He must have got in when the janitor arrived."

"He never made a sound," Dan said.

Anand said, "The dagger is silent."

By the time Dan regained consciousness, the Assassin had bound him hand and foot. "That's when he started with the knife. And his fists. I finally passed out…and woke up in the grave. He threatened to leave me there to die."

"What did he want?" Phoebe asked.

"The same thing they all want." Dan cast a wary glance at Anand. "The source of the soma lotus."

"No cell phone reception down here," Anand said. "He probably didn't receive word from Bukhara until later."

Phoebe turned to Dan. "But certainly you told him. Didn't you?"

"The source? No. I don't know where it is."

"You don't *know*?" I said. "You mean you didn't tell Baghestani?"

"No."

"Dan, please," Phoebe said. "There's no sense keeping it secret any longer."

He turned his weary gaze to her. "Why do you think I'm here?" he said. "Believe me, if I knew the place where the seeds came from, I would have told him long before he stuffed me in that grave."

We stared at him, dumbfounded. "But you're the one who found the fresh seeds," I said. "That's why all these people have been after you."

"I didn't find the seeds," he said. "I stole them."

Phoebe riled up. "So *that's* why you didn't tell me."

"Who did you steal them from?" I asked.

"A Swiss mountaineer named Felix Fiore."

"I met him!" I said. "In Rome. He's the retired CEO of a pharmaceutical company. He's been trying to track you down."

Phoebe stared at Dan as if she didn't recognize him. "You really have turned into a *thief*," she said.

"I told him I'd return the seeds if he told me where he got them."

"I was wrong then," Phoebe said. "You're an extortionist *and* a thief."

"I'm a scientist, Phoebe, despite what you think. I'm looking for answers—"

"You've put yourself and all of us in danger. I don't see how—"

"Please, not now," I said, amazed at how quickly they'd fallen back into bickering. "We're wasting time. What about Baghesta—"

"Afraid you're right," Anand said, vigorously wiping the pry bar to remove his fingerprints. "The doors will open any moment now. If we don't clear out of here, we risk arrest for murder." He placed the bar in the grip of the dead Assassin, then rose and turned to me. "Please. Show your brother."

I'd almost forgotten. Pulling the camel out of my pocket, I told Dan, "This is from a Tamerlane chess set that belonged to Professor Baghestani. It looks to be made from the same jade as the cenotaph upstairs. Does it mean anything to you?"

Dan turned it in his hand, mystified.

"Two spaces diagonal, two straight," Phoebe said.

He pondered, still puzzled.

"It's Bactrian," I said. "Camel caravans? The Silk Road? *Anything?*"

Finally he shook his head, looked at us, and shrugged.

"Well then," Anand said. "It would appear we've arrived at a dead end indeed."

71. The Scientist

A block away from the mausoleum we spotted the Iranian's car: no surprise, a black Mercedes, tinted windows and all. A click of the key fob confirmed it. Within seconds Anand was chauffeuring us down another broad, tree-lined boulevard, heading toward Samarkand's tourist mecca, the central square known as the Registan bazaar. With only the caravan camel as a clue, Anand had decided he wanted a map of the ancient Silk Road route.

No one had any better ideas.

In the back seat, behind the tinted windows, Phoebe quickly set to work patching up my brother. I turned around and watched, trying to comprehend the fact that we'd actually managed to find him. Alive. It was a great relief and, despite his abysmal condition, a joy to finally see him again.

Phoebe soaked his shirt with bottled water and used it to wipe the dried blood from his chest. After swabbing the cuts with disinfectant, she plastered them with the last remaining bandages in my kit. The wounds, though painful, were not too dangerously deep, and despite the beating he'd taken, no bones appeared to be broken. It was clear the Assassin had wanted to keep Dan alive—at least until he got some answers.

I needed a few myself—starting with Tamerlane. "Why the tomb?" I asked.

Dan winced as Phoebe dabbed a contusion at his temple. "Sorry," she said.

"It's all right," he said. "I much prefer being tortured by

you."

"Don't be so sure," she said. "I'm just getting started."

"Promises, promises."

Their bantering bothered me. "Dan—why the tomb?"

"Baghestani believed Tamerlane must have known a good deal about soma. The Sufis—"

"Ahmed Yasawi—the bronze cauldron?" Phoebe wanted her theory confirmed.

"Yeah," Dan said. "He looked into that. The connection very likely came through Tamerlane's Sufi imam. But it might have been even simpler than that. For centuries rumors of a sacred soma plant had passed with the caravans along the Silk Road. Tamerlane was bound to have heard—"

"Hold still," Phoebe said. She spread a butterfly bandage over an inch-long split on his cheek. "There. Just try not to smile."

"Impossible when I'm looking at y—" He winced as she wiped dried blood from his chin.

"That help?" she said.

"You're a sadist."

"I thought that's what you liked about me. Answer your brother's question."

"What question?"

"Tamerlane," I said. "The Silk Road. You were saying there would have been rumors."

"Yes. Many believed the soma plant still grew somewhere in Asia. Baghestani said Tamerlane searched for it during his ransacking invasion of India, and was looking for it again, toward the end of his life, when he turned his sights on China."

"The terminus of the Silk Road," I said, glancing at Anand.

"Indeed," Anand said. "China was once the richest kingdom in the world."

"The Celestial Empire," Dan said. "Ultimate prize for the Mongol warrior who'd never been defeated in battle. He planned and prepared the invasion for years. It was to be his final campaign."

"I thought the invasion never happened," Phoebe said.

"It didn't," Dan said. "Not long after he embarked with his

army, severe winter snowstorms brought the march to a halt. Tamerlane fell ill with a fever and died. He was 69 years old. His body was carried back to Samarkand and interred in the mausoleum."

"So he never found the place where the lotus grew," I said.

"Baghestani believed he did," Dan said. "He just never made it there himself."

"What do you mean?"

Dan watched warily from the corner of his eye as Phoebe applied a salve to the abrasion on his jaw. "Like I said, Tamerlane had spent years preparing the invasion. That was his usual method. His planning was meticulous, and he placed a premium on collecting good intelligence. A net of spies had fanned out across Asia into China—traders, craftsmen, laborers, wandering hermits, itinerant monks, dervishes, fakirs, Sufis. For years they reported back all they saw or heard. His most trusted emir, a man named Allahdad, developed a detailed survey for the king, of every city and village, every tribe and castle, every river, mountain and desert he might encounter."

"And you believe they found the source of the lotus," I said.

"According to Baghestani, when Tamerlane died, the intelligence was passed on to his grandson, Ulug Beg, the eventual heir to the throne in Samarkand."

"The one who built the tomb," Phoebe said.

I thought of his final resting place at the foot of his grandfather, just as Tamerlane rested at the foot of his imam.

"Ulug Beg's writings about the tomb are deliberately obscure," Dan said. "Baghestani was trying to decipher them. They seem to suggest that some form of tribute was left in the grave, in honor of his grandfather's final, unfulfilled desire."

His unfulfilled desire. That was the sense I'd had, standing over his grave: that the insatiable Conqueror of the World, his dreams curtailed at last by death, was condemned to spend eternity beneath a block of stone.

"If there was something in the grave," Anand asked, "wouldn't the Soviet archaeologists have found it?"

"Baghestani read their records. They make no mention of soma, or of any maps or information related to the lotus. He thought they must have missed something, or possibly been censored. Baghestani petitioned the Uzbek government to allow him to open the grave. They refused."

"Not surprising," I said, "given what happened the last time."

"Of course that didn't stop *you*," Phoebe said. She was cleaning crusted blood from his ear.

"I'm determined," he said.

"So was Tamerlane," she said. "The truth is, like him, you're afraid."

"Here we go. Afraid of what?"

Phoebe stopped fussing with his ear. "Afraid of dying before you find this thing you're dying to find."

Dan stared back, blinking.

"Registan Square," Anand announced, pulling the car to the curb.

We peered out through the tinted glass. A vast expanse of open courtyard stretched out beneath the high facades of three massive monuments—former madrasahs, or religious colleges, their entry arches soaring between pairs of minarets. One building formed the far end; the other two, flanking it, mirrored each other perfectly across the empty space. The vastness and the symmetry evoked a sense of calm. Tourists meandered leisurely. Vendors hawked their wares. We seemed a million miles from the murder in the tomb.

But Anand remained uneasy. "Wait here," he said, unlatching his door. "If you see the police, or anyone suspicious, don't hesitate, just drive away. As quickly as you can."

He left the engine running. We watched him cross the square.

"RAW?" Dan asked.

"That and more, I imagine," Phoebe said.

"He looks like the mountain men I met in Nepal. Only he's

evidently got a bigger appetite."

"He told us he was born in Kathmandu," I said. "But he's lived most of his life in Delhi."

Phoebe tried to reassure Dan. "He saved our lives," she said.

"More than once," I added.

We watched Anand pause to briefly scan the square, then disappear into the darkness of a madrasah's towering portal.

"That school was built by Ulug Beg," Dan said. "If he knew it had been converted into tourist shops, he'd be turning over in his grave."

I thought again of his modest block of marble, set at the foot of his grandfather's massive block of jade. "Did you say Ulug Beg's writings about the tomb were *deliberately* obscure?"

"There's no other way to describe them," he said. "The tribute was implied, never specified. As though he were hiding something."

"The source of the soma, you mean."

"Ulug Beg was a brilliant astronomer and mathematician," Dan said, "with a passion for medicine and philosophy, and for poetry and music and the arts. He never had the military ambitions of his grandfather. After seeing all the terror Tamerlane wrought, he must have thought it best to leave the soma hidden."

"Maybe he was right," I said. I was beginning to feel a kinship with this fellow, Ulug Beg. Especially in comparison to his psychopathic granddad. Better to be a stargazer mapping out the heavens than a warmonger piling up pyramids of skulls. "If soma's been hidden for centuries, why bring it out into the world again now?"

"I don't want to bring it out," Dan said. "I just want to find it."

"Why?"

He looked at us as if he were debating whether to say.

Phoebe grew impatient. "Dan?"

"I think..." He paused, looking uncomfortable. "I think the source of the lotus plant is the kingdom of Shambhala."

"Shangri-la?" I said.

"You can't be serious," Phoebe said.

"The monasteries of Shambhala were reputed to hold the most powerful secrets of the sages of the East—"

"Shambhala is a utopian myth," Phoebe said. "Like the Garden of Eden or the Fountain of Youth."

"It may have once been a real place," Dan said. "If I could discover where the soma plant is grown, it might tell me where that place was—or is."

"So you believe Shambhala really exists," Phoebe said.

"I want to find out if it does. I don't 'believe' anything. I told you, I'm a scientist. I trust only my experience—what I can prove or I can see."

"All this you've put us through," I said. "People killed. You tortured. For what? Why is it so important? Why does it matter to you?"

"It matters," he said. "I'm sorry about what's happened. I didn't mean it to. But I can't help myself; it's just the way I'm wired. I have to know the truth."

That word again.

"Ever heard that saying," Phoebe asked: "A wise man sees as much as he ought, not as much as he can?"

Dan stared off thoughtfully at the madrasahs in the distance. "What do you see—out there? Minarets? Madrasahs? Look at the basic structure. See those giant portal arches? Every major madrasah, every traditional mosque has one. It's a basic feature of Islamic architecture—it represents the gate to paradise. Over the portal of the madrasah he built in Bukhara, Ulug Beg inscribed a quote from the Hadith: 'It is the duty of every true Muslim, man and woman, to strive after knowledge.' For him the search for truth was the path to paradise. Ulug Beg ruled Timur's empire for nearly half a century. It was a golden age of learning and science."

"Another paradise on earth," I said. "A Muslim Shangri-la."

"Not everybody thought so. Even his own son felt he'd gone too far. Ultimately, Ulug Beg was beheaded by religious reactionaries."

"Some things never change," Phoebe said.

I agreed. "One man's utopia is another man's hell."

We gazed off across the plaza. Phoebe asked, "I wonder if Anand's all right?" He had yet to emerge from the madrasah.

I noticed a group of vendors nearby, their wares set out on the flagstones. "I'll be right back," I said.

Something had caught my eye—something dark and gleaming.

72.
Kukri

I crossed the short distance to the cluster of trees where the vendors sat cross-legged in the shade. Among the items on display—silk slippers, jewelry, painted porcelain tiles—one seller had laid out a lacquered chess board arrayed with the traditional pieces. The black pieces looked similar to the camel in my pocket.

The secret is right before your eyes.

I picked up the black king to have a closer look. It was indeed tinged inky green, that same exquisite night-jade color. Sinister, yet seductive. So black it seemed to suck in light, so sensual it made you want to clutch it.

Fear, I thought. And *craving*.

Black jade embodied the antithesis of soma. The opposite of fearlessness. The converse of contentment.

I thought again of Tamerlane's somber cenotaph, the black block installed over his tomb by Ulug Beg. With the same dark luster as this king in my hand, the stone expressed the yearnings of the howling corpse beneath it, exuding a gleaming emptiness, a sort of vivid void.

Was it not the perfect tribute to his unfulfilled desire?

A wizened Mongoloid face peered up at me, curious at my expression.

"Where was this made?" I asked.

"Jay!" he said emphatically.

"Yes. But *where?* Where does the jade come from?"

"Xitoy," he said.

It sounded like some magical, Oriental kingdom. Or maybe just a Samarkand toy store. "Where is…Xitoy?"

The man slowly raised his arm and pointed toward the street. "Tha' way," he said.

I looked and saw nothing. No store, just the street.

The man deadpanned his fellows. They slapped their knees and laughed.

"Xitoy eez China," one man said. Another cried, "Made een China!"

Amid their laughter, a horn beeped; I turned toward the car. Phoebe rolled her window down and gestured off behind me.

Across the square, two tall, bearded men shuffled toward the madrasahs. One of them limped, severely. Both were wearing dirty clothes, tattered and disheveled—dark vests over white kaftans and baggy pajama pants.

Black turban. Checkered turban. The Taliban men we tossed from the train!

Phoebe frantically waved me to the car. They'd kill us if they spotted us. I casually set down the chess piece and started walking toward her, resisting the temptation to break into a run.

The two jihadis paused and scanned around the plaza. Praying they wouldn't see me, I turned my face away and strode on quickly toward the car. Phoebe's tinted window rose, concealing her from view. I raced to the driver's door. Just before I climbed inside, I stole another glance.

The two men were rushing toward Ulug Beg's madrasah. Anand had emerged from the portal. Struggling to fold up a map.

"We've got to get out of here!" Phoebe cried as I climbed behind the wheel.

The men were snaking through a crowd of tourists. Anand had still not noticed them.

I threw the car in gear, hit the gas—and rammed up over the curb.

"Jack?!"

"We're not leaving without him," I said. Rumbling over the flagstones, I headed straight for Anand.

Pedestrians fled our path in a panic. Anand saw us coming and turned to look behind. Emerging from the crowd were the two jihadis, one limping, the other at a run.

"He's got a gun!" Dan shouted.

The limper in the black turban paused to raise his pistol, aiming directly at Anand.

Tourists bolted, screaming.

"Get down!" I shouted. Dan and Phoebe ducked. I swung the car around Anand, skidding across the flagstones and blocking the Pashtun's shot. The bullet pierced the rear windshield and ripped the front-seat headrest. I flinched as a second shot sparked the rim of my door.

Despite his bulk, Anand moved fast. He jumped into the passenger seat without my even stopping. But as he reached to close his door, the jihadi in the checkered turban grabbed hold of his arm. The man ran alongside, tugging at Anand.

I hit the gas, then slammed on the brakes—an old woman with a walker stood petrified before us. We skidded to a stop at her toes.

Another gunshot zinged the trunk.

The jihadi swiped a pocket-size dagger at Anand. In a flash Anand pulled a machete from his jacket and slashed across the Pashtun's chest.

The man fell backwards, wailing.

Stunned, I wheeled away from the lady with the walker and floored it across the square. Two more gun blasts echoed behind us. I cringed behind the wheel, but no bullet struck the car. Hurtling over the curb, we flew back onto the pavement and roared off up the street.

I glanced into the rearview mirror, my heart pounding furiously. Dan and Phoebe raised their heads. Anand pulled out his handkerchief and coolly wiped his knife.

"Where did *that* come from?" I asked.

"From a very talented blacksmith in Surya Benai."

The weapon looked as vicious as a *Hashishin* dagger, but longer, and made out of ordinary steel. Curved slightly inward, the blade broadened toward the tip and stretched the length of his forearm.

"A kukri knife," Dan said, peering over the seat. He slapped my shoulder. "You just rescued a Gurkha, Jack!"

"Former Gurkha," Anand said, sliding the knife back into its sheath. "And one most grateful for your gallantry."

I returned his gaze incredulously. The gratitude in his glistening eyes betrayed no lingering tension, as if he'd just awakened from a catnap. "Gurkha—what is that?—like a Ninja?"

Anand giggled.

"They're legendary," Dan said. "Bravest of the brave. 'Better to die than be a coward' is their motto. It's said that if a man claims he's not afraid of death, he's either telling you a lie or he's a Gurkha. Which brigade?" he asked Anand. "Nepalese or Indi—?"

Phoebe interrupted, peering out the back. "The police will be looking for us—we've got to get rid of this car."

My hands still trembled uncontrollably on the wheel. I couldn't seem to focus on the street signs. "I don't even know where we're going," I said.

"I do," Dan said. "Make a right at the next corner. Circle back to Tashkent Road and take it north to the edge of town. We're going up to Ulug Beg's Observatory."

"What now?" Phoebe asked. "A lecture on astronomy?"

I began to imagine some long-forgotten camel constellation. Or maybe a Silk Road lodestar. And of course there was that story about soma and the moon—

"You think it's where Ulug Beg hid his secret?" Anand asked.

"No," Dan said. "It's where I stashed my car."

73.
The Observatory

When Ulug Beg built his hilltop observatory in the 1420s, it was the biggest and best equipped in the world, with a colossal marble sextant hewn into the rock, a huge rotating quadrant mounted on curving brass rails, a rooftop azimuth-calibrating circle, a massive concave solar clock integrated with the sextant, and a scholars' library consisting of some 15,000 books. A cutting-edge research facility, Dan asserted, the Stanford or Scripps of its time.

Which is why it was torched and razed to the ground by the same fundamentalists who beheaded Ulug Beg. All that remains today is what was carved into the earth: the giant semicircular trench of the sextant, excavated in 1908.

A tall, white-marble plaque nearby displays the astronomer-king's epitaph:

Religion disperses like a fog,
Kingdoms perish,
But the works of scholars remain for an eternity.

"*Some* scholars, anyway," Phoebe lamented. "Most I've known are numskulls." As Dan glowered, she smoothed down the bandage that loosened on his cheek. "Or criminals," she added.

"Certainly beats Tamerlane's epitaph," I said. *"Do not disturb, or else!"*

Anand neatly summed up the two contrasting kingships: "Tamerlane used his religion to seek more power," he said. "Ulug Beg used his power to seek the truth."

Here we go again, I thought, and spoke the thought out loud: “Truth alone triumphs.”

This delighted Anand, who seemed surprised I knew it. “*Satyameva Jayate,*” he said. “‘Truth stands invincible.’ The national motto of India!”

“Dr. Fiore translated it for me. It was on Maya’s government stationery.”

Anand became dispirited at the mention of her name. The memory of Maya seemed to weigh on him. “She was a practicing Buddhist, you know.”

“I didn’t know,” I said. “Unusual occupation for a Buddhist.”

“Not all Buddhists are pacifists,” Anand said. “Many at times have been quite violent. But Maya often did feel conflicted.”

I thought of her crawling up the staircase to save me. “I’m sorry to admit it, but I’m glad she wasn’t conflicted in Rome. I wouldn’t be here now.”

We continued walking toward the parking lot where Dan’s rental car sat waiting. For safety’s sake, we had abandoned the Mercedes in a neighborhood nearby and hoofed up the hill to the observatory.

I asked my long lost brother how he had come to meet Felix Fiore.

“We met at a Gyuto monastery in northern India,” he said. “You’ve heard of the city of Dharamshala?”

“Where the Dalai Lama lives?”

“They call it ‘Little Lhasa’—home to the Tibetan government-in-exile. Fiore and his granddaughter had traveled there for a mandala ceremony.”

“The mandala in your sketchbook?” Phoebe asked.

“We’ve been trying to figure out what it means,” I said.

“So have I,” Dan said. “I’d heard about it from a Frenchman I met, an ex-monk who’d studied with the Gyuto Order for years. He said it was the most extraordinary sand mandala he’d ever seen. Every spring, a small group of Tibetan monks trek down from the mountains to construct the elaborate mandala in the sanctum of the monastery’s temple. It remains undisturbed there for exactly three days before it's deliberately destroyed. Only a select group of the monastery's monks are allowed to set eyes on it. I had to sneak into the temple in the middle of the night to be able to make those sketches."

"Fiore go in with you?" I asked.

"Dr. Fiore is a Gyuto monk himself—the Tibetans consider him a lama. He arrived with the mandala makers."

"With his *granddaughter?*" Phoebe asked.

"Yes," Dan said. "In fact, it was through Govindi that I gained access to the temple."

Phoebe eyed him curiously. "Really. *Govindi.* I wonder how you managed that?"

"She appreciated my passion for Tibetan Buddhism," he said.

"Your—" Phoebe stopped herself. "It's funny you've never mentioned this woman before."

"I haven't seen her in 18 months."

"So you're counting, then."

Phoebe looked miffed. I wondered: Was she *jealous?*

We reached the rental car; Dan popped the trunk. From deep inside a backpack, he pulled out a Ziploc bag. "These are yours," he said to Phoebe, handing her the seeds. "Tell Karakov he has me to thank for keeping them from the Assassins."

The Aryan seeds looked dark and shriveled. "So I take it you're not afraid they can germinate," Phoebe said.

"Not those," he said. "I sterilized them." He fished out another bag of similar-looking seeds. "I'm keeping this portion for myself. And these"—a third bag—"I lifted from the monks."

He tossed the bag to me. It contained several dozen light-gold seeds, dried, but plump and hearty. "Just like what you sent me in Rome," I said.

"I knew if I was captured they'd be taken from me," Dan said. "I sent you those few for safekeeping."

Phoebe took the bag and squinted at the seeds. "Was your girlfriend an accomplice in this caper, too?"

"Govindi? No. In fact she tried to kill me."

It appeared he wasn't kidding. "Because you stole them?" I asked.

Dan hesitated. "Because the seeds were a part of the mandala."

Phoebe grimaced, incredulous. "You *stole* them from the *mandala*?"

"Talk about bad karma," I said.

"Your brother doesn't care about karma," Phoebe said. "Or the ten commandments or the Hindu dharma or the Buddha's eightfold path. Why should he bother to restrain himself? He thinks he can have his 'spiritual experience' and ignore all those silly rules."

"The experience is the basis of it all," Dan said. "Direct apprehension of the transcendent truth—"

"Tell that to the men who want to kill you. They seem to be ignoring all those silly rules, too."

"Or believing in a bunch of silly ones."

"That only proves my point. The 'experience' can be misconstrued—"

"Excuse me," Anand said, interrupting. "I'm confused. You said you took the seeds from the mandala. But wasn't the mandala made out of sand?"

"The mandala was constructed in the traditional way, by trickling grains of colored sand, but the lotus flower the Buddha held was formed entirely of lotus seeds. When I saw that, I knew I was on to something."

"What made you think they were from the soma plant?" I asked.

"I only had a theory," he said. "It wasn't until I could test them against these"—he held up Karakov's dark, shriveled seeds—"that I knew the lotus of the Buddhist monks was the same as the ancient Aryans'."

I had trouble reconciling the connection. "Why would teetotaler Buddhist monks have anything to do with the Aryans' soma?"

Dan set a seed on the palm of his hand. "You could say the Vedic Aryans planted the initial seed of Buddhism. Soma gave them courage, but taken in heavier doses it could be a real trip. I believe it was the catalyst that turned their warrior culture inward. Early Hindu seers began probing human consciousness, exploring ways to make permanent the 'invincible' state of mind. Over the course of centuries, they developed various meditation techniques that came to be known collectively as *yoga,* a Sanskrit word meaning 'yoke'—'to bind together.' The idea was to yoke one's limited self to the unlimited *ground of being*, what the Hindus called Brahman, the all-pervading divine. With years of diligent practice, yogis hoped to break free from the dream of *samsara*—the relative world of suffering and desire—and awaken into a permanent state of enlightenment."

A dusty breeze swept over the hilltop. I peered out over the city below, where several killers had just been hunting us. One had been slashed with a knife in the square; another—Dan's torturer—had been shot dead in the tomb. The world of samsara was no make-believe dream. Yet from this lofty vantage, those events did begin to seem somehow slightly dreamlike, and I knew they'd only become more so as my memory of them faded, like washed out photos from the first world war, its purpose long forgotten, its passions absurd.

"Siddhartha Gautama came out of this tradition," Dan was saying, "and developed his own radical innovations. Guided by his own experience, taking absolutely nothing on faith, the Buddha realized he could not honestly affirm that the yogic state was divine. He even disputed the instinctive assumption of an inner, autonomous 'self.' Our identity, he asserted, was fluid and contingent, like a burning fire or a flowing stream, never exactly the same from moment to moment. It was therefore indescribable, not a self, but 'no-self'; what the Buddhists refer to as 'emptiness.'"

I thought of the black void of Tamerlane's gravestone, and pulled out the black jade chess piece. "So is that what the camel means—we're nothing?"

"Emptiness does not mean nothingness," Dan said. "It means being emptied of the false sense of 'self.' No 'I,' no 'thing' stands completely independent and apart. It is only our thinking makes it so. That's living in samsara—the illusion of separateness."

I tossed him the camel. He responded instinctively, catching it. "That thing is separate," I said. "So am I and so are you. And if you need reminding, so was the guy who nearly tortured you to death."

Dan's eyes darkened at the memory. "I'll be the first to admit...I felt completely alone." He viewed the camel on his open palm, his hand still trembling slightly. "And yet I know it isn't so."

Anand held out his hand, and Dan gave him the piece. The Gurkha studied it closely. "There's a famous phrase in Sanskrit, said to be the sum of all Hindu philosophy: *Tat tvam asi.* 'That art thou.'" He handed the camel to me.

"Okay," I said. "I'm the camel and the camel is me, and everything is empty, and we're all part of one great big cosmos. But meantime we got to live down here on Earth, where people are killing each other over a lousy lotus."

"That's the nature of samsara," Dan said. "Constant change and conflict. The trick is to find the pathway through it. That empty, open path is nirvana, 'the Refuge of the Buddha.' But finding and maintaining that state of mind is a difficult endeavor. Like the journey to Shambhala. That's why this sect of Buddhists kept the soma plant, I think. To give their novices a taste of what they're looking for—to offer them a glimpse of enlightenment."

Dan's theory about soma had a certain logic to it, but something about it still bothered me. "How could this group of Buddhists be the only ones that still have the lotus?"

"I'm not really sure," he said. "But somewhere during the course of the past three millennia, this particular lotus species vanished. My guess is, it was deliberately destroyed. In ancient Persia, the reforming firebrand prophet Zoroaster condemned the intoxicating haoma ritual. The religion he established replaced haoma with a much milder stimulant derived from the ephedra plant. It's still in use by Zoroastrians today. Something similar happened in India with the rise of Hinduism and the renunciations of the yogis. Buddhists in particular would have wanted soma suppressed—to prevent the plant's misuse or its exploitation in war. So the religious function of the lotus flower became entirely symbolic. Soma was eventually replaced with *padma*, the beautiful *Nelumbo nucifera* lotus, the so-called 'Sacred Lotus' of India."

"Is *padma* a stimulant, too?" I asked.

"*Padma* contains alkaloids that are mildly psychoactive," Dan said, "but nothing like the experience attributed to soma. My theory is that soma interacts with serotonin-2 receptors, affecting the fear response, the survival instinct, and the sense of one's physical boundary—all interlinked in the oldest and most primitive part of the brain. Basically, the sense of one's 'self' is transcended. You're left to experience the boundlessness of pure *being*."

"As if touched by the divine," Anand added.

"Or by chemistry," I said.

"We're bio-chemical organisms," Dan said, "enmeshed in a material world. How else could a brain reach beyond itself except by reaching through it?"

Anand agreed. "Nirvana is in samsara," he said.

"Exactly. The Sacred Lotus represents enlightenment on earth. *Padma* grows up out of the muck, its leaves repel the muddy water and its bud blooms into perfection."

"Om mani padme *hum,"* Anand said.

"'The jewel is in the lotus,'" Dan translated. "It's considered the most important Buddhist mantra of all. Emptiness, divineness, nirvana—the jewel—is right here, before our eyes, within our mucky world. For Tibetans the jewel is a diamond, the symbol of perfection. Like the Tibetan 'diamond thunderbolt' adapted from the Aryans—"

"Your Vajra!" I'd nearly forgotten about it. Digging it out of my pack, I tossed it over to Dan.

His eyes lit up at the sight of it. He fingered the curved prongs that formed the two hollow spheres. "This represents everything I've been talking about. The Buddhist turning inward to contemplate the void. Emptiness within suchness. The union of opposites. Yoking the blood-and-guts world of samsara with the timeless world of nirvana." He centered the

Vajra on his outstretched finger, delicately balancing the spheres. "One who achieves enlightenment rests with equanimity in both—"

The Vajra slipped off his finger—he grabbed it in midair. He seemed delighted to have this "no-thing" back in his possession. "Govindi gave me this Vajra...before we fell out. Theirs is a *Vajrayana* sect of Buddhism—the 'Vehicle of the Diamond.' They use special means and practices to accelerate the process of awakening."

"Special means?" Phoebe said.

We all turned. Phoebe had been quietly studying Dan. "Now I know why you never mentioned her."

"Govindi?"

She turned to me. "*Vajrayana* is better known as Tantric Buddhism, Jack. I think I'm beginning to understand your brother's sudden 'passion' for it."

Dan visibly blushed. "Sex is only one area of tantric practice, Phoebe. And it's actually not used all that often."

"Of course not. Special means need special circumstances. Like a willing woman for one—"

"Tantra is merely a means—"

"*Please,* Professor, enough with the lectures. Tantra is about restraint, though I'm sure you convinced Govindi that's just another rule to break."

"Govindi didn't need convincing! She's not so strong-willed like—" Dan stopped himself, realizing what he'd just admitted. "Like you."

Phoebe stared at him, her suspicions confirmed. She glanced at me, then back at Dan. "It turns out I'm not so strong-willed, either."

Dan's eyes slowly narrowed. "Really?" He turned to me with his mouth open.

I shrugged.

"Excuse me."

It was Anand. "I hope you don't mind," he said. "This is most...fascinating. Quite exciting, really. But I remind you, we do live—as you said—in the world of time. And I'm afraid our time at present is quickly running out."

Dan tried to shake off his shell-shock. "Yeah," he said. "Of course."

The moment he looked away, Phoebe and I exchanged a glance. *Could it really be that easy?*

Anand in the meantime was asking Dan, "Can you tell us whether the monks grew any lotus at the Dharamshala monastery?"

"No, there's no pond," Dan said. He still seemed to be trying to absorb the revelation from Phoebe. He turned to her. "I couldn't very well tell you about Govindi without having to tell you everything."

"Like the fact that you'd fallen in love, you mean, and never bothered to mention it?"

"If I didn't keep my involvement with the monks and her quiet, their secret would have gotten out in no time. You remember what happened in Greece—"

"That was hardly my—"

"Please," Anand said, growing impatient. "What about their orchards, their vegetable gardens?"

Dan shook his head. "I searched. There were no water plants anywhere on the premises."

On the sun-baked hood of Dan's rental car, Anand unfolded his English-labeled, "Silk Road" tourist map. "If that's the case," he said, "one could assume the monks from the mountains carried the seeds down with them."

"Most likely," Dan said. "I assume the mandala is remade every year for the benefit of the exiles in India. I think it's a ritual of confirmation, verifying the soma lotus is alive, that's it's still being actively cultivated."

"In Shambhala," I said.

"That's my theory," he said.

Anand's fat-fingered hands fanned out, flattening the creases of the map. "The only question then is where."

74.
The Source

Standing around the map, the four of us peered down like gods over Asia. Red lines traced the ancient Silk Road from the eastern shores of the Mediterranean Sea, across the Middle East and the Land of the Stans, deep into the vastness of China. South of these lines, in the northern neck of India, Anand's roving fingertip skated to a stop. "Dharamshala is here," he said, "in the foothills of the Himalayas. You're certain these monks came down from the mountains?"

"That's what Govindi told me," Dan said. "She wouldn't say from where."

The crescent sweep of the Himalayas—the famous "Roof of the World"—formed a long, formidable border with Tibet. From east to west the mountains stretched some 1500 miles, with yet more ranges thickly stacked above them to the north.

"Well that certainly narrows things down," Phoebe said.

Dan looked it over despairingly, the night's torture still in his eyes. "I'm sorry," he said. "This is why I'd hoped to find an answer in the tomb."

Anand moved his finger to the city we were in—Samarkand, in southeast Uzbekistan. "How does the camel go?" His finger moved diagonally down, then across. "Afghanistan, Pakistan, and...India,Tibet."

Phoebe exclaimed, "Two countries diagonal, two countries across!"

The four of us stared down, wondering.

"Seems a bit of a stretch," I said. Still, it was all we had to go on. I took the chess piece out of my pocket and placed it down on Tibet. "Camel in the mountains?"

"Fish out of water," Phoebe said.

Dan agreed. "I can't see how the lotus plants could survive the Himalayan winter."

"And it still leaves an awful lot of ground to cover," Phoebe said.

"Even more than you think," Anand said. "Since the occupation, Tibet is considered a province. Officially, the country that camel's in is China."

"Where Tamerlane was looking," Dan said.

The four of us surveyed its immensity. "Third largest country in the world," Phoebe said.

The absurdity of it reminded me of the street peddler's joke. *"Xitoy,"* I said.

"What?" Dan asked.

"The Uzbek's name for China. In the square, a man was selling chess…" I broke off.

"What is it?" Dan asked.

I picked up the camel.

"Jack, what's wrong?" Phoebe asked.

"The secret is right before your eyes," I said.

"What do you mean?" Dan asked.

"It's what your torturer said when we showed him the camel," Phoebe said.

Dan took the chess piece. Looked at it. Looked at me.

"You thought Ulug Beg left some clue inside the tomb," I said. "But what if the clue was the tomb itself? What if the clue was the jade?"

Phoebe eyed the camel. "The largest block of jade in the world."

"Where did it come from?" I asked.

"India, supposedly," Dan said. "But no one really knows. Some believe it was mined in Mongolia. Others—"

"China," I said. *"Xitoy."*

"It's certainly possible," Dan said.

"More than possible," Anand said. "It's actually quite likely. Long before they began trading silk, the Chinese were trading jade. In fact, the Silk Road in China actually followed what used to be the ancient Jade Road."

We all stared down at the red, ropy lines, each knotted with scattered oases.

"Maybe the monks didn't just come *down* from the mountains," I said. "Maybe they came *over* the mountains."

Anand pushed his fingertip north from Dharamshala. "The nearest route across would put you down about here," he said.

Dan set the camel down on the spot—the Silk Road just north of Tibet. The road at that point had split into two, a north and south route around a large, empty basin, ringed by a conga line of mountains.

"The Taklimakan Desert," Anand said. "The Uyghurs call it 'the Sea of Death.'"

Given my recent preoccupations, the emptiness of it intrigued me. Except for the rivers that died into it, and the name "Taklimakan," the desert itself contained not a mark.

I asked Anand if he knew what the name meant.

"'The place of ruins,'" he said. "It may be the most dangerous desert on earth. No one, nothing lives there. It's deeper inland than any desert in the world. The empty heart of Asia."

No wonder the caravans circled it, I thought. Avoiding the ultimate void. It reminded me of the dark void of Tamerlane's tomb. And the so-called "emptiness" of the Buddha—

"Oh my God," I said. The Buddha. Hand raised. Holding up the lotus. "Right before your eyes!"

75.
The Empty “O”

I ripped into my duffel bag and dragged out Dan’s drawings. Pages fluttered down over the map. Scanning them quickly, my eyes fell on the Buddha. I centered the page and arranged the various mountain pages around it.

“Look,” I said. “He’s sitting alone in empty space. Holding up the lotus. He’s not in a square fortress—he’s surrounded by a ring of mountains.”

The others closed in around me, shifting their gaze between the drawing and the map.

“And the fingers of his right hand touch the earth,” Phoebe said.

“He’s pointing!” I said. “Between those two rivers.”

“Here,” Phoebe said, indicating a city on the Silk Road route at the southwest rim of the desert. Two rivers from the mountains bled out on either side.

Dan lit up. “Khotan!” he said.

“You know it?” I asked.

“I know about it,” he said. “It used to be the *kingdom* of Khotan—the Silk Road’s cultural capital. And a thriving center of Buddhism, and of Buddhist philosophy and art. There’s a legend the city was founded by the son of Ashoka the Great.”

I remembered Fiore mentioning the famous Indian emperor. “Maybe Ashoka’s son brought the soma lotus with him,” I said. “Maybe Khotan is your Shambhala.”

“It’s an excellent candidate,” Dan said, quickly warming to

the idea. "There were many Buddhist cities along the ancient Silk Road. But Khotan had hundreds of monasteries and thousands of Buddhist monks."

"It's hard to picture Shangri-la in the desert," Phoebe said.

"Khotan was the largest, most fertile oasis," Dan said. "Wealthy from trade, and very tolerant and diverse. Nestorian Christians, Indian Hindus, Chinese Taoists, Persian Zoroastrians—all were welcomed equally. The city took to heart the Buddha's message: he wasn't trying to create a new religion; he was trying to create a new *civilization*. The idea may have reached its zenith with Khotan. Its citizens were highly cultured and sophisticated. And elaborately polite—they greeted each other by genuflecting. The place was luxuriously sensual and open. Women wore pants, not veils, and rode horses like the men. The people staged great parades and celebrations. Painting and music and poetry flourished."

"Sounds like the Buddhist paradise to me," I said.

"The city is no paradise now," Anand said. "I was on an assignment there—with Maya—two years ago, monitoring the Uyghur uprising. It was not a happy place."

"They're rioting again there now," Phoebe said. "I saw it on the news in Bukhara."

"Uyghurs resent the Han Chinese as much as Tibetans do," Dan said.

"But they're far more likely to use violence," Anand added.

"They're not Buddhists?" I asked.

"The Uyghurs are Turkic Muslims," Dan said. "Khotan remained predominantly Buddhist for more than a thousand years. But around 1000 A.D. the kingdom fell, and the Buddhist monks were all driven out."

"The Muslim invasions," Anand said. "Similar to what occurred in India."

Dan said, "I remember, there's a famous verse in Turkic, praising the kingdom's conquest. 'Like river torrents, we flooded their cities, we captured their monasteries, and shat on their statues of the Buddha.' "

"Lovely," Phoebe said. "I hope it rhymes in Turkic." She was surfing for info on her cell.

"I believe there's only a tiny Buddhist enclave there now," Anand said. "They maintain a monastery on the outskirts of the city. Maya tried to visit it, but they wouldn't allow outsiders."

"Listen to this," Phoebe said. She'd pulled up the Wiki entry. "'Khotan is famous for its high-quality nephrite jade,'" she read. "And those two rivers? One is called the Yurungkash, the White Jade River, 'alluding to the white jade recovered from its alluvial deposits.' The other river is called…" She looked up at us, her face alight—"The Karakash. Anyone want to guess what that name means?"

Anand and Dan and I exchanged gleeful glances. "If 'Kara*kum*' means 'the Black Desert,'" I said, "I think we've got a pretty good idea."

Phoebe continued reading. "The monastery you mentioned? It lies by the shoreline of the Karakash."

Dan's eyes glowed. "It may be the last vestige of Shambhala..."

"It has to be the source!" I said.

"If it is," Phoebe said, "the Iranians are probably already there."

I'd forgotten about the stolen manuscript. The Assassins knew as much or more than we did.

Dan looked suddenly stricken. Staring down at Khotan. "Dr. Fiore will be with the monks," he said. "Govindi will be with him." He raised his haunted gaze to us. "It's all my fault," he said.

Phoebe and I glanced at each other. Anand laid a hand on Dan's shoulder. He eyed the three of us gravely. "We've got to hurry if we want to save them."

76.
Invincible

Within minutes we were on the road again. Anand, riding shotgun, cell phone to his ear, was speaking in singsong Hindi and English to his RAW office back in Delhi, requesting they facilitate our visa applications and help expedite our entry into China. At the same time, on her cell, Phoebe booked us flights—from Tashkent, the Uzbek capital just north of us, to Ürümqi, the provincial capital of northwestern China, and finally over the desert to the city of Khotan, known to the Chinese as Hotan.

Shouting above the din of telephone chatter, Dan fed me directions as I steered us out of town. Before long we were cruising through the countryside. I borrowed Phoebe's cell when she finished and put in a call to Faraj. Oddly, he didn't answer. I left a message telling him we were heading to Hotan, China. Then I dialed Harry Grant.

"Jack?"

"Where are you?"

"The hospital," he said. "Just got here a few minutes ago." He sounded distracted.

"Is Faraj there?"

"You haven't heard from him?" he asked.

"Not since yesterday."

"The nurse said he left in a rage. Very distraught. He must have—"

Beside me in the car, Anand was still talking into his cell, and asking Phoebe for passport numbers and flight information. I couldn't hear Harry Grant. "What did you say?"

"He left. Last night. They said he was very upset. He'd been by her side almost constantly. They said he just couldn't believe—"

"Is she with him?"

"Oriana? I thought they said they called you—"

"What happened?"

He paused. "Oriana died last night."

"What?"

"Massive hematoma. Lower thoracic—"

"My God."

"She was under heavy sedation. Probably was never aware—"

"How could it happen? She was recovering—"

"Her spleen had been nicked by the dagger. The surgeon thought he had sewn it shut, but it opened yesterday, bled out before anyone knew. When the nurse finally noticed, last night..."

"I can't believe it."

"I'm sorry. It's my fault. I should have gotten here—"

"No," I said. "I shouldn't have left her. It's just...there's been so much happening."

"Did you find your brother?"

"Yes." I glanced in the mirror. Dan was silent, watching me. "He's here with us now, safe."

"That's good," Harry said. "I'm glad."

Having overheard my end of the conversation, Anand and Phoebe had stopped talking. I was staring out at the road ahead, but not really seeing the road. Hazel, I thought. Her eyes. Light brown with a tinge of green. "I should have been there," I said.

"You did what you had to do."

What I had to do.

"Tell me where you are now," Harry said.

His voice sounded far away. I wasn't sure I should answer.

"Jack. Please. You have to let me help you. These men have killed too many people."

Too many people. Way too many. And now, beautiful

Oriana…

"She was more than a friend to me," Harry was saying.

"I know," I said.

"Then you must let *me* do what I have to do."

I thought of the two men I'd shot in the pit, the men who had stabbed Oriana. The runt had grinned at me as he died. Amused by my fear and confusion. He had no doubts, no fears, no qualms—*only what he had to do.*

"Oriana would have wanted me to help you," Harry said.

"But she's not the reason, is she?"

"Reason for what?"

"Your obsession with killing these men."

Harry was silent.

"Who was it?" I asked. "Someone close?"

He waited a moment. "An Iraqi ex-pat, living in London. She came back to Baghdad to run for office. I was sworn to protect her. Bravest woman I ever met. Thought she was invincible."

Invincible. "No one's invincible," I said. "Those who pretend to be end up dead." Maya, Saar, Oriana. Next up probably Harry Grant. What drove these people to do what they did? What made them risk their lives?

"What color were her eyes?" I asked.

"Her *eyes?* Brown. Dark brown, almost black. I remember she—" He stopped himself, paused a moment. "She was remarkable," he said.

Dark-eyed. Brave. Headstrong. Invincible.

"Do you know which one of them killed her?" I asked.

"Yes. Ali Mahbood."

"The guy from Kahrizak Prison?"

"Vanitar's old boss. Second name on the list."

"How do you know it was him?"

"The way he killed her," he said.

"Cut her throat?"

"No. It was...much worse than that. A method he developed at the prison. Now it seems all of them are doing it."

I flashed on Saar, disemboweled in the trunk. "Oh, my God, I'm sorry," I said. "Please, forgive me for asking."

Grant was silent. "It isn't vengeance, Jack. It's my duty. I feel...responsible."

His duty. His dharma.

"I just feel like shit," I said.

"That comes first," he said.

Phoebe laid a hand on my shoulder. I returned her gaze in the rearview mirror. I looked at Dan and Anand.

I don't want these people to die, I thought. I don't want any more killing. But the killing, I knew, was not over yet. Along with Ali Mahbood, there were still half a dozen *Hashishin* on the loose—including Vanitar, eager for revenge. And all of them undoubtedly now heading to Hotan.

"Jack—"

"We're on our way to Tashkent," I told him. "We're flying to the city of Hotan, in China. There's a Buddhist monastery there called Kutana, on the banks of the Black Jade River. We think it's the source of the soma lotus. The monks there may be in danger."

"From the Iranians?"

"They've got the same information we have," I said, "only they got it one day earlier."

Harry thought for a moment. "Who is with you now?" he asked.

I glanced in the mirror. "My brother. Two friends."

"They armed?"

"No. Anand says we'll never get firearms past the Chinese customs authori—"

"Who is Anand?" he asked.

I looked at the man beside me. "I told you. A friend."

After a pause Harry said, "Be careful, Jack. The police won't be any help in Hotan. At the moment, they've got their hands full."

"We've heard," I said. "What will you do?"

"I've got to make some arrangements here. There's going to be a lot of questions. But I'll be on the next flight out to Hotan. Try to keep safe 'til I get there."

"Okay," I said. Then added: "I'm sorry…about Oriana."

"Me, too," he said. "Me, too."

I shut the cell. Looked at the road. Glanced in the mirror at Dan.

Dan was staring at me. "You shouldn't have told him," he said.

Hotan was in chaos. Business and tourism had ground to a halt. The airport teemed with fleeing Chinese. Using Faraj's old passport as ID, I paid in cash for a rental car. On the drive out to the monastery, I returned the call from Duran.

He didn't answer; I assumed he was in flight. I left him a voice-mail message that would have fooled the devil himself. It seemed almost indulgent to keep stringing him along, but the American might prove useful in helping to stop Mahbood, I thought. And once I had the lotus—the Ayatollah's prize—I could at last take vengeance for my brother.

Ending Duran's pointless life would be an act of kindness. Such a trusting dupe. More boy than man, I thought. Lacking any conviction, led only by his lust. Was he not the very embodiment of his country?

77.
Xitoy

It wasn't until our plane set down in Ürümqi that I finally heard back from Faraj. As we waited in line to be processed for entry, Phoebe noticed his message on her cell—he had called during our three-hour flight from Tashkent. She listened to the message for what seemed a full minute, a look of fascination on her face.

"What is it?" I asked when she finally finished.

She shook her head in disbelief, hit replay and handed me the phone.

Faraj's voice strained over road noise and wind: *My friend Jack, I pray that you receive this. Last night, I return from dinner, I see a bearded man driving off in a black Mercedes. It is Ali Mahbood! I run to Oriana's room. Her stitches are leaking. The nurse says she is bleeding, inside. I cry to Allah, my heart is breaking. But they cannot save her. I tell them she is murdered, but they do not believe me. So I go, myself, to find Mahbood.*

At the airport, only one place rents this car. They tell me he is going to Karshi, he is taking the midnight flight to Hotan. I am following him. I will follow this murderer wherever he goes. Insha'Allah, I will find him, Jack. For Oriana, I—

"End of message. To keep this message, push—"

I closed the cell. "Where is Karshi?" I asked.

"Couple hours south of Samarkand," Phoebe said. "It was the first city I tried to book us through."

"To Hotan?"

"Yeah, there's a direct flight. Only problem: It left early this morning."

"Faraj must have taken it," I said. "I wonder if he's caught up with them." Our flight to Hotan wouldn't leave for several hours, barring visa delays. I called Harry Grant and left a message on his cell relating what Faraj had told me. A short while later, he called me back.

"Your friend was right," he said. "Someone cut a wire coat hanger and slipped it through her stitching. They found it in the trash bin, coated with her blood."

Grant was calling from the road. It so happened that he, too, was on his way to Karshi. Booked on the midnight flight to Hotan, he wouldn't be arriving until late in the night. "Please stay out of trouble 'til I get there," he ordered.

I didn't respond.

"Jack?"

"Yeah?"

"Ghurkas are brave. But like you said, no one's invincible."

"What…?"

"Just be careful. Please tell that to Mr. Pandava as well."

He hung up. I looked at Anand.

As I had expected, I arrived too late. Through binoculars I saw a Mercedes parked before the walls of the Buddhist monastery. Mahbood and his men were already inside. So be it, I thought; my chance will come. Who are we to question the workings of the Lord? A servant does his best with what he's given.

Soon a second Mercedes-Benz drove up and parked at the monastery. Two bearded Hashishin emerged. Mahbood had flown them in from wherever they'd been stationed—Damascus? Beirut? Baghdad? Kabul?—uprooting them from imbeds that may have taken months, from roles they had meticulously constructed. All that careful effort had been tossed aside for this: to reclaim the lotus from the Buddhists, and to replenish for Mahbood the pure drink of Paradise.

I alone would stop him, and secure the living lotus for the Grand Ayatollah. Together we'd rebuild the Hashishin!

The two men scanned the surrounding plains, then disappeared inside. For half an hour I waited, debating my next move. Suddenly I saw Mahbood drag out an old white-bearded monk, trailed by an entourage of protest. He forced the monk into the car, slashing a young woman, robed in crimson, who physically tried to stop him.

A nun! A girl! Do Buddhist men have no honor? The monks stood by and watched as she put them all to shame.

I followed Mahbood's Mercedes at a quarter mile's distance, until at last the car pulled off onto a desert road. Driving past the turnoff, I parked along the shoulder and climbed out with my binoculars. For several minutes I tracked the trailing cloud of dust until it faded. Then I grabbed the goatskin and prepared a place for prayer.

No sense keeping close; I'd follow soon enough. Mahbood had entered the Taklimakan, Satan's Sea of Death. For me, a careful strategy of patience seemed most fitting. For Ali Mahbood, the traitor, there would be only one way out: God's scimitar—my dagger—the glinting gate to Hell!

SAMSARA

78.
Kutana

The worm of fear twisted, spinning its silken thread.

Across the rice fields, the white walls of the Kutana monastery shimmered in the heat, and the tiered roofs above them seemed to hover. Orange dust in the air turned the sun into the moon, a milky pail of soma for the war god. Anand said it was typical of Taklimakan towns, bathed by the windblown dunes of the desert, but we had seen smoke columns rising from the city, and I wondered now how long those angry fires would keep burning, and if the sun would soon be blotted out. The moon-like sun, the saffron sky, the gleaming irrigation channels watered from the river—all appeared imbued with a dreamlike unreality. Only the very tangible tension made it true.

Our Range Rover idled with the a/c rattling while we waited, and watched, and debated what to do. Some forty minutes had passed without us coming to a decision. Dan had grown impatient, Phoebe more reluctant, I increasingly uncertain, and Anand…

Anand wouldn't say. He was peering silently across the fields through a pair of miniature binoculars. Even without them I could see the Assassins' raven-black car, parked beside a nondescript, dust-covered sedan, and an aged white cargo van, windowless in back. While the van and dusty four-door likely belonged to the Buddhist monks, no one had any doubts about the Mercedes.

The growing anxiety took a toll on my temper. "What is it

with these assholes and their fucking black Mercedes?"

"Vanity," Phoebe said. "They should be driving a hearse."

Anand held his binoculars steady. "Perhaps they hold a deep respect for German engineer—"

"I can't sit here any longer," Dan said. He threw open his door. "I'm going in."

"Wait!" Anand called.

"For what? Their throats to be—"

"Someone's coming out."

We peered into the haze. It took a moment before I could spot him—a squat monk in a red robe, scurrying toward the vehicles.

"Curious," Anand said, following with the glass. "He appears to be alone."

The monk opened the door to the cargo van and climbed behind the wheel. Blue fumes belched out the back. Within seconds he was stirring up a dust cloud.

"Follow him!" Anand ordered.

I threw the Rover into gear and lurched into a U-y, heading back to where the dirt road met the paved road we were on. We were just west of the city of Hotan, by the ragged shores of the Karakash, and very near the site of the ancient oasis, the kingdom's lost capital, Khotan. The glorious city of wood and clay had long ago rotted underfoot, and now the once-famous "Buddhist paradise" was nothing more than irrigated farmland. Only Kutana, a 19th-century monastery, stood amid the wind-blocking poplars on the plain.

For a man dedicated to the contemplative life, the monk was in one heck of a hurry. I drove at high speed to catch up with him. "Where do you think he's going?" I asked.

"From the direction," Anand said, "you'd have to guess the city."

I pulled up behind. "What now?" I asked Anand.

"Let's see if we can get him to stop."

Aside from our two vehicles, the unlined road was empty. I hit the pedal and pulled up alongside the van. The young monk shot a frightened glance at us. He had a pudgy moon-face, with short black hair and thick black brows. Anand lowered his window and waved for him to stop. The driver slowed slightly. Then, reconsidering, he stepped hard on the gas. Black smoke billowed from his tailpipe.

"Stop him!" Anand shouted. "Pull out in front!"

I floored it and slid up alongside him again. The man stared forward, pedal to the floor, too scared to risk even a glance at us. We were flying near 100 km/h, our Rover rumbling noisily over the heat-wrinkled road, the van's rotten exhaust pipe howling. Just as I started pulling ahead, another vehicle appeared coming toward us out of the haze.

A farm truck, stacked with hay. Quarter mile and closing.

I hesitated. Floor it and cut in front of the monk? Or slow down and fall in behind?

The hay truck's horn sounded. "Take it!" Dan shouted.

Phoebe shouted, "No!"

Before I could make up my mind, the monk's van suddenly slowed. I quickly cut in front of him. The farm truck whistled past.

"Our monk's a good Buddhist," Anand said.

Riding now in front of him, I gradually reduced our speed, forcing the van to slow. Anand and I gestured for the monk to stop. Resigning himself to fate, he made no further effort to avoid us and pulled to the side of the road.

Anand and Dan jumped out of the car. I waited behind the wheel with the engine running, watching the monk in the mirror.

"He's not going anywhere," Phoebe said, peering out the back. We climbed out to join Dan and Anand, standing outside the monk's door.

The door was locked, his window shut. He watched us from behind the glass, his black brows arched in fright.

Anand put his palms together over his heart and bowed his head to the monk. *"Tashi delek,"* he said. Dan, Phoebe and I followed his lead, nodding to the young monk silently.

He flattened his palms together and nodded in return, but continued eyeing us warily.

"Please," Anand asked, calling through the glass, "could we possibly talk with you a moment?"

The man shook his head, no.

Anand briefly gazed at us, then turned back to the monk. "We know that evil men have come to your monastery," he said. "That is why we have traveled here—to help you."

The monk's gaze fell as he considered it a moment. Then he looked back up at us and shook his head again. He seemed to be convinced there was nothing we could do.

Anand stood back, opened his jacket and drew out his knife. For a second I thought he might smash it through the glass. Instead he laid it flat across the palms of his hands and displayed it openly before the monk. "My name is Anand Pandava," he said. "I humbly place myself at your service."

The monk stared at the kukri. His widening eyes rose slowly to Anand's. Mouth agape, he reached down blindly and opened up his door. He stepped out, still gaping, and stood before Anand.

"My name, Jamyang," he said.

79. The Fifth Assassin

Crouched in the back of the cargo van, Dan and I peered ahead through the windshield as Jamyang nervously drove us toward the monastery. The Mercedes and the dust-covered Volvo sedan remained where they'd been in the lot; apparently no one else had departed. Nor did anyone appear outside the monastery walls. The wooden entry door was shut, the windows all shuttered. In the hazy half-light of the soma-moon sun, the scarred, bleached building looked forbidding.

Jamyang parked the van beside the other two cars. He turned to look beside him at Anand. "Fear, like fire," he said.

"Yes," Anand said. "Like fire."

Anand was wearing a doctor's white coat, at least one size too small for him. The red tilak had been wiped from his forehead. He pulled a stethoscope from a medical bag and hooked it around his neck. After a quick scan of the shuttered monastery, he turned to peer back into the darkness at us. "Are we all clear on the plan?" he asked.

Dan didn't answer.

"Jamyang will hide the keys to the Volvo," I said. "Dan and I'll take care of the Mercedes, then wait here 'til you come out. How long do you think it'll take?"

Anand eyed the entry door, then looked back at us again. "Quarter of an hour," he said.

"What if you don't come out?" Dan asked.

"Then they'll come out, looking for you. The moment you see them, start the van and leave. They won't be able to chase you without the cars. You can meet up with Phoebe and return with the police."

"Jack can go for the cops," Dan said. "I won't leave this place without Govindi."

"Then you may never leave this place at all," Anand said.

According to Jamyang, Dr. Fiore's granddaughter had been stabbed by the leader of the Assassins—a man they called "Mahbood"—when she intervened to stop him from taking Fiore away. Mahbood drove off with him in a second black Mercedes, while Govindi and the monks were kept as hostages. Where the doctor had been taken, Jamyang couldn't say. But in the hours since, Govindi's condition had worsened. The Iranians, for some reason intent on keeping her alive, sent Jamyang to Hotan to retrieve the monastery's doctor. The rest of the monks—more than forty in all—remained under the watchful eyes of three armed *Hashishin*. If Jamyang did not return—or brought back the police—he was told his fellow monks would have their throats slit.

This is why Jamyang had been so terrified to talk with us. And why he now appeared anxious and uncertain.

"Jamyang, are you ready?"

The monk searched Anand's eyes as if he thought they might reveal the source of the Gurkha's courage.

Anand gripped his shoulder. "Introduce me as the doctor. I'll handle it from there."

We had accompanied Jamyang to the hospital in Hotan, a scene of utter chaos. With truckloads of riot victims arriving by the minute, the medical staff and E.R. had been completely overwhelmed. But Dr. Tzu, it turned out, was a Buddhist monk himself, and committed to the welfare of his fellows. When he heard from Jamyang that their lives were in danger, he agreed at once to Anand's risky scheme, and rode back to wait in the Rover with Phoebe, parked now on the distant road across the paddy fields.

Jamyang gazed up at the ghostly walls, struggling to still his fear. At last he turned to Anand and nodded. The two men exited the van.

From the back, Dan and I watched through the windshield

as they walked toward the entry door. Anand had transformed himself. He looked nothing like the bear of a man we had met on the train to Samarkand. Limping arthritically, he meekly ambled forth in his tight-fitting coat, hunched over and shrunken down as if he'd aged and withered. Dr. Tzu's medical bag dangled from his hand. I noticed Jamyang peek at it. Buried inside was the kukri knife.

Anand intended to kill the three Assassins.

Jamyang opened the door. As they entered into the darkness, Anand threw a glance back at us, in warning or farewell. The door closed behind him. A terrible thought struck me that we'd never see him again. Just the mere imagining provoked a pang of grief. Anand remained a mystery but had somehow touched my heart. Perhaps because he'd risked his life in order to save mine. I had done the same for him, and now I wondered why. We hardly knew each other. My affection for him was, in truth, a kind of fascination. At the duality at play in him, the constant contradiction. The sacerdotal warrior. The sybaritic spy. His joyfulness and lethality. His serene lack of doubt. It seemed the lightness of his spirit came from somewhere deep.

I wanted to know him better. I didn't want him to die.

We waited several minutes before opening the rear doors of the van and quietly slipping out. Dan kept watch as I crept to the Mercedes. Hiding behind it, I took out my Damascene dagger and crawled to the right rear tire. Anand had suggested I stab through the sidewall to avoid the steel wire under the treads. It took several blows before I finally broke through. The tire unhappily hissed.

I looked to Dan. The coast was clear. I scrambled to the left rear tire and slashed it like the other. With a whoosh it slowly emptied. The car appeared to sink.

Still no one at the monastery door.

I turned around and peered across the irrigated fields. In the distance, barely visible through increasing smoke and haze, the Range Rover wavered, a glinting mirage. Phoebe, I knew, would be watching through the glasses.

I waved to her.

Just as I did, a black car drifted past. On the same empty highway as the Rover. Slowing to a stop, it pulled a sudden U.

My heart leapt into my throat—I'd seen this act before. I scurried back to the cargo van. Dan was still crouched behind it, watching the entry door.

"Look—on the road!" I said.

We watched the car slowly roll up to face the sitting Rover.

"Late arrival," Dan said grimly. With three Assassins in the monastery, and Mahbood off with Fiore, we knew at least two more *Hashishin* were unaccounted for.

"It could be Vanitar," I said. I had asked Jamyang if he'd seen a man with a slight scar over his lip. He said he hadn't noticed.

The driver climbed out and started walking to Phoebe's door. From the distance, through the heat waves, he was little more than a blur.

Phoebe threw the Rover in reverse.

The driver rushed after her. She turned to drive away, but running he caught up with her and the Rover suddenly stopped.

"What'd he do?!" I said, rising to my feet.

Dan pulled me down. "Careful!" He glanced back at the monastery, then peered across the field. "He's got them," he said.

The man was hauling—or helping?—Phoebe out of the car. The doctor emerged from the other side to join her. From the distance it was difficult to see their interaction.

I imagined the worst. "He'll kill them both," I said.

Phoebe and the doctor were moving toward the Mercedes. We watched as the driver opened the rear door and the two of them climbed inside.

"C'mon!" I said. I started into the van.

Dan grabbed me. "Wait!"

The black car rolled off up the highway. "For what—?"

The driver turned onto the dusty road that led to the monastery. "He's bringing them here," Dan said.

80.
Doubt and Uncertainty

I could hear the car coming but couldn't see it—I was lying face-down on the ground, hidden underneath the Volvo. Dan and I had hurriedly improvised a plan, but the second we split apart I started entertaining doubts. What if the car wasn't a Mercedes? I thought. What if the driver wasn't an Assassin? Had we really seen Phoebe being forced out of the car? At that distance, we couldn't tell how they had interacted. Maybe she had discovered he was a friend.

It could be Faraj, I thought—he'd reported being on the trail of Mahbood. Even Harry Grant might have already arrived. Or called in someone else—perhaps the CIA. We'd seen no hint of them since the flower peddler in Rome. Harry had said it was possible they had gotten a man "inside."

Then again, I thought, it might be Vanitar.

Lying under the Volvo, I began to shake again. Sweat dripped off my face making craters in the dirt. In my hand, the iron tire wrench felt peculiarly cold and heavy. I wondered if I had the nerve to actually bludgeon this man to death.

All I could see when the car came into view were the tires and the trimmed black bottoms of the panels, shrouded in a whirlwind of dust. The vehicle came to a stop on the other side of the van, which was parked beyond the flat-tired Mercedes beside me. When I heard the engine shut off, my pulse began to throb. Peering through the gap beneath the parked row of cars, I saw the driver's feet hit the ground and heard his door slam shut. He opened the rear door, and two more pairs of feet joined his, one pair clearly Phoebe's, the other Dr. Tzu's. They all began walking toward the monastery.

Halfway there the man stopped. His feet turned in my direction.

I gulped, throat dry. My teeth freakily chattering. A fly buzzed my ear. The man said something I couldn't hear, then started heading toward me. Phoebe and the doctor hesitantly followed. The man's polished shoes—black laced leather under neatly creased slacks—paused a moment in front of the cars, then entered into the space between the Mercedes and the Volvo. They finally came to a stop less than one yard from my face. I gripped the iron tire wrench in terror.

The man's dark hand suddenly lowered into view. But instead of reaching toward me, the fingers turned away. They stroked the Mercedes' slashed sidewall.

I exhaled silently. The hand quickly withdrew. Now the shoes moved to the other side of the Mercedes, where I assumed the man must have been inspecting the other flat. He backed off, paused a moment, then walked very deliberately to the cargo van's front door. I heard him try to open it, but the doors in front were locked. The man marched toward the rear doors.

Inside, Dan was waiting.

This was it. Time to move. I slid out from under the Volvo and crept behind the Mercedes. Peering through its windows, I saw the van's rear door swing open. I gripped the wrench and charged.

Dan thrust a fistful of dirt into the man's face. His hands went to his eyes and his head swung away.

I raised the wrench to strike him, but couldn't see his face. Was it Faraj? Was it Harry? Was it Vanitar?

The man turned. Steel flashed—

Dan plunged the crescent dagger deep into his gut. The man bent over, retching. The blade poked out his back.

The four of us stared at the corpse on the ground, curled, fetus-like, bleeding into the dirt. He'd finally stopped moving.

Though the dirt Dan had thrown still covered his face, his eyes were frozen open, and with relief I saw the man was bearded.

He wasn't my friend Faraj, and he wasn't Harry Grant. In his hand was a Damascene dagger.

Phoebe, teeth clenched, clutched her upper arm. Blood trickled out through her fingers.

"Are you all right?" I asked.

"Imagine," she said, glaring down at the Assassin. "He thinks he's going to paradise."

The kind-faced Chinaman, Dr. Tzu, stared at the body in silence. I bent down close to look at the man's mouth. Blood was dribbling out of it. I saw no scar above his lip.

Dan removed the dagger from the corpse's hand, and turned with it to face the monastery. In the rush of the attack, the bandage on his cheek had fallen off, and the cut there now bled freely. He didn't seem to notice or to care. In fact his battered face looked flushed and excited, as if the brutal killing had aroused him.

"Something's gone wrong," he said. "Anand should be out by now."

"Stay cool," I said. "You heard what he—"

"What he told us doesn't matter if he's dead." Clenching the dagger, he headed toward the monastery.

"Dan!" I hissed.

He ignored me.

"What the hell has gotten into him?" Phoebe said.

Govindi I wanted to say.

"Aiyah!" Dr. Tzu reached for something on the floor of the van, lying beside Dan's open backpack. He brought it to his nose and sniffed it—a small glass vial, empty. A worried look of recognition settled on his face. He handed the vial somberly to me.

The glass was streaked with a milky coating. It smelled like fresh-cut grass and honey. Phoebe took the vial and examined it closely, and her eyes shifted over to the monastery.

Dan was plunging in through the doorway.

"There's no stopping him now," she said.

———

The cut below Phoebe's shoulder had been given as a warning, following her failed attempt to escape in the Rover. The gash was deep enough that stitches would be needed. In order to stem the bleeding now, Dr. Tzu was wrapping it with a strip of white cloth torn from the dead man's shirt.

"I'm sorry you've been dragged into this," Phoebe told the doctor.

He looked at her in surprise. "No sorry."

"No happy either, I'm sure," I said.

We were crouched behind the cargo van, trying to decide what to do. Six tense minutes had passed since Dan had gone inside. I was watching the entry door intently.

"Maybe he was right," I said. "Maybe Anand's been killed."

"If so, Dan is next," Phoebe said. "Then they'll come for us."

If so, if not, maybe, maybe not—the fog of uncertainty blinded us with fear, and fear hobbled us with more uncertainty. Every move seemed dubious and unpredictable. If we could see clearly what had to be done, we'd be more than halfway to doing it. Clear vision gave conviction, and conviction gave courage. Clarity was a clarion call.

That was Anand's secret, I decided. Seeing the truth of the matter. Information, intelligence, strategy, a plan. He had asked the doctor to diagram in detail the monastery's physical layout: the monks' cells, the temple, the prayer hall, the kitchen, where they were keeping Govindi, where the monks were being held, where the Assassins were stationed, where he could hide if he had to, how he might quickly escape. He had asked all kinds of questions about the three Assassins, and even more about the backgrounds and experience of the monks. After listening carefully, he had figured out a plan. A clear vision of action to embolden him.

By now, I thought, that vision had most likely gone to hell. Nearly thirty minutes had passed. And my lunatic brother had been added to the mix, jacked up on his home-made brew of soma. There was no telling what I'd find if I entered in there now. So I cowered behind the van with Phoebe and the doctor, straining for some vision to embolden me.

I didn't have to wait for long.

A red-robed monk slipped silently out the door. I recognized at once it was Jamyang. He stole across the lot, glancing nervously about, black brows piled up with tension. When he reached us he was out of breath. "Dr. Tzu…must come now."

"What happened?" I asked. "Where's Anand?"

"He kill one man, wound another. Wounded man escape."

"You said there were three of them."

"Third man in prayer hall. Wounded man there, too."

"With the monks?"

He nodded nervously. "Man say he kill them unless we bring doctor."

I looked at Dr. Tzu and Phoebe.

The doctor headed off toward the monastery. Jamyang followed.

"Wait!" I grabbed Jamyang. "What about my brother? He just went in a few minutes ago."

Jamyang shook his head—he didn't know. He gently moved my hand from his shoulder, then hurried off after the doctor.

Phoebe and I looked at each other. "You better wait here," I said. I turned to the body on the ground behind us and rolled him onto his back. Grabbing hold of the dagger, I yanked it out of his gut. The sound it made repulsed me.

When I turned back, Phoebe was taking up the tire wrench. "I'm going with you."

I hated to think of her facing their knives. "You can't—you're bleeding."

"So was Dan."

"Dan is crazy."

She glanced at the bloody knife in my hand. "So are you. Cowboy."

She hefted the wrench with her good right arm. It reminded me how she'd thrown me in that tower back in Bukhara.

Together, we headed toward the monastery.

81.
Death Chant

Behind the entry door, a short, dark passage led to a large, open courtyard. Phoebe and I peered out guardedly from the shadows. A low sound resonated like a humming hive of bees—the guttural murmur of the monks' chant. Where was it coming from?

Against the wall on either side stood the two-tiered arcade of the monks' quarters, chalk-white cells roofed with unpainted timbers. In stark contrast, before us blazed the oxblood red and mustard yellow of the temple and assembly buildings, with staircases rising to high-set doors, and sweeping, green-tiled, pagoda-style roofs, their corners curled to the sky.

"There," Phoebe said, pointing. "The prayer hall."

Jamyang and Dr. Tzu were rushing up the stairs. The hall seemed to be where the chant was coming from. I noticed, emblazoned on the façade above its wood-pillared porch, the chariot wheel chakra—Ashoka's Wheel of Dharma.

Beneath it, Jamyang rapped the red double-doors. One of the doors opened and the two men meekly entered. A bearded Iranian emerged—dark suit jacket, open collar, and in his hand, a dagger. The Assassin scanned the courtyard. Phoebe and I drew back.

The throb of chant again subsided as the prayer hall door swung shut. We crept out from the shadows. For the first time I noticed the sound of trickling water.

A round, stone-rimmed pond, fed by an open channel,

occupied the center of the courtyard, its surface green with lily pads. In the middle, like an island, a stone Buddha rested on a giant stone lotus.

"The center of the mandala," I said. Even the Buddha's hand gestures appeared exactly the same: right hand reaching to touch the earth, upraised left hand holding a sculpted lotus. I quickly scanned the pond for the soma plant. Pale pinks, yellows and whites abounded, but there were no red-and-gold flowers to be seen. "It's not here," I said.

"Jack!" Anand had emerged from a cell to our left, bearing the body of a monk in his arms. His white lab coat was streaked with blood.

Weapons drawn, we hurried to him.

"Drop those," he ordered, "and get her out of here, quickly." He held the body out to us—a woman!—she was alive.

"Govindi?" Phoebe asked. She tossed aside her tire wrench, I dropped my dagger, and we took the woman into our arms.

"She's lost consciousness," Anand said.

Sleeping Beauty, I thought at first glance, and wondered if she really was a nun. Though she wore the customary crimson robe, her head had mercifully not been shaved and her feet were clad in sneakers. Her face appeared a pretty blend of Asian and Caucasian, with jet-black hair pulled into a pair of girlish pigtails, and beaded necklaces glittering in the open cleft of her robe.

I couldn't take my eyes off her face. "Gabby," I said.

"What?" Phoebe asked.

"I know this woman," I said. "I...met her...just a few days ago in Rome." I remembered leaving her asleep in her bed. Now her robe felt damp in my arms. When I looked at the palm of my hand I saw red.

"Right arm and abdomen," Anand said. "Wrap them and get her to the hospital at once." He started across toward the prayer hall.

"Where's Dan?" Phoebe called.

Anand looked back. "When he saw what the *Hashishin* had done to her, he went charging out after them."

Phoebe and I glanced at each other.

"Go now," he said. "Hurry." He crossed the courtyard, drawing out his blade, and disappeared into the passage between the prayer hall and the temple.

With Govindi growing heavy in our arms, Phoebe and I headed for the exit.

"What about Dan?" she asked.

I was afraid to answer. With the soma and the sight of Govindi in his head, he must have gone into a rampage. The two of us peered up warily at the prayer hall. The building seemed alive with the insect drone of the monks. Even the painted wheel appeared to pulsate.

"Didn't Jamyang mention a rear door?" I asked.

"That must be where Anand—"

The entry doors of the prayer hall suddenly crashed open. Dan staggered out, bloody dagger in his hand.

"He's been cut!" Phoebe cried.

Blood drained down from his un-bandaged face and streamed from a gash on his arm. He stumbled forward, delirious. At the top of the stairs, he collapsed.

We set Govindi down in the passageway and started across the yard toward the stairs. The chant of the monks echoed out from the hall. A large man appeared in the doorway. Face bloodied, blade in hand, the Assassin lurched toward Dan.

Phoebe screamed in warning. We raced across the yard.

As Dan struggled to his feet, the Assassin swung his crescent. Dan wheeled to dodge it, but the knife slashed across his back and his eyes bulged in pain. Teetering, he dropped his dagger and tumbled to the bottom of the stairs.

We reached him as he came to a stop, face-down. Phoebe crouched beside him. The long scarlet gash had opened up his back. In the blood I glimpsed the white of his spine.

"Daniel!" Phoebe struggled to turn him over. I dropped to my knees and helped her. When we finally saw his face, his eyes looked dead as stones.

"Oh, God," Phoebe said.

The Assassin gazed down in triumph.

I could see he was not Vanitar, but a giant of a man with a

broad, flat face and ears the size of an elephant's. Slowly, I rose to my feet.

The giant lifted Dan's dagger off the floor and tossed it out over the stairs. It landed with a thud on the ground in front of me.

I stared down at the bloodstained blade. Phoebe, cradling Dan, peered up at me. "Jack. You can't."

I looked at her. The terror in her eyes. Dan lying dead in her arms.

I bent down and picked up the knife.

"No," she said. "Please!"

I started forward, as if in a trance. Dragging my foot up the first step. I took it, slowly, then took another. Then, more slowly, another. My gaze rose up to the Assassin.

He stood on the platform watching me. A ravenous look on his face.

Phoebe pleaded behind me. The chant of the monks seemed to petrify the air. My legs grew thick and heavy. I tried to raise my foot up, ascend another step. The leg turned solid as cement.

I couldn't move.

The Assassin, watching, smiled.

Anand burst out the doorway behind him, bloody smock flying and kukri in the air, a mad butcher erupting from an abattoir. The giant whirled to face him. They launched into a swirl of feints and flashes, a storm of lightning strikes. Steel gnashed steel. The slashing crescents hooked. With a single, sudden, sweeping pivot, Anand sent the Assassin's dagger flying and impaled the man's throat with his kukri.

It stuck. Anand released the knife and the man reeled back, hands swatting vainly at the handle. Gurgling, choking, he turned to get away—and toppled over the rim of the landing.

I felt the earth shudder as the body hit the dirt.

The guttural dirge of the monks droned on, a zombie din of death. The Assassin lay twisted with his face toward heaven, the kukri still jutting from his throat. Nothing of him moved but the outpour of his blood. His bulbous eyes seemed locked in awe—of black-cloaked Death, or Allah.

I descended the stairs in dread. Phoebe was still cradling Dan's head in her lap. "Your brother is alive," she said.

Alive and in a state of shock. At least that's how it seemed. We feared the slash across his back had damaged his spinal cord. Although conscious and alert, he appeared numb to what must have been excruciating pain, would not move his limbs when we asked him to try, and repeatedly failed to respond to our questions. He remained almost creepily detached and observant, watching us move and talk around him without moving or speaking a word himself. Phoebe was frightened for his life.

I thought it might be the soma. Prayed it might be, actually. Dr. Tzu said the soma might be alleviating his pain, but he wasn't sure why Dan was not responding.

He and Phoebe were on their knees, preparing Dan for transport. Watching them, I felt a sense of helplessness and shame. "Dan didn't hesitate for a second," I said. "I couldn't even bring myself to move."

Phoebe looked up from him. "I'm glad you didn't," she said, "or you'd be lying dead beside him now."

We loaded Dan into the cargo van on a wood plank employed as a stretcher. Govindi lay semi-conscious on the floor beside him, moaning intermittently and calling out a name: "Ätti." The hospital was less than half an hour away, but with riots still raging in the smoke-plumed city, Dr. Tzu said an ambulance was out of the question, and so it was decided that Phoebe would drive while the doctor worked in back to keep his two patients alive.

"Ätti…"

Dr. Tzu pulled shut the van's rear doors. I escorted Phoebe to the driver's seat.

"Swiss-German," she said. "She's calling for her grandfather."

Dr. Fiore. The Swiss mountaineer. Student of religion, connoisseur of plants. Pharmaceutical CEO turned Tantric Buddhist monk. I remembered him wading serenely through that clover pond in Rome—and wondered why his granddaughter had wanted to sleep with me.

It hadn't been for sex. I was knocked out. Govindi must have spiked the carafe of red wine we shared.

"What's wrong?" Phoebe asked.

"My phone..."

"Your cell? You told me—"

"That night I met Govindi in Rome—that's when I started having problems with my phone."

"You think...she bugged it?"

"She was working with Fiore. They were hoping to locate Dan."

"You can't blame them, Jack. They're trying to keep the lotus from these butchers who misuse it. We have to do whatever we can to help them."

As usual, she was right. "We'll find Fiore, I'm sure of it." But I spoke with a confidence I didn't really feel. Jamyang had said the monks were not told where the old man had been taken. Our only hope was the injured Assassin tied up in the prayer hall; Anand was up there now trying to get the man to talk.

I opened the driver's door for Phoebe. "You just take care of these two," I said.

She nodded in agreement but seemed preoccupied. "Remember Dan said he wouldn't leave here without her? I guess he really meant it." She tried to smile at the irony, but her eyes were welling up.

Sympathy overcame my own jealousy. "I know you still love him, Phoe—"

"Love him?" She hopped in the van. "I hate him. All this time I stayed away from you—and he was in love with Govindi!"

I laughed. She started the van. For a moment, we looked at each other.

"It's my fault," I said. "I'm sorry I didn't—"

"Please. Don't be sorry. And don't be a hero, cowboy. Make sure you come back."

"I will," I said.

"No...I mean… Come back *to me.*"

Her blue eyes glistened, displaying that naked longing I had glimpsed the night before. It struck me like a thunderbolt. A Vajra to the heart. That place inside of her was that place inside of me. I suddenly imagined the two of us would never be apart.

"I reckon' I ain't never leavin' you, Slim."

She leaned out and I kissed her. A tender kiss that lingered, that filled us both with longing, that did not want to end...

82.
Womb

The monks had stopped their chanting. A silence hung over the courtyard, deepened by the trickle of the lotus pond and the stillness of the vigilant Buddha. I mounted the stairs of the prayer hall. A faint humming caught my ear, like a lingering echo of the monks' chant. Below, on the ground where it had fallen, the corpse of the Assassin hosted a frantic orgy of flies. Two red-robed monks laid the wood plank down and prepared to move the body. One of the men looked up at me and I saw that he was Jamyang.

He nodded a bow. I nodded back. Just another day in Shangri-la.

Inside, huddled in shadow under avenues of pillars, a sea of scarlet monks squatted silent on the floor. Dim sunlight filtered down from above, through air reeking of burning butter and layered with the blue haze of incense. The glow of flickering butter lamps, blazing by the hundreds, lit paintings and carvings of bodhisattvas and saints gazing down from darkened niches in the walls. The walls themselves, and even the pillars, were draped with fiery fabrics—deep-dyed yellows, crimson reds, incandescent oranges—luminous up in the sunlight but dimmer down in the shadows, so that despite its airy heights, the room felt warm and womb-like.

Up front, under the gaze of an enormous golden Buddha, Anand paced slowly back and forth. I made my way toward him. The meditating monks, bald-headed boulders, eyes focused inward, paid no mind as I quietly padded past. Anand appeared to be mulling over the problem of the Assassin. Propped against the golden Buddha's massive lotus throne, the wounded Iranian sat on the floor, hands and ankles bound with rope, white shirt soaked with blood. His head hung down with his chin on his chest; I wondered if he might be unconscious. But then I saw that beneath his brow he was following me with his eyes.

Was this Vanitar? My only glimpse of his face in Rome had been in the dark on the roof, and later through the rain-fogged window of the Alfa. I paused to look at this man now as he raised his gaze to mine. His eyes were black and menacing. The untrimmed beard reached high across his cheeks; the moustache scowled beneath his nose. The skin of his face was pocked and dark. I saw no scar at his mouth.

"Where is Vanitar?" I asked.

The assassin peered up at me, silent.

Anand stopped pacing. "Won't say. Won't say where they took Dr. Fiore, either. In fact, he won't say anything at all."

The killer's stare shifted from Anand back to me. I wondered if Dr. Tzu had given him pain medication. He appeared to be enjoying our predicament.

I looked to Anand. "What are you going to do?"

"What do *you* think we should do?"

The casual tone of his question annoyed me. "Aren't you supposed to be the expert at this?"

"At what?"

"I don't know—interrogation." I glanced at the sea of faces behind me, then moved in closer and whispered to Anand, "Can't you *make* him talk?"

He answered in a loud voice, "Are you suggesting torture?"

Was he trying to embarrass me in front of the Buddhists? "Not at all!" I said.

"Good. I'm quite certain our friends here would not approve of that. Far preferable, I would think, to simply kill the man."

I thought he must be joking. But Anand dramatically pulled back his jacket and drew out his kukri knife. I was shocked to glimpse a wet stain of blood above his waist. Anand had been stabbed. Was this some kind of payback?

He stepped toward the Iranian. The man stared up, defiant. Anand rested the tip of his blade in the hollow of the Assassin's throat.

My heart pounded. I thought of the grinning runt in the pit. "Wait—"

Anand paused.

"Death is exactly what he wants," I said. "It's a part of their code. Woolsey said the *Hashishin* would rather die than to submit. Threatening to kill him will not make him talk."

"I don't expect him to talk," Anand said, still holding the blade to his throat.

"Then what—?"

"Ask yourself why the Iranians wanted to keep the young woman alive," he said.

"Govindi? I don't know." It clearly had been a risk to send Jamyang for Dr. Tzu. "Maybe they promised her grandfather they wouldn't let her die."

Anand peered calmly into the cold stare of the Assassin. "I suspect these men have no interest in keeping promises to Buddhist monks."

The enfeebled Iranian retracted his lips, presenting a glimpse of his teeth.

"They must have wanted Govindi as a backup," I said, "in case Dr. Fiore misled them."

"That would imply that she must know as much as her grandfather knows."

"Where they grow the lotus, you mean?"

"If she knows where, would it not seem highly likely that others know as well?"

"What others?" I asked.

Anand withdrew his kukri blade and turned his gaze on the monks. "Indeed." He had their full attention now; all eyes were on him. "Who among you can tell me? Where is Dr. Fiore? Where was he going with the Iranian?"

A few of the monks glanced at each other, but no one dared to speak.

Anand asked louder: "Where did the doctor go?"

The younger monks in the back eyed each other timidly. Up in front the elderly lamas guiltily dropped their gaze.

Anand sheathed his kukri knife. He raised his right hand, open-palmed—the gesture of good intentions—mirroring the *mudra* of the golden Buddha behind him. "What you have seen here today is only the beginning," he explained. "Many more lives are at stake. Many innocent people will die. If you refuse to help us, their blood will be on your hands. We must stop these killers now—before they steal the secret you've protected for so long."

He waited. Silence. No monk returned his gaze.

With a flourish Anand unsheathed his knife. He set it once again at the wounded man's throat. "Speak up now," he told the monks, "or right here, in front of your Buddha, I swear I will kill this man."

The Iranian trembled, staring at the blade. My heart was banging wildly.

"Aiy!"

From the back, near the doors, a lone monk hurried forward. The sea of faces turned to him. Anand withdrew his blade.

It was Jamyang. The young monk came rushing to a halt in front of us. Glancing at the lamas, he turned his anxious face to Anand. "Lama Fiore, he ask… He tell us—no talk. No talk anyone."

Anand eyed him silently.

"But why?" I asked. "He knows what these men want. Surely he knows they'll kill him for it?"

"Lama Fiore no afraid of death. He say for no one to follow him."

Anand and I exchanged a glance. He looked again at Jamyang. Then he peered into the wintry eyes of the shriveled old monks in front. "Buddha once said, 'I don't believe in a fate that falls on men however they act. But I do believe in a fate that falls on them *unless* they act.'"

The sitting monks' fossilized faces remained inscrutable, their eyes betraying nothing.

"We are not willing to allow Dr. Fiore to die," Anand said.

"Not when there's a chance we can stop them from killing him." He turned with his knife to the Assassin and lifted the blade to his throat. "This man, too, claims he is not afraid of death. Are you willing to allow *him* to die?"

Anand peered down at him and prepared to plunge the knife. The man stared back into his eyes.

Jamyang and I looked to the lamas. Tense seconds passed. Finally the oldest lama lifted a frail finger into the air.

"Stop!" I told Anand.

The lama struggled to rise. Jamyang hurried to his side and, together with another monk, helped the elderly man to his feet. Together they approached Anand.

Anand sheathed his dagger. He put his palms together and bowed to the man. The lama's eyes glittered in a deeply furrowed face. In a high, frail voice, he spoke some words I could not understand but assumed were probably Tibetan.

Jamyang translated. "He say you same—like the bearded children." He nodded toward the Iranian, who appeared to have passed out.

"Believe me," Anand said, "we are not the same." From his inside jacket pocket, he drew out three Ziploc bags—the lotus seeds belonging to Dan and Phoebe. "This is the entirety of soma seeds we've been able to find so far," he said. "I want to return them to you." He held them out to the monks.

The lama eyed them as Jamyang translated. He gave a subtle nod, and Jamyang received the bags.

Anand spoke directly to the lama: "Our only intent is to stop these men. And save the doctor's life."

The lama seemed to grasp the words without waiting for Jamyang's translation. He spoke something in Tibetan, then shuffled off with the other monk while Jamyang remained behind. We looked to him expectantly.

"He say the Taklimakan thirsty. Your blood, their blood—drink it all the same."

Behind us, the sea of monks resumed their deathly chant. The womb-hall throbbed like a beehive. Anand had to shout to be heard. "Fiore went into the Taklimakan?"

Jamyang nodded. "Before they come, he destroy all the

lotus. Bury seeds in desert."

"Where?" Anand asked.

Jamyang's eyes flitted between us. "Rawak," he said.

Anand looked puzzled. "The Rawak Stupa?"

Jamyang nodded.

"You know it?" I asked Anand.

"It's a Buddhist ruin in the desert," he said. "Maya told me about it."

I'd seen these monumental *stupas* in India—giant, dome-shaped mounds housing relics of the Buddha. They were places of prayer and pilgrimage, like Christian reliquaries. "You say the seeds are buried there?"

He nodded. "In Buddha's jade medicine box."

"Black jade?" I asked.

He nodded enthusiastically. "Yes! See—box no here." He pointed toward the lap of the golden Buddha. Anand and I moved closer. The Buddha's giant left hand lay open on his lap, his upturned palm and fingers bent around some missing object—what very well may have been a black jade box.

"Medicine—the elixir," I said.

Anand and I looked at each other. "We need to hurry," he said. He turned to Jamyang. "Can you—?"

Jamyang was bent over the slumped Assassin, feeling his wrist for a pulse. He looked to us and shook his head.

Another one lost to paradise.

83.
Fire in the Mind

From what we could understand from Jamyang—and the description Maya had given to Anand—the Rawak Stupa formed the heart of a vast Buddhist temple complex built on the banks of the Black Jade River in the Third or Fourth Century A.D. It was eventually abandoned and fell into ruin as the course of the river shifted and the dunes of the Taklimakan Desert rolled in. The Hungarian archaeologist Aurel Stein excavated the remains in 1901, uncovering nearly a hundred clay statues of Buddhas and bodhisattvas, with indications that several hundred more once existed. According to Jamyang, the massive Buddha in the monastery's pond was a replica of one of those disinterred by Mr. Stein. The original statues, along with the temples, were destroyed by treasure hunters and the brutal desert winds, eventually dissolving into dust. All that remains today, like a punctuation point, is the eroded brick mound of the stupa.

The last surviving ruin of Shambhala.

Jamyang, after some coaxing from Anand, agreed to take us there. I shouldn't have been surprised. Courage engenders charisma, I'd learned. The young monk seemed to share my fascination with Anand. As he drove us over the grasslands at the fringe of the Taklimakan, he asked the Gurkha why he'd been sent to find the soma plant.

"My government has an historical interest," Anand replied. "But more importantly, they want to keep it out of the hands of terrorists and assassins."

"No," Jamyang said. "I mean…Why they send *you*?"

Anand peered out the grimy windshield of the Volvo. "These Iranians are men of the knife," he said. "I understand their way of thinking. That's why the agency sent me."

I couldn't help but wonder if it had more to do with Maya. "Did they ask you, or you ask them?"

He glanced over his shoulder at me. "I usually don't go on this kind of mission anymore. Unless I ask for it."

I gazed into the haze. The grass was thinning out. Sand filled the empty spaces. "What *is* their thinking?" I asked. "The *Hashishin*, with their knives."

He didn't respond straightaway, but after several moments, as we ground our way up the gravel road, he began to reminisce. "My father was an officer in the Gurkhas. He trained at Sandhurst in England. I had a kukri knife in my hands from the day I learned how to walk. He wanted me to become accustomed to it—to 'make a friend of fear,' he said. He'd grown up in the mountains, and he fought alongside the British in the Second World War. First Battalion, Second Gurkhas—Cyprus, then North Africa.

"The Germans had a genuine fear of the Gurkhas, a reputation my father was eager to promote. He'd have his men slip into a German barracks at night and, in silence, slit a dozen throats. Every other soldier had only his boot laces cut. When they woke up in the morning and found the men on either side of them dead, they'd reach for their boots in a panic, see the severed laces, and know that they could easily have lost their lives as well."

"Like leaving a dagger on their pillow," I said.

"Indeed, the same effect," Anand said. "The weapon is in truth not the kukri or the dagger. The real weapon is fear. Fear can deter an enemy from taking any action at all."

I thought of my paralysis on the steps of the monastery. "Did the trick on me," I said. I held up my hand. "Look—I'm shaking even now. My dad probably should have kept a steak knife in my cradle."

Anand chuckled, then grimaced in pain. He'd wrapped his belly before we'd left, enough to staunch the bleeding. I asked if he was all right.

"Occasionally I need to be reminded," he said. "Fear does have its reasons."

"I could do with a whole lot less of it," I said. "I wish I'd taken some of Dan's soma juice."

"Oh no," Anand said. "A drug like that is far too dangerous. Look at what just happened to your brother. The mastery of fear can be a terrible thing. Think of suicide bombers. Kamikaze pilots." He glanced at Jamyang. "Even those Buddhist monks who in protest set themselves on fire. The absence of fear is perverse and unnatural."

"I thought it's what people call courage," I said.

"Courage is resistance to fear, not the elimination of it. Fear is a kind of pain, an anticipative pain, like the 'ache' of desire. It brings energy, intensity, strength. In a way, you might even say it's the source of courage. If you're able to accept it, you can work with it, use it."

"Like fire," Jamyang said again.

"Yes," Anand said. "Like fire. You can warm yourself with it, you can cook your food with it, or you can burn your house down." He glanced back at me. "Or you can set your camels ablaze and spur them into battle."

Tamerlane, the Earth Shaker. Courage run amok. His egomaniacal ambition and self-serving religious faith had extinguished the normal flickers of fear. All that remained to frighten him, like the looming pit of his grave, was the terror of an unfulfilled desire.

What a contrast, I thought, from the monkish life of Jamyang. The Buddhist lived his days like a psychological fireman, damping down the flames of passion that routinely flare up in the mind. Greed, resentment, infatuation, fear, instead of being kindled into blazing obsessions, were snuffed out at inception before they leapt out into the world.

The warrior king and the meditating monk. One had an ego the size of Asia; the other's would fit on a pinhead. The Scourge of God sought to conquer the world, the Buddhist to conquer himself.

"What about you?" I asked Anand. "How does a Hindu

handle his fear?"

"With prayer," he said. "And practice."

"With the knife? Or meditation?"

"A little of both, I would think. One aspires to reside in Brahman—even as one acts in the physical world."

"Is Brahman God…or emptiness?" I asked. "—Wait. Don't tell me." I imitated his accent. "'A little of both, I would think?'"

Anand laughed, then cringed again with pain.

"You sure you're all right?" I asked. I knew full well he wasn't.

Slowly, he sat upright, gritting his cig-stained teeth. "*Sat-chit-ananda:* infinite being, infinite consciousness, infinite bliss. Brahman. Hellishly difficult abiding there with this bellyache," he grumbled.

I peered out the windshield worriedly. Our talk had eased the tension, but his torment brought it back.

"End of road," Jamyang announced.

Ahead, parked cars materialized in the haze. A flame of terror licked my spine at the sight of a black Mercedes.

84.
Dharma Road

The three cars were parked near an old stone well surrounded by disintegrating brushwood shelters. Aside from the automobiles—the Mercedes, a Citroën, and a battered SUV—the oasis looked deserted. We climbed out of the Volvo into an utterly lifeless silence. It took a moment before I noticed, standing off in the haze, a mammoth-sized, double-humped Bactrian camel. The camel was tethered to a post, and a seat had been lashed to its back. Uncannily inert, the beast stared off indifferently across the sea of scrubland dunes.

From this oasis, Jamyang had said, a camel-driver could be hired to make the journey to the stupa, several miles farther into the desert.

"Better bring extra water," Anand now told the monk. "Looks like we'll be walking."

He went immediately to inspect the cars, while red-robed Jamyang shuffled to the well. I trudged past the empty shelters and headed out toward the camel. The odor of dung grew pungent. Straw lay scattered at the animal's feet and clung to its coffee-colored fur. Its miniature cousin still resided in my pocket, and as I reached my hand in to clutch the silky jade, the living beast turned its languid eyes on me, as if it had expected I'd be showing up by now.

"At long last we meet," I said. "*Salaam alaikum*, Camel."

Camel kept his frown.

"I'm Lawrence. Of Chicago."

It leisurely shifted its gaze toward the well. Blankets

padded its wood-frame seat and saddlebags hung from the frame. The camel's ear looked chewed. I noticed tethers dangling from the other hitching posts, and several piles of fresh dung gleaming on the sand. A chaotic collage of footprints and hoof prints trailed off into the dunes.

Why had this camel been saddled up and left behind? I wondered.

Anand had joined Jamyang at the well. As I approached, they turned to me grimly.

"What is it?" I asked.

They waited for me to look. At the bottom of the well, some forty feet down, a man in a white dishdasha lay dead. Even in the dimness I could see his bloody throat.

"The camel driver," Anand said.

"Why?"

"Jamyang says Fiore knows the way to the stupa. Apparently Mr. Mahbood felt he didn't need a guide."

I looked toward the cars.

"The SUV belongs to the camel driver," Anand said. "According to the rental papers, the Citroën belongs to your friend."

"Faraj?!"

"He must have arrived sometime after them. The engine is still warm."

"He's following them," I said. I peered off in the direction of the tracks. "Why wouldn't he take the guide's camel?"

"Crossing on foot would be stealthier," Anand said. "The same should hold true for us." He looked me and Jamyang in the eye, as if ferreting out any doubts. "Are we ready?"

Jamyang hesitated, then nodded.

I looked back at the cars. Something still troubled me. "What do you think happened to Vanitar?"

"I don't know," Anand said. He tramped off briskly, calling back, "When we find Mr. Mahbood, you can ask him!"

Jamyang and I exchanged a look. Then reluctantly followed the Gurkha.

———

Beyond the oasis, the dunes grew deep and bare of brush. We trudged up and down the trail of tracks, with Jamyang now doggedly leading us, his robe a red flame against the dust-laden sky. The silence was all-consuming. It seemed to swallow the swish of our steps and stifle Anand's labored breathing. I worried about his wound and glanced back frequently to check on him. He held his belly as he walked and kept his eyes fixed on the ground, attentive to every step.

Finally I slowed and walked beside him. Hoping, I suppose, to reassure myself, I asked again if he was all right.

He glanced at me with a painful grin. "I trust I'm not merely raising dust."

The phrase triggered a memory. "Maya said that to me in Rome. Something about the traveler…hesitating. Raising dust on the road."

"It's a quote from the Buddha," Anand said. "'Do what you have to do, resolutely, with all your heart.'"

I remembered Maya reciting those words that sultry night on the roof. At the time it felt invigorating. Now it just seemed sad. "Unfortunately, for Maya," I said, "it didn't serve her well."

"Oh, I don't know," he said. "It served her purposes well."

"*Dying*, you mean? She was stabbed by a man from the CIA."

"Maya was fulfilling her dharma, her duty. She believed in the end that's all we are: the actions that we take. The ultimate result is beyond our control."

I felt a sour resistance. "Whatever Maya thought she was doing," I said, "she ended up killing—and being killed by—an ally. That wasn't her dharma—that was a tragedy."

"That's life in samsara," Anand said. "We live in uncertainty and illusion. Even when we do see clear, the view is always limited, like a page torn from an infinite mandala. We must see the truth as best we can and act upon that truth. That's really all we can do."

"Is it?" I said. "Maya would have been better off not getting involved at all. Maybe the lamas are right."

"Right for them, perhaps. But Maya's dharma was Maya's

alone. That's the road she chose. Remember: she did live long enough to kill a key Assassin—perhaps the very worst. And doing so, she saved your life. Maybe many lives."

We walked along in silence.

"That line you laid on the monks," I said, "about a fate that falls on men unless they act? Was that really a quote from the Buddha?"

"I was rather hoping the monks would think so. In fact, it's from G. K. Chesterton, a big-bellied British Buddha—though he actually didn't think much of Buddhism at all. The English called him the 'Prince of Paradox.'"

A man of opposites—how fitting. "That's a perfect name for you," I said.

"I should say…I've been called worse. We are all of us double inside."

His voice had grown weaker. Although stoically plowing ahead, Anand was clearly suffering. "Do you want to rest?" I asked. We'd been walking for nearly an hour.

For a moment he appeared to be considering. Jamyang turned a hopeful face to him. "Go back?" he asked.

Anand slowed to a stop. "Water," he said.

I pulled out the big plastic jug from my pack. He took a healthy gulp, then held it out for Jamyang. The monk shook his head, "no." Anand handed it to me. I took a swig and capped it.

We peered out over the path ahead. A breeze caressed the camel tracks trailing off into the haze.

"Raising dust," I said.

Jamyang looked to Anand. "We go back Kutana?"

With intense self-containment, Anand held his gaze on the horizon. "Walk on," he commanded.

And so we did. Resolutely. The three of us snaking across the bald-headed dunes...until a mile or so later Anand Pandava finally collapsed.

85.
To Kill a Man

The wound was on his left side just beneath his belt, a smile of a slit some three inches wide. He had hurriedly taped it shut before we departed from the oasis, but with all the walking and bleeding the adhesive had given way, and the cut now bulged with a coil of his intestine. Jamyang pressed it back inside, bloodying his fingers, then held the slit together as he dried it with his robe. I stretched out several lengths of tape and sealed it up again. His skin felt chilled and clammy. We rewrapped the cloth bandage around his waist, then laid him back to rest against the gentle slope of the dune.

The wound had stopped bleeding out into the sand, but he was still hemorrhaging internally. His face looked pale, his eyes staring vaguely. He was conscious, but groggy from shock. "A moment," he muttered. "Just…a moment."

Jamyang watched him worriedly. He had only come this far because of Anand, whose confidence and courage had been contagious. Seeing him falter now suddenly undermined his will. The world appeared even more dangerous than he'd thought.

The monk laid out Anand's kukri knife neatly in its sheath. He noticed the sand beside it was blood-soaked. Scraping up a handful, he held it out to me. "Taklimakan thirsty."

The old lama at Kutana had been right.

I turned and peered ahead into the haze, struggling to control my own mounting sense of dread. The wind was picking up. The hour was getting late. We were standing in the middle of the empty desert, no cell phone reception, no ambulance to call, no way to save Anand if he fell further into shock. A full-blown dust storm might whip up in an instant. Nightfall would bring a bitter cold. And out there ahead of us, at any moment now, returning with the jade box of soma lotus seeds, Mahbood might appear, dagger in hand, ready to further slake the Taklimakan.

For a long moment I stood there, debating what to do: try to keep Anand conscious and send Jamyang for help, or sling the man between us and try to walk him back to the car.

I crouched down beside him. "How do you feel?" I asked.

The luster had left his eyes. His face was losing color. "Long road," he said.

"Looks like it ends here."

"Mine does," he said. "Not yours."

The suggestion rankled me. "There's no way we're going ahead without you. No way."

"Not Jamyang, perhaps." He looked with tenderness at the monk. "He's on a different road."

"Enough already with the roads," I said. "I'm starting to think you got stabbed in the head. Look around you—there's no 'road,' there's no 'dharma.' We're in the middle of the fucking desert! If we don't get you to a hospital, you'll die."

"Anger is good," he said. "It can help subdue your fear."

"Did you hear what I just said?"

"Yes," he said. "If I stay here, I may die. But for sure I will die if I try to move."

He was right. That he'd made it this far was astonishing. "Then we'll send Jamyang," I said. "He can bring you help."

Anand gazed off despondently. "There isn't time," he said.

The words were tinged with pity; a plaint, I sensed, not for himself, but for my own predicament. Anand had faced the truth. There was nothing more he could do. It had taken him less than a single minute to accept the fact he might die.

Clearly, the onus had fallen on me.

I stood up. My mind ablaze. Frantic for some answer. I looked back down the way we'd come. Then peered ahead at the trail.

Jamyang stepped up beside me. I asked, "How much farther to the stupa?"

He paused a moment, considering, then turned to me and shrugged.

"You told us it was only a few miles," I said. "It feels like we've walked five."

"Perhaps is…not so close," he said.

It occurred to me suddenly that he really didn't know. He had only made the trek once, several years before—while riding on the back of a camel.

How far *had* we come? Even I had no idea. Anand's pace had slowed us down; some deep sand as well. And in the desert, distances were difficult to judge, especially—

"Take this."

We turned. Anand was holding out the kukri.

"I wouldn't know how to cut a loaf of bread with that," I said.

"Take it."

I did. Reluctantly. The knife felt weightier than the dagger in my pack, with the blade loaded heavily toward the tip.

"To cut bread, use a bread knife," Anand said. "To kill a man, no blade can best the kukri."

"Unless it's in the hands of the *Hashishin*," I said. "I don't stand a chance in a knife fight."

"You're right. You must kill him before any fight begins."

"How?"

"Stealth. Surprise. Deception."

"Easier said." I practiced slicing and stabbing the air.

"Keep your wrist straight," Anand suggested. "The blade is angled down. To stab, thrust forward, like a punch. Or better, raise the knife like an axe…bring it down hard through the skull or the shoulder."

The idea repulsed me. "I won't have the nerve," I said. "I won't be able to do it."

"You will," he said. "When you see what must be done, you'll do it."

"What makes you so sure? You don't know me."

"You saved my life in the square."

"That was an impulse," I said. "I don't know what got into me."

"What got into you was already there—you simply got out of the way. When you see clearly what must be done, you don't take the action. The action takes you."

The action takes you. "So 'I' have nothing to do with it?"

"You have your body, your brain, and your weapon. But the most important thing is your decision to use them. That decision must be made sometime well before the battle. You have to make a choice. In that place deep within yourself. That when the moment comes, when you have to act, you will do whatever is necessary."

"Kill him, you mean."

"Resolutely. With all your heart."

"Right. You said you're double inside? I've got like a whole convention going on."

"Just keep it simple," he said. "You won't be able to think."

I looked at the knife in my hand. *Down hard through the skull. Down hard...*

"What if I miss?" I asked. "What if I blow it? What if it's him coming after me?"

Anand frowned in thought.

"That's it, then, right? I'm off to paradise?"

He stared off vaguely into the desert. "There is…one thing you could try."

"What?"

He looked at me. "You'll think me a nasty man," he said.

As if I didn't already.

86.
What You Have to Do

Detachment. Enlightenment. The calm of self-surrender.

I felt about as far away from these things as a cipher under a spotlight cowering on a stage. My spotlight was the desert sun; the stage a pit of sand. I ventured out, locked inside my separateness. No state of cosmic oneness could be conjured into consciousness. No sense of being "empty" or divine. I was not infused with a sudden burst of valor, nor did a bold clarity of vision spur me on. Uncertainty and trepidation stalked my every step. Frantic second thoughts continually boomeranged.

I had left them the jug of water, and already I was parched. Dehydrated and fatigued, how long would I survive? Would I be in any shape to face the murderous Mahbood? Would I be able to muster the courage to actually kill him? If it did turn into a knife fight, what did I think I would do? Anand's wicked idea had seemed deranged. And even if I did survive, surely I'd be injured. How would I keep from bleeding out with all those miles to march? Night would fall. I'd be lost. The cold alone would kill me.

Even the supposed urgency of my cause now fell into doubt. Was stopping the Iranians here really worth my life? Was saving the old doctor up to me? This was not Phoebe I was marching out to rescue. This was not my brother, or Oriana or Anand. I was risking my life to help a man I barely knew. And to confront a man who'd take pleasure in disemboweling me.

Fear pervaded the desert. Not selflessness, not Brahman.

The faith of Anand and Jamyang could not dispel the air of doom. In fact it seemed to border on insanity. Were these two monks really pilgrims on the road to the so-called "Truth?" Or credulous dupes deluding themselves with visions of invincibility? My last glimpse of them, stranded and defenseless, made me think even the old Gurkha must have fallen into doubt.

Still…I walked on. Deeper into the desert.

God, give me strength. Keep calm and carry on.

Prayers and exhortations, the weapons of the weak. Woolsey no doubt recited them on the way to his execution—futile mutterings to save him from his separateness. But he, too, was wrapped inside an envelope of skin, as easily slit open as a valentine.

Though I walk through the valley of the shadow of death, I will fear no evil, for thou art with me. The prayer welled up, unbidden. *He leads me in the paths of righteousness... I will dwell in the House of the Lord forever.*

The House of the Lord. The Refuge of the Buddha. The Infinite Ground of Being. All noble names for that walled paradise, the Kingdom of Heaven Within. A place that now seemed to have vanished, if ever it truly was there.

Here, now, in *this* place, set upon this desert trail, trekking toward my fate, I was enmeshed in the dream of samsara, the dream we all are dreaming, the "truth" that is our lives. That dream now seemed the only truth. Nothing lay beyond it. Not God, not Brahman, not paradise. Not a heaven above or a kingdom within. Not even a dream of awakening.

My heart raged inside me as if struggling to escape. If what is here is all there is, and nothing lies beyond it, then why forfeit my separateness, why sacrifice myself? My separateness was all I had—my skin, my soul, my life. Why wasn't that worth saving?

The thing to do seemed all too clear. Halt this fatal march. Return to Anand and Jamyang, go find Dan and Phoebe. Save my friends, save myself. Fight another day.

I stopped. Looked back.

Phoebe. My love. *Come back to me*, she said.

The low sun cast shadows into the hollows between the dunes. The atmosphere had cooled. The haze that hung so long in the air had lifted like a veil. A vivid stillness replaced it. Above me the sky shone a violent blue. The ochre sea beneath it seemed to shimmer.

I'd been walking for nearly an hour, maybe even more. Around me, in all directions, empty desert stretched out as far as I could see. Infinite and strange, yet claustrophobically real, it seemed as if I'd awakened in the bell jar of a dream, my skin prickling with perspiration, my breath a hollow whispering.

You have to make a choice...

I turned and peered ahead at the camel tracks trailing off into the shadows.

He leads me in the paths of righteousness...

Paths that lost so many: Maya, Oriana, Sar, Woolsey. Names that seemed to gnaw at me. Lives severed, incomplete.

That place in you, that place in me...

Could I bring myself to abandon Dr. Fiore and Faraj? Let the butcher Mahbood walk away with the seeds? The Assassins commit more murder?

Do what you have to do, resolutely...

The path seemed to tug me like the current of a river. Before I was even aware of it, I was trudging ahead on the trail.

Why did it seem I had no choice? What was it kept me going?

Honor? Pride? Ego?

Or dharma, duty, selflessness. Submitting to the will of God. Acceptance of my fate.

I was on that dharma road connecting East and West. Assert the self? Surrender the self? It seemed I must do both. My heart insisted on it.

God. Brahman. Emptiness. The Truth. Perhaps they're only the names we give to the need we have for meaning. Or perhaps they are the names we give to the Source of meaning itself.

I walked on.

87.
Go Deeper

I had been watching Mahbood from the ridge for nearly half an hour. His progress had been slow. The short-handled spade, designed for planting tent stakes, was ineffective digging in the deep, compacted sand. He appeared to have reached about four feet. How far down would he go?

At the wall beside the stupa, the white-haired monk sat bleeding. Mahbood had beaten him within an inch of his life and threatened the old geezer with his dagger. But the pigheaded Buddhist had resigned himself to death, and now the Assassin—without his precious knife—was back down in the hole again, digging away with his spade.

Anger and impatience fueled his endeavor. Until my shadow fell on him, he hadn't noticed my approach. "Kind of you to dig your own grave," I said.

Mahbood turned, slowly, squinting up at me as if I had long been expected. "Deeper," he said, nodding toward the monk. "That's all the old-fart will tell me. 'Go deeper.'"

The monk sat silent, eyes swollen shut, the white of his beard a wet crimson.

I picked up Mahbood's knife and tossed it away. "Six feet should do it," I said.

"Any deeper than that, I'll let you take over." His insolent gaze dropped down to my dagger. "Unless you're above digging ditches now."

I glanced again at the monk. "I did your dirty work at Kahrizak, Mahbood. Only I never enjoyed it like you did."

"No? How about now? Have you enjoyed taking the lives of your brother Hashishin?"

"My brothers have been misled. In Bukhara, they tried to kill me."

"They serve the Ayatollah. If you have a problem with that, you should take it up with him."

Mahbood went back to his digging.

I considered various ways to bring the devil's life to an end. Quick slash across the carotid? Slow puncture to the spleen? "You'll have to take it up with your Maker," I said. "The Ayatollah will have nothing to do with you."

"You speak now for the Ayatollah? Now that you sacrificed Arshan?"

"My brother was killed by the hand that betrayed him. I speak for the Bringer of Judgment, who takes your soul by night and knows all you've done by day."

Mahbood paused, resting his shovel on his shoulder. "You quote the Koran like a pious little mullah. All your fancy talk from Qum. You sound as pompous as Faraj—"

"Faraj lied. I speak truth. Isn't that simple enough for you?"

"Faraj lied about Islam. He spoke the truth about you."

I swung my dagger at his neck. In a flurry his shovel deflected the blade and his fist came down on my foot. The fist held a wedge-blade dagger. I howled and fell to the ground.

Mahbood pulled the short blade and stuck it up under my jaw, one jab away from my jugular. His sweating face breathed into mine. "People can lie under torture. But they can't lie for long. In the end I always find out what a man really believes. Peel back the layers of his lies."

A cool steel blade slipped under my shirt—Mahbood's other hand had my dagger!

"What do you believe, little brother Vanitar? That your beautiful young mother really died giving birth? That your limp-dick old daddy was a saint?" The fire in his eyes seemed to burn into mine. "Mirrors don't lie to you. Faraj spoke the truth. It's obvious why the two of you looked so much alike—"

"It's a lie!"

"Faraj's father fucked your mother, and your father killed them both."

"Lies!"

"Lies?" The razor edge of the crescent slowly sliced across my belly. "Is that all you can say? Where's the fancy words now? Quotes from the Koran? Tell me again how proud you are of your father, the shahid, the murderer who avoided jail by joining the Basij—"

"Stop—!"

"Just one of thousands slaughtered in the human wave attacks. Another nameless casualty in another pointless war."

"My brother said—"

"Your brother hid the truth. He wanted to protect you. Your 'piety,' your 'virtue.' Your dream of becoming an imam. But your friend Faraj spilled it all out in his rage at you in prison." The point of the crescent dagger pierced the skin beneath my ribs. "Yet still you refused to listen." He was going for my spleen. "Still you refuse to see—"

A cry cut the air like the shriek of a hawk. Startled, I stopped to listen. The utterance had undoubtedly been human. A silence followed, then voices. Two men in an argument beyond the dune ahead. Not English—Persian? One voice accusatory. The other seeming to plead.

I raced up the dune to its wind-carved crest. Peering over, I saw them in the shadowed depression below. A bearded man with two daggers—the Assassin, Ali Mahbood—was advancing over Faraj, who scrambled on his backside along a freshly dug pit.

The pit resembled a grave. It lay at the base of an ancient ruin, a 20-foot-high stupa of creamy, crumbled brick. Rising roundly by tiers to a flat-topped peak, the great mound stood surrounded by a decaying courtyard wall, half drowning under undulated dunes. Two saddled camels stood just beyond the wall, indifferent to the goings-on within.

Faraj had been stabbed and was bleeding. On his knees now at the edge of the pit, he seemed to be imploring the Assassin to spare him.

Where was Dr. Fiore? I wondered. Already buried?

My pulse pounded frantically, fear now riding on a razor's edge of panic. I slipped off my duffel bag and pulled the kukri knife. The wooden handle slithered in my grip. My hand was shaking violently.

———

Mahbood stood above me, boot dagger in his left hand, my Damascene in his right.

"I betrayed no one," I said. "The Hindi...the American...it was they who killed Arshan."

"Of course. Your friends."

"No...I swear—"

"They were listening, in Rome. To every cell phone call. That's how they got our numbers—"

"Who?"

"Who?" He laughed. "The Christians In Action, you idiot. Your friends—the CIA!"

———

Stealth. Surprise. He doesn't know I'm here.

Staying hidden, I slid feet-first back down the slope and crept around the dune toward the stupa. The two men, concealed now behind the courtyard wall, became a pair of disembodied voices. I crawled to the wall and crabbed along its base, heading toward the place where I could breach it—a wind-blown sand-heap reaching to its rim. I scrambled up and peered into the courtyard.

Mahbood now had his back to me, with Faraj at his feet. Holding daggers firmly in each hand, he spoke as if delivering a death sentence. Faraj stared up dazedly, too feeble to resist, his hands struggling in vain to stop his bleeding.

The fear now came alive in me, the hairy worm erupting like a chrysalis in birth. Cracking, unfreezing, it burst in fluttering spasms through my belly and my limbs, wings beating frantically, urging me to run away—or take the plunge and fight.

Now. The moment. *What I had to do.*

88.
Now

The fear took me with it, an exhilarating wave, propelling me up over the wall and down the leeward slope. I charged toward the Assassin, raising up my kukri like a madman with an axe. All thought fled. The sudden storm of energy completely overwhelmed me. Surging like the rush of some enormous, flowing force, it carried me along with it, propelling me into what seemed a kind of parallel dimension. A tunnel out of mind. Dreamlike, yet real. At once floating beyond myself, watching from above, while racing in slow motion through a tidal wave of terror. Would I live? Would I die? Did it even matter? The only thing that mattered was to kill the *Hashishin*.

Down hard through the skull—

Faraj's gaze shifted as he saw me rushing toward them. Mahbood sensed me coming and whirled—

I brought the knife down hard and straight, but did not strike his skull. His Damascene dagger, its blade a crescent hook, caught the kukri with a clash and sheered the steel aside.

The deflection sent me careening and the knife flew from my grip. I tumbled into the pile of sand dug up from the pit. Grit stung my eye. My vision suddenly blurred. Looking over I saw Faraj rise up to defend me, but Mahbood quickly turned and slashed the dagger across his chest.

Faraj collapsed. The Assassin turned to me.

A cold terror struck my heart. *I am going to die.*

He moved slowly toward me. I tried to focus through the tunnel vision of my fear. His brow brimmed with sweat. The sun glared behind him and his face fell into shadow. Only his piercing eyes shone clear.

The eyes darted toward my knife, half-buried in the sand. I leapt across and grabbed it, but when I tried to stand up, my left ankle gave way and the leg quickly collapsed. A warm numbness suffused my foot. Had the ankle somehow twisted? I looked down to see a gash across the backside of my boot. Blood was filling up the heel and leaking out the slit. Mahbood had slashed the tendon between the heel and the calf. The touch of his dagger had been so swift I'd neither seen nor felt it.

He moved toward me now in silhouette, like an elongating shadow. Slowly, unhurriedly, as if in pity for me—or savoring my death. His gleaming eyes betrayed a kind of single-minded madness. The fervor of a predator intent upon its prey. The unflinching concentration of a psychopath.

Soma, I thought. The man had drunk the Kool-Aid. He had the very same look on his face that Dan had displayed at the temple. Calm, steel-eyed certainty.

Anand had warned me not to fight, not with him residing in that deep, dark place. Untrained, unskilled, now injured, I had only one chance against the invincible jihadi: goad him out of his god-like state and exploit his own ego to kill him.

I scrambled away on my backside just as Faraj had before me, dragging my useless foot through the sand, clutching the kukri knife, until I backed against the cold mound dug up from the pit. Glancing into the gloomy hole, I saw that it was empty.

The Assassin stepped before me, his daggers dripping blood. *Full of strength. Sharp-weaponed. Irresistible in battle.*

My heart thrashed inside me like an animal encaged. My legs shook uncontrollably. I uttered some fretful noise like the bleating of a sheep.

"You are slain already," he said, his mocking voice serene.

I pressed back against the mound and tightened my grip on the kukri.

He glanced at the Gurkha knife and grinned. "Bravest of the brave?" He made a show of sharpening his crescent dagger's edge by swiping his short blade back and forth across it. "Do you know what I do to brave men?"

I flashed on Saar's corpse.

"Tell me something, Gurkha. Tell me if it's true." He tossed aside the short blade and felt his crescent's edge. "Is it really better to die than be a coward?"

He peered into my eyes, waiting for my reply.

Do it now, I told myself. *Do it now or die.*

I spit in the Assassin's face.

He stopped. Stunned. The gob of spittle trickling. Momentary disbelief transforming into anger. In that very instant, as he bristled into rage, I launched a punch with all my strength, aiming the kukri at his heart.

The blade cracked through his ribcage, plunging deep into his chest, until it stuck in hard bone, a sudden, stony stop. Had it struck his spine? I did not try to pull it out, but backed away in horror.

No blood at all came out at first. Everything seemed frozen. The embedded blade, the bulging eyes, the visage gaunt with shock. He stood for several seconds staring blindly into space. Was he dead? I wondered. What is it he sees? Hell? Paradise? The forbidden face of Allah? Or Buddha's unknowable nothingness, his truth at last unveiled.

Whatever secret he saw remained so. As the dark bloom of red blood spread out from the blade, the Assassin dreamily dropped to his knees and toppled face-down in the sand.

My gaze rose dizzily beyond him. There, against the wall, hidden in its shadow, sat a meditating, red-robed Buddha. I had been so focused on Faraj and Mahbood I had not seen him sitting there before. Recognition came with a shock. Fiore's white-bearded face had been bloodied and the neck of his robe torn askew. Despite the killing that just occurred, he remained cross-legged in the lotus position, and his puffy eyes stayed shut. He did not appear to be breathing. In fact he sat so utterly motionless I thought he was probably dead.

Faraj stirred under the shadow of the stupa. I started crawling toward him. An excruciating spasm electrified my leg. Blinding light seared a spiky circuit through my head. The contraction of the calf muscle had torn apart the tendon, and the pang sent a shockwave through me. I cried out and collapsed. My body started trembling and I broke into a sweat. Struggling to endure the pain, clutching at the sand, I swallowed up gulps of air and gaped in concentration, writhing finally onto my back and glaring up at the sky.

Please, please...

I waited for it to subside. Clenching fistfuls of sand. The sky peered down indifferently, an icy eyeball blue, while the creamy mound of Buddha's bricks, an upturned breast of stone, offered dry succor to the empty air, a gesture as vain as my pleading.

Another shadow fell over me. A beardless silhouette, Mahbood's dagger in one hand, a goatskin flask in the other.

"Faraj."

He continued staring down at me. Sweaty, bloody, grimacing, he looked on the brink of death.

"Water," I begged.

It seemed to take a moment for the word to reach his ears. As if his mind were miles away, mulling some unanswered question. Or wondering how he had come to be here, in the desolate Taklimakan, the Sea of Death those wary caravans so long avoided.

At last he dropped beside me and opened up the flask. I sucked from the goatskin greedily. The slaking of my thirst helped divert me from the pain. But when I suddenly realized the liquid wasn't water, I shoved the thing away.

"Soma?"

A delay before he nodded.

The torn tendon throbbed, sending tremors up my leg, nudging me to the border of unconsciousness. I clung to the sand. Praying for relief. Until...miraculously, the pain began to fade. Heat radiated from my belly through my throat. The warmth seemed to calm my body down.

I sniffed the concoction. Sweet, herbaceous milk. *Of heaven, of water, of thousand-fold wealth, who the gods have made for their drinking, most sweet-flavored, invigorating, dripping, honeyed, causing happiness—*

I drank. Great gulps of it. The answer to my prayers. God's

gift to the Aryans. The *Hashishin's'* "pure drink."

Warm juice trickled down my chin. Nodding thanks to Faraj, I gave the goatskin back. Faraj drank the last of it, then wiped his milky mouth.

I stared at him. At his mouth.

A scar above his lip.

Faraj saw me staring. He rose up on his feet.

My gaze drifted down to the dagger in his hand. Then climbed back up to his face. The face began to fade. *"Faraj?"*

"No," he said, his voice far off. "I killed Faraj in prison."

The words sounded wrong. Distant, distorted, nonsensical. Was that a bloody grimace, or was he actually grinning? His face had lost focus. The light had grown too dim.

"Vanitar," I whispered.

Then it all went dark.

89.
Nirvana

I awoke to a nearly lightless sky, an inky cobalt blue. The sun had sunk behind the dunes, yet light still lingered on the summit of the stupa, which glowed like a golden throne. The twilight seemed to magnify the strangeness of the place. A tranquil silence permeated everything.

My leg was still in pain but the pain seemed more remote, as if the wounded limb had been somehow disconnected, or my mind been uncoupled from my body. Fearing movement might dissipate this palliative illusion, I lay perfectly still on my back in the silence, peering up past the stupa at the emerging moon and stars, and savoring the sensation of spaciousness they seemed to unlock within me.

The night I crossed the Caspian Sea, the stunning sight of the stars above had triggered a kind of panic, a terrifying realization of the never-ending emptiness of space. Now I experienced a similar astonishment, but here, in the last remaining ruins of the kingdom of Shambhala, the awe that had gripped me that night on the boat was replaced with a blissful calm, and the dark infinity of the blueness above seem to lift my soul into heaven. Everything emptied out of me—pain, fear, regret, desire—all faded in a fusion of inside and out, as if thought itself had disintegrated and the act of perception dissolved. All that remained was the One: the deep, darkening, infinite blue, brightened with glittering pinpoints of light and the wink of my own lunar eye.

Tat tvam asi. That am I.

I have no idea how long my state of cosmic bliss endured. It may have been mere seconds. Or a minute. Or an hour. But now a sound came to my ears that narrowed my awareness. A soft swish, or lashing sound. Gentle. Or cruel.

Welcome back, I thought. Back to the world of time and pain. Back to the dream of samsara.

90.
Irresistible in Battle

"Go deeper," he'd told Mahbood. But how much deeper? The white-maned monk refused to say. He would not condescend to speak with me.

What illusion in the Buddhist mind makes them think they are superior? They who have no fear of God—who have no God at all! Instead they talk of emptiness, and sit and drone like crickets. They let the Chinese steal their country, and now they wander the earth like Jews. They say everything is nothing and nothing is everything, then hold out their beggar's bowl and instruct us on compassion.

The old one sits there, eyes downcast, staring at the sand. No doubt he sees the universe in every little grain. But had he not seen Allah's hand in the killing of Mahbood? How the naïve American—yet again—had acted as an unwitting instrument of God? And how my life once more was spared, while yet another liar was cast down into Hell?

No. The Buddhist won't see what's right before him. Like a child, he hides behind his eyelids, pretending he's invisible, that blindness makes him safe and that darkness is the Truth.

But Truth is the light that comes down to us from Allah. I could feel it at that very moment filling up my soul.

Leaning down, I whispered a quote from the Koran into the old monk's bloody ear. "Truth has arrived, and falsehood perished, for falsehood is by its nature bound to perish."

With that, I took up the shovel and slowly climbed down into the hole.

The swishing sound was Faraj—Vanitar—shoveling sand from the pit. His head bobbed up from the hole with each expelling toss. Yet he was working slowly, seeming feeble and fatigued. I'd seen how badly he'd been cut. What was it kept him going? His desire for the seeds? Or fear of that deep darkness he kept hidden in his heart?

Lying face-up now in the sand where he had fallen, with a slit in his chest where the knife had been removed, the man I had stabbed was no longer a man: it was a lifeless corpse. Beyond it, Fiore sat locked in the lotus posture. He looked like a bloodied Buddha sculpture propped against the wall. Was he breathing? I couldn't tell. I prayed he wasn't dead.

Vanitar had taken the kukri, along with the crescent dagger. But across the sand lay the dead man's short blade, casually discarded, the goatskin flaccid beside it. Given that I could neither stand nor walk, Vanitar must have assumed I was no longer any threat. But why had he given me the painkilling soma? To keep me from passing out? Why had he not simply killed me to avenge his brother's death?

Suddenly I knew the answer. There could be only one reason for keeping me alive.

Five feet. Still nothing. Does the monk tell lies with his silence?

I will go one foot deeper. If that does not uncover it, I'll open Duran, slowly, in front of the old monk's face. The mute may shut his eyes to it, but the screams will make him speak.

Dragging my foot, I crawled toward the dagger, a dull gleam in the dark. Spasms of pain triggered lightning in my head. I winced but kept on moving; it seemed I had no choice: do what I must to protect myself or Vanitar will kill me.

My severed tendon flared with pain, but the thought of dying sparked no corresponding flare of fear. Fear had emptied out of me. There was only what had to be done. I may have been down in the muck of things, but part of me clearly was not.

Another pitch of sand settled on the pile beside the pit. I heard a dull clank, and turned to see that Vanitar had disappeared into the hole. With his obsessive single-mindedness and reckless lack of fear, the *Hashishin* had dug in over his head!

Just past six feet the shovel struck a rock. A black rock, or so it appeared, until I got down on my hands and knees and brushed aside the sand. The flat, polished stone surface gleamed in the twilight, reflecting my dark silhouette against the sky above. Feverishly I clawed away the dense sand all around it. Oblong, a foot in length, several inches deep, the object finally came loose. I held it up for a look.

A box made of black jade. Intricately engraved. The sliding lid locked in place. A keyhole with no key.

As I reached for the short-bladed dagger, I heard a cry from the hole, a howl of pain and anger. I grabbed the knife and hurriedly crawled—on one knee—toward the pit. My best chance to kill Vanitar would come as he tried to climb out.

The lid would not slide loose. The heavy box, thick as a block, repelled the blows of my blade. Even using the tip of the kukri, I could not prize the lid. Finally, jamming down the point, it slipped and sliced my hand. I wailed in a fury.

I thought of the Buddhist, sitting smugly silent. Bristling, I realized that he must have the key.

Stealth. Surprise. The only chance I had.

Dragging my bleeding ankle behind, clenching the knife in my teeth, I clawed my way across the sand, creeping toward the hole. *Sharp-weaponed, irresistible in battle, attacking, slaying his foes—*

I spotted something moving. A pair of hands pushing an object out over the rim of the hole.

The jade medicine box! I eagerly crept toward it.

———

Exiting this deep trench was not going to be easy. My foot could find no purchase in the crumbly sand walls, and there was nothing at the top that I could hold to. I struggled in vain to clamber up the side. My fingers clawed the rim. Sand tore loose and cascaded to my feet. With each attempt, I lost more strength. Finally, I collapsed.

Lying on the floor of the pit, I waited to catch my breath. Blood had drenched my shirt and belly—the devil Mahbood's handiwork. He had skillfully punctured my spleen—

The knives—of course!

I scrambled to my feet. The crescent lay half-buried. The kukri stood erect. I extracted it, turned it flat, and jammed it into the wall. This would be my stair-step. The crescent would be my rail.

———

I reached for the jade box.

The Damascene dagger suddenly swung out of the hole and plunged down before me, hooking deep into the sand.

I stared at the blade in shock. Vanitar rearranged his grip and pulled himself up to the rim. The moment he did, he saw me.

With a yell, I lunged—dagger in hand—burying my blade in the back of his neck.

Vanitar cried out. I backed away in horror.

Locked in a grimace, the knife still poking out of him, the Iranian collapsed back down into the hole, hauling his crescent dagger with him.

A silence fell over the site. I listened with growing relief. Despite the terrible thing I had done, I felt a surge of triumph. *Irresistible in battle! Attacking, slaying his foes!*

I crawled forward to peer into the pit...

———

The Old Man had said he could trust me. Me, and me alone, of all of them.

I cannot displease him. I must do what I must do. Retrieve the lost lotus. Avenge Arshan's death. For the Old Man, for the Mahdi, for the Glory of Islam!

Reaching back I extracted the stinging dagger from my neck. Blood sang from the wound, and the song gave rise to a rage. I flung the paltry knife aside and grabbed the Dagger of God.

May the Lord curse the American and get Hell ready for him. He and the devil monk are about to face the Wrath of Allah.

"Allahu Akbar!"

———

With a shout Vanitar burst from the hole, his bright dagger flashing. I rolled aside as the blade slammed down, catching my shirt in the sand. Still halfway in the hole, Vanitar raised the knife again. I scrambled back and away. The crescent crashed down between my legs. I turned and scuttled toward Fiore.

The white-thatched monk sat motionless against the garden wall, exuding a deathlike calm. Even in the twilight I could see wet blood on his beard. Somehow I thought he *had* to be alive.

Fear had reignited. I had no weapon now. As I scurried toward the monk, I glanced back at the hole. With his dagger spiked in the sand, Vanitar had hauled himself out onto the ground. Starting on all fours, he struggled to his feet. For a moment he stood staggering against the evening sky, its blueness turning nearly black behind him. He bent down for his dagger and could barely pull it out. Then he reached down and lifted up the black jade box.

I crawled over to Fiore and peered into his face. Still I couldn't tell if he was breathing. "Doctor—he's coming for us. Please. Wake up."

Nothing. No reaction. The Buddha of my dream.

Vanitar lurched toward us. The knife hung from his hand. I thought, if I could stand up, I might beat him back, or tackle him and try to take the dagger. But I could not stand up. My ankle wouldn't hold. And with all the blood I'd lost I'd grown too weak.

I looked again to Fiore. His swollen eyes still shut. Which one of us, I wondered, would the crescent fall on first?

91.
Like Water

Vanitar walked unsteadily toward us, holding the jade box and the scythe-like dagger, his shadowy figure more distinct with every step. When finally he stopped and stood teetering above us, I found myself horrified at the condition he was in. Blood drained down his shoulder where he'd pulled the knife from his neck, and below the ribs his soiled shirt glistened blackish red. His face, gaunt and pallid from the loss of so much blood, gave off a ghoulish glow like the moon above his head. The scar he had managed to conceal for so long now looked like the trace of a kiss on a corpse.

Only his eyes looked alive. They flared wide and white, desperate with desire, craving this precious thing it seemed he could not live without.

I couldn't help feeling pity for him. Perhaps I simply could not shake the bond I'd thought we had. He had been Faraj to me, my ally and companion, a role he had performed with great conviction. Could that better part of him really be so dead and buried? Could the bond I felt have been completely false?

Vanitar's gaze fell on the immobile Buddhist monk. "The key," he uttered.

I realized then the box he held still remained unopened, and turned to see if Fiore would respond.

He did. Slowly. His eyes gradually opened as if waking from the dead. His lungs once again took in air. He raised his gaze to Vanitar and observed him for a moment. Then, in his soft and gentle voice, he spoke to him in a language I assumed must have been Persian.

Vanitar looked stunned.

A thunderbolt struck me as I stood before the monk. It came not from the words he spoke, but from the voice that spoke them. In the same flawless, formal tongue I'd been hearing from the Ayatollah, he was quoting a Persian Sufi poet, a favorite of Faraj:

"All the hundred and twenty-four thousand prophets were sent to preach one word. They bade the people say 'Allah,' and devote themselves to Him. Those who heard this word by the ear alone let it go out by the other ear; but those who heard it with their souls imprinted it on their souls and repeated it until it penetrated their hearts and souls, and their whole beings became this word. They were made independent of the pronunciation of this word; they were released from the sound of the letters. Having understood the spiritual meaning of this word, they became so absorbed in it that they were no more conscious of their own—"

*I had stopped listening to the tale he was telling. All I could hear was the familiar sound of his voice—*the voice of the Ayatollah! *The same voice I had first heard through my brother's mobile phone, the voice I had presumed belonged to the Old Man back in Qum, the voice I had submitted to, the voice I had obeyed.*

They had gotten Arshan's phone number the very night he died! The "Ayatollah" calling me had been this sly imposter—a Buddhist monk who lied in perfect Persian.

"You must follow my instructions," he had ordered back in Rome "—and my instructions only. Trust no one but me.*"*

I flushed away my phones. Cut off contact with Mahbood. Killed Hashishin I'd thought had turned against us.

But I'd believed in lies. Mahbood had spoken the truth. He'd been taking orders from the true Ayatollah. I had been recruited by this devil!

Vanitar's look of disbelief had soured into a rictus. "Who are you to speak to me of Allah?!" he asked in English.

Fiore answered calmly. "I speak only of the Truth that lies behind the word."

"What do you know of the Truth? You're with the CIA. You've been telling lies to me for days."

I turned to Fiore in astonishment. "You're with the CIA?"

The doctor methodically unfolded his legs and achingly rose to his feet. "It would be more accurate to say that the Americans are with me." He looked directly at Vanitar. "They don't seem to share your fascination with our lotus. Their only wish is to see your cult of Mahdism destroyed."

Vanitar peered back at him, a deathlike, ghostly glare. "The *key*," he demanded.

Fiore looked down at the jade box and the knife in Vanitar's hands, then back up into the desperate eyes that glared at him. Although Fiore himself had been badly beaten and bloodied, he seemed to have retained within a great reserve of strength. He reached out slowly toward Mahbood while opening up his hand. On his palm lay a blackened brass key.

Vanitar seemed surprised at how readily it was offered. With a wary look, he took the key and tried it in the keyhole.

The lock turned. The lid slid open.

As Vanitar peered into the box, he seemed to grow delirious, unsteady on his feet, his face disintegrating into despair. The box slipped from his hands, landing open in the sand. He gazed at it, bewildered.

"It's empty."

He said the word in English and I saw that he was right. There were no seeds, no lotus flowers. Nothing at all in the box. He looked in desperation at Fiore.

"The Truth is like water," the monk said gently. "It needs a vessel to carry it. But you mistook your vessel for the Truth."

Vanitar seemed to hang on the word, struggling to comprehend it.

The Truth.

What Truth? I'd believed in lies. Lies about myself. Lies about my father. Lies about my mother's honor. Lies about Faraj.

At Kahrizak I had killed Faraj because he spoke the truth.

My legs gave way. I dropped to my knees. Fear drained all the life from me. I was being hollowed out, emptied into the sand. There'd be nothing left...

"Nothing."

On his knees before the monk, visibly bleeding to death, Vanitar looked like a supplicant who had lost the ear of God, or a saint who suddenly realized he'd been confessing to the devil. The zealotry that lit his eyes had melted into uncertainty, and his face now reminded me of Faraj again, the boy who had been his childhood pal, the man who had been my friend. Vanitar had tortured and killed that friend in prison. How had he lived with that sin?

Lies. Falsehood. The comfort of illusion.

Truth has arrived, and falsehood perished. I am left naked and alone. Fatherless. Motherless. My half-brothers dead. One of them, my dearest friend, killed by my own hand.

All is lost. I am lost. I do not know who I am.

Vanitar turned to me, desperate now for some way out, a way to hold on to what he believed in spite of all that had happened. But when he saw me looking at him—with curiosity and compassion—a flash of panic crossed his face. On impulse he gripped hold of his dagger and attempted to raise the blade. But the weight of the weapon was too much for him; he no longer had any strength. I laid my hand on top of his and gently pressed it down. Offering no resistance, he let the knife fall easily, then raised his eyes to mine.

I did not look away.

I gazed into Duran's eyes and saw the way he looked at me, as if I were still Faraj, garnering his high regard, eliciting his pity. It frightened me at first. His eyes were like a mirror. But then I fell deep into them, like limpid pools of water, sinking into him somehow, seeing from his eyes. Gazing at me openly, without a trace of fear, it seemed he saw himself in me, or me inside of him.

Peering into his eyes, I felt I all but disappeared. Time came to a stop.

"You are perfectly safe now," Fiore was saying. "Everyone must taste death..."

The Buddhist monk was speaking, but his voice slowly morphed into the haunting voice of Faraj. Faraj, my brother. Reciting a line from Rumi:

"We become these words we say, a wailing sound moving out into the air..."

Vanitar's gaze climbed slowly skyward. *"Allah,"* he whispered, and with that last exhalation of breath, the last of the *Hashishin* keeled over, dead.

92.
Home

Night had descended on the Taklimakan. Beyond the wall the camels stood against the starry sky, while the stupa loomed above like a monument to darkness, and Vanitar's corpse, lying out before us, offered its last drops of blood to the sand.

As Dr. Fiore delicately wrapped the slit across my ankle, he explained how the CIA had approached him that final night in Rome. Aware that the Assassins were searching for the lotus, they had been listening to my cell phone calls in hopes of locating Dan. In the process they discovered that Dr. Fiore and his granddaughter were trying to do the same. When they began to pick up the calls and numbers of the Iranians as well, they decided to join forces with Fiore. Given his intimate knowledge of the Iranians' language and religion, they approached him to play the starring role of the Ayatollah in Qum.

"We are close to the same age," he said. "And they knew a lot about him. His teachings. His temperament. His apocalyptic vision. They said the Old Man and his *Hashishin* were a major destabilizing force throughout the Middle East."

It didn't take long for Fiore to decide. He'd have access to CIA intelligence and surveillance capabilities, vital aids to track down Dan and get his lotus back. And if he managed to trick Vanitar into turning on his own, he could flush the other assassins out and destroy the *Hashishin*.

The doctor quickly agreed to the scheme, but under two conditions: that they would supply the intelligence, under his direction, and that the soma lotus would be left in the hands of the Buddhist monks alone.

To his surprise, the Agency agreed. "Iran, Iraq, Syria, Russia—not to mention Al-Qaeda and the Islamic State—the hands of the CIA are plenty full these days. Stopping the Assassins was high up on their list, but chasing after a lotus flower? They just didn't get it."

"Do you trust them to keep their word?" I asked. "I know my brother wouldn't."

He thought for a moment before he replied. "The Americans have displayed a lack of wisdom on occasion. There is no one in this world can see all ends. But one thing they don't suffer from is a deficit of courage. You proved that yourself unmistakably today."

Despite the enduring effects of the soma, my ego swelled with a sweet surge of pride, punctured by a pinprick of uncertainty. "I can't help wondering if we'd all been better off...if I'd done what you first suggested and just gone home."

Fiore finished wrapping and looked me in the eye. "You *are* home," he said. He gradually gathered himself to his feet. "Rest here for a moment. We've another long journey ahead of us."

With that he trudged off to retrieve the two camels and a bamboo ladder he had hidden in the sand. I laid back and stared up at the stars.

You *are* home.

Oddly enough, I knew exactly what he meant. We were far out in the desert in the cold of night; I was badly injured and unable to walk; Anand was probably dead or dying and Jamyang in despair; it was miles back to the car and still more miles to the hospital, where Phoebe was frantic to save Dan and Govindi, while all around them the rioting city was going up in flames.

And yet...

I felt right at home.

Blame it on the soma, or perhaps the loss of blood. Call it the House of the Lord. The Refuge of the Buddha. The Infinite Ground of Being. Madness. I lay safe in the center of the mandala, halfway between East and West, suspended in a state of equilibrium, a human being balanced on the finger of God between the worlds of eternity and time. Faced with the prospect of death and calamity, my soul remained stoical and calm, the same calm I'd tasted at the sight of Vinny's Christ, or the Rembrandts in Steinberg's foggy shop window, everything intimately vivid and real, yet somehow transparent and infinite, too, as if cruel samsara were a dance through nirvana, as if God inhabited everything and the Buddha was in the world.

The doctor sidled by with the bamboo ladder. A fire-trailing meteor rode the sky. A sudden spark of pain sent a spasm up my leg. A camel raised its muzzle to the stars.

This might be my last night on earth, I imagined. Or the beginning of a magnificent new life. One simply must go forward without knowing, guided only by the longing of the heart. For what is courage, after all, but love overcoming fear?

I closed my eyes a moment and at once I fell asleep. Unafraid of darkness, or of death.

93.
The Cry

"Jack!"

I awoke beneath the ancient oak. Wind tearing through its branches. Dan and Phoebe gone.

Phoebe's cry came faintly to me, borne inside the gusts. *"Jack! Come back to me!"*

I could not see her anywhere; she'd vanished in the air. *"Phoebe!"* The wind snatched my voice away. The heaving branches creaked. I cupped my hands around my mouth and cried out, *"Phoebe!"*

"Jack. Wake up."

My eyes snapped open. The red-robed Santa Claus doctor peered down at me. I sat up, wincing as the pain returned to my leg.

We were still at the stupa.

"You were calling for someone," he said.

The lingering sound of her cry troubled me. "Just a dream," I said.

"Well...now you are awake."

Behind him, the moonlit camels waited languidly. The night, utterly still, seemed magical, unreal. "How do I know that for certain?"

"Pain," he said. "You don't feel pain in dreams. Only fear. That's why you're supposed to pinch yourself to see if you're awake."

"Then for sure I'm awake," I said. "How do I stop the pinching?"

"Pain is inevitable," he said. "But suffering is a choice. Ready to join the caravan?"

I nodded toward the bulging sack slung over his shoulder. "We going by camel or reindeer?"

He dropped the bag in front of me and dusted off the sand. "When you get back to Rome, I want you to do me a favor. Keep your eye on that pond in the garden. If you discover the lotus is growing there, tear it out and destroy it."

I remembered him wading immaculately from the depths of that muddy pond. The seed pod I'd tossed from the roof—*that's* what he'd been up to.

"Why destroy it?" I asked.

"We won't be needing the backup," he said, untying the top of the sack. Inside it looked like a thousand eyes staring out of the dark—hundreds of lotus seed pods, each sprouting multiple seeds. "We harvested these three days ago, before we destroyed our plants."

"Where did you hide them?" I asked.

"There," he said.

I turned to see the bamboo ladder poking up from the pit. *"Down there?"*

"Yes."

"Then why didn't Vanitar find it?"

"Vanitar didn't look deep enough."

We had not traveled more than half a mile from the stupa, retracing our tracks in the sand, when the two of us caught sight of a glaring star on the horizon. Distracted momentarily from my "suffering" on that camel, I felt like a Wise Man on the journey to Bethlehem. But then the star grew brighter and a sound reached our ears—the unmistakable whir of a helicopter.

Scanning the sands with a spotlight, the chopper appeared to be tracking the route we had taken north from the well. Had the Iranians conspired with the Chinese? I wondered. Had they spotted Jamyang and Anand? The large aircraft looked like a troop transporter, painted in sand-colored camouflage. The beam of its light soon locked on us. We squinted up blindly from our saddles, uncertain whether to wave in welcome or flee off into the dark.

As the great bird descended, a fierce squall of blowing sand threw itself against us. I covered my face with an elbow. Amazingly, the camels resolutely held their ground, treating the brutal onslaught like a sandstorm. I squinted into the nettling wind and saw a man emerge, bending to avoid the scything blades. An upheld arm covered his face until he stood below me. Then Harry Grant busted into a smile.

"You're invincible!" he shouted.

I grinned and showed my bandaged ankle. "Not quite," I said, then nodded toward the chopper. "How did you manage—?"

"Beijing doesn't want their internal troubles attracting America's attention. They're anxious to fly us the heck out of here."

"Have you seen Dan?"

"He's going to be all right," he said. "No damage to the spine. Govindi's okay, too. I saw them with Dr. Tzu at the hospital."

"Thank God," I said. "My friend Anand is up ahead. I had to leave—"

"They're on the chopper!" Harry cried. "We picked them up on the way—"

"He's alive?!"

"The guy's a former Gurkha, Jack—old soldiers never die!"

Dr. Fiore was trying to coax his stubborn camel to the ground. Staggering out of the cyclone, clutching his robes in the wind, Jamyang spotted the lama and gleefully raced across to help him.

"Jack?!"

The voice sent a thrill through me. I peered into the storm. "Phoebe?!"

Holding down a headscarf, she emerged from the swirl of sand and started rushing toward me, shouting out my name again, almost in a scream.

That naked cry of jubilation pierced right through my heart.

It answered the only question I had, maybe the only question that really matters about love. The only question that matters about anything.

Is it true?

In my rush to dismount, I tumbled into the sand.

Phoebe fell beside me. "Are you hurt?" she asked.

"Yes!" I said happily. "It's excruciating!"

She looked at me as if she feared the fall had cracked my head.

"It means I'm not dreaming!"

She grinned. "You sure?"

I stared into her baby blues. "I'm absolutely certain."

"So am I," she said. She lowered her mouth toward mine. "You fell off your horse, cowboy."

"Call me Easy, Slim."

We kissed. The two of us. Merging into One.

AFTERWORD
& ACKNOWLEDGMENTS

While *The Assassin Lotus* takes its starting point from the world's oldest religious text still in use today, the ancient *Rig Veda* of Hinduism, its true inspiration was the later and more widely known Sanskrit classic, the *Bhagavad Gita*. Composed in India between the fifth and second century BCE, the *Gita* tells the story of the warrior prince Arjuna, who pauses at the brink of a terrible battle to consult with his charioteer and guru, Lord Krishna. The divine Krishna urges Arjuna to overcome his doubts and to fulfill his earthly duty as a warrior to kill. According to Swami Vivekananda and, more recently, the Maharishi Mahesh Yogi, the essence of the book is succinctly expressed in Krishna's initial exhortation to Arjuna (verse 2.3): "Do not yield to unmanliness, O son of Prithâ. It does not become you. Shake off this base faint-heartedness and arise, O scorcher of enemies!" What seems a simple call to courage is actually a summoning of Arjuna's deeper Self, a concept that requires another 699 verses to fully explore its logic and meaning. For what is courage, exactly? And how do we summon it within ourselves?

Montaigne said that courage was "the strangest, most generous, and proudest of all the virtues." The ancients saw it as the essential trait, without which all other virtues were impossible. In fact, as C. S. Lewis put it, "Courage is not simply one of the virtues, but the form of every virtue at the testing point." For this reason courage—or the lack of it—lies at the heart of every story ever told. From Homer to Hemingway to Harry Potter, it is bravery makes the hero. But the *Gita* was the first story to examine where that bravery comes from and to try to understand just what it is.

A list of American descendants of this genre would have to include Stephen Crane's *The Red Badge of Courage,* or Harper Lee's *To Kill a Mockingbird,* or more recently, the works of Steven Pressfield. All address the conundrum of courage directly. Stephen Crane saw his Civil War novel as a "psychological portrayal of fear." With a remarkable turn of phrase, he describes the sudden surge of valor in battle as "a temporary and sublime absence of selfishness." The adjective *sublime* is key: it suggests a kind of transcendence, an inspirational grandeur and awe. At the same time courage contains a dark, manic quality, what Crane calls "the delirium that encounters despair and death, and is heedless and blind to the odds." The blindness is in truth a kind of single-minded vision. In Harper Lee's novel, the attorney Atticus Finch explains that true courage is "when you know you're licked before you begin, but you begin anyway and you see it through no matter what." T. S. Eliot expressed a similar sentiment: "For us there is only the trying. The rest is not our business." The ultimate result lies beyond our control, and in the end it almost doesn't matter. What matters is to act. That's a principle that in the past has been proudly embraced by Americans. In the heart of the heartland, the Nebraska Cornhuskers play football in a stadium engraved with words might have come from the lips of Lord Krishna: "Not the victory but the action; not the goal but the game; in the deed the glory."

This notion of acting without expectation—a central theme in the *Bhagavad Gita*—is the core of Eastern philosophy and the very definition of self-sacrifice. "Be free from vain hopes and selfish thoughts, and with inner peace fight thou thy fight" (verse 3.30). Finding the source of that inner peace is a spiritual quest that charts its course through all the major religions, and achieves its highest expression in our greatest works of art. Think of Michelangelo's *David.* Single-minded calm in the face of impossible odds. The beauty of the sculpture resides in the way it so perfectly captures that sublime quality of selflessness that Stephen Crane wrote about, a sublimity that hints at an answer to the question, "How could a mere boy do this?"

It is our deepest mystery, one that must be plumbed again in every generation. Juan Mascaró, in the introduction to his translation of the *Bhagavad Gita* (Penguin Classics, 1962), writes that "Sanskrit literature is, on the whole, a romantic literature interwoven with idealism and practical wisdom, and with passionate longing for spiritual vision." *The Assassin Lotus* is a 21st-Century American writer's attempt to carry on that noble tradition, a challenge I often found outstretched my meager talents, yet one that I felt I could not give up on, if only to avoid feeling cowardly. As no less a hero than Amelia Earhart wrote, "Courage is the price life exacts for granting peace."

Heartfelt thanks to my dear friend, author/publisher/producer Ken Atchity, for bucking up my courage and for keeping me on track. And of course for reminding me: "In the writing the glory."

A huge thank you to my good pals Debrah Neal and Roy Freirich, brilliant story analysts and two of the very finest writers I know. Your notes and generous support have been invaluable.

Special thanks to photographer/videographer Larry Scher, my very first buddy in the business in LA. I truly appreciate all the help you've given me over these many years.

"Jai Guru Dev" to my lifelong friend, electrical engineer-cum-yoga-radio guru, Dan Waterloo, who has aided me enormously in all things technological.

And lastly, a merging-into-one kiss to my beautiful wife, Joanna. It was you who made it possible to "see it through no matter what." Your love is the root of my courage, always.

—D.A.
Los Angeles ~ Memorial Day, 2014

ABOUT THE AUTHOR

DAVID ANGSTEN is the author of two previous novels, *Dark Gold* and *Night of the Furies*, published by Thomas Dunne Books/St. Martin's Press. In his former life he traveled the world as a video and film director, and for years wrote riveting screenplays that, after cheerfully star-trekking through the galaxy of Hollywood, forever disappeared into the black hole at its heart. He believes two things have saved him: forty-plus years of meditation practice, and marriage to a clinical psychologist. David now resides with his wife in West Hollywood, where he presumes to be an authority on the art of self-deception, lives in constant fear of re-inflaming his tennis elbow, and seems to take a perverse pleasure in describing himself in third person.

Tat tvam asi—him be me.

FINAL NOTE TO THE READER

An adventure thriller about Eastern mysticism runs the risk of alienating its two most obvious audiences. Thriller readers may have little interest in religious or spiritual matters, while students of Eastern religion and philosophy will likely be put off by violence and killing. But hopefully readers who have made it this far have seen that this mixing of the sacred and profane is partly the point of the story, and that the act that makes a hero can be a link between the two. If you've found it a tale worth telling, I hope you'll take a moment to share your thoughts with other readers on Amazon.com. A review there—however brief—would be extremely helpful, and much appreciated by yours truly. I also invite you to follow me on Twitter **@DavidAngsten**, friend me on **Facebook**, and email me at **davangsten@gmail.com** (please note: no "id"). My author website is **DavidAngsten.com**, and my blog "Be Here Now" is at **davidangsten.blogspot.com**.

As a writer, I'm useless without readers. It would mean a lot to me to hear from you.

—D.A.

Made in the USA
Coppell, TX
03 October 2020

39149544R10270